BLACKHEART KNIGHTS

BLACKHEART KNIGHTS

LAURE EVE

Jo Fletcher
BOOKS

First published in Great Britain in 2021 by

Jo Fletcher Books
an imprint of
Quercus Editions Ltd
Carmelite House
50 Victoria Embankment
London EC4Y 0DZ

An Hachette UK company

A CIP catalogue record for this book is available from the British Library

HB ISBN 978 1 52941 191 1
TPB ISBN 978 1 52941 176 8

10 9 8 7 6 5 4 3 2 1

Typeset by Jouve (UK), Milton Keynes

Printed and bound in Great Britain by Clays Ltd, Elcograf S.p.A.

FSC www.fsc.org MIX Paper from responsible sources FSC® C104740

Papers used by Jo Fletcher Books are from well-managed forests and other responsible sources.

For the real Red,
multi-talented artist, fabulous friend and constant source of inspiration,
who is better looking than the Red in this book.

PART I

It always begins with desire.
It is our fuel. It is our fire.
Quote from the Caballaria Code

CHAPTER I

Senzatown
Nineteen Years Ago

Knight-in-training Lillath o'Senzatown scrapes her foot backwards across the ground, gravel piling up in a mound against her heel.

The sounds of those shifting stones are lost in the quiet hum of the desiccated building behind her. The building houses a power relay, a simmering electricity monster caged in thick stone. It is one of hundreds that sit in miniature wastelands like this one, strewn far and wide across the depth and breadth of London.

Lillath's lean calf visibly tightens as she shifts her weight downwards and raises her other foot inch by painstaking inch into the air. Next to her stands Lucan, another knight-in-training, his arms folded and his face creased in a tutorial frown. Their best friend Art is sprawled out in a chair in front of them both, watching with an amused look on his face.

'What is this?' he says. 'You look like you're fighting under water.'

'That's actually the best way to practise.' Lucan holds a finger aloft. 'Our trainer makes us do these movements over and over in the salt pool every morning. My muscles scream for hours afterwards.' He turns back to Lillath, paused with her leg in the air, striking a crooked balance. 'Lower and shift forwards on to front foot, bring right arm round to describe an arc, palm edge first.'

'It's like you swallowed the instruction manual whole,' Lillath mutters as her movements follow Lucan's dictation, limbs-in-treacle slow.

Lucan ignores this. He has a prodigious memory. It is highly likely he read said manual cover to cover and now leafs through it in his head as if the real book exists on a shelf in his brain.

Art draws on his sicalo, breathing out blue-tinged smoke in a long plume while he watches his friends, noting the shapes their bodies describe against the stone-and-cement backdrop. A tutor once told him that he made a habit of surrounding himself with oddities rather than more obviously useful allies. It was said at the time with some measure of disapproval, but Art had decided to take it as a compliment. After all, in his opinion his friends are quite spectacular.

Lillath has the kind of confidence most only dream of and enough charm to file down its sharper edges. Her most constant trait is that she always seems to know what anyone is thinking, enforcing a level of honesty around her both annoying and admirable in equal measure.

Lucan's careful studiousness extends into the way he approaches life. He anticipates two steps ahead of all the people who underestimate him due to his diminutive size and unobtrusive nature. He has a few very particular requirements to be at ease in life, but it is a small price to pay for the talent he brings to the world.

'At this rate, your demo is going to last until past evemeal,'

Art says. 'You'll both be striped for lateness and I'll get a bitching from Hektor. You know how well he does that.'

Lucan frowns. 'First of all, "striped"? It's a Caballaria training ground, not a prison. No striping goes on.'

'Really? Not even a swift thwack across the legs with a practice sabre to teach you your place?'

Lucan looks irritated. 'Art, our trainer is Si Vergo. Remember, Vergo the Valiant? The incredibly famous ex-Caballaria knight? He's a great man—'

'Even great men can make errors of judgement.'

Art watches his two friends pause in their demonstration. He knows what they're thinking. It skitters across both their faces, and for a moment he fancies he can actually see the thin thread of thought that unites them against him.

Must be nice, he thinks, *not to feel alone.*

'It's not like we're working directly for *him*, you know,' Lillath says.

Art smiles humourlessly. 'You're both training to be knights,' he points out. 'Knights serve the King.'

'Knights serve London before they serve the King.'

'There's no difference. The King *is* London. London *is* the King.'

They trade back and forth, but the words have lost their meaning with repetition. It is a mountains-old argument between them.

Art flicks the end of his sicalo into the dirt, shifting on his chair. He found the chair in the small dump sat in the scrub behind the power relay building, along with the rest of the four-set it belongs to. The set is well moulded, carved out of expensive slicker wood, but one leg has been severely chipped, presumably enough to displease, and the whole lot has been thrown. Doubtless another set was bought the very next day. The imperfect ones have been left here, where the unwanted gather dirt.

He knows how they feel.

As the most northwestern of the seven districts that make up the sprawling city-state of London, inner Senzatown is relatively easy for Art to travel to from the country estate he calls home. He and his friends don't meet very often, but when they can, they come to this little dump. They found it in their wanderings just over a year ago, realised how non-existent its security was and henceforth claimed it as their territory. Security is always non-existent around the wilder areas of London.

If Si Hektor, Art's guardian, found out that he went city dump-diving in his spare time, he'd likely have the world's calmest aneurysm and threaten to lock Art up in the country forever – a hell he is reluctant to risk. It's not that he dislikes the country, exactly, it's just that it's so saintsforsaken *dull*. Nature is too pretty and jewel-like for his taste, but stark, sharply formed places like this have a kind of dark, grim beauty that stirs his soul. Spindly weeds poke through the cracks in the cement, those most hardy of urban plants. There is a loneliness here, yes, but also a tenacity that he admires. Power relay buildings might be ugly to look at, but they function as the insides of the body – vital carriers of the life spark that keeps everyone alive.

These are the city's haunted places, areas often claimed by the encampments of the homeless, their makeshift tent-towns nestled in between buildings still tumbledown and crumbling from the last civil war. Street foxes, orphans whose numbers far outstrip what few hostel beds the district has scraped together, do a meagre trade in frisking the unwary.

Yes, Art knows the risks, and he knows what Hektor would

say about it, but no one around here would ever recognise his face. Besides, he never comes here alone. He has his friends.

A rippling rattle interrupts the training demonstration. The chain-link fence ringing their private little Kingdom for the afternoon sounds off like a metallic alarm. Lillath and Lucan pause, their gazes seeking the source of the noise, but Art doesn't move.

Later, analysing every moment and thought of that day, burned as they are on his brain, he will wonder why. Why he doesn't turn. Why he doesn't even look up.

Did you already know, somehow? Did you feel it?

'T'chores, Garad,' Lucan calls. 'You're unforgivably late.'

The fourth member of their group, who was supposed to have been here an hour ago, darts through the fence's battered gate and comes to a stop before them, cheeks ugly-flushed. The sound of dragging breath carries over the power relay's constant hum.

Garad is a huge cat of a human, a full head taller than the other three. Only sixteen but already a beautiful fighter, their most fervent wish is to enter the Caballaria, competing in the arena for justice, fame and glory. Most hopefuls fail the notoriously brutal training, but the group's tacit agreement is that Garad is most likely of them all to become a knight.

'Sprinted all . . . the way . . .' comes a tight gasp. 'They're right . . . behind me.'

Then something happens to stop Art's heart.

Garad sinks to one knee on the dirt ground in front of his chair.

'You churl, what are you doing?' Lucan says, astonished.

Art knows, but the knot in his chest is too heavy to let his voice out.

'Art,' Garad says, and then halts. 'Sire—'

The air roars, drowning out any further words. Outside the dump, just beyond the chain-link fence, gravel spits and runs underneath the tyres of two enormous bikes. They are show machines, their hinds glossy-polished, their engines cut to give out growling revs instead of quiet purrs, chosen for ceremonial occasions when their riders wish to be both seen and heard.

The riders themselves drop their kickstands, plant their feet on the ground and stride through the chain-link fence, which vibrates gently with their passing. They are in full black cycle gear, their leathers sporting a silver sword emblem on each shoulder that only more fully draws the eye due to its coy size. If that were not enough to dissuade any casual threat – and it should be, touch the royal guard the wrong way and risk execution – the bulky swell of gun holsters at their hips would do the job.

Their arms rise. They lift off their helmets to reveal the gently sweat-sheened faces of a man and a woman Art has never laid eyes on before. An ebony scabbard arrows heavily downwards against the woman's leg.

'Your father,' Garad hisses, rising hastily as the two riders approach the group. 'He's—'

'Dead.' The word is choked out through Art's protesting throat.

Lucan sharply inhales.

'Oh fuck,' whispers Lillath.

'Artorias Dracones,' pronounces the man when he is close enough to hear. His gaze passes briefly over Art's friends, eyes having to slide up a little to accommodate Garad's height into his line of sight.

Art is stuck to the chair. He is made of it and it is made of him.

'Yes,' he says. His voice sounds steady to his ears. Later, he'll be grateful for it. Later, it will develop into a skill he'll come to rely on, that his body automatically delivers such outward calm in moments of high stress.

Echoing Garad, both riders sink to one knee.

The woman undoes her belt as her head hangs low, popping open the scabbard and withdrawing a slender sword. It has been made to look good on display, set high on some opulent wall in the royal palace. In the bright, flat air of some nameless urban scrubland, it looks cheap and glittery.

'Your father,' the woman begins in a carefully formal voice. 'Marvol has taken him into his arms, and he now passes the heavy burden of his life's task to you.' She pauses. 'Do you accept?'

Marvol. The Death Saint.

All his life, this awful potential has been lurking in the dark, surfacing in the smallest part of the night to curl the depths of Art's stomach . . . but still, it was never supposed to happen. His father is – *was* – a strong, healthy man. He also has – *had* – his young wife, the Lady Orcade. He wasn't supposed to die before she could give him a legitimate child. That had been the entire point of their marriage.

Art is the product of a scandalous, illegally conceived union. He might be innocent of the crime, but the shame of it has followed him all his life, staining his soul before he'd even had a chance to tarnish it himself. It should not be possible for him to take over from his father – and yet here it is, the impossible possibility, kneeling in front of him in the dirt.

Art could say no. He could tell them to toss their glittery sword in the nearest hydropower lake and watch the shine eaten eagerly away by the grime floating on its surface. Unfortunately, there is no other path for him. He is rich and he is safe, but he has never known the giddy terror of choice, and he has nowhere else to go.

Sat in his rejected chair beside a small city dump, with the electric hum of a crumbling power relay and the smell of mildewing furniture in the air, seventeen-year-old Artorias Dracones becomes the new King of London.

And he is *really* fucken unhappy about it.

CHAPTER 2

Caballaria Arena, Rhyfentown
One Year Ago

The challenger has their head covered in a black face-hood, a ragged strip torn out for their eyes and another for their mouth.

They wear engineer's tape wrapped around their knuckles, and it goes in careful overlaps again and again all the way up to their wrists. A raggedy, oversized jumper hangs from their slender frame, stretched enough to expose collarbone to the air. Black, nondescript trousers. Boots that look too heavy to give them much speed but might pack a heft if they smacked you in the face with their foot.

A cheap, cobbled-together look, but then challengers come in all shapes and sizes. Some are kitted out like rock stars already, their rich families providing. Some are desperateers off the streets, starving and ready to take a beating if it means they might get in a stable for a few nights, even a fourth-rate stable. A lot of them think they're hot shit. Most of them are scared.

Not this one, though, not so much. They have no visible shakes in their outline, and they walk well. The simple light board showing each fighter's information pronounces their name to be 'Red'. Nothing more, nor less. If they have no family or district name then they're an orphan, a street fox. They show none of the fear that must be coiling uneasily inside their guts, which in itself is a good sign. It indicates that they're good at acting, and showmanship is half the battle in becoming a Caballaria knight.

The small arena should be half empty, should only be filled with those mad fans who come to all their local bouts, rain or shine – but today the arena is packed out, because today is special. No one was even supposed to know about why today is special, but the whisper somehow got out and made its way around all the local bars faster than the take-up on a round of free drinks.

The audience shifts and grunts and brays in the stalls, protected from the spitting rain by tattered canvas overhangs. They wince whenever a challenger gets beaten down, but it's a wince of greed, of expectation, of dark pleasure. They wince through sharp grins and bared teeth.

The scouts are up there too, checking out new talent for their stable owners. One or two of the biggest stables are usually represented at outer district challenger bouts such as this one by a greener scout hoping to score big with a brand-new find.

They huddle in the private box, surrounded by opaque walls and the best view of the arena pit below, sipping on cheap whisky more like hot engine grease and making buys from the winners of each fight. Sometimes from the losers, if they see potential and are working to a low budget. They're hoping maybe there's a glimmer of talent there that could be coaxed out with a bit of training. If not, each pick is out in two weeks. Some stables offer more of a trial period than that, but most don't.

The challenger is stamping on the damp arena ground in the

cold, waiting for their opponent to make his grand entrance. Entrances are always important, even in a shit-tin challenger bout like this, and the Sorcerer Knight must know that better than anyone.

He is the reason those without tickets are pressed up to the fence three-deep outside, braving the wrath of the arena guards to get a glimpse of the most famous Caballaria knight in London, and perhaps all Seven Kingdoms. He is the reason the seats are sold out, even the drenched ones outside of the overhangs. People around here wouldn't be able to afford tickets for the big, important tournaments that he normally fights in. Those they have to watch on the glow screens in their local bar like everyone else, yelling and cussing and throwing their trick coins at the betting agents.

They always pick this apart in the pre-fight talks – why the Sorcerer Knight sometimes fights in a routine, new-blood tourney like this one. Some of them think it's because he's bored. It must get dull, knowing no one can beat you – maybe he's looking for a surprise. Others say that it's because he's done something to hack off his stable and this is his punishment, downgraded for the day in bouts that are so beneath him they aren't even mud on his boots.

Neither of those reasons is the truth. The real reason that he chooses to fight in places like this is because he's looking for other people like him. It's an open secret, what he's up to. A rumour never officially confirmed but known all the same.

The doors at the end of the little arena slam open. The crowd roars, their multi-voice crescendoing, pummelling the air for a mile around. They've seen him fight twice already today but they're still not tired of it – and neither is he, by the looks of things.

The challenger known only as Red stops pacing and stands, waiting. They are still, very still, as the beautiful monster approaches them.

The Sorcerer Knight. Scourge of the Godless. London's Left Hand. He has a few names, and he has earned them all. It is a cool, wet autumn day outside but he wears only trousers, his bronze skin picking up a sheen from the falling rain. His boots are soft, not the clumpy style of the challenger's, undoubtedly made from the finest of materials. Light but fully waterproof, and lined with the tiny needle knives that he favours to make his kicks deadlier. He has the best weapon-makers in London falling over themselves to give him their pieces of art. Their names get up on the glow screens when he fights in the big, showy dispute bouts that draw watching audiences in their millions, and then the weapon-makers can hang a sign in their shop saying 'as worn by the Sorcerer Knight'. They make very good trick off his fame.

As they near each other, you can see the challenger is tall – at least enough to not look like a scrawny child in comparison like most do – though they're a little too rangy to stack up against the solid, loping wall of muscle heading their way.

They stand, facing each other. There are no fancy light shows or music intros – no wasting it on a bout that won't even make it to the glows. An electric whistle sounds through the arena's tinny speakers, and that's it.

It begins.

It is careful, at first. The shouts of the crowd die down as they watch the circling. The challenger isn't a show-off, and the Sorcerer Knight is going to give them every chance to shine in order to be fair to such a mismatch. In a real fight, with heavy stakes, it might already be over.

Then they clash.

The first surprise is that the challenger isn't down. The hooded figure backs off fast, wary. Still, as they meet again the crowd beast knows it'll be done soon, and it begins to shuffle, rustle, mutter. The challenger is not bad enough to be entertaining and not good enough to be interesting.

Except if you know what to look for.

They clash again, and every time they do the challenger looks less like they're going down. It's not until at least three minutes in that people start to work out what they're doing.

They're testing.

Silence rolls across the crowd. Everyone has their eyes trained on the pair and their mouths glued shut.

Then just like that, it stops being a dance.

The pair are going at it, now. The challenger is fast – and damn, thinks the crowd, they're *good*. They whirl like a dirt demon across the sanded concrete. No one has ever lasted this long against the Sorcerer Knight in a bout like this. The challenger has unusual moves, odd spins and slides. Excitement blooms, thickening the air. Surely this street fox can't be the one to beat the unbeatable—?

No, they can't.

The Sorcerer Knight lands a punch so fast and savage that it can barely be clocked before the challenger is down against the far wall. Usually that would be enough for them to stay put, but this challenger staggers upright, still fighting. The Sorcerer Knight wraps a hand around their throat to keep them still.

Give up, the crowd thinks.

No one is supposed to die. A heavy, painful world of legal and financial chaos would rain down on the stable owner if one of their knights killed another, especially in a tourney shown on the glows where the world can see. They might even cut the knight loose as punishment. In no-glows bouts like this it would at least get the killing fighter some major fines, and it can be a career-ruiner.

It happens, though. In the raw heat of a clash it's hard to tell between stopping someone for a minute or stopping them for good.

The challenger is still fighting. Their leg comes up and their knee slams against the Sorcerer Knight's side, again and again – but nothing budges. They are struggling, getting weaker, one palm braced on the Sorcerer Knight's chest. The crowd mutters, satisfied they can see the end.

Then that strip of exposed mouth moves and they choke out—

something

Their hand bunches into a sudden, tight fist and their lips form silent sounds that are lost in the arena noise – but what happens next needs no translation. The Sorcerer Knight reels back as if violently shoved, pitching on his feet and collapsing on the ground behind him, gloved palms bracing his impact. The challenger hasn't even touched him.

It takes a couple of seconds for the crowd to work out what has happened, and by the time it reaches them it has faded to no more than a cold, wet gust of air. But it is there, undeniable.

Magic.

The whole arena is frozen.

In the midst of the crushing silence, the Sorcerer Knight levers himself back up to standing, takes two loping strides to the challenger and pulls off their home-made face-hood.

Out tumbles a fall of long, tangled black hair that drips down past the challenger's shoulders. Though her admission form says she is eighteen years old, she only just about looks it. Her skin is a creamy brown and her eyes are hard black coins set in a pointed face that could look good enough for the glows with the right kind of paint. She is graceful, clearly talented. She has everything the Caballaria could possibly want in a potential fighter knight.

Except for the magic, of course.

This challenger girl is playing a very dangerous game, and she knows it. You can see the fear in her shivering frame, now, even as her expression hardens in defiance. She raises her hand as if to try a move. It gets halfway up before the Sorcerer Knight whips out a knife from the belt on his thigh and slams it into the challenger's shoulder, leaning into her like a lover, the knife pinning her flesh against the crumbling wall behind. The challenger lets out a guttural, infuriated scream.

The Sorcerer Knight turns his back on her and faces the scout box.

'Magic,' he says, addressing the group huddled within the box's depths. 'You saw it.'

Nothing.

Then a voice like a sputtering, revving cycle rolls out from the dimness. 'I didn't know she was a godchild.'

It's the unmistakable voice of Faraday, one of the oldest Caballaria scouts around. Only those closest to the box will have heard it, but it moves through the crowd like a forest fire.

The canniest of the fans will realise that this was never destined to be an ordinary challenger bout. The most famous knight and one of the most famous scouts in London, both coincidentally in nowhere-town together?

Faraday could have had his pick of the richest stables, but he seems to prefer working in the down-and-dirty grime of the streets. He said in a rare interview that it's more exciting, spotting dark-horse talent from the outer-city dregs. Originally from some prim, shiny northern Kingdom, he defected to London when he was young. The nastiest commentators like to bring his northern roots up when one of his finds isn't doing so well in a bout.

Ah, well, comes from a shithole, all he's going to scout is shit, right? they joke.

'She's mine,' says the Sorcerer Knight.

Protests float out from inside the box, but they die down in the face of his unrelenting stare.

'Fine,' says the sputtering-cycle voice of Faraday, eventually. 'Sold.'

Faraday was the one who sponsored the godchild challenger's entry. He is the one who gets to sell her.

The other scouts' voices rise in protest.

'You can't do that!'

'The rules!'

'It's in the very Code of the Caballaria!'

'Fuck the Code,' says the Sorcerer Knight.

This blasphemy hits them hard. He is well known for not pandering to procedure – it's one reason he's so popular – but this might just lose him some favour.

The challenger is trying her hardest not to make a noise, but her strained panting fills the little arena. The knife juts out of her shoulder. The crowd neither shifts nor breathes, trying to catch every sound of the argument.

'The godchild is illegal,' splutters another scout. 'She should be *arrested*.'

Those closest to the box register the misstep before the scout does. There are muffled gasps.

'I wasn't aware that the mere existence of godchildren is against the law,' the Sorcerer Knight says in a tone of flat calm.

The scout flounders. No one dares help him.

'Not illegal for being a godchild, of course not, but the magic she used is – it's the law. It's . . . the *law*.'

A colder voice joins in. 'Can someone just lock the girl up so we can move on to the next fight, please?'

'She won't be arrested,' the Sorcerer Knight replies. 'She's still underage. That means her magical transgression only counts against me, and I'm entirely uninterested in opening a dispute. I'm only interested in sponsoring her entry into training.'

Silence.

'No fighter can sponsor another fighter,' the cold voice states.

'My stable owner will arrange it on my behalf.'

My stable owner, he says, as if there is anyone left in the Seven Kingdoms who isn't aware of just who it is the Sorcerer Knight fights for.

'Are there any other bids?' asks Faraday.

The box is silent. They are afraid of the Sorcerer Knight, and of the power he wields. No one in their right mind would bid against him.

'We will have to verify this with your *stable owner*'s seneschal,' comes the cold voice.

'Then do it,' replies the Sorcerer Knight, unconcerned, 'but at the same time as someone does something for the challenger bleeding out behind me. I'm not interested in damaged stock.'

The Sorcerer Knight turns to the panting challenger. She looks as though the only thing stopping her from falling on the ground is the knife in her shoulder pinning her up. Her mouth gives a sour twist as she hawks deep in her throat and spits at him.

The arena is silent, lost in admiring horror.

The Sorcerer Knight regards her for two or three long

seconds. The crowd holds its breath – but all that happens is that he turns and lopes away, disappearing back through the doors.

Medics trundle into the pit and swarm around the sagging, grey-faced girl. The crowd cranes its collective neck. The knife tip is slid snug between two bricks. It might not be good to move her, but they don't have much of a choice. One medic brushes the knife handle with the tips of his fingers, but his gentleness likely comes from fear of touching something that belongs to the Sorcerer Knight, as if it is either sacred or cursed – people never seem to be too sure which it is they believe more. Even that soft barely-a-touch sets the challenger wincing, her face streaked with sweat.

'Just pull it out!' calls someone from the crowd.

And like that, the silence breaks. The noise fumbles, swells.

'Go on.'

'Hurry up!'

'Pull it out!'

Pull

it

out

Pull

it

out

chants the crowd beast.

The medics try to ignore it, try to be professional. The set of their shoulders means they know best, but the trouble is, they probably don't. Tournament medics are different – the best in the land – but outer-city arena medics are another tale.

Anxiety is a thick, clotted taste in the mouth of the crowd. Now the Sorcerer Knight wants her, they're all for the risky little street fox. They need her to be all right. The medics can feel it too. If they screw this up, not only will they incur the displeasure of the Sorcerer Knight, but – more importantly in London – the crowd.

In the end, one medic has to put a foot up the wall next to the knife in order to clip the tip with an evil-looking pair of industrial shears, while two more hold the challenger up tight in case she faints and tears her shoulder open from the downward weight. Awful seconds tick past while the medic wrestles the shear points in between brick and flesh, scrabbling as gently as they can to gain purchase, the air filled with the challenger's hoarse cries.

Then, all of a sudden, it is done. The challenger sags, passing out, and the medics catch her before she hits the dust, laying her out on a stretcher to the backdrop of the excited muttering that fills the air.

Red. She only came in with one name, but it will be everywhere by morning. It will be the most famous name in the whole of London.

She'd better be ready for this.

CHAPTER 3

Blackheart
Nineteen Years Ago

Not long behind the two riders with their glittery sword comes a whole transport fleet from Cair Lleon, the palace of London's King.

They arrive to spirit Art away from the lot and towards the life that he never wanted. Garad, Lucan and Lillath, his friends, his lifeline, are left behind. He is too dazed to protest, bundled into a slick black quad, the two riders who first broke the news accompanying him on the back seats in silence.

A numbed Art tracks the outside world sleeting past through the smoked glass. Dazzle-blind riots of emerald green and electric blue light stripe his face as the quad moves through the ups of Senzatown, its richest and flashiest area – and only two streets over from its downs, its poorest and most notorious.

The streets are empty, cleared moments before by the bikes that precede them like a shoal of leathered sharks herding a ponderous whale. Even though the official news of the King's death will not be released until that evening, the curious crowds, pushed all the way back to shop windows, know something is up.

For years afterwards, they will tell each other where they

were that day. A few of them will remember the fleet of quads and realise they saw him go past. They will assume that Art rode inside with a straight back, the heavy knowledge of his destiny in his eyes, perhaps a tear or two tracking down his cheeks for the complicated feelings the death of his father had arisen in him. They would never assume that he had sweated against the dark leather seats the entire ride there, concentrating on quelling his swelling need to throw up.

Perhaps it looks much like complicated feelings, from the outside.

A lifetime later and his quad reaches the border checkpoint between Senzatown and London's nucleus, Blackheart, from which the city-state's seven districts radiate out like spokes on a wheel. Once again, the way has been cleared ahead of time, and the retinue slides through border control as if greased, the guards pausing to give rather disparately executed versions of the royal salute.

And now they are in Blackheart. Infamous, brooding Blackheart. Twenty-four million people's lives are shaped by the power in this area. Cair Lleon squats at its very centre, its famed dark lava-stone spires cutting into the skyline like a constant wound. Now those spires seem blanketed in deathly silence.

Art's quad rolls up the endless, empty driveway, the sprawling complex of palace buildings filling his eyes gradually to the brim as they approach. He had been dreading some sort of formal retinue in rigid rows, saluting as he passed. The absence of anyone at all is eerier, and does nothing to dispel the feeling sizzling in every cell of him: unwanted, unneeded, unnecessary, un.

You are an un-human, Art, and you are not supposed to be here.

He feels a sudden wild hope. It could be a joke. Why the fuck it would be, he can't yet see, but no matter – he'll walk through the doors and his father will be standing there in the echoing hallway that Art has only ever seen in pictures, because despite being the King's son he has never once been allowed to cross the palace threshold, to feel the cold rolling from the steelstone walls himself and set his flesh furring.

His father will laugh at him – *such a good joke* – why the fuck it would be, he doesn't know, but no matter. It will feel exactly like one of those nightmares that convince you its reality is yours for several moments after waking, laying its sticky sour claim to your brain until you manage to shake it off. And the relief when you realise that it isn't true, that it isn't your life – that gorgeous, blossoming relief.

But there is no relief waiting for Art.

The two riders lead him from the quad and up the steps to the towering front doors, three times his height, built of thick grey metal and lacquered with a dull silver sheen. They take him through a normal-sized side door, hidden from the view of the steps, and inside, the darkened cavern of a giant awaits him – but his father is not there, and it doesn't feel like a joke any more.

No one is there to meet him. What little light there is filtering down from the high bird's-nest windows feels empty and blank, as if the palace itself knows that its master is dead, and that his replacement will never be able to measure up.

Art is herded through a long corridor, the boots of his two guides – guards, jailers – clomping heavy in the hush. Eventually they reach a wooden door, no different to any of the rest they have passed, and usher him into a small room beyond, one of the many parlours the palace has that serve as calm and quiet waiting rooms.

The concrete floor is muffled soft by plush, dense rugs. Discreetly embedded glow projectors light up the walls with beautifully rendered image-captures of past rulers, frowning down at the living from the realm of the painted dead. The far wall is animated with holographic footage of important Caballaria fights of the recent past.

And then, right there on the wall, is his father.

Uther Dracones, the warrior bear, showing off his Rhyfen-touched form, broad chest heaving as he whirls a double-ended short spear above his head. He fought in two inter-district wars. He saved lives and ended countless more. He might have been hated by many, but he was *known*. He had lived, booming and unafraid.

Except for his mistakes. He had always seemed very afraid of those. Now here is perhaps his biggest, standing in his palace, come to claim his power.

Art watches the holographic footage play and shift, roving on. Now the light image shows his father young, having not long been sworded King. There is a man standing next to him, small and prim in comparison, dressed in the soft leathers of a style fashionable in Gwanharatown, his origin district. There are black strips on his shoulders and a jacket patch sporting a silver sword emblem sitting right over his heart, denoting his allegiance to his King.

The footage narrows in with vulturous greed on the man's mild-looking face. Art knows that face so very well, tracing its bone shapes as easily as those of his own parents. The face belongs to one of the most notorious Londoners ever to work a court. His name was Edler Feverfew. He was a godchild, and without him Art would not exist.

The story of how Artorias Dracones came to be begins just

over seventeen years ago on the fifth night of the Festival of Light. It was during King Uther's now infamous peace tour, a month-long ride around the Seven Kingdoms, designed to cinch each nation beneath the belt of togetherness after a spate of murderous and devastating terrorist attacks by Kembrian separatists.

The last stop on the tour was Kernow, the southwestern-most Kingdom, remote and beautiful and proud and poor. Its Queen, Meraud, was a rare Christian but tolerant nevertheless, and enjoyed the Saith Festival of Light as much as anyone.

Among those of the Queen's court introduced to Uther on the festival's first night was the Laerd Gorlais, one of Meraud's closest advisors. Gorlais had his wife with him, a statuesque tech strategist named Ingerna. Everyone who was there that night – and many more who weren't, as these things always go – swore that King Uther could not take his eyes off her.

She, apparently, was not similarly afflicted.

It was said that Uther approached Ingerna in private and made his desire for her known, but she rebuffed him. He threatened her. She told him if he cornered her again she would stick the organ that did his thinking for him with a needle knife, King and peace tour be fucked. Gorlais was the only man she wanted, and the only one who could have her.

So Uther decided that if he couldn't have her as Uther, he would have her as Gorlais.

Enter Edler Feverfew. The most powerful thwimoren for a hundred years, Edler's godchild skill was in illusions. He could have you convinced a cup was a rat. He could make a building disappear before your eyes. He could make anyone look like anyone else.

Some say the idea to fool Ingerna was all Edler's. Others

decry Uther as the mastermind, claiming that he forced his sorcerer pet to the plan. Either way, the end result was the same and the conspiracy carried out by both, so what did it matter who first came up with it? Edler used his magic to make Uther look exactly like the Laerd Gorlais. This was how Uther gained entrance to Ingerna's bedroom without any alarms being raised.

After that . . .

Uther liked a challenge

Uther liked to hunt

Uther liked to chase the most reluctant kind of cunt

Art fights a sudden surge of bile that stings its way up his throat.

He first became aware of the rhyme about his conception when he was eight years old. His guardian Hektor had a distant cousin come visiting during one hot, breathless summer to scrounge money and favour. The cousin's twin sons lured Art out to the orchard while the adults were preoccupied with the business of getting drunk in the games room. Once they realised that Art had no idea of the sordid rumour behind his origins, they proceeded to relate the story to him in graphic detail. They couldn't remember all twelve verses of the rhyme offhand, so their sing-song was punctuated with more prosaic explanations that tumbled out of their gleeful mouths.

Edler's illusion apparently held fast for the entire week that Uther stayed at the Kernowyen court. Opinions were divided on whether Ingerna realised at some point and had to be forced, or whether she was oblivious until Uther left. Either way she fell pregnant, and by then knew enough to know the baby was not her husband's.

Some months later she made the journey to London, appearing at Cair Lleon visibly swollen and armed with astounding accusations. Uther immediately denounced her story as a ridiculous lie, and she had no evidence to prove otherwise. Kernowyen court officials would swear under interrogation that they had seen no one but Gorlais near her and, in a final crushing blow, her own husband sided with the King.

Rejected, humiliated, furious and alone, Ingerna disappeared from public view, carrying the most controversial baby in the Seven Kingdoms away from the craned necks of the world. Unforeseen health complications led to tragedy, and she died soon after giving birth to Artorias.

Only after her death did Edler choose to come forwards. Rumour was that he and Uther had a bitter falling-out, and in revenge Edler went straight to the news glows, corroborating Ingerna's story by relating what Uther had forced him to do in order to seduce and ruin a passing fancy.

Edler's decision to expose them both was deemed bafflingly suicidal. He was arrested for treachery against the King of London, but not for illegal use of magic – to admit that would be to admit that there could be some truth to his story – found guilty, and exiled, along with his entire family. He disappeared overseas and reportedly died not long ago, leaving behind an overblown legend.

No matter that the Caballaria justice system conveniently found Uther innocent of all charges. The damage was done. The scandal clutched his heels for the rest of his reign, and the people shook their heads in sorrowful, gleeful condemnation. *Magic corrupts*. Everyone knew this. It was one of the hardest-learned lessons of history, and yet there were always those like Uther who thought themselves immune, the exception to the rule.

The world turned, finding newer scandals to bask in. Ingerna Gorlais became an icon of tragedy. Artorias Gorlais, in apparent pity, was quietly claimed by Si Hektor Caballarias Pendennis o'Senzatown, a rich, retired knight with an impeccable reputation and no children of his own to care for.

Si Hektor's honour found the subject of his new ward's origins far too distasteful to address. His household were kind and affectionate to the child Art, if a little careful, a little distant – emotions he would come to understand once he realised just who he was and how much they protected him from the outside world.

Art knows he is still talked about. He is a thick knot on the string of recent history, a half-closed clamshell the birds like to peck, magpie-fascinated by the shiny thing that was never supposed to exist.

The male knight clears his throat, startling Art from his contemplation.

'Please wait in here . . . Sire,' the knight says. 'Someone will be with you soon. They'll be able to explain things.'

The hesitation before the *Sire* is telling, as is the phrase *explain things*. Art might be King, but it is only a temporary state, a legal move to maintain stability until an official Caballaria tournament can be held. Now his father is dead, the seven families who control the seven districts of London will have the right to claim the Sword that rules them all.

It will be chaos. It usually is.

'We can get the projector shut off,' the male knight says, uneasy.

'No.' Art's voice is absent, cool. Again he wonders at his own outward appearance of calm. 'You must forgive me. I never even asked for your name.'

The knight looks startled. He and the woman exchange glances.

'Madoc, Sire.'

'And yours?' he asks the woman, gently. They are both twice his age.

'Tepta.'

'Thank you. This situation can't be easy on either of you.'

'I . . .' Madoc checks himself. 'No, Sire.'

The door opens and a slim, hawkish server in neat-cut clothes enters with a silver tray balanced on his palms, his soft shoes noiseless on the floor rugs. He sets the tray down on a low table in front of a deep red divan. On it is a teapot carved from mottled grey bone, a thick glass goblet and a plate of flat, dense cakes.

'While you wait,' murmurs the server.

Art stares at the tray.

'Do you have any Pollidori whisky to go with that?' he asks.

Hesitation. Out of the corner of his eye, he sees Madoc shift very slightly in his stance.

The server inclines his head. 'How do you have it?'

'Double fingers and chips.'

The server is lost. 'Double fingers and chips' is northern Senzatown slang and doesn't make sense in a Blackheart room.

'Two standard measures,' Art amends. 'I don't know how you serve your ice here, but if it's in pieces as big as half a thumb, I'd like two of those.'

The server nods his head again and retreats.

Servers. Can't he just go to the kitchens himself and pour his own drink? He'd never find them, he supposes. The palace is famously labyrinthine, with new servers requiring weeks of training just to learn how to navigate it all without getting lost. Art wonders if they offer the same training to each new ruler. Uther's legitimate successor would have grown up here, of course, and already known it intimately.

'Someone will be with you soon,' Madoc says, and the two knights make their exit.

The projector purrs on, just audible above the crushing quiet.

It is only then that Art realises his cheeks are wet.

CHAPTER 4

Bone House, Blackheart One Year Ago

'Awake, are we, mine gory-eyed celebrity?'

The words are delivered in a cracked machine kind of a voice.

Red opens her eyes.

The room is unfamiliar. She gazes up into an impossibly high ceiling crossed with steel girders likely almost as wide as her. Light stripes the white sheets blanketing her body, falling through a tall window framed with pikes and curls of black iron.

Red opens her mouth to speak but her voice is stuck like dry, choking bread in her throat.

'You're in a Blackheart bone house,' says the voice helpfully, guessing at her next question. 'They transferred you as soon as they could be sure you wouldn't bleed to death if you were moved.'

Blackheart. The word gets her motors revving.

'I'm . . .' she tries, clears her throat. It doesn't much help. 'I'm *inside* Blackheart?'

'It's that easy,' Faraday agrees, leaning back in his chair. 'All you needed to do was risk your life, and now you're a saintstrue trickster.'

Trickster, one of many slang names Londoners use for themselves. It comes from trick, the Seven Kingdoms-wide monetary system that uses electric power as its currency. First dreamed up in London, of course, and they never want anyone to forget it.

Then there's *mongrel*, a name Red finds particularly confusing. In other Kingdoms it is a pejorative used to describe something badly made of many parts, but Londoners actually seem to be proud of the term. What kind of people are proud to be mongrels?

'My shoulder,' she croaks.

'Nothing long-term. You're still in the game.' Faraday shrugs. 'Doctors don't know how he managed it, but he barely damaged you. Give it a few days and you should be fine.'

The ghost of the screaming fire that had engulfed the nerve-ending map of her arm as the knife went in still haunts her flesh, waiting for her to move too fast so it can come back to life and scream again. A stab wound like that should have ended her chances of entering the Caballaria this year right there and then. She thought it had.

She dares to hope. 'How's that possible?'

Faraday gives a humourless smile. 'Magic?'

Relief closes her eyes. 'What happens to me now?'

'You were clever enough to impress one of the most powerful men in London with your little performance,' Faraday says. 'You're to be moved straight into a stable. They ain't even going to bother with a trial period, as you're already a decent enough fighter. Just as well since you'll miss the trial period anyway, what with being holed up here 'til your shoulder can take the six-month beating it's about to get during training. And you won't get no favours. You don't pass training and you're out. Use magic even once, even just a little puff of air, and you're out.'

His voice has a lilt of pride to it. There are only fourteen known godchildren in the whole of the Caballaria, and none with the rare magic that Red possesses. It makes her exotic, immediately more fascinating than the hundreds of other knights who join the ranks every year. Faraday will likely dine off being the one to find her for quite a while.

Training to be a Caballaria knight is hell, so the stories go, and most trainees drop out before the end of it. Red will not be one of them. She will win. She must. There is nothing else.

'Good timing, your stunt,' she hears Faraday say. 'Another couple of weeks and you'd have been illegally unregistered.'

Red does not reply. The timing was deliberate – maximum exposure, minimum risk of prison. Something about Faraday's speculative tone suggests that he knows that.

'Shame they changed the law on it,' he remarks. 'Used to be they registered the kids as well, not so long ago.' He snorts. 'Eighteen years old, my arse. *Twelve* is old enough to know right from wrong.'

Registering a godchild means putting them on a list – their name, background, magical ability – and tattooing them in permanent ink, so they can never hide what they are. Red has seen old footage of screaming children being forcibly removed from their crying parents and tattooed, branded like cattle before their magic had even settled. Eighteen is young enough to be registered, no matter what Faraday thinks. You get a month's grace from your birthday to apply for your tattoo, and hers is in three weeks time.

Londoners love tattoos. They all cover themselves in permanent art both pretty and ugly – visual allegiances, remembrances, celebrations. To them getting a tattoo is as casual as buying new boots, but Red has never had one before. When she is registered she will be forever scarred, unable to hide. She pushes it out of her mind. Sacrifices must be made.

'Well, at least I don't have to travel far with a busted shoulder,' she says.

Faraday cants his head. Understanding dawns on his mountainous face.

'You ain't going to be staying in Blackheart,' he says. 'You've been assigned to Rhyfentown Public training grounds. It's the district I put down next to your name when I entered you. It's where you were discovered. That's how it works.'

'What? Why? The Scourge is the one who's sponsoring me and he's a Blackheart knight. Why won't I be where he is?'

'Slow down, girl,' Faraday says, gentler. 'He might have arranged your sale, but that only means your training is being funded by his stable instead of Rhyfentown money. They ain't exactly going to let a stranger with no background just dance merrily into the King's own district, are they? You're going to have to prove yourself twice as much as the rest, three times. You got a real disadvantage, Red. You're a godchild. You ain't going to be trusted.'

'They trust Wyll, and he's probably the most famous godchild there is,' Red retorts.

Faraday is all amusement. 'Oh, it's *Wyll* instead of the Sorcerer Knight now, is it? Your old pal *Wyll*?'

'He stuck a knife in me. I'd say we're close.'

Faraday lets out a rumbling laugh. 'You caught his attention, but that's about it. If you think that's enough to get you close to him, you're all backwards.' He pauses. 'I'll be interested to see how far you get without him sussing out what you're really up to.'

At this, Red refocuses. Her gaze, having been clambering the walls in thought, switches to the lithe, craggy man before her.

Careful, careful.

Faraday raises a brow. 'Oh, you thought I was stupid. Well, people do. I don't mind, makes things easier for me.'

'I'm not up to anything,' Red says. 'I just want to be a knight. It's been my dream since—'

'Neh, I remember the speech you gave me when you came begging for help in getting entered. Listen, why d'you think I took you on? Cos you're a godchild?' Faraday waves a dismissive hand. 'Not that interesting when you can't even legally use your magic to fight with. But everyone joins the Caballaria for their own reason and I can tell that you've got a good one. Don't know what it is, but I'm curious to set you loose and find out.'

He knows. Shut his mouth. Permanently.

Red can feel her temper rising at the potential threat. Violence sparks to life inside her, flickering its hungry flame – but between the pain she is in and the drugs they have her on for it, she won't be able to harm him much.

'Curiosity kills,' she says.

Faraday tuts. 'Not here, little fox. In London, it goes "curiosity saves" – and you're in London now, girl.'

He levers himself up from the chair and dons the thick grey coat slung across its back.

'I'll be watching your progress, Red o'Rhyfentown, with much interest.' He pauses. 'And I won't be the only one.'

His departing footsteps echo on the dark tiled floor.

Caballaria records officially show that Red is an orphan with no family name – but now that she has been picked up from the challenger bout by Rhyfentown's own public Caballaria training grounds she becomes o'Rhyfentown, taking on the name of that district as a marker of her new allegiance. It is a temporary naming. She only gets to keep it if she passes training.

The Sorcerer Knight looms large in her mind. The sheer awe-inspiring sight of him up close, sinewed and blank-eyed as he fought, locks Red down into the sheets and quickens her heartbeat. There is no question in her mind: she gave it everything she had in the fight, but that bastard had just been toying with her, watching her dance herself into a pointless frenzy when he could have put her down any moment he liked.

Or maybe he had been letting Red show off what she had. If the Sorcerer Knight had been bored, he'd have ended it three minutes into the fight. Who could say for sure, except for the knight himself? His face had been stone, hard and unreadable throughout – until right there at the end. Red had felt the hand around her throat, that heaving, muscled torso inches away as those fingers squeezed slowly, gently, into her flesh. Red had forced her gaze up into those gold-rimmed eyes and seen them widen in shock as the magic had done its work and forced him off.

Everyone knows about his obsession with finding other god-children. It was the best way to get his attention, and it worked like a charm.

Red has spent her life in preparation for what comes next. This is the most dangerous game she has ever played. If she wins, she'll get the reward that she has craved since she was eight years old. The prize, the meaning of her hard-edged existence. If she wins, she'll be free.

But if the Sorcerer Knight finds out what she's up to before then, she'll be dead.

CHAPTER 5

Cair Lleon, Blackheart
Nineteen Years Ago

It is the clock that finally breaks him.

It stands in the corner of the room like an overseer. Its casing is graceful fluted wood, its face cold white electric light. The minutes swim up to its surface from the black depths, killing time with silent efficiency – until the hour, where it emits a calming succession of rippled notes, crushed together and spread like jam across the air.

The third time it happens, Art snaps out from his torpor.

Three hours ago he was deposited here like the world's most unwanted guest. Tea and whisky long since drunk, two cakes eaten in an attempt to stop his stomach cramping up. He rises, irritated. Wait? How long for? What in seven hells is happening out there?

They haven't locked the door. Was it a test to see how long it would take him to leave of his own accord, or did they assume he'd just do as he was told and stay like a good dog?

The corridor outside is empty, the world beyond it long fallen into darkness. Art shuts the door quietly behind him and manages to stop himself creeping like a naughty child, telling his legs to take slow, purposeful strides.

Until he hears voices, and his courage fails him. He is not going back to that room with that fucken clock. An armoire with a jutting side panel is between him and the voices. He'll just slip in behind it, not quite covered all the way, but enough, hopefully just enough, not to be seen in the dim lighting—

—and there's no time to find a better place, anyway. The voices are just ahead of him and getting closer.

'. . . he's seventeen.'

'He's not even of age,' another voice retorts. 'It's ridiculous, giving the Sword to some child who won't even know what to do with it.'

The voices are round with Romish vowels, the edge of each word sharp and precise.

'Have you seen the pictures they've been showing of him on the glows? Not much of a kingly way about him, neh?'

'Nanette, it's hardly his fault. He wasn't brought up right, was he? Bundled off and hidden away in the countryside all his life.'

The quiet swish of feet fills Art's ears and the feel of bodies prickle his skin, bodies walking right through his just exhaled breath. They haven't even seen him.

'He won't last, anyway. Stephanus said he overheard half the members of the Consilium plotting away in the long room.'

'Oh, fantastic,' groans the voice of Nanette. 'The city's already dancing on razors as it is. Uther made sure of that. I'm not sorry he's dead, and frankly, neither's most of Blackheart, whatever they say in public.'

'Keep it down,' the other voice hisses, 'or I won't tell you about the betting game the kitchens have just started up.'

Nanette sounds amused. 'Already? Fast work. Which family you laying trick down on, then?'

The voices melt into the distance as their owners, servants by the sounds of it, move down the corridor and away from Art. The last thing he hears is the offhand voice of Nanette.

'Poor god-touched kid. He'll be eaten alive.'

Art stays behind the armoire while his heart struggles and heaves.

Eventually he feels calm enough to leave his hiding place. Retracing his steps from earlier on takes an age, but eventually he reaches the cavernous entrance hall.

If he can get outside, he can find the garages. He can take a bike – only knights can ride them, but Hektor himself taught Art how – and get the hells out of here . . .

'Si Dracones, please stop.'

He hadn't noticed them when he first came in, but the front doors have guard knights before them, of course, standing in the cool, echoing chamber like statues. Gun holders are slung casually at their hips. Sword emblems twinkle mutely on their shoulders.

'Si is incorrect,' Art replies. 'I'm not a knight, and I'm never planning to be.'

The guard knight hesitates, paralysed by the unfamiliar waters of etiquette they now swim in. How does one address a temporary, probably-not-going-to-be King?

Art presses his advantage. 'I'm going out.'

'Can't let you leave,' the knight says.

'I'm still going.'

The knight's hand moves slowly, feather-touching the handle of his gun.

Art laughs, hollow. 'You're going to shoot me? Surely not, I only just got here. At least give the rest of them a chance to take a crack.'

'It's my understanding that you always had a distaste for the fight,' a voice echoes from behind him. 'Hence your refusal to enter knight's training. With things being the way they are outside right now, I'd have thought you'd want to stay here, where it's safest.'

Art doesn't turn, instead waiting for the owner of the voice to draw level with him and make themselves known. Force them to come to you: Caballaria power play for beginners. Sadly, this player is better than he is, for no one materialises in his line of sight.

He turns at last, seceding.

Standing framed by an archway at the edge of the hall is a short woman with bladed metal legs. Art knows who she is – Brune Vastos Burdokke o'Evrontown, one of the King's oldest and most well-known inner-circle advisors. Her iron-grey hair is clipped to her skull at the sides, with a longer mass of slick quaff rearing atop her head. Her leg blades protrude from the bottom of short, severe trousers, catching the cold light in quick slices.

'And what is it like out there?' Art says.

Introduction formalities be damned. She certainly hadn't bothered.

Brune appears to think about her answer. 'Complicated, Draconitas. Complicated.'

The diminutive is supposed to put him in his place, he supposes. Draconitas – little Dracones. Still a child in her eyes, with all that implies.

'Is that why you're inside too?' he asks.

She smiles. 'An old dog can still bite.'

The most well-known thing about Brune – apart from the loss of her legs due to a bomb attack in her district during the last civil war – is that, like Art, she never entered knight's training either. She is a vastos, a civilian advisor, and the only one of his father's inner circle who was never a fighter of any kind. This in no way impacts just how intimidating she is.

'Nevertheless,' Art replies, 'I'm leaving.'

'Are you?'

'Will you really shoot me?'

Brune nods to the guard. 'In the thigh. He's a great shot. I promise it will only incapacitate.'

Art, still riding calm, considers his options.

'Then I have a request,' he says at last.

'We shall try our best to meet it.'

'I've been stuck alone in a little room for three hours. Tell me what's going on.'

'Arrangements are taking a while,' Brune replies. 'It was unexpected. I'm sorry for our inability to keep you entertained.'

Art nods, careful not to acknowledge the lie in her eyes.

Stephanus overheard the inner circle in the long room, plotting away.

Trouble is afoot.

'Then let me fetch a couple of playmates to amuse me while the adults do the hard work,' he says, his voice light.

Brune is all regret. 'Too risky, I'm afraid.'

'Not at all. They were security-vetted as soon as they applied for Caballaria training, which means they can enter Blackheart, and I'm sure someone as important as you are can expedite their entry into the palace. Garad and Lucan, their names are. There's also Lillath – she's about to ditch the glamour of knight's training to become an advisory vastos instead, which I suppose means she wants to be like you, some day. They were all with me at the Senzatown dump where you picked me up. I'm sure you know exactly who I mean, just as I'm sure there's at least one palace minion whose job it is to keep tabs on every association I've made since the rather unfortunate night of my birth.'

Brune hesitates.

Art pounces. 'What?'

'They might have already made their presence known a little while ago. They were turned away.'

He breathes out. *Thank you, thank you, friends. You've given me a rope.*

'They'll just come back,' he tells Brune. 'They may even go to their parents and complain. You know who Lillath's parents are, right? I'm sorry to say that they might make a bit of a fuss. Take it further, maybe even to a news glow. After all, they have no idea what you're doing with me in here, since you haven't let me talk to anyone. You did kidnap me off the street.'

She looks entirely unimpressed. 'Don't be childish; you came of your own free will.'

'Oh,' he says doggedly, 'but I *am* still a child, as you so rightly pointed out, and so are they. They're pretty silly. Dramatic, even. Tiresome, I know, but when you're an unwanted bastard, you take what friends you can get.'

Silence.

Art forces his mouth into a smile.

Brune cants her head.

'Then by all means, let's head any tantrums off at the pass,' she says. 'We'll see if we can get them to come and keep you entertained.'

Art dips into a polite bow. Not all fights are with fists.

Caballaria power play for beginners.

Brune is commendably fast.

Art is back in the waiting room with the maddening clock,

but at least he now has a whole bottle of Pollidori whisky on the tray in front of him, with four glass goblets and a miniature hill of ice chips in a cold cup.

Soon enough he hears voices filtering through the wall, clambering over each other in grating knots. The door opens and a harried-looking vastos is closely followed by Lucan, whose head is turned back in the act of tossing words over his shoulder to Garad, who enters next with their head bowed to duck cleanly under the lintel. Bringing up the rear is Lillath.

'Shut UP, Lux,' she puffs, and in the next breath, 'ART.'

'ART,' Lucan echoes in a glad shout. 'Fuck the saints, you're all right.'

Their vastos escort physically flinches at this casual blasphemy. Art wants to let loose a giddy laugh. They're here. They're filling the dead, stale air with their noisy life and he is no longer alone.

'Art,' Garad echoes finally, face creased in clear worry.

The trio halts, uncertain.

'You came.' Art exhales, feeling a grin split his face. He rushes towards Garad and wraps his arms around their torso. He feels Lillath crowd close, one hand on his back. Lucan hangs back as always, never good with touch. Art turns his head against Garad's chest and looks at him.

'I love you all,' he says softly.

Lucan nods, relief shining in his eyes.

'You *punched* a guard knight,' Art says.

Garad uncomfortably nurses a whisky glass.

'They just took you,' Lucan protests. 'No one would tell us anything. We followed you as best we could, but when we got to border control into Blackheart they wouldn't let us in, not until we started waving our Caballaria IDs, and then getting to the palace took forever because the streets are crazy right now, and then when we got here they turned us away at the gates, like everyone else, and, well—'

'Garad lost their temper,' Lillath supplies drily. 'Lucky we weren't all arrested.'

'Not in that chaos,' Lucan cuts in. 'Those guards had their hands full.'

'I . . .' Garad subsides. 'I was worried. It's a mess outside. The things they've been saying on the glows . . .'

'A mess?' Art echoes.

'They announced the King's death not long ago, and it all went a little crazy.'

'Of course it did,' Lucan says. 'People are saying your candidacy for the Sword won't be legal.'

'Oh honestly,' Lillath snorts. 'He's hardly the first child to be born under the shadows of scandal or magic.'

Lucan's gaze turns to Art. 'They say it was moldra lagha that took your father's life.'

Moldra lagha. Marvol's Law, the Death Saint's most famous surviving edict. It is the only judicial instance in which a life can be taken in vengeance for a life lost, and only taken by someone proven to have a personal relationship with the murdered. A life for a life, a re-balance of the scales.

It was said that Saint Marvol introduced moldra lagha to try and curb the violent impulses of the nation, forcing people to think twice about taking a life, lest theirs be given up in forfeit. In Art's opinion, the law doesn't really work and never has. Humans continue to do what they do best – namely, killing each other for power that only exists because everyone believes it does.

'Uther died of heart problems,' Garad says. 'His entire personal medic team confirmed it.'

'So they say,' Lucan mutters, 'but how many living people had a death grievance against him?'

'The biggest problem we've got,' Lillath interjects, 'is that right now the most likely candidate to be the next King is Agravain Welyen. That's what shits *me* up.'

Garad looks horrified. 'He'll never get the Sword.'

'He *is* the King's brother-in-law. Was, sorry. Anyway, Alaunitown might riot if he doesn't. They haven't had one of their own at the top for the best part of fifty years. No one wants another damn civil war – we're still crippled from the last one.'

Lucan snorts. 'You can count on it if the Welyens are in charge. You know what'll happen? They'll make half of London into a slum that they own. Then they'll kick everyone who isn't a tech corp out of the other half, so they can make room for more tech corps. The city'll be dead inside ten years. Their family motto pretty much translates to *fuck everyone who isn't us*.'

'You know how it goes. Every ruler's death creates space for the seven families to start scrabbling for control.' Lillath's voice darkens. 'At least back when we had succession, it meant we didn't have to go through *this* every time.'

'Saints, Lil, you're a bloodliner?' Lucan exclaims. 'I can't believe—'

Art lets their argumentative voices drift away from him as he sinks back against the divan. How many times have they idled nights away together like this, putting the world to rights for hours and hours with a bottle between them? It used to be one of his favourite things to do.

But this is no longer theory. This is his life, *his life*, and he only gets the one.

He knows it is cowardice, and selfishness, and a million other terrible, ignoble things. But he also knows that London is far better off not putting some bastard kid in charge who absolutely no one will follow. His entire being shrivels at the thought of that weight.

He'll do what he can to calm things down in the meantime, assuming he is even allowed to do that. Of course he will. And then in a month's time, when they announce the Caballaria tournament for the Sword of London, he gets to wake up from this nightmare and escape.

For the first time in hours, Art feels his heart rise out of its misery. He may have to enter the fight to be King, but that doesn't mean he has to win.

He can lose. Deliberately.

CHAPTER 6

From Blackheart to Rhyfentown
Eleven Months Ago

The knight arrives with a roar that streaks across the quiet street and tails off like a sound comet behind their bike.

They come at nightfall, head to toe in snake-green leathers adorned with metal pins, badges, tiny hanging charms and a fabric neck collar patterned with grinning, stylised cat heads. Each trinket speaks to this knight's passions and allegiances, Red knows, but damned if she recognises any of them – except the one patch sewn into their right shoulder: a bright orange sunburst, a classic symbol of the Saith saint Rhyfen. The patch has been done in a cartoonish design that Red finds faintly vapid, a rather ill-fitting style for a religious symbol.

At least it identifies the biker, though – this is a Rhyfentown knight, and Red's ride out of here to her new home for the next six months. She's been kicking her heels in the hospital's draughty entrance hall, waiting for the pick-up she'd been told would be here an hour ago.

The biker's fingers drift skywards in a lazy salute. Their voice is muffled by the opaque screen of their helmet, which they haven't taken off. It completely covers their head, obscuring their face and hair.

'Ready?' they say.

Red is back in the outfit she wore when she fought the Sorcerer Knight. Her black undershirt and jumper have been washed clean of her blood, at least, and her boots are keeping her feet warm, but she's drowning in the greatcoat Faraday insisted on giving to her to ward off the encroaching winter chill – it's too big on her, letting in too much sharp air. She's tired, nervous, and her still tender shoulder aches in the cold.

'And you are . . .?' she asks. Don't people in this violent pit of a city even greet each other properly?

The biker taps the sunburst pin on their leathers.

Red is baffled. 'I'm just supposed to trust that? More to the point, you haven't even asked me who *I* am. How do you recognise who you're picking up?'

A hand extends back, a wave to the streets at large.

'Your face is all up in the sky,' the biker replies. 'You're pretty hard to miss, cub.'

Silver winks in their gloved hand – a trick coin. They push it into the bike's power slot, purring the engine into life. Then they point to the back seat.

Get on.

Prickling with unease, Red does so. Only knights ride trick bikes. It is the easiest way to spot one, prowling their way through the city streets like sleek cats. Many wear helmets with smoked view screens to hide their identities – though the only knights famous enough to be recognised are the ones who fight in arenas, so hiding their faces is only an invitation for people to assume that they are one and pay them even more attention. It is all part of the deliberate fame games of the Caballaria that Red finds both irritating and entirely pointless.

She is not a knight – *not yet*, she reminds herself – so this is the first time she has ever been on a bike. The Rhyfentown knight has to know that, but no mercies are granted. As soon as Red's thighs slide up against the back seat grips, the knight upkicks the engine until it gives an electronic scream. A show-off mod, Red thinks – normal trick motors are smooth and silent, barely a purr to them.

Over the keening whine, the biker turns back and shouts through their helmet, 'I go fast!'

The bike bucks and they're off, speeding down rain-slicked suburbia, no doubt followed by the eyes of startled paper shufflers peering out from their neat little apartments, the rooms behind them filled with the wails of their woken babies.

Red leans forwards into the buffeting wind, head angled towards the biker's back in front of her, thighs already starting to burn from the death grip she has around the machine's flanks. Every mild corner turn has her convinced that she is about to slide off and smash bodily into the ground. The engineer's tape around her hands is too slick against the back seat's metal pommel, and the harder she grips, the quicker her fingers slip.

This biker likes to be noticed. It irks Red – her default mode is to blend into the background. As they approach the bridge that will get them across the Thames River and into the starting tip of the vast pie wedge that is the district of Rhyfentown, however, all notions of stealth go up in flames.

Because up in the sky, ghostly against the clouds, is a face as big as a god's.

It is Red's face.

The giant projection moves as she watches, lines of pain etched across its cavernous mouth and forehead. Then it flickers, juddering to the moment her face-hood stretches off her features as the Sorcerer Knight rips it away, forcing her black hair to tumble out, strands of it sticking to the sweat on her skin. Another flicker, her exposed lips are moving, and the next moment is of the Sorcerer Knight as he falls back on to the arena floor.

The headline that lights the clouds underneath her face is in glowing crimson letters:

GODCHILD V GODCHILD!

And flashing underneath that like starbursts, the words:

UNKNOWN CHALLENGER ALMOST BESTS
SORCERER KNIGHT WITH ILLEGAL MAGIC

The curse Red spits is whipped away by the wind as soon as it leaves her mouth. Faraday had said local challenger bouts weren't recorded, not deemed entertaining enough for the main Caballaria glow shows – but apparently, hers had been. They must have found out that the Sorcerer Knight would be there that day. Her only goal had been to catch his attention, not the entire city's. Will she have eyes on her now, on every move she makes?

The thought pours cold bile into her belly.

The bike reaches the bridge, slowing down into the back-end of a traffic jam. Drivers lean out of their quad windows, yelling at other drivers up ahead who can no more move out of the way than pull a lever, flip their vehicles into tanks and roll right over the stationary mess.

'What's going on?' Red says into the back of the biker's head.

'Nothing,' the biker responds. 'Just a regular Tuesday.'

'Saints.'

The biker laughs. 'I think they figured opening up the district borders would *help* the traffic problem, but it just made everyone want to move around all the damn time. Don't you worry, though, we got ourselves a workaround.'

The bike slides into the gaps between quads like it's been greased, pulling stares along with it. Red ducks her head further into the safety of the rider's back, wishing her coat had a hood. The knight's face is covered – plus they have the added advantage of their visage not currently being echoed by an enormous news projector flickering over their heads.

Having minutes ago decided to detest bikes, she now appreciates the ease with which they can weave through a jam, much like their riders weave in and out of everyday life, touching the same roads as the rest of the city but somehow above them, elevated. They clear the bridge jam and slip into the streets beyond, thronged with people who, used to skirting fast traffic on autopilot, angle absently out of the bike's way and then turn to gawk as they belatedly realise that a knight just went past.

The biker's green leather back is lost under a riot of moving colour as adverts and shop signs blink and gyrate overhead, crowded thickly on the sides of the buildings, overlapping each other and projecting out into the air above the heads of the shifting crowd below. Flashing blue fish signs for the seafood dens, slithering bright green snakes wrapped around pulsing red rods for the hedgewitches, white lightning daggering downwards over and over for the electric charge-up kiosks. Holographic mannequins swing their hips behind flecter-glass storefronts to beckon in foot traffic, the latest light-up fashions blinking down their legs.

Winding through it all are signs of the Caballaria. Silvery sword symbols jut up from the sides of the betting shops that project shifting announcements of recent and upcoming fights into the street air:

The Black Cat v Florian the Giant

Salia Senzatown v Ego's End

Rogue Two v The Fisherman

London is a maddening jumble of a place, a million images and ideas all demanding attention, sucking a little bit of life and energy from each passing body. How anyone copes with it for long, Red does not understand. She grew up far away from its madness, if not its influence. It will never be her home. As soon as she succeeds in what she came here to do, she'll be gone. This thought is what will get her through the next few months.

Soon enough, she'll be gone.

The innermost point of Rhyfentown begins, as does each district, from the central coin-shaped area of Blackheart, then widens and widens the further out they ride. A good half hour later, heading north at buffeting speeds, and they are only just approaching their final destination.

This part of Rhyfentown is quieter than the riot they have left in their wake, but no less crammed. They turn into a narrow side street away from the main boulevard and ease past a row of cheap and cheerful eateries. The biker pulls them up just outside a tiny Alban meat bar. Despite its size and the late hour, it's popular – a crowing, laughing crowd mills inside, pressed up against the bar's see-through window front.

When the knight actually parks the bike and throws the kickstand out with the tip of their boot, Red assumes this is a pit stop for food, or a quick errand. Why it couldn't have waited until after their journey's end is not hers to fathom.

'We're here,' the biker says over their shoulder.

Red doesn't move. *Here* is barely more than an alleyway, a streak of wet pavement glistening under the glow of the shop signs. There is absolutely no way Rhyfentown's public Caballaria training grounds are *here*.

The biker turns in the saddle and pops lightly off the bike, stretching out their limbs. Not until they are standing does Red realise just how small they are.

'I don't understand,' she says eventually. 'Where are the training grounds?'

The biker gestures upwards to a tall, narrow building squeezed in between the meat bar and a bike repair kiosk. They lift up their gloved hands and tug off their opaque helmet with a groan. Underneath the helmet is the face of a woman with bright blue-tipped springy curls that graze her chin, each tendril glowing ghostly in the street lights against her dark brown skin. She shakes her head like a wet dog, making the curls dance and shudder.

'Tell me honestly,' she says to Red, 'how shit does my hair look?'

Red is mute.

'I'd ride helmetless if I could get away with it,' the knight continues, 'but my Caballaria insurance won't let me. It's the whole "head cracking open like an egg if I come off the bike" thing. I used to scoff about it, because when I was a cub we used to ride pushbikes, and we all rigged up home-made trick motors on them to hawk them up like everyone does at that age, right, so I spent my delicate formative years doing bewbies with a motor between my thighs.' She catches Red's confused expression and mistakes it. 'Bewbies, you know, "back-wheel balances"? Don't know if people say that anymore, but that's how the Rhyfters I knew when I was growing up used to call them. So when I first started learning on a proper bike, I told them, "I don't need a helmet, are you high? I've ridden years without a helmet." But they just laughed at me.' She grins. 'Turns out real bikes go a hell of a lot faster than rigged up pushbikes. All you'd get falling off a pushbike is road burn, maybe some bruises. Fall off a real bike without a helmet and you likely lose your brains. A free tip from one street fox to another.'

Red has taken the chance to examine the woman thoroughly as she chatters away. At first she isn't sure, because it couldn't possibly be – but it's the woman's flippant mention of Caballaria insurance that starts it, and identifying herself as a street fox seals it.

No wonder she was hiding underneath that helmet.

Standing all casual in the middle of a regular alleyway as if it were utterly normal for her to do so is Finnavair Caballarias o'Rhyfentown, the fighter knight known as the Fair Fae. Like Red, she famously has no family, having grown up in one of the many orphan hostels that sprang up in between each of London's civil wars.

Street fox knights are still rare enough for people to make a fuss of it. Soon after passing training, Finnavair quickly began a winning streak of bouts that got her shooting up the ranks. A ten-year veteran of the public Caballaria circuit, she is, without a doubt, one of the most popular fighters it boasts. Or at least, she was – there has been a rumour circulating about her going private in favour of a more lucrative career.

She gestures to the narrow building next to them.

'It looks small from the outside, but it's big, trust me. There's a bike park underneath the building we could have ridden into, but I'm not stopping for long, just delivering.' Her dark eyes light on Red's face, finally sensing the pause. 'How are you doing there, cub?'

She is a foot shorter than Red, at least. So much smaller in person. She is famous for using her size and youthful appearance to throw off her opponents. She is famous, full stop.

'I'm sorry, why in seven hells are *you*—?' Red swallows, searching for a less aggressive form. 'I'm trying not to be rude—'

Finnavair tips her head. 'I'm appreciating the effort. Why is someone like me giving you a ride, you mean? Well, it's nice to get out in the fresh air sometimes, you know? They don't like me going out by myself much nowadays. And I trained here, of course, grew up on Rhyfentown streets. Felt like swinging by my old dis', seeing how it's doing. Plus – you're an orphan like me, and now you're famous overnight. Seems we have a lot in common.' She laughs. 'I was curious, truth be told. I wanted to see you up close.'

She reaches a gloved hand up as if to touch Red's cheek, but Red ducks back, alarmed. She has a celebrity knight out to play fetch and games with her, one who talks too much and too fast, all easy and offhand as if this is normal, as if they know each other. It's as if someone is determined to surround her with flashing lights when all she wants to do is hide. This was not the plan.

This was not the plan at all.

Finnavair stops her hand and her mouth opens, but luckily they are both saved by a shout.

'Fin!' A lean man hangs out of the meat bar's doorway. 'What's this, you slymonger, you never said you'd be back this way any time soon!'

She turns to the shouter, a wide grin peeling across her face. 'Surprise visit,' she calls cheerfully.

The man shades his eyes with a hand and peers down the street. 'But where are all the capturers that follow you round these days?'

'Shut your pie-hole.'

'Hoy, our cwen is gracing her humble old dis',' says another voice behind the lean man. 'Anyone got any flowers to throw at her feet?'

A ripple of laughter and whoops rolls inside the meat bar, knocked from wall to wall. Whatever a cwen is, it speaks of clear, easy camaraderie, a warmth that doesn't reach Red the outsider.

'Bastards,' Fin mutters affectionately under her breath.

The bar leaks people out on to the street, and Red feels curious glances tossed her way, the stiff, drab nobody standing at the shining Caballaria darling's side.

'You too famous for a drink?' the lean man says to Fin.

'Can't,' Fin replies with obvious regret. 'I slipped out to fetch this one, and I'll be missed soon.'

'Do they not know where you are? Just as sly as ever, I see.' Up close the lean man is all points like a cricket, a head of slicked-back dark hair adding to his angles. 'So who's your silent package?'

'*Pfff,*' a curved ball of a woman exclaims from behind him. 'You had your head in your arse the last couple of days, Frome? That's that godchild challenger who made the Scourge fall over.'

Despite her sinking heart at the recognition, Red feels a prickling at the woman's choice of words.

'It was a lot more than just a falling over,' she says, then immediately regrets it.

The crowd hoots like a bunch of malevolent owls.

'She's got a tongue on her, this one,' Fin says over the noise.

'She can be a taunter,' someone else calls.

Red bites back a retort. She is no taunter, one of those who uses words as well as weapons to trip up their opponents in a bout. In Red's opinion, words have little power against a well-placed fist.

'Don't take it wrong, cub,' the lean man named Frome says easily. 'You were making him dance with you even before your little magic display. That's more achieved in one challenger bout than most have managed in a whole tourney.'

'Not true,' a girl stood next to the round woman pipes up. 'I don't understand why everyone always goes on about the Sorcerer Knight as if he's untouchable. He has *lost* bouts, you know, and opponents land blows on him all the time.'

The round woman snorts. 'Please. Everyone knows he rolls over the bouts he loses, when he's trying to game the outcome—'

'You been watching those stupid conspiracy theory glows again?' the girl retorts. 'The stats alone—'

'No stats after hours!' Frome bellows over their rising voices, and they both quiet, sheepish. 'Especially not over food, Rhy stab us.' He glances at Red. 'Speaking of, you must be starved. Join us? The stew here is the best in the dis'.'

'I ate before we left,' Red says.

Frome waves a hand dismissively. 'I'm buying.'

Red entered the Caballaria an orphan, so she supposes that it's natural to assume she has no trick to pay her way. The man means it as a kindness, but Red cannot bear kindness.

Especially considering what she has come here to do.

'I'd just like to find my room,' she says.

The awkward pause that follows this lets her know that she misjudged her tone.

'Oh, neh,' Frome replies. 'You must be tired. Shoulder still fucked, no? Don't worry, we'll go easy on you in training.'

A laugh ripples through the small crowd at his back, exposing his lie.

'Fin,' Frome says, 'you got time to show her inside?'

'For sure,' Fin replies. 'I'll come find you before I leave.'

'You'd better.' He looks at her bike. 'Or I'll let someone steal it.'

She tosses him a very explicit gesture and then starts towards the building without looking back for Red, who follows her, feeling like a pet dog trotting obediently in her wake.

She clears her throat, casting around for small talk.

'So this is your old district,' she says. 'You don't fight for a Rhyfentown stable any more?'

Fin's small mouth has a faintly amused cast. 'No, I'm Blackheart now.'

Red's pulse gives an eager skip. She's a Blackheart knight?

Make nice. She could be a way in there.

'Congratulations,' she offers. 'That's quite a promotion.'

For the ambitious, getting into a Blackheart stable is the top of the top, a wild sky dream for everyone on the bottom rungs, but Fin gives no indication of her feelings on it either way. She climbs up the three steps to the building's front door and presses a small orange button set into the wall. Muffled chimes sound from inside the building.

'Do you know the Sorcerer Knight?' Red asks.

Fin shrugs. 'No one knows the Sorcerer Knight. Not really.'

It's the sort of generically mythologising, overly dramatic thing they say about the Scourge on the glows, and it's disappointing. Fin probably hasn't even met him.

She might not be so useful, after all.

The front door opens and Fin leads the way in. The tiled corridor beyond is draughty and softly lit, the high ceiling lost in darkness. Fixed to the walls on either side are soft lamps in the shape of small, fat sunbursts. Red is led through the muffled darkness and into a small waiting room. Simple steel chairs line the sides, with rows of bookshelves recessed into one wall.

Fin stands, arms folded. 'Someone will be along to collect you and take you to your room,' she says. 'I'd best be off.'

She is unimpressed with Red. That much is clear.

'Si,' Red says, unsure how to delay her.

Fin cuts her off. 'Just Fin.'

Red gives up. 'I'm sorry if I've not behaved right,' she says. 'I'm not good at . . .'

'Talking?' Fin asks, but her voice is softer.

Offer her a truth. She seems the kind who likes honesty.

'I know I came in off Rhyfentown streets,' Red tries, 'but I grew up outside London. In the north, near the Glems border. Things are . . . strange for me, here.'

Strange, loud, grim, dark, bright, too much, too everything.

Fin cants her head. 'You're a northerner? They never said that on the glows. No wonder it was Faraday who sponsored your entry. Well, you're brave.'

Red is guarded. 'Why?'

'A northerner. A street fox. A godchild. Odds couldn't be stacked further against you, cub. At least I'm only one of those things, and I've found it tough enough.'

Red searches for how to reply. 'I want what I want,' she says eventually.

Fin seems to understand. It is another well-known London saying that Red has been careful to pick up. They applaud the ambitious here, even when it means that others must be fucked over in their wake. The Caballaria rests on the same simple principle: for there to be a winner, there must always be a loser.

Fin appears to reach some sort of conclusion about her. 'My advice?' she offers. 'Make friends. You'll need allies to survive, especially during training. For what it's worth, I hope you make it through. If there's one thing the Caballaria loves, it's an underdog with guts. Play it right and they'll lap you up.' Her eyes are warm as she regards Red. 'Just don't pull any more magic stunts that could land you in jail, neh?'

This time, she doesn't try to touch Red. The soft creak of her leathers is the only noise in the dark little waiting room as she leaves.

Make friends. There doesn't seem much advantage in such advice. Everyone in this world is out for their own gain, so why pretend otherwise?

From here on in, Red fights among her enemy.

CHAPTER 7

Blackheart
Nineteen Years Ago

'They're nervous around you. That's probably what it is. It's stage fright.'

Art slumps his forehead to the table.

'Lux,' he talks to the smooth metal surface inches from his lips, 'for someone normally so clever, you are, at this moment, I'm sorry to say, talking complete shit.'

Lucan leans back in his seat, defeated.

It has been a long, long morning.

A tournament for the Sword of London has finally been called, and the relief is so palpable it can almost be smelled on the air. Only the Caballaria can safely see the city through the many-armed deadlock they have found themselves in. The announcement has dampened the restless streets, gifting a temporary, tenuous peace. Though bars are still being busted in every district for breakouts of unsanctioned fights between passionate citizens rooting for one champion over another, at least it's only happening about once a week, and not every single night.

London waits. For now.

Each of the seven districts have formally declared their candidates to be the next King or Queen. Each verified candidate has been busy choosing a champion, a Caballaria knight who will fight for their right to rule. The next ruler of London will emerge from the arena as chosen both by the will of the saints and the indisputable power of the Caballaria. Fights are not always won with fists, but in cases like these, the saints apparently like fists best, and therefore whoever wins only does so with their grace and favour.

To Art's utter dismay, his bid for the Sword, as his family's most viable candidate, has been swiftly approved. Rival possibilities are thin on the ground. His father's only siblings were both lost in the Rhyfentown district bombings twenty years prior, and everyone else, Lillath informs him, is either too young or too far removed from Uther's bloodline to be considered fit. No one really believes he will win, but for the sake of keeping the peace, they are letting Art play. Uther still has his supporters, who have now – despite his salubrious status – transferred their allegiance to Art.

There are now only three days left for each family to name their champion, and Art is the only candidate who hasn't yet chosen his. The problem lies in finding a half-decent champion who is actually willing to fight for him.

'Being nervous,' Garad says, 'doesn't excuse complete lack of talent.'

Their chest rises and falls, shirt dark at the armpits and creased in a long, wet groove down the middle of their back. They have been working hard, but not as hard as they should have been. The private training room that has been serving as the group's audition room for Art's champion now smells of sweat overlaced with the faintest tang of blood. Garad has been sparring with each hopeful so they can show off their abilities, trying to go carefully on them – this is an audition, after all, not a real bout – but in their opinion, some of these so-called fighters deserve a future scar or two.

Lillath is thoughtful. 'I liked the girl with those lovely body-art flames going all the way up her arms.'

'She lasted less than two minutes against Garad,' Lucan says. 'I timed it.'

'I didn't say she was good. I said I *liked* her.'

'Leaving Lil's eye for bed-fillers aside,' Art says drily, 'do we think any of them can actually fight?'

'What about the juggler?' Lucan posits.

Garad gives a derisive snort. 'The *juggler*? What kind of idiot takes time out in the middle of a bout to throw his weapons up in the air? I could have skewered him twice over while he fooled about with those shiny blunt knives of his.'

'It was great showmanship,' Lucan says reasonably. 'It's how he's been taught.'

'You don't want some prick tossing knives. You want someone who's going to *win*.'

'I want someone who's going to *lose*,' Art corrects. 'I just don't want someone who's going to humiliate me doing it. I have my pride.'

Garad cuts their arm through the air, tossing their broadsword on to the ground. It slithers madly across the cement and batters the far wall, shattering the fragile peace.

Here we go again.

Art raises his head and leans back in his chair, steeling himself.

'If there's something on your mind,' he says calmly, 'by all means voice it.'

Garad wastes no time, blood still up from the last fight that ended moments ago. 'Your pride,' they spit. 'If you had your pride, you'd try and win this instead of slinking away with your tail between your legs.'

Art is a still water pool to Garad's roaring mountain river.

'Agravain Welyen has Borin the Bloodless fighting for him,' he replies. 'You recall, of course, how dear Borin got his name? Because in the last war, while all the other battle knights around him got chopped in half on the daily, he didn't even get scratched enough to draw any blood. He's the greatest Caballaria champion anyone has ever seen, with an undefeated streak longer than the Thames.'

'Twenty years ago, maybe,' Garad says doggedly. 'He's old, he's past. Everyone knows it.'

'The odds running on him are ridiculously favourable. The odds running on me are laughable, and well they should be. He's going to win, Garad. The only way he loses is if he gets bought off, and I'm pretty sure someone like him doesn't need the trick. Every other district has declared champions who range from ball-clenchingly terrifying to at least surpassingly good, and I'm left with the embarrassing dregs because no decent Caballaria knight wants to risk their career to fight for the god-touched mistake. And frankly, why should they? I was never meant to rule.'

'You saintsdamned soft spine,' Garad shouts. 'All your life you've talked about making things better for everyone, not just the ones rich enough to afford it. You know exactly what'll happen if Agravain gets the Sword.' They point an accusatory finger at Art. 'You've had one of the finest educations that trick can buy. You've spent your entire childhood studying history, war, governance, damn . . . even *philosophy*. You're clever, you're kind, and you know what it's like to be an outsider. To be excluded just because of the way you were born. How many times have you said that the only way to change things is by having the power to do it? And now here it is, that power handed to you on a fucken plate, and you're running. You're *running*.'

Garad finally loses steam and their finger drops. They claim not to be able to use words so well, but once in a while they somehow manage it all right.

It is not the first time Art has heard something like this. Brune has taken him aside more than once, ostensibly for a little private one-on-one that begins as coaching and ends with her trying to understand why he's not out there romancing and oiling up the court's veteran power players, attempting to win support. His arguments that 'nothing good ever came from courts filled with sycophants in it for their own gain' just earns him a condescending look. *This is the way you gain power*, says the look, *this is the game*.

But Art doesn't want to play.

At least Brune seems willing to give him a chance. More than once over the last few weeks he has detected a tiny flicker of burgeoning respect in her eyes, modulations in how she speaks to him – though she is careful to give no hints of this in public.

'I mean to lose this tourney, Garad,' he says quietly, 'but if you don't want to be a part of it . . .' He turns to Lucan and Lillath, both stock-still in their chairs. 'I understand.'

'You defy the saints if you try to game it,' Garad says. 'It's blasphemy.'

Art gives a heavy sigh. 'It's how it's always been.'

'So you're gaming it because everyone else does? What a noble argument.'

'No, I'm gaming it because it's the only way out of a duty not one Londoner wants me to have, including me.'

Garad shakes their head, pushing the heels of their hands across their forehead in frustration. Art has always loved his friend for their idealism, but when it swings too far towards naïveté it does tend to grate.

Lucan speaks. 'Garad should be your champion.'

Art frowns. 'What?'

Garad's hands freeze. '*What?*'

'Garad. Your champion,' Lucan repeats.

Lillath barks a laugh. 'Lucan, go get some fresh air.'

'Listen to me,' Lucan says, his voice maddeningly calm. 'In an even match, the Caballaria is almost never determined by strength. This is why for important bouts, the fighters are matched as evenly as possible, yes? If you're an atheist, it's pure bastard luck that determines the outcome. If you're not, it's the will of the saints.'

'There's no even match in this,' Lillath argues. 'Borin's going to crush everyone. Simple.'

'Not necessarily,' Lucan says patiently. 'He *is* old. Now, we've got the richest, most elite candidates throwing their weapons into the ring, so that pretty much means all the champions are going to be the best fighters in London. Maybe even the Seven Kingdoms. That's about as even a matching as it gets, wouldn't you say?'

Art massages the bridge of his nose. 'Where are you going with this, Lux?'

'Say Garad is your champion.' Lucan holds his tutorial finger aloft. 'Now, that's *uneven* matching. Not yet out of training, no Caballaria tourneys to their name, not even an official bout. *We* know they're an amazing fighter, but no one else does. So:

Garad is likely to lose – apologies, Gar – but at least you know they'll lose well. Your pride is intact and you can slink off into the night. But in the unlikely event that Garad *wins* . . . well, that's the will of the saints. How can you argue against the saints?'

'I'm an atheist,' Art says, his voice bone-dry.

'Then they're the most amazingly lucrative odds you've ever seen, and you can lay down a bet on Garad, make yourself a ton of trick before you're forced to take the Sword.' Lucan's smile is wide. 'Give your winnings to charity, if you like. Start your reign with a positive bang. Anyway, you don't really think they're going to win against Borin, do you? You said so yourself – he's the greatest Caballaria champion anyone's ever seen.'

Art growls, 'Stop goading me.'

Lucan sensibly falls silent.

Art dares to look at Garad. 'Tell me you think this is the stupidest idea you've ever heard.'

Garad has fallen eerily calm. 'Actually,' they say slowly, 'I don't.'

Art closes his eyes. 'Fuck.'

CHAPTER 8

The Dungeons, Rhyfentown
Eleven Months Ago

A sudden sonic violence throws Red so hard out of deep sleep that she ends up toppling halfway to the concrete floor before she even realises she is awake.

Silvers seem to customise their glow-screen alarms with as much loving detail as their bodies and their clothes. The sound they choose to wake up to in the morning is a cultivated one, saying as much about their personality as their earrings, their jacket patches and their skin art. Many record their own voices, or buy the voice of their favourite glow actor, as if they can pretend that the actor lies next to them like a lover, murmuring them into gentle wakefulness. Some choose songs as their alarm, others bird calls or the soft patter of rain.

Some absolute *bastard* has set Red's glow-screen alarm to the sound of an industrial jackhammer.

POUND POUND POUND POUND goes her heart, in tune with the deafening, bowel-loosening hammer currently making her entire room vibrate. It takes her a few terrifying seconds to confirm that is not due to a construction team drilling a hole in her own floor.

Frantic and electrified, she yells, 'STOP, SHUT UP, I'M AWAKE,' but she can't even hear her own voice over the noise. She scrabbles to the glow screen, dancing over it and waving her hands.

The buzzing silence left in the alarm's abrupt departure is almost as deafening.

Red cautiously begins to relax each twisted muscle, but just as she reaches the point where terror starts to flip over and become anger, a loud thump from the wall only feet away from her sets her jumping.

'What the fuck,' comes a muffled screech from the room next to hers, as the owner of it pounds their adjoining wall for emphasis. 'What. The. *Fuck*.'

And now at least one of her fellow trainees, whom she has yet to meet, will hate her on sight.

Good.

Red's overwhelming first impression of Rhyfentown's public Caballaria training grounds is of a strange, tall rat maze.

The building is made up of floors and floors of long corridors, endless doors and darkness, and what it seems to lack in width it more than makes up for in both height and depth. The first few floors are the living quarters, modestly furnished rooms that each trainee sleeps in during their time there. The building knows an ebb and flow, a constant swelling and receding tide of bodies as more hopefuls are picked up in the yearly local challenger bouts and deposited within its walls, only for many to fail or drop out within the two-week trial period. A month down the line and the floors will be half empty. Near the end of the six-month training and it's a ghost town.

Red's own room is simple and to the point. A single bed,

wardrobe, desk and washbasin. A battered little glow screen fixed into the wall shows her schedule. The wardrobe holds three outfits. One is a thin, slippery, figure-hugging two-piece. The other is looser, a black shirt and trousers designed for bigger movement. The final one is a series of connected armour plates, made from a lightweight material entirely flexible through its many joins. Two coats, one short and indoor soft, the other a longer, thicker waterproof. Each piece of clothing sports a small, woven patch decorated with the Rhyfentown sunburst design. Soft, pliable shoes and hard boots complete the minimalist range.

This floor's washroom is several doors down from Red's bedroom. It is communal in the fullest sense of the word, sporting dull metal shower tubes fastened in a long row down one wall, but no divide of any kind between them. It is also the darkest, most cavernous washroom she has ever seen, covered in an endless mosaic of indigo tile that is broken up only by the shower tubes and a surprisingly large number of regular drain-hole grilles set into the middle of the floor.

'So the blood don't show up,' grunts a naked trainee, catching the look on Red's face when she enters. The trainee is a hulking mass of a human, with exquisite tendrils of black tattooed line art covering most of his skin, showing off the fact that he has endured hours upon hours of pain. It is a badge of honour, a tactic designed to intimidate.

He gives Red a cold grin and shoulders past her on his way out.

Red stands, draws her breath in slow, lets it out slower. It is her very first day of training. If she wants to get through this, she needs to be calm.

A hurried shower does nothing to take the edge off her

nerves. Luckily she's the only one in there. Apart from the hulking trainee who was in here before her, she is up and about earlier than the rest of this year's intake.

The reason is because she has an appointment with a tattooist before breakfast.

Her schedule didn't list the reason why it had to be before breakfast, but she already knows. They don't want to run the risk of her puking half-digested food across the room. She might be new to tattooing, but she has read up on it. Most Londoners get their first tattoo when they're younger than she is. Tattoos are regarded as much a part of their rituals of customisation as their clothes patches or hair styles. Only godchildren don't have a choice about it.

Red had known going in that this would be an unavoidable part of her journey. The registration law was supposed to be a way to bring godchildren out from the underground, legitimise them, open them up to respectable jobs and normal lives. No employer would hire a godchild without knowing exactly what magic they had – would anyone be okay working alongside a telepath who could pick up on your private thoughts without you knowing, or get inside your head and make you do whatever they wanted? – and so registration was born.

It's only fair, argue the commons. *Don't want godchildren using their magic to get ahead without us even knowing about it. It's about equality.*

The more paranoid glow shows put the estimate near half a million, but no one really knows how many unregistered godchildren there are currently across the Seven Kingdoms. Still, half a million people out of the total population of near eighty million makes them rare enough.

The back streets of every district are filled with godchild

soothsayers, dispensing their bits of prophecy for trick coin. It is a rite of passage, of sorts, to dare to visit one when you're barely more than a cub and get your fortune told. Every so often there have been half-hearted attempts to crack down on the fortune-telling black market, but in reality the soothsayers of London are a major tourist draw. They are regarded as mostly harmless, their fortunes being vague and all-purpose at the best of times.

No, registration is really for those much rarer godchildren with talents like Red's. The truly dangerous ones who can move things without touching them, create illusions more real than life or lift thoughts straight from your head. They can do anything to you.

It's about equality, the commons repeat. *That's all.*

But it is far more about the balance of power, and while electricity might be its currency, power is the wheel on which London turns.

Back in her room after her hasty shower, Red chooses the loose shirt and trousers to dress in and the heavy boots for her feet, feeling like she needs weight to anchor her to the floor. She checks the scratched glow screen attached to her wall again and again, memorising the route to her appointment, and then leaves her room.

The corridors are silent. She makes her way slowly, a strange sense beginning to steal over her. It feels like no time has moved on since last night. It feels like nothing has changed. There is no new-day sensation. What if whoever messed with her alarm set it to seem like it was going off in the morning but in reality it's still the middle of the night? There is no one else around. Where is the nearest daylight? How does she check?

Red halts in the middle of a stairwell as the realisation hits her.

Last night's impassive guide kept referring to this building as 'the Dungeons' rather than the 'training grounds', as if it was a moniker everyone should instinctively know even if they have never been here before, but she hadn't understood why until just now. Her corridor, her room, the cavernous washroom, this stairwell – none of them have any natural light.

There are no windows anywhere in this entire building.

When she resumes her course, she finds her feet going faster, responding to her pounding pulse. It is a ridiculous thing to be afraid of. Of all the things she has endured and will in the months to come, this will surely not be the hardest. If she can't even get through—

Up ahead of her, a door opens.

'Ah, there you are,' says a woman. 'Come in, come in.'

Red doesn't hesitate. Hesitation is weak.

The rubbery surface of the eggs on her plate glisten just a little too much in the dining room's bright electric light. Red pushes the plate away.

The tattooist was surprisingly kind, but nothing could have prepared her for the needle. A buzzing, invasive sensation like a swarm of microscopic bees trapped under her skin, rolling through her nerves in waves.

It is a small tattoo and it sits on her upper neck, just behind her left ear. The ink the tattooist used is a muted grey, barely visible until a special kind of light reveals it. The design is an inoffensive symbol, an undulating cross-hatch of thin, curved lines. A pretty kind of scar, but still a scar. It will never come off, and she had no choice.

Red has been designated as a pelleren, the name for someone who can move objects without touching them. The registrars probed her background, asking her questions on when she had first begun to notice her ability, how it had manifested in the past, if she had tested it out in any useful ways to explore its limits.

She told them that she was an orphan, having lost her parents in a bombing when she was three. That she grew up in a hostel in a sizeable but isolated town near the Glems border. Her life changed when, aged twelve, she got into a violent scuffle with another hostel kid. She learned two things that day. One, that she was a godchild. Two, that she had a natural talent for the fight.

She came to London a few days before the yearly challenger bouts were due to start, armed with what travelling money she had managed to scrape together from the hostel patrons. She came here because all she had ever wanted was to join the Caballaria; it is the only thing that has ever meant anything to her.

She left out all the really interesting parts of her story and lied about the rest of it. If they noticed the holes, they made no sign.

The Dungeons dining room is full of trainees at breakfast, a sea of stranger faces. There's not much talk – a little low conversation here and there. The air is full of tense energy. They are each on a path that will see most of them fail to become a knight, and now they have one more to add to their number. They size her up, some openly, some surreptitiously. She feels eyes slide her way, but no one approaches.

The first hour after breakfast finds her in an uncomfortably warm room deep in the bowels of the building, full of hulking, humming machines edged in glow light. Next to them are two women dressed in impractical outfits that can only mean they have nothing to do with training her to fight. One has a row of bells fixed to the bottom of her skirt that tinkle sweetly every time she moves, like an aural warning system. When the hem lifts as she shifts in her seat, Red catches sight of boots so heavy that they put hers to shame.

The other woman wears her saffron-yellow hair in a long, arrowing plait. Her clothes, her hair, her make-up seem designed to guide the eye down her form like water. They call themselves *flow*, an aesthetic popular in Rhyfentown right now, which favours simple, soft lines of minimalist grace. This flow has a sharp, eagle-like face thrown into even greater relief by the hard light from the portable glow screen held in her hands.

'Name,' she says.

'Red o'Rhyfentown.'

'Age.'

'Eighteen.'

'And you're a pelleren, correct?'

'Yes.'

'Adjust readings for elevated body temp,' the flow mutters into the room, and the other woman nods. 'Now. Step up to me, please, and take all your clothes off.'

Red hesitates. No wonder the room is so warm. Like a pig being prepped for market, she must be weighed and measured, poked and prodded, every detail of her body noted. It has become her main commodity. This is going to happen on a weekly basis as long as she is still in training so her physical changes can be tracked, which means she'd better get used to the sensation.

Show no weakness.

She pulls off her clothes and then stands gazing at the far wall while the flow walks around her with a glow measuring tape, wrapping the thin strip of light around various parts of her body and noting down each measurement. There is no sensation of touch from either the woman or the measuring tape, and her voice is absent. She must have done this hundreds of times with hundreds of bodies, over the years.

The woman's gaze snags on the patch taped to Red's neck, spotted with tiny flecks of blood from the fresh tattoo. She wonders just how many of the bodies this woman has processed belonged to godchildren. Hardly any, judging by the way she lingers on the tattoo patch.

'Dominant hand?' she asks.

'Excuse me?'

'The hand you fight with.'

'My left.'

'Oh, just like the Sorcerer Knight!' the woman with the belled skirt says cheerily, the top of her head just visible above the humming machine bank she sits at. 'Did you know there's only fourteen registered godchildren in the whole of the Caballaria right now?'

'Yes,' Red says.

The flow clicks her tongue. 'Of course she does, Ano,' she says impatiently. 'Why wouldn't someone like her know a thing like that?'

Someone like her.

The flow fits a bulky bracelet around Red's left wrist. The bracelet is a wide band of dark leather encasing a hard, boxy bundle. Three small buckles strap it tight to her flesh. It sits cold and awkward against the nodule of her wrist bone.

'You've trained with a monitor before,' the flow states.

Red shakes her head.

The flow frowns. 'What, never?'

'They didn't have them where I come from.'

The flow's gaze clears. 'Oh, of course – the north.'

An orphan hostel, actually, Red wants to say, *where they don't have the trick for gadgets like this* – but the bracelet's alien weight on her wrist has temporarily dampened her fire.

'It's pretty basic,' the flow says. 'It measures your energy output – godchildren have higher base-level readings, you know, and of course when you use magic, the readings shoot through the roof – and then they'll collect the data from it after each of your fights.'

'It's just to make sure you don't cheat,' Ano, the belled-skirt woman, chimes in.

Every one of the fourteen godchild fighters wears a similar monitor, as much a part of their aesthetic as their weapons and hair. The Sorcerer Knight's own bracelet is a sleek, muted black thing which probably cost more than the annual budget of this training ground. As with the tattoo, the bracelet is simply part of the deal, next on the list of trials Red must endure to reach her goal.

She becomes aware of the flow's gaze. Her pupils are nothing but disturbing dark pinpricks swimming in white irises – customised lenses, Red presumes, but the effect is grim.

'Are you all right?' the flow asks her.

It sounds kind.

Red gives a quick nod.

The flow examines her a moment more, then closes off her glow screen with a snap.

'All right, we're finished. You'll be able to access all the information we've collected on the screen in your room, and it will be updated with your latest stats after each session with us. Which means that you can put your clothes back on, and we'll see you next week.'

'Not if I fail training,' Red says.

The flow regards her. 'I somehow doubt that's going to happen with you.'

Before she can compose a reaction to this, the flow turns her back and walks over to the woman with the belled skirt. Red hurriedly pulls on her clothes. She turns at the door, expecting them to be huddled over a screen together, so it jolts her to see that both women are watching her. The flow's pinhole eyes are still uncomfortably blank.

'You should run,' she says. 'You've only got five minutes to get to your next session.'

Red remembers from her schedule that her next session is in a room fifteen floors up and mentally curses this strange, towering edifice she has voluntarily trapped herself in.

'T'chores!' the woman with the belled skirt says cheerily. 'Have a successful first day!'

'Thank you,' Red stammers, and flees.

The ascender machine that is supposed to take Red to her first-ever group fight session is a huge birdcage of twisted metal that judders alarmingly into life when she pulls its spark lever. She holds on to the vibrating bars and finds herself wondering what it will feel like to fall tens of floors to her death.

She reaches the right floor without incident and wipes a curl of sweat from her forehead with the heel of her hand before continuing on. Between the hot, strange measurement session and the sprinting she had to do in order to get up here on time, she's feeling more than a little uncomfortably slick, and she doesn't want anyone to mistake exertion for nerves.

Because she is absolutely not nervous.

It isn't until she opens the door to the training room that she realises it isn't a room at all – it is the rooftop of the building. Cold air slices her face, whipping past her and slamming the door shut out of her shocked hand.

For one heart-freezing moment she thinks she has made a mistake.

No. No mistake. She sees the evenly spaced figures ahead of her, hears the shout of an instructor, the end of their words bitten off by the hungry wind. The group stands in the shadow of an overhang which marks the edge of the building's solar panel farm. Sturdy metal sheets tower above them all, glittering in the cold light, faced towards the morning sun in impassive rows.

The training room for this session is down on Red's schedule as 'practice space 34', which had hardly indicated the damn rooftop. As she approaches the group, she notices every single one of them is snugly wrapped in a copy of the short coat currently hanging uselessly in her wardrobe. The wind cuts less in the space under the overhang, but she can still feel her fingers galloping valiantly towards numb.

And eyes on her, turning to track her progress.

They have already had two weeks to feel their way around this place, their schedules, each other. They are gradually filling their moulds here. Red is oozing out over the sides of hers, sloppy and blind.

'Hoy, trainee,' says the instructor, his arms folded. It is the thin man from last night's meat bar, the one Fin was so friendly with. He is also, Red notices with some bitterness, in a coat. 'Time to work that shoulder.'

'Feeling warm, godchild?' calls a voice from the paired crowd. One or two laughs follow.

'They're more hot-blooded than us, didn't you know that?' says another.

Red keeps silent, working to un-tense her jaw.

'Shut your flute, Kay,' mocks the instructor. 'You were an hour late to your very first session because you couldn't even find your way up here. That's a touch more embarrassing than being underdressed.'

'This place is a rat maze,' the luckless Kay protests. 'How's anybody supposed to? Come to think of it, how did the god-child find it? Been here before, have you?'

Red scans the crowd and finds the one talking. Saints alive, the blustery Kay is built like a bull. Perhaps best not to antagonise him right away.

'Never in my life,' Red says evenly.

'She's still late,' someone else snorts.

'My measurements session overran.'

Kay looks her up and down. 'You're tiny,' he roars. 'What the shit is there to measure?'

A girl bursts out laughing.

'Enough,' the instructor calls. He faces Red, gives her a short head bow. 'My name is Daedalas Caballarias Frome o'Rhyfentown. My name to you will most often be "Si Frome". Occasionally you may wish to amend that to the longer and more formal version of "Fuck You, Si Frome", which will no doubt rise unbidden to your mouth at least once over the course of your time here.'

'For anyone who's had their head jammed into their arses over the last couple of weeks, this,' Frome sweeps a hand out in Red's direction, 'is the now infamous Red o'Rhyfentown, who narrowly escaped jail to get her hind into a training ground.

She gambled and she won. Now we'll see if her gamble pays off.' His hand sweeps back to the crowd. 'These are your fellow trainees. You're two weeks behind every single one of them. Now you just have to survive the next six months.'

The most evil smile Red has ever seen splits Frome's face in two.

'Also,' he continues cheerfully, 'your shoulder is still tender, you're undernourished, underweight for your body mass, you've spent the last few days wasting in a bone-house bed instead of using your muscles and your physical system is currently compromised by the cold because you didn't think to bring a coat with you this morning. Each of them has a head start on you in every possible way.'

He gestures to a lithe woman with a carefully styled strip of thick orange hair running down the centre of her head to tickle her neck. The woman steps forwards. Held loosely in her hands is a thin length of metal piping.

Red flinches as something freezing cold brushes her knuckles. Frome is holding out a similar length of piping, prodding her weaker fight hand with its end. She takes it automatically, then glances up at him.

'Defend yourself,' he says simply. 'I don't want flashiness, I want simple. I want to see how you move. Begin.'

Orange Strip lunges for Red, delivering a whack to her forearm that rings inside her flesh and begins a furious, creeping burn, lighting up each nerve ending as it goes. Orange Strip moves back as Red gasps and wrenches away, and the rest of the group melt back against the wall to give them their dance space.

Red grapples for the pipe with her other hand. Thank the saints her opponent went for the wrong arm.

'You know what I heard?' Orange Strip says, her voice

pleasant as she shifts slowly from foot to foot, easing and centring her balance. Her eyes catch on the bulky bracelet around Red's wrist. 'I heard that sometimes you godchildren lose control and you just can't help your magic coming out.' *Magic* is said with the same tone most might use on the word *turd*. 'But even if it's a mistake, even if you didn't mean it, you still get kicked out of the Caballaria. Ain't that right, Si Frome?'

'No second chances in this game,' Frome murmurs in reply. He's taken a stance alone, off to the side, his arms folded and his face watchful.

Orange Strip laughs, carving a figure of eight with the end of her pipe. Red just watches, easing herself back into a poised balance, coaxing her frozen muscles into alertness.

This time, she sees it when Orange Strip lunges, switching her hips to the side to avoid a vicious jab to her guts. Adrenalin leaves shaves of metal in her blood, cutting her up on the inside.

'They might be afraid of you out there,' Orange Strip says, pale eyes wide to catch any little movement, 'but in here, one little bit of puffery and you're gone. So what are you without your magic?'

Red is all gritted teeth. 'A fucken ace fighter who's about to knock you on your back.'

Jeers burst from the crowd, growing in strength as she simply waits, doing nothing of the sort. The bracelet pulls her arm down, a new weight she hasn't had time to adjust to. She strikes forwards and Orange Strip evades easily, returning to a centred balance with a grin on her face.

Good. Let her get cocky. Red doesn't push forwards, but waits instead. It earns her a goading from the crowd. She ignores it.

They clash twice. Unless Orange Strip is faking, which she

may well be, she has the widest, most obvious tell when she drops into guard—

'Enough tender licking,' Frome calls. 'Step it up.'

He has barely finished his sentence and Red is already there, ducking under her opponent's softened guard as the idiot pays too much attention to her instructor, delivering a crushing swipe to Orange Strip's shoulder that crumples her to the floor. Her pipe clangs hard to the ground and rolls away.

'Oh look,' Red says. 'Now *your* shoulder hurts, too.'

Orange Strip's face is stretched in pain. She glares up at Red from her position on the freezing ground. Her breath clouds on the air.

'Sneaky cheat,' she says darkly.

Red feels a gorgeous, joyful rush at the sight of her opponent hurt and beaten and hissing like a cut cat. It is an old friend, that gorgeous rush, and she welcomes it in.

'Again,' Frome orders.

Orange Strip hauls herself to her feet. She is given her pipe back and switches it to her uninjured hand, carving a figure of eight with as much ease and grace as before.

Ambidextrous. Fantastic.

This time Red goes in, but there's no ducking under the solid guard that comes up and the clang from their connecting weapons judders agonisingly up her nerves.

They dance.

To her credit, Orange Strip is more careful this time, but Red – belly gnawing from the hole left by the breakfast she didn't eat, neck aching from the tattoo she never wanted, wrist stinging from the bracelet that watches her body like a naughty child – stops fighting the rush and with a glad, hot sigh, gives her body what it wants and lets go.

The roaring wave that follows gets her through the next few seconds. Three furious strikes later and her opponent is back on the ground, all pretence of equality gone. Orange Strip isn't the Sorcerer Knight. Orange Strip isn't who Red most ardently, desperately desires to have on their knees before her.

Orange Strip is just in the way.

Red hears someone mutter a soft oath, thick with a glotted Rhyfentown accent. She heaves in a shuddering breath, coming back to herself. So calm now. Such beautiful, peaceful calm. The calm that comes after letting go is a craving she has always been too afraid to voice, because she knows what it makes her.

A monster.

'Well,' Frome says into the silence, sounding satisfied, 'now you all know why she caught everyone's attention. It wasn't about the magic, children. In the Caballaria, it'll never be about magic. It's about the fight, and it roars in her heart just the same as yours. Shae and Dekkard – you're up.'

Red backs out of the fight space, only now aware again of the eyes on her, the mutters behind hands. As the lesson continues with a different pair, she feels a presence at her elbow.

'That was beautiful,' says a mouth near her ear, close enough that she feels hot breath tickle.

She pulls away from the heat and turns to find a shaven-haired girl with sultry, heavy-lidded eyes standing close.

'Sela,' the girl murmurs.

Red gives a wary nod. 'Red.'

'How d'you learn to fight like that?' Sela asks.

'My hostel was run by an ex-Caballaria. She favoured the ones who could fight. Gave us regular training.'

'A brutal upbringing.'

Red shrugs, unwilling to invite scrutiny.

Sela tips her head. 'I've never met a godchild before.'

'Lucky you.' Red concentrates on the fight before them.

She hears Sela laugh. 'Don't worry, I'm not one of those fetish types. Magic doesn't make me hot. But a woman who can handle a weapon . . .'

Red glances at her. Sela has a faintly suggestive smile on her face.

'Ignore the others,' she advises. 'People are often afraid of what they don't understand.'

'You think you understand me?' Red shoots back.

'Not yet. But give me time.'

Sela turns her back and moves away, leaving a baffled Red staring after her with a flush on her face that cannot, truthfully, be totally blamed on the aftermath of the fight.

Hours later, a bone-weary Red stumbles back into her room, and the first thing she sees within its welcoming darkness is the scratched glow screen on her wall, lit up with a new message icon.

She presses on the icon and it opens up. Confusingly, the sender appears to be anonymous. The building's glow network is a closed circuit, Red knows – nothing from the outside gets in or out – so it has to be from someone within the training grounds.

The message itself is just four words long:

Impressive first day.
Wyll

The Sorcerer Knight.

He is not in the building. He can't be. All would be uproar if he was.

Maybe someone on the inside is sending him information and relaying his messages for him. They have all been warned that training sessions are recorded for playback and study. What if someone sent the Sorcerer Knight the recording of Red's fight this morning? It would make sense for him, wouldn't it, to check up on his investment. Reassure himself that he bet on the right dog.

In the safety of her own head, Red can admit to occasional moments of doubt before now. It had seemed so impossible to achieve, catching the attention of the most famous knight in the Seven Kingdoms. Yet here it is, evidence in hand. The Scourge is watching her.

And she is one step closer to her revenge.

CHAPTER 9

Cair Stour Arena, Blackheart
Nineteen Years Ago

The morning of the tournament for the Sword of London dawns bright and sharp.

Art has not seen or spoken to Garad for seven days straight. Following the rules of the Caballaria, all nominated champions are sequestered, not only from those for whom they fight, but from the world. They use the time to prepare in solitude, employing trainers for last-minute tactics and training if they so wish.

Garad has asked Si Vergo, the hulking master from their training grounds, to visit each day. They have asked for no other visitors. Family and friends are barred, according to tradition. All ties to the parts of each champion's life that is not Caballaria have been temporarily severed. For them, the fight is now all that must exist.

Art has been reliably informed that the palace underbelly has its own secret betting pool going on, and that the odds on Garad winning are outrageously low. Their entry into the tournament was a fraught process. It took two independent tutors from Garad's training grounds to sponsor them, and hours of cajoling Garad's family to persuade them to sign the waivers that disavow Blackheart of blame in case of injury or death during the tournament.

Art has been kept entirely out of it. Garad is the determined one, the one arguing their way in and bullying the right bureaucrats to bend the rules – rules, Garad keeps pointing out, that are already half out the window in this unprecedented situation. Art himself is an unprecedented situation. It seems to make sense that his champion should mirror this.

In fact, Garad has taken to being Art's champion in a very unexpected way. The others just laugh when Art brings it up – 'How have you never noticed that Garad's head and heart both belong to the Caballaria?' Lillath said when he pointed it out – but Art realises that he had no idea up until now just how deep the fight runs within his friend.

It has been keeping him up at night. The evening before the tournament sees him awake until the early hours, staring up into the dark, heart turning in a slow, awful churn of dread.

What if it goes wrong, and Garad dies? It's rare, but it happens.

Art will have killed his best friend for a Sword he does not want.

'Tell Garad to pull out.'

Lucan blinks sleep away, pulling his long indoor coat tighter around his body.

'Art,' he says with a croak. 'How in seven hells d'you get out of the palace?'

Art jerks his head towards the door. 'They'd only let me out if I was accompanied by an armed guard. There are two of them standing in the corridor out there, so don't make any loud noises, neh? They startle easily.'

They are in the cavernous kitchens of the Caballaria training grounds at Villiers Street, where Lucan – and until the past week, Garad – has been living. It is barely a ten-minute bike ride from the palace, but from the way the guards had looked at him, you'd think he'd told them he was off to a Wardogs bar to get his face pummelled for fun. Even temporary Kings apparently do not take unscheduled trips in the middle of the night.

Lucan sinks on to a chair opposite Art, who is sat beside the still glowing embers of a slumbering fire. The palace rooms are riddled with such open fire grates – though only in the private wings, he has noticed. The rooms housing those vastos who live within Cair Lleon walls, as well as the public halls and meeting rooms, all sport electric chandeliers and heating systems laced into the walls for light and warmth. Fire is pure opulence and sheer waste.

By all reports, his father loved fire.

'Tell Garad to pull out,' Art repeats.

Lucan shakes his head. 'I can't.'

'Well, I can't, can I? It's going to be a bit obvious if *I* try to pay a visit, but couldn't you ask Vergo, or sneak in or something . . .?'

'Art, the tourney champions are all in a fully guarded monastery. You know this. I can't sneak in, there's nothing to sneak in behind. They barely believe in furniture in those places.'

'Get a message to them, then.'

'I understand that you're worried—'

'I'm not worried,' Art spits. 'I'm terrified.'

Lucan is silent.

Art slumps back. 'Lux. What have I done?'

'We.' Lucan's voice is soft but unyielding. 'We all decided this together, remember? If you ask Garad to pull out now, you'll ruin their career before it's even begun. Garad takes honour very, very seriously. You know that. You've always known that. They'll hate you for it. They'll never forgive you.'

'They already hate me. And if anything happens to them, I'll never forgive myself.

'Garad's made their choice.' Lucan gives him a steady look. 'The least you can do is to help them see it through.'

Cair Stour, London's most famous Caballaria arena and the largest in all Seven Kingdoms, rears into the sky like an indifferent god. Sprawling heavily across the landscape and drawing the gaze, it is built on the site of an ancient cathedral, now long gone into the dust of past wars, and sits a convenient five-minute quad ride away from the palace.

Rather than the expected fanfare, Art insists his arrival be as anonymous as possible – and Brune has, surprisingly, agreed. On the day of the tournament, Art is taken out to the arena an hour earlier than anyone else from the palace, travelling there in a sleek, anonymous quad flanked by a cadre of guard knights. Cair Stour's wide boulevard is already packed with people camped out to catch a glimpse of every arrival they can. His quad causes much stirring and excitement, but with smoked windows and no official markings, the crowd has no way of knowing who might be inside. They crane their necks and strain their eyes at the back windows, trying in vain to catch the tiniest glimpse of a face.

Art surreptitiously lowers himself in his seat.

His quad circles the arena's vast bulk and he enters the building through an unremarkable private entrance near the back, thankfully empty of any watchers. Inside, an air of strange, reverent silence drapes blanket-like over every stone. History is being made here today, and the building itself seems to know it.

Art is led to the Eye, the opulent private area reserved for citizens of the palace and only accessible via a private ascender activated by a key. The box is the loftiest of all viewpoints in the entire arena, the main room of the very top floor. Art is stationed there by himself with a resplendent array of food and drink to wait it out, bored and twitching out of his skull.

Temporary Kings still get the best seat in the house, it seems. He is right at the front, close enough to touch the balcony edge that hangs ponderously over the arena floor. His chair is high-backed and cordoned off from the rest of the Eye by swathes of charcoal silk draped between metal spike stands. Two entirely silent guard knights flank him at a barely respectful distance. The entire set-up screams *do not approach.* Over the next hour or so, Art sits and listens to the rustling and murmurs swelling at his back as the box slowly begins to fill up.

He has never felt so alone in his life.

For the duration of the tournament, he will be sharing the room with people who have, until now, pretended that he doesn't exist. He has been kept away from most of them during his short time living at the palace, like a fragile glass oddity to be studied and discussed, but not to be interacted with, which risks making him human and real. Current precarious protocol demands that no one approach him without a formal invitation, and the only one well placed to do so is Brune, who hasn't arrived yet.

This whole absurd situation, he thinks, may at least provide some entertainment.

Night falls and the stands below begin to fill, clogging up the vast, echoing arena space with a roaring buzz of noise and life. Huge projections of each champion flicker across the sky above the fighting pit, moving through recorded loops of their attack stances, their most famous finishing moves, their favoured weapons. Patterned neon spotlights rove over the pit, streaking the sand and concrete over and over in a hypnotising dance.

It all seems so far away from the lofty heights of the Eye. The crowds below cannot see into the box – it is protected by a one-way screen – but Art can see out. He is removed, floating above the world like a numb and serene balloon. He wonders idly which moment will bring him crashing back down to earth. Will it be when Garad steps out into the arena?

Will it be when they lose?

Roving capturers rake along the heads of the packed, seated crowd. The cream of London is here from each of the seven districts, and the capturers are eager to pick them out for the giant glow screens stood at each arena end, keeping the status-obsessed members of the crowd entertained at their favourite game of people-spotting.

The rest of the stands are filled with Londoners from all walks of life. Tickets were offered in lotteries held at every district. Half the crowd is here because of the luck of the draw – each successful applicant security-vetted, of course, or they'd have never even made it through Blackheart's famously strict border control.

Art finds his gaze drawn to the Alaunitown section of the stands. High up in the sky-seats sit the Welyen family, sequestered from the rest of their fellow district citizens by transparent flecter-glass walls and impassive guard knights with gun-belted hips. As the supposed descendants of Saint Alaunis himself, the entire district bows to Welyen influence – influence that much more cemented with the marriage between Orcade Welyen and King-in-the-Ground Uther Dracones.

The arena captures greedily focus on the man sat next to

Orcade. It is Agravain, her older brother and the absolute favourite to win. His chestnut hair is slicked back from his face today, exposing his soft, rounded features. He wears a high-collared white coat threaded with copper wire, in traditional Alaunitown colours and style. Peeking through the folds of his coat is a poorly hidden knife scabbard secured with a hip sash.

Any Londoner has the right to carry a personal weapon, but they are outright banned from Caballaria arenas and bars. The only people who should be weaponed here today are the guns and the swords – the arena's guard knights and the fighters themselves. Agravain Welyen likes to flaunt his ability to break the rules with no consequence. Such is his privilege. He lounges in his seat with breezy confidence, laughing at something his grandmother Irena has just said in his ear.

Orcade is not laughing. She looks young and composed next to her braying brother. Her marriage to Uther was deemed one of political and economical superiority on both sides, heartily approved by all the official pundits, but Art has often found himself wondering what Orcade herself felt about it. Marrying a feared and hated man three times her age, moved like a chess pawn in the game of power that her family plays so well.

Perhaps it had been her idea. Perhaps she had been happy about it.

One thing is clear. Choosing to sit with her family in the Alaunitown section instead of the Eye is an undeniable statement, and one commentators are no doubt crowing over right now. Orcade does not approve of her dead husband's bastard son trying to take the Sword.

Or perhaps it is more to do with choosing the winning side.

Just beyond the arena buzz a roaring can be heard, like the

constant swell of a far-off sea. It is the noise of the crowd outside Cair Stour, made up of less lucky citizens clamouring for a piece of the action, heads tilted up to the smaller glow screens ringing the arena's outer gates from on high.

Every so often the sea of people is broken by betting agents standing on makeshift plinths, taking in dozens of bets faster than most can talk. They have their own shorthand language, which they croak and roar above the noise as they exchange trick for paper slips with slippery flicks of the wrists.

All this is repeated across every Caballaria bar in the country. If any of those bars have faulty or broken glow screens they will be shut tonight, bitter at the loss of the best night's takings in twenty years. An official bar or an arena is the only way most people get to see a Caballaria fight live, and no one in their right mind will be missing this one. Every single Londoner for the years ahead, no matter the outcome, will need to be able to say that they saw this Sword Tournament with their own eyes.

Art delicately sips his watered Pollidori, trying to push down the nervous bile clambering up his throat. The first round draw has been favourable to Garad – they are matched against a champion with the second-worst odds in the tournament – but they have never fought in an arena, never even fought in a bout that counted for anything at all, never mind so much.

With moments to go until the tournament is scheduled to begin, Brune appears beside Art with a tired grunt. The last few weeks' preparation for this momentous event have been taking their toll. Still, she looks good decked out in her finery, a form-fitting body suit coloured in deep purpura that hugs her trim frame. Her draped trousers are wide and flowing, split up the sides to her thighs to show off her bladed legs, and her silver hair is swept stiffly backwards into a regal cockscomb.

Ever to the point, she gives him an appraising glance and says, simply, 'Ready?'

'No,' Art mutters.

She nods and turns her face out to the arena, the roving spotlights playing across her skin as they sweep past.

'Good,' she replies.

Before he has time to wonder what could possibly be so good about such an admission, the roving arena lights dip together all at once, diving like birds to the ground.

'SEVEN CHAMPIONS . . . ONE WINNER . . . WELCOME . . . TO THE TOURNAMENT . . . FOR THE SWORD . . . OF LONDON!'

It is the voice of the nuntias, Cair Stour's famed showmaster, amplified a hundredfold by the speakers fixed to each towering column of the arena. The aural boom is deafening as he moves ponderously through each champion's stats and pairings.

Up above, the projection of Garad flexes, drawing their broadsword slowly across the clouds.

Throw the first bout, prays Art. He doesn't care about his pride any more. *Garad, if you can hear me, throw the first bout and get out of there.*

But when it is finally time for their fight, and the nuntias calls their name, and the electric bells ring and the lights flash, circling down to the pit, Art knows his prayer has gone to waste.

Because Garad looks spectacular.

Both giant glow screens fill with their form as they stride out into the fighting pit, greedily drinking it in. They are dressed head to toe in dense, close-fitting armour made up of tight white platelets that resemble fish scales and catch the light in a thousand ways, dazzling, winking, making their outline seem sleek and supple and wet.

Garad's family is not rich, not even close. There is no way they could have afforded such an outfit – they had already been saving half their lives to pay for Garad's knight training – but Lillath's family, the DeHavillands, are embarrassingly wealthy. Art hisses his held breath out through his teeth. No wonder she's been avoiding him recently, the sneaky cat.

Garad raises their broadsword in one hand and the nuntias struggles to be heard over the beast of a roar from outside the arena. The elite among the crowd shifting in the stands might be too nervous to voice their approval of this young, glittering fighter for fear of taking some sort of publicly political stance, but the rest of the city knows a Caballaria champion when it sees one, and fuck politics. This is not the appearance of someone who intends to throw the first bout.

Garad is playing the game.

Seven champions make uneven rounds, so one fighter is always chosen by random lottery to sit out the first round. If the world were fair, then Garad, the untested, would have been given that chance, but another family's champion was picked, so they – and five other fighters – must endure the full three bouts.

Their first opponent, Helyan the Merciful, is short in comparison – though probably a decent height up close; everyone looks short compared to Garad – with an even keel of wins and losses to his tally. His charcoal-grey outfit is trim, neat, unshowy. Built for fighting and not prancing about, Art thinks with a sinking heart. This knight is a veteran of the Caballaria and he is here to win. He favours an evil-looking mace as his weapon of choice and its spikes trail wavy lines in the gritty sand scattered across the pit floor.

A capturer closes up on Garad's face. It has been dusted with mother-of-pearl powder, gleaming along each bone line, a carved statue. His friend has never looked so beautiful.

So young.

The starter bell sounds and the lights stop their dancing, settling to light the pit in a steady stream, ready for the fight.

The second bell sounds – and they clash.

Garad, unused to controlling an adrenalin surge which must feel like a tidal wave, goes in too hard and loses their footing, managing to tumble into a roll. The error of a green, a complete novice.

Art cannot watch.

He feels eyes on his back, drinking in every twitch of his head, but he cannot watch.

All around him the noise sea rolls and swells with whoops and gasps, covering any sounds of the fight. He waits, eyes lidded, heart a pounding drum. The first-stage bouts of a tournament are usually over fast. The quicker you get your opponent under threat of a killing blow, the quicker it is done and the more you have to give for the later rounds. Why isn't this one over yet? Why are they not calling time?

And then, just like that, they do.

A triumphant shout goes up from the pit, its tail drowned in the roar that follows from the stands.

'You might want to take a look,' Brune says into Art's ear. 'Your champion just won.'

Art's eyes snap open. Both fighters are on their backs, but Garad has the edge of their sword against Helyan's unprotected neck, and their feet pin his arms to the ground. Helyan's mace lies feet away, abandoned. He is done.

The crowd's volume dies down expectantly.

A moment of stillness.

'I yield,' comes Helyan's clear voice.

Underneath the renewed roar, Art watches Garad lever themself to standing. The sheen of their outfit is dulled from sand and dirt. They turn slowly, seeking something. When they find themself facing the unmistakable bulk of the Eye, and Art, head on, they slowly raise one fist and touch the opposite shoulder. It is a salute only ever raised to Kings and Queens. The Caballaria crowd lets loose.

Art just about manages to stop himself from sinking down into his seat.

'FOUR. CHAMPIONS. LEFT ... ONLY ... ONE ... WINNER!'

After an hour's break for refreshments, in which Art is served the most delicious spiced pork stew that has ever tried to seduce his tongue, and of which he barely manages a mouthful, the second round begins.

The round that will decide who goes into the final fight.

Garad's odds have shot up since their first win, but in the next fight they are up against a crowd favourite – the Lady Lyonesse, a knight whose tragic, romantic backstory has made her a recent darling of the circuit. Accusations of her attempts to milk this for all it's worth in the public eye are neither here nor there. This is the Caballaria. This is the game.

Brune leans into Art, her face set to casual as if to discuss the weather.

'So much whisky on a young and empty stomach?' she murmurs.

Art glances at the bottle on the little table beside him, now decidedly much more glass than liquid. He forces another mouthful of cold stew past his protesting tongue.

Brune gives a satisfied grunt. 'Remember, show no weakness.'

She returns to her seat behind him and starts an animated conversation with some palace dignitary sat next to her. Art swallows down another forkful of pork, and then half-chokes on it as Garad re-enters the pit. An unfettered roar from outside the arena greets their appearance. The dirtied, dulled, scaled white armour suit from their first bout has been discarded for a new version, this one the colour of deepest ebony. It makes them look like a black cobra.

How the fuck much did the DeHavillands spend on these saintsdamned costumes?

The electric bells sound out, the audience quietens and Art's stomach attempts to climb out of his throat.

Here we go again.

At least this will be the one Garad will throw. They have saved him face by winning the first bout and made a grand beginner's name for themself in the process, nicely kick-starting their Caballaria career. It will all be over soon.

The Lady Lyonesse is the first to strike, whirling across the sand with a speed that leaves Art breathless, her twin rapiers brandished – but Garad is ready. This time Art forces himself to watch, and as he does, he has to marvel at his friend's form. Their armour is a miracle of design, clearly metal, judging by the ringing sound when the Lyonesse scores a brief strike against Garad's torso, but of such a tight, sinewy construction that it hugs the body and allows Garad all the freedom of movement they would have in regular training clothes.

As the fight progresses, a sickly kind of doubt begins to bloom in Art's mind. It grows legs as the Lady Lyonesse is forced to one knee to avoid a sweeping blow from Garad's dulled-edge broadsword. The Lady is outmatched. Visibly, obviously outmatched.

Unless Garad is suddenly struck with terrible luck, they are going to win.

No. Garad is smart. They have studied the Caballaria since childhood. They'll find a way to throw it without making it obvious. It will happen. The fight goes on, and the Lyonesse is clearly tiring, but it's okay. It's okay. They're just looking for the right moment. 'Pull a muscle', feint a little too obviously, lose your footing, clumsy up your follow-through – there are a hundred ways to lose, Garad.

Lose, Garad.

Garad does not comply.

The Lyonesse overextends a thrust and skids, falling, just a little too tired to correct fast enough – and she is down, and Garad's sword point is digging at her heart.

The romantic, tragic Lady's face is full of venom.

'I yield,' she spits.

'Let me through *right now*.'

The guard knights stationed in the dingy corridor leading to the champions' underground resting area are skittish, and with good reason. This momentous night already has everyone's nerves strung up tight, and on top of that, they now find themselves confronted with the boyman who may yet be their King before the night is through.

'Sire—' one begins, then falters, protocol strangling him. 'Si—'

'Oh, for fuck's sake,' Art shouts, 'I don't care what you call me, just let me through to see my own saintsdamned champion!'

'It's against the rules,' another firmly states.

Art considers pulling the I'M PRACTICALLY YOUR KING, YOU IDIOT card, recoils from the idea in horror and attempts to clear the red mist of fury currently fuzzing his brain.

He sighs.

'I apologise,' he says. 'Things are . . . difficult at the moment, you may appreciate.'

The guard, visibly confused at Art's apparent lack of enthusiasm for how well his champion is doing, is mute.

'Art?' comes a cautious voice.

Lucan's head pokes out of a door along the corridor.

'You're not supposed to be down here,' he says unnecessarily.

Art raises his arms. 'Really?' he asks the ceiling, astonished. 'Well, how stupid of me to put all that effort into escaping the Eye and arguing my way past every single security level. I'd best just trot meekly back upstairs and get to work on the beer and pancakes I've left waiting to go stale, hadn't I?'

Lucan appears to assess the situation. He moves into the corridor, letting the door behind him click shut.

'Si,' he addresses the two guards, 'do you take bribes?'

The guards, possibly used to a little more subtlety, exchange glances. The quicker of the two nods. Transactions are briefly discussed and finalised. As the guards stroll up the corridor just out of sight, Art brushes past Lucan and opens the door.

Garad is in the room beyond, sitting on a plain stool, stripped to the waist while a tourney medic stitches up a nasty gash in their side. Underneath the harsh strip lights it is much easier to see the toll each fight has taken so far. The pale tiles underneath the stool are streaked with watery blood. Garad's skin is pallid and tired. They give Art a cursory glance, and then go back to staring at the wall opposite.

Art stands, anger drained at the sight of them, battered and sliced open.

For him.

'Garad,' he says, his voice quiet. 'What are you doing?'

Behind him, he hears the click of the door as it is opened, letting in a slice of crowd noise that echoes down the corridor's stone walls. The door shuts and the noise is cut off.

Lucan stays behind him. Probably anxious to be out of the firing line.

'I'm doing my best to not humiliate you,' Garad replies.

Art points outwards, towards the pit. 'Borin the Bloodless just won his second bout without appearing to break a sweat. That means you face him in the final fight, which is in less than an hour.'

'You have a gift for stating the obvious.'

Art struggles to keep his temper. 'You should have thrown against the Lyonesse. You know that.'

'Careful,' Garad says dully. 'Tongues wag.'

'I've been well paid not to gossip.' The medic's calm, muffled voice drifts around Garad's torso as he attends his work. 'And I'll thank you to remember that I'm also loyal.'

Lucan had said that his family had offered up the services of their own private – and highly expensive – medic for the tourney, rather than use those on offer from the arena itself. Better trained. Garad isn't the only one putting their neck on the line for him. His other two friends have tangled up not just themselves but their own families in this, too.

The medic finishes up in the silence, carefully swiping the neat wound with a disinfectant pad. He stands up and fills the little sink in the corner with water, rinsing his tools. Garad leans back with a wince and begins to cover their hands with white grip tape, winding it in slow and deliberate rows.

'I've glued and stitched the wound, but it'll likely tear at some point during the bout,' warns the medic. 'It won't hold for long.'

'I know,' Garad says.

'When you feel it tear, don't get cautious – just go flat out. It won't matter, then, and if you finish up quicker you'll lose less blood.'

'Yes.'

Art's stomach roils uneasily. He is not a fighter. Never has been. Oh, he's enjoyed watching Caballaria bouts just like everyone else, and just like everyone else he has studied the Code, the ancient, thousand-page-long tome that explores the art of the fight. He has read every single one of its lean, poetic philosophies, its morals and myths, its beguiling stories.

But in front of him is its hard, blunt reality. Torn, battered flesh and pain. Out there a wall exists between the watchers and the fighters, a wall made of glittering lights and glorious skin paints and the performance – enough, sometimes, to make an atheist believe in gods again. In here, however, the wall is gone. In here there are only humans, and humans break.

'Garad,' he says, 'for saints' sake – look at me.'

But they won't. He watches them pull on gloves studded with metal tips that would make a punch draw blood.

'Art,' comes Lucan's anxious voice behind him. 'The arena team are coming back in a minute to talk to Garad about the final bout. You'd better go.'

'Garad,' Art tries again.

Garad flexes their fingers, their voice distant.

'I'll see you afterwards,' they say, and then after that, nothing more.

*

The electric bells sound.

'TWO. CHAMPIONS,' screams the nuntias. 'ONE. WINNER.'

The crowd noise slams into Art's ears, drowning all else. He feels nothing. It is a strange and comforting sensation.

'... WINNING STREAK,' the nuntias shrieks, but not even those enormous speakers can get him above the roar of the Caballaria beast. '... CHAMPION OF CHAMPIONS ... THE *BLOODLESS*!'

Garad's final opponent steps into the arena.

Even from this distance he is an ogre of a man. The glow screens fill up with him, capturers having to pull out hastily and refocus at a greater distance to get all of him into their sights. He wears a chainmail torso wrap rumoured to be fashioned from port docking rings. His long black hair skirts the small of his back. Tonight he has it pulled into a tail that will shiver and splay into the air when he moves. His muscles are giant, stacked boulders. Famously, he also favours a broadsword, which is currently lifted in one hand and rests against his chest, jutting up above his head. An even match of weapons with Garad, at least.

Borin does not belong here, in this time of neon-drenched glass and steel. He belongs on a misty, mud-sucking battlefield, swinging an axe into howling monsters like in the legends of before. Cair Stour is one of the largest landmarks ever built, but it looks too small to contain him. He fills it from side to side just by standing still. He pulls all eyes towards him.

But then Garad enters. For the final bout, their skin-tight armour is silver. Silver, flashing pure and bright, the colour of trick, the colour of London. There is no trace of the wound that has opened up Garad's side in their expression, no trace of the bruises and the exhaustion that lined them such a short time ago. Underneath the arena lights, all reality is washed away.

The opponents face each other.

Garad, the most physically imposing human Art has so far met, looks like a matchstick in front of Borin, one he will reach out and snap in seconds. Garad's lips move, the words lost. Capturers zoom hastily towards their face, trying to catch what they are saying, but too late. Borin's own mouth is pressed closed – and then it opens, and he replies.

'What did they fucken *say*?' someone behind Art shouts, decorum forgotten in the heat of the moment. 'Why they don't put mouthpieces on the fighters, saintsdamn it, I'll never understand—'

The cacophony only grows as the fight takes hold of everyone there, faces stretched and eager as they pour all their emotions down into the pit. Art is only vaguely aware that his heart is trying to kick its way out of his chest.

The first bell sounds.

Garad's sword lifts, scoring the sky.

And Borin's drops, scattering sand in a blast around its hilt from its impact with the ground.

For a moment, confusion unfurls from the crowd – did he *fumble* it? – but then he sinks slowly to one knee.

All noise dies, dies, dies away.

Borin raises his empty hand as a fist into the air, echoed by his giant counterparts on each giant glow screen. His voice, when it comes, echoes the crumble of rocks in a landslide.

'I yield.'

The clamour is sudden and immediate as thousands of voices let loose.

Capturers light on the Welyens, screaming out into the arena, having watched their champion deliberately, unambiguously and very publicly throw the most important bout of his and their lives.

There are calls of 'void' and 'illegal'. There are shouts of denial.

Garad is a statue.

In the chaos, a figure detaches itself from the ring, the hidden, sunken area surrounding the pit where Caballaria officials, medics and trainers oversee each bout. The figure crosses the sand, the white colour of its jacket marking it out as an impartial adjudicator from the arena team. It takes a long, long time for the noise to die down, but die down it does as the crowd gathers itself, waiting for what happens next.

The adjudicator reaches the pair and bends next to the kneeling Borin, talking to him. A capturer closes in, picking out the face of a middle-aged woman, lined and serious. The crowd strains to hear, but it is no use.

She stands up, brushing sand from her trousers. Then she turns and nods at someone in the ring.

A moment later, the voice of the nuntias suddenly blasts out through the speakers.

'GARAD GAHERIS, CHAMPION OF ARTORIAS DRACONES . . . WINS.'

The crowd beast roars, incoherent.

Soon enough, this will become one of the most iconic images in the history of the Caballaria: the hulking, grizzled shape of Borin the Bloodless, on his knees with his sword in the dust, his impassive, scarred warrior face turned up to the silver angel before him. The young champion standing lithe as a birch tree, their own sword lowered, the tip tracing a pinprick in the sand by their side.

The arena glow screens are filled with Agravain Welyen. He has stood up in his seat and his soft face is scrunched in utter fury. As Art watches, giant glow-screen Agravain holds his arm out straight and slowly squeezes his hand into a fist, the gesture of promised death.

His arm is pointing straight towards the Eye.

Art hears Brune swear under her breath, sudden and vicious, and then he feels someone grab his shoulder and wrench him out of his chair. He has time to see Brune speaking across him, calling over the noise, before he is pulled out of the Eye and surrounded by a phalanx of guard knights in the narrow corridor beyond.

'Get him out, get him out,' he hears someone say, and there is no time to protest, he is dazed, swept along, walking so close to the knight next to him that he can feel his thigh gently grazed by the gun in its holster slung around their hip.

'Wait,' he hears himself say. 'What's going on?'

'Taking you back to the palace, Sire,' the guard next to him says, eyes elsewhere. 'Quad's waiting outside.'

'What about . . . where's Garad?' he asks.

'Doesn't matter right now. Sire!'

The knight barks an alarm but Art is already gone, darting through the distracted bodies around him that are steeled for an attack from the outside and not within. *Garad*, his mind urges him numbly, and he obeys. The upper tier of the arena is serviced by its own ascenders but Art takes the stairs, hurling himself through the door and clattering down the cement, two, three, four stairs at a time. He feels like he's flying.

'Artorias!'

'Sire!'

The shouts come, but they come from above and he is

arrowing down to ground level, down to the pit. Now he hears the chanting drifting through the walls, muddled and confused, words lost, only clashing rhythms to feel.

There. A cluster of arena guards in front of that door. No words this time, no arguments, he simply *is* getting through. Astonished by the sight of the boy who just became their King barrelling towards them, they don't even protest. He pushes through them and wrenches open the door into the sunken ring beyond, and unlike the echoing, empty corridors that lead to it, this place is buzzing with people, and the crowd chants are inhumanly loud this close, and he stops just inside the door, trying to work out how in seven hells he gets out to the pit from here—

'Art!'

A silver angel is hemmed in by a knot of white-jacketed arena team people all talking at once, trying to be heard over the noise.

'Art,' the angel calls again, and their voice is so tremulous that it breaks through the remnants of the numb shield Art has been hiding behind.

Garad fights out of their knot and Art comes forwards, and somewhere in the vague, unimportant distance that is the rest of the world, he sees people moving back from them, allowing them to meet in an empty space of their own, a circle ringed with silent faces.

Up close, Garad is too real to be an angel. Their armour looks incongruous outside of the pit, as if they are on their way to a costumed ball. Their eyes are too bright and their short hair hangs in damp, limp tails.

Art opens his mouth, but finds he has no idea what to say.

Garad waits, tall and guarded and self-possessed.

'What did he say to you? Borin?' Art asks at last.

The white-jackets of the area ring lean in to hear.

'That he thought you should be King,' says Garad. 'That he thought . . . it was the right thing for London.'

It sounds good. Too good to be real, perhaps – but who knows how it feels out there in the pit, with the theatrical weight of a nation on your shoulders? Art imagines Borin rehearsing it beforehand, that craggy visage mouthing the words into his dressing-room mirror.

'Can he really do that?' Art asks the ring at large.

'Yes, Sire,' comes a voice from his left. 'Borin has willingly forfeited. The rules on forfeiting are clear, they were changed and updated at the request of your father . . .'

The voice falls silent.

'I am not my father,' he says calmly.

Garad's voice is low. 'No. You'll be a thousand times better than he ever was.'

If the watching circle of white crows is shocked at this, no one makes a sound to display it. Their gods are the champions of the Caballaria, and Garad, right now, is their god.

This is too much. How does anyone become the ruler of millions without collapsing under the weight of so much power?

'Don't you want to win some before you lose?' Garad asks, as if they can sense his turmoil.

It is an old and well-known expression. Fight, it means, fight for what you believe in and what you desire and what you want to be true. Win as many fights as you can until your final bout with the Death Saint – the one fight everyone is guaranteed to lose.

Make your life count for something, because this life is all you get.

Art steps forwards, inches away from his coiled and waiting

friend. At least he won't be alone in this. There is Lucan, there is Lillath. There is his fierce, loyal champion, watching him with anxious eyes.

'You just helped make a King, Garad,' Art says. 'How does it feel?'

Garad lets loose a relieved, sobbing laugh, pulling him into their arms. After a moment they sink to one knee, but Art refuses to let go, sinking with them to the ground. The King's champion is his equal. Let everyone watching know it.

Garad presses their forehead against Art's. Their face paint is streaked with sweat. The touch of their slippery skin against his is the truest thing he has ever known.

'Feels good,' Garad whispers to him, eyes bright. Hands come up and grip softly around the back of Art's skull, tightening their connection. 'My brother. I'll follow you, gladly, until I lose for the last time. You know that, right? You've always known it.'

Art's own hands rise to rest on top of Garad's, fingertips digging into the spaces between theirs.

'I know it,' he whispers back.

For better or worse.

Artorias Dracones is King.

CHAPTER 10

The Dungeons, Rhyfentown
Ten Months Ago

Strobe lights in the sky spell her out for all the world to judge.

Against the misty clouds above London, Red's name is a waning wisp of a word, as if she could fade from existence any day. Framed signs that seem to float on the air give away all her secrets, written in screaming neon.

The purr of the bike under her thighs and the grip of the waist in front of her draws her back to earth. They ride, Red and Finnavair, they ride a streak across the world. A soothing, whistling breeze rushes past Red's skin. An ache starts up in her core, rolling out across her body, the ache of the freedom of miles eaten up underneath her. On a bike, no one can stop her or tell her what to do. A knight follows their own rules. Normal structures collapse in their wake.

They ride.

Red clutches her arms tightly around Fin's slender waist, feeling the press of leathers against her bare wrists. She is not supposed to want this escape. She is running, but she has forgotten what it is she runs from and why, and she does not want to remember. She feels Fin's gloved hand on hers and relishes the touch, the nearness of another. Fin is freedom, and she pulls Red towards it.

Then she turns back in her seat, facing Red full on, and the dream plummets into a nightmare. Because it is not Fin's face she sees, but the face of her mother.

The bike judders and then flips, flinging them both away. Red skids across the ground and the bike lands on her, crushing her at her neck and pinning her body to the floor. Her throat collapses slowly, crumpled as easily as a paper tube. Her lungs won't inflate. Her throat won't open. She tries to move. Tries to tug. Wrench. Shake. She pulls, pulls, *pulls*, but nothing happens, nothing happens. She can't breathe. She is a spider impaled by a pin, its legs curling up as it shudders weakly towards death. The vice weight trapping her is not a bike but arms, a woman's arms, thin and implacable, while at her throat she can feel a deadly razor-edge of steel, slicing open her skin—

—and then she wakes, sweat-streaked and shaking.

She struggles and heaves towards normal breath. She is not trapped. She is not helpless. She is here, alive in the darkness of her room, safe and alone—

No, not alone. There is a ghost in the corner of the ceiling.

Red stares at the shivering, draped shape. Then she croaks, 'Light.'

Her bedroom lights fade up, rendering the mysterious banal. The ghost is nothing more than a bed sheet. It has been pulled off her legs, off her bed, and pushed impossibly into the corner of the ceiling, hovering, pinned by some unknown force.

It's you doing it, you idiot.

She blinks. The sheet drops to the floor in a tangled heap.

Fuck. It's not the first time that has happened, her magic leaking out of her while she sleeps, but it is rare, and it is always because of a nightmare that, no matter how it begins, ends the same way: a woman's arms pinning her down. A slice of death prickling at her throat.

Red feels herself thrum with its aftermath. If she doesn't find a way to calm down, its threat will follow her all the next day until she is too afraid to speak, never mind fight, just in case her magic pushes its way out of her without her control. Then – goodbye, knighthood.

Sweat dries on her skin, itching. A shower. She'll take a shower, try to wash the dream off her soul. She levers herself out of bed and roots around for a towel. She needs space. She needs the breeze, the stars. Saints, she even misses the bright, sticky glare of the neon street signs. It all lies just beyond one windowless layer of stone, just one wall between her and the world, but the wall might as well be miles wide. They do not leave this place. This place does not leave them.

It is more than a month since Red began her training at the Dungeons. Days have been turning into weeks with alarming speed, and in their turning Red's world has been shrinking smaller and smaller, until it clings close to her like a claustrophobic second skin.

Nothing from the outside is allowed to penetrate the Rhyfentown public training grounds. The longer this goes on, the easier it is to believe that there is no longer any kind of outside. The trainees' bedroom glow screens are configured to contain elements of only this world, inside this building: their fight recordings, their statistics, their improvements, their lapses, their trainers' comments, their diets, their alarms and schedules. No news. No entertainment. No messages from family or friends. Nothing that is not about the life they are living in day to day.

'It's a cult, is what it is,' one trainee had muttered at breakfast a couple weeks ago, an irritable man called Herthen with a mean left hook that sinks his opponents in one – when he can catch them with it. His eye sockets are lean with dark shadows. 'They push your body until you're too tired to think, and then they push your head until all you can remember, all you can put in it, is the Code.'

If it is a cult, Red had thought, *the entire Seven Kingdoms was lost to it long ago.*

Kay the Bull, the hulking trainee who had teased Red in her first training session and now often went out of his way to sit with her at meals, had bristled. 'That's the point, isn't it? You want to be in the Caballaria, you give up your life for it. You don't half-be a knight, sometimes, when you feel like it. It's all or nothing.'

Herthen just shook his head, muttering into his coffee cup, 'A true convert.'

Herthen didn't last much past week two. One morning at breakfast there was an empty space where he should've been, and a gruff announcement in the day's first training session that he had dropped out.

He was the first, but he was not the only one. By week four half of them are gone – several from sheer exhaustion; a few from injuries bad enough to take them out of the running for too long to complete their training satisfactorily. At least, this is what the rest of them are told.

Half-hearted jokes are made – 'Are they really dropping out or have the kitchens run out of decent protein sources?' and 'My brother heard a rumour that at the Senzatown training grounds they have a cemetery in the cellars for the ones who don't make it through' – but each time another space at the breakfast table appears, determination screws ever tighter in each of the remaining trainees' chests.

They have made it this far. They cannot fail now.

Despite her determination to get through it alone, Red has found herself drawn to several of her fellow trainees. Kay is all roaring aggression in a fight, but beyond that he's proved to be generous company, and he has a knack for making her laugh. Then there is Sela Delaney, the sultry, shaven-haired girl she encountered after her first-ever training session.

Sela seems to take special delight in goading Red. She flirts during their bouts, riling her opponent even more when her blood is already hot from the fight. They are often paired, good at exploiting each other's weaknesses – Sela's footwork can be messy and ill-formed; double weapons tend to confuse Red – and their sparring has a playfully fraught edge that the other trainees, always on the hunt for entertainment, only encourage.

It is often hard to tell how serious Sela is. She seems to find everything terribly amusing and likes to throw out careless, outrageous opinions designed to ruffle spines. Then she either puts the offended back in their box with some scathingly light wit, or surprises them with a gift to make them like her again. An extra bread roll at dinner. A new book. A bottle of expensive sword oil obtained via the Dungeons' illegal trading market that brings in goods from the outside world.

Red has tried her best to ignore the market's existence. She once refused a sweet from an illicit bag of frozen jellies offered to her by Sela, and thereafter it's been her rival's favourite game to play: what temptation will finally make Red crack? But Red will not crack. She cannot afford to risk her place here. What if the Scourge sees? What if it disappoints him?

'You're a law dog, Red,' Sela once remarked at dinner. 'Trotting obediently inside the rule lines.'

'If I was, I wouldn't beat you so often, would I?' Red had retorted. 'You're a low cheat.'

Sela just smiled as if the insult was a compliment.

Inside the Dungeons, the only sign of the arrival of night outside is when every light in the building switches from a frosted yellow-white brightness into a cool, blue-tinged dimness. Red edges out into the dark corridor from her bedroom in search of a shower. When she reaches the communal bathroom she can hear the faint but unmistakable noise of splashing water. It is close to midnight, but someone else is in there.

She stands for a moment, undecided – but the dream arms squeezing her body and the dream knife pricking her throat surface in her mind like the bloated body of a corpse in a river and she gives an involuntary shudder. Nothing will do but to try and relax or she'll never get back to sleep, and running water helps.

When she pushes open the door, it takes a moment to determine who it is. Their trim outline is clouded by steam. They turn their head at her noise.

Sela.

Red's pulse gives a nervous skip as she crosses the slippery tiles and chooses the showerhead right next to her. She is rewarded with a lazily impish grin.

It is late, and the showers are loud. Red lets the water streak her body, enjoying the feeling of it drumming gently across her back, keeping her gaze fixed on the drains in the centre of the floor.

Sela came in before her, but still her shower runs.

Just as it starts to feel awkward, Red hears a metallic creak from the space beside her, and the shower shutting off. Suddenly self-conscious, Red turns away from Sela and back to the wall, water bouncing off her arms as she holds them close to her chest and stares at the tiles.

'Can't sleep, Pel?' she hears Sela ask.

At first she despised the nickname – short for pelleren, her godchild designation – but now she feels an annoyed kind of affection for it. Strange how much louder Sela sounds with the knowledge of night beyond this room, and all those sleeping bodies. They might be the only two people awake in the whole building right now.

'Not tonight,' Red tells the ground.

'Bad dreams?'

Red flinches. She wants to throw out a light-hearted retort but her throat closes up.

'Sorry,' Sela murmurs. She sounds, for once, genuine. She rallies. 'I know what your dream was about. It was me, pounding your face into the dirt yet again. I'll bet you woke up all a-fright.'

'You've won precisely forty-seven per cent of our bouts,' Red manages to say, grateful for the lifeline. Irritation is a good tool for dispelling fear. 'I'm not afraid of your less than half a victory at pounding my face into the dirt.'

'Want to give me a chance to even the score?'

Red turns her head. Sela is standing close, skin streaked wet, her outline thick and rich and inviting under the cavernous bathroom's dark blue light.

'Now?' Red says. 'In the bathroom?'

Naked?

'Seems like a useful way to pass the time to me.' Sela shifts her weight, pulling Red's gaze downwards, travelling over her wet curves.

Red swallows, fighting a sudden rush of hungry yearning.

'I'm not—' she begins. 'I don't want to fight right now.'

'No?' Sela is maddeningly playful. 'What do you want to do right now?'

'Sleep?' Red tries.

'You sure about that?' she asks with a great smile on her face.

Red feels her heartbeat pound hard.

'I've noticed something about you, when we fight,' she hears Sela say softly.

'What's that?' she manages to say.

'I've noticed how much pleasure it gives you.'

Red is mute.

'You look embarrassed,' the girl purrs. 'You shouldn't be ashamed of it. It's just set me wondering if you get the same kind of pleasure in the other kind of fight.'

'The other kind of fight?'

'You know exactly what I mean. I've seen the way you look at me when we're close up. Like you could just as easily fuck me as fight me.' Sela inches closer. 'Tell me I'm wrong.'

An unsettling thrill runs through the depths of Red's stomach.

'We can't,' she mumbles.

'Ah, yes. The law dog gives a little bark.'

'They could fail us if they find out.'

'No matter how tough training might be, it hasn't managed to kill us all from the waist down yet, has it?' Sela says. 'They know that. Everyone's been at it. Shae and Kitani even sneaked up to the rooftop the other night. The trainers all look the other way.'

She is so close now that she fills Red's vision from side to side.

Don't, Red wants to say, but the rest of her body is ignoring her. She feels faint. Her skin seems to buzz under the bathroom's hard darklight. The buzz builds up, pushing insistently from the inside of her skin, itching, maddening. It only earths itself when Red's hand reaches out around the back of the neck in front of her and grips it hard. She is rewarded with Sela's faint gasp, which echoes off the tiles.

The effect is immediate. That angry wasp buzzing under Red's skin dips to a softer, heated trill as her fingers dig into flesh.

Sela's mouth is open in a pleased grin. 'Ha. Does that feel better?'

She seems to know something hidden that Red cannot see. She speaks a language Red has yet to learn.

I don't understand this, Red wants to admit. *What do I do?*

'You're such a tense little rule-keeper,' Sela murmurs under the running water, her eyes wide. 'Let me help you relax.'

Red feels the trail of strong fingers on her belly, slow and soft, as if taking care not to startle her. The fingers skate lower, lower, tickle past her inner thighs – and then slide inwards, gently prising her open. She lets out a pained, humiliatingly obvious gasp.

'How wet you are,' Sela whispers in her ear.

'It's the shower,' Red croaks.

'No, it's not.'

Sela reaches her hand behind her and clasps it over Red's on the back of her neck, as if to make sure it stays there. Then she begins to slide downwards, settling on her knees.

Red can feel the short hairs at the girl's nape tickling her palm. The sudden thrill of warm breath on the soft skin of her thighs. Slippery cool tiles against the warm flesh of her back. The hot, slick tongue of the girl kneeling at her feet, pressing its way inside her, lapping her up like a cat at milk.

The rush, when it comes, is so much like the sensation of a fight that she can barely tell the difference.

CHAPTER 11

Cair Lleon, Blackheart
Nineteen Years Ago

The Swording chair is high-backed, curving graciously over his shoulder blades like furled wings.

The celebrated artisan who made it as a gift to her new King sculpted it to his exact measurements. No one taller than Art can sit in it as the wooden curls will dig into their flesh, stopping them from straightening their spine. Garad has already tried, folding into it like an awkward spider, to get him to laugh.

The crown Art will wear during the ceremony has been made to the precise circumference and landscape of his head. It is fashioned from twisting, bubbling spires of jet-black glass, shaped by running carefully directed electric bolts through basalt sand and then polishing up the result to dark gleaming points. It is beautiful and menacing. It is power.

He hates both the chair and the crown. He hates the grand lies they tell about him.

A knock comes at his bedroom door.

'Enter,' he calls.

It has taken him weeks to speak at all, as he worked out early on that if he doesn't give permission the knocker is not allowed to come in, and he gets left alone. Palace staff are now wise to it, however, and the household rule has been changed. These days they knock twice, wait a respectful thirty seconds in case he is any kind of *busy*, then enter regardless of whether he calls out or not.

The tall bedroom door creaks ominously as it opens. Apparently a former Queen had it done deliberately so the noise would alert her if anyone was trying to get into her bedroom, and presumably not in order to give her a surprise back rub. A happy thought.

Fortigo Balanchine, personal steward to the new King, pokes his head around the door. The son of a famed Caballaria trainer, he has never been interested in the fight himself, instead becoming a palace vastos at the age of nineteen, a controversially young age to be accepted into Cair Lleon's prestigious retinue. In a dry twist he is now, at twenty-one, nearly four years older than Art. Apparently nineteen is considered too young to serve a King, but not too young to be one.

'Sire,' comes his even, measured voice, 'you have about twenty minutes before the quads arrive. They will come to collect you from your receiving room. Once outside the palace, you'll be accompanied by guard knights every step of the way.'

One of the reasons Fortigo passed his vastos training so young is his innate unflappability. The passionate tides that pull most others in every direction barely mark a swell in him. It is a skill to be prized and put to good use in such a place as Cair Lleon. Art has never seen him look worried.

Until now.

Fortigo has a slight crease in his forehead. Art finds his own pulse, not exactly settled before Fortigo's appearance, climbing in response. What is not being said hangs in the air between them. No one expects violence today, but they have prepared for it, nonetheless.

'Thank you, Fortigo,' he replies.

'Sire.' Fortigo pauses, a space that could be filled with calming platitudes, but he doesn't do Art the disservice. The space itself is enough to indicate his feelings.

The door shuts.

The Swording of Artorias Dracones is being shown live on glow screens across London and the Seven Kingdoms, the first-ever news event to be so. It has taken weeks of negotiation with teams of representatives from every major glows network. The only screens the general population have access to are communal – the towering public information pillars at the centres of cities, towns and villages, and the smaller but no less blocky versions dominating one entire wall of every Caballaria bar.

Such a thing as a portable glow screen does not yet exist. It isn't possible to make them small enough, never mind the current astronomical expense involved in their creation – but the technology is close. It will take a few more years before they can be made affordable for everyone, but that is, he has been assured, the goal.

Art likes to imagine a future with free-flowing information, accessible to everyone, regardless of status or wealth. A grand, impossibly ambitious idea, and something his father had apparently dismissed as a pointless pursuit – but Art likes impossibly ambitious ideas. He likes the sensation of something stretching out far beyond him, its ripples still felt even after he is gone.

He faces the full-length mirror in his bedroom, trying to see what the rest of the country will see. For the next two hours, there will be no escaping his face. It will loom out at everyone relentlessly, creased with crushing awkwardness. He hopes he doesn't sweat too much.

This damn live glow show was all Lucan's idea, so at least Art knows exactly who to blame.

'It's important for everyone to see you,' Lucan had argued. 'You should be a real person to them as well as a symbol. They'll like you more if they can see that.'

'I don't want them to like me, I want them to ignore me,' Art had sourly replied. 'I want this entire country to continue being a big sea of everyone getting on with things just fine. No one needs some privileged fool in spiky headgear being symbolic at them.'

'And a cape,' Lillath had supplied.

'What?'

'The cape. You know about that, right?' Her gaze had slid to Lucan. 'You told him, didn't you? The Swording cape? It's so impressive. It's made of thousands of tiny lights embedded in the fabric that give it this amazing silvery glow – what?'

Art had sucked in a deep breath.

'I am not wearing a *fucken silver cape*.'

He has won the cape argument. The traditionalists will grumble and judge and drip poison, but then again, what about his ascension to the throne has been in any way traditional? Better to be consistent.

Staring at himself in the mirror, Art fruitlessly smoothes his hair, but there is nothing more to be done there. His hair is its own fuzzy creature and will not be bid, preferring instead to give the impression of a perpetual escape attempt from his scalp.

Giving it up, he leaves his bedroom and walks into the receiving room next door to await his fate with sweaty, heart-hammering composure. Pacing across the room's dark lava-stone tiles and deep cushioned rugs, Art finds himself staring at the frescoes dominating every wall, something he has been doing frequently in the run-up to this day.

They were painted two hundred years ago, well preserved with layers of careful lacquering. Each fresco panel, stretching up to the ceiling and tickling the floor, slowly unfolds the history of the Saith, the seven sainted founders of modern London.

It begins in a time when godchildren ruled.

Back then, godchild rule always was and had been. There are not many surviving records of life before them – they were careful to control as much as they could in the thousand years of their domination, and destroy whatever they disagreed with – so their origins are left to historians to squabble and theorise over, while the nation's collective memory is more simply divided into two distinct eras: Godchild and Saith.

The fact that always struck Art was how few of them there were in comparison to commons. Even the most generous estimates had never projected more than a tenth of the entire population as godchildren, and yet their control had been absolute. It was hard to rise up against a people who could pluck your secrets right out of your protesting head.

Godchildren were favoured above commons at every turn, securing indefinite places of prominence and power. The literature of the time was filled with jokes against commons – lighthearted, of course. A friendly ribbing between peoples, which often became a discussion over their inferiority. Which then often became a discussion over whether they even needed the same rights as godchildren. Which then became a fact that they did not.

Not many godchild rulers have been marked well in history,

but few were so universally feared and hated as the very last, Fria Lysander. An intelligent, hugely charismatic girl with an unprecedented talent for not only reading but influencing the minds of almost everyone around her, Lysander soon became famous, and the girl gradually grew into a woman who had only ever experienced life as an idol, the self-possessed eye of a frenzied storm.

A cult formed around her and swelled inexorably, its tidal wave pulling her into power, despite her relatively humble origins. By her late twenties she had swept aside the old King, a weak man with a vague talent for soothsaying which did nothing to help the majority of the populace climb out of the abject poverty they were kept in.

Fria easily took the throne, claiming the system corrupt beyond repair, and established herself and her most fervent followers in its stead as a fairer, more democratic ruler. She would represent everyone, she declared, not just the rich and influential. Justice and prosperity would flourish. Those were the passionate promises she made.

It was subtle at first, as these things go.

Technological development was slowed, and then all but stopped. Any research on godchildren, scientific or historical, was banned. Communications tech was cut off from the general populace and reserved for the elite, as was any weaponry more sophisticated than a sword.

Under these restrictions, the first seeds of the modern Caballaria were sown.

Commons might have had no extraordinary godchild talents but they were not weak, there were far more of them, and they were part of a nation with an innate talent for violence. Underground fighting circuits had always existed and now they blossomed, mutating from a way to indulge the Seven Kingdoms' love of the artistic sport into training grounds for rebellion. Pockets of insurrection sprang up, hesitant at first, their boldness growing in jerky fits and starts. These insurrections were always quashed, but continued oppression swelled the numbers, and over the decades, momentum gathered . . .

And then came the moment, several hundred years ago, when the tide of history turned.

Art's gaze travels across the next few panels, paintings depicting the rise of the Saith. Seven commons from disparate backgrounds who joined forces to take bloody civil war to Fria and her son Jost, her equally despotic successor. The names of the Saith are etched into the collective brains of every Londoner alive.

Evron the Gentle Saint.

Rhyfen the Fierce Saint.

Marvol the Death Saint.

Senza the Just Saint.

Gwanhara the Fair Saint.

Iochi the Slippery Saint.

Alaunis the Canny Saint.

The shell of London, all that remained after the Lysanders' regime had been toppled, was remade, divided into seven districts named in honour of the Saith, each developing its own culture and tastes and dialects and ways.

The Saith outlawed familial succession, instead establishing a more democratic way of deciding who ruled. No one Saith family could hold London for more than a generation – unless they proved themselves the best candidate to do so. The Caballaria would ultimately decide. London needed strength at the top, but it also needed mercy, justice, compassion, creativity, cunning and intelligence. Its King or Queen would rule with six others as their most trusted advisors, and those six would represent the entirety of London, not just its elite.

It was a beautiful idea.

Art imagines how grand their hopes must have been for it: a sharing of power between seven people, a fair system to determine who should rule. Now it has descended into civil wars and infighting. The Saith has ended up dividing London into seven instead of bringing it together. If history has taught Art anything, it is that humans have a horrible habit of poisoning every good idea they have as they put it into practice.

'It's our nature,' Lillath once said. 'We made up honour and justice to beat back the dark in our own hearts, but the universe doesn't care about our desperate little stories. The universe has never heard of honour.'

But Art does not believe that. He cannot believe it.

He wonders what the Saith were like in person. Whether they stood in rooms like this and pulled apart every variable, every possible decision. Whether they dutifully brushed their teeth. Drank until they passed out. Whether they got to the end of their lives and knew their time had been well spent. Whether they would have done any of it differently.

History has transcended their status as fallible humans into saints, protectors, icons of ingrained worship. How does a human being become such a thing? Did they have something special that marked them out, or was it a messy combination of unrelated happenstances? Art does not believe in fate, but in choices. What haunts him is whether he is making the right ones.

'Brushing up on your ancestry?' comes a voice.

Art turns to find Orcade Welyen standing framed by the doorway that connects the receiving rooms to his bedroom.

For a moment he just stares at her.

'How did you get in?' he blurts, composure scattered to the four corners.

Orcade lifts her chin, faint amusement wafting around her face like the remnants of perfume. 'This may come as a shock to you, but I'm quite familiar with the King's rooms. Including all the secret ways into them.'

Art takes note of the plural. There is only one secret way in that he is aware of – an emergency exit of sorts that sits behind the main wardrobe and leads into an underground tunnel running through the bowels of the palace – but his father's famous paranoia would have doubtless made sure there was at least one more escape route that no one knew about.

No one except his wife.

It is the first time in Art's life that he and Orcade have been within speaking distance of each other, never mind alone together. She is dressed in a beautiful dove-grey justacorps, finishing in a high, stiff collar, studded with tiny jewels made of jet, that underlines her jawbone. Soft slashed slate-coloured trousers swirl around her legs to graze the rugs, and her high-heeled boots sport an intricate brocade pattern up their sides. Her pale-butter hair has been streaked with silver and entwined with a charcoal comb, from which swing several crystal droplets that wink in the light.

Every part of her speaks of a demure kind of wealth, the kind so rich that it feels no need to be showy. She might still be in official grey mourning colours, but it is the new King's Swording day, after all, and a little tasteful celebratory sparkle is called for. The Welyens have balanced her perfectly between regal and respectful. They likely employed one of the best and most expensive clothes artists in London to dress her for the occasion – Safiero, perhaps, or Dala deLaia – palace officials will be sure to supply the name to the hungry news dogs at the post-ceremony glows interviews.

Orcade crosses the room, joining Art in front of the panel depicting the Saith standing together in a gloomy, cavernous room of Lysander Castle, having taken it in the final bloody conflict. After the war was over, Lysander Castle was torn down and Cair Lleon built on its blood-soaked ground.

'Is it strange to look at your great-however-many-times-grandfather?' she asks, her fingers reaching out to brush the face of Rhyfen. A soldier by trade, he was the fiercest and most warrior-like of the Saith. He had led the war against the Lysanders as its general. There is no room for passivity in Art's genetics. His is a fighter family.

'As strange as it is to see yours, I imagine,' Art says to Orcade.

Though each of the Saith family's bloodlines aren't exactly crystal clear nowadays, the Welyens claim to trace their lineage directly from Alaunis, the Canny Saint. Alaunis is said to have invented a weapon, an iron sword he named Calevel that could somehow disable a godchild's talent. Most modern historians assume this to have been highly mythologised. There is still no tech on earth that can reliably do anything like that, even all these years later. Biologically, godchildren are still quite the mystery.

Still, the story of Calevel is the legacy of Alaunis – patron saint of inspiration, experimentation and innovation. Technology companies often use his name and his colours, creating their logos around his legend.

'I have to confess, I've never really felt any kind of connection to Rhyfen,' Art murmurs as he gazes at his ancestor.

'My, you're as honest as they say,' Orcade replies, the hint of a tease in her voice. 'Not many would-be rulers of the Seven Kingdoms would admit to that.'

'London,' he corrects. 'I don't rule the Seven.'

'London is the First Kingdom. The rest come underneath its grimy boots.'

I think the other six Kingdoms might disagree.

Or not. There is no denying that a dizzying amount of the Seven Kingdoms' power, wealth and influence lies with London. He could really do without the reminder right now, however.

Art watches Orcade studying the fresco.

'What happens to you, now?' he asks. He realises he has no idea.

'I get to fade demurely into the background and live out my days being a royal ornament,' she says.

Her eyes are as clear and sparkling a blue as the summer-sky-coloured bottles that house his favourite imported Etruthan wine. It is a curious, rare colour, and up close, quite startling. She has the deliciousness of a too-fresh apple – full and round and crisp and sharp. Even though that is all Art realises he has ever seen her as, all she has ever been allowed to be, demure ornamentation does not suit her.

'You'll still live here, in Cair Lleon?' he asks.

'Don't be silly. The widow and the bastard son under the same roof? Imagine the gossips.' She sounds faintly amused. 'You know that we've been kept away from one another deliberately.'

Art fights an uncomfortable flush.

'I'll go back to my family,' she continues, 'to be wheeled out for special occasions when they need to show me off. Shuffle off and die in the corner of a pretty townhouse.'

'Why would you let them do that to you?' Art asks, baffled.

She gives him a pitying look. 'That's just how it is.'

'You could go into the family business.'

One of London's biggest tech corporations, Leoma, owns a full third of the vast wind and solar fields that power the city-state, and the Welyens own Leoma.

'Dull,' Orcade says dismissively.

Her fingers trail the heavy curtains hanging beside the panel they gaze at together.

'It was an impressive feat, you know,' she says. 'Your winning the Sword. Your chance really was ever so slender. The saints like an underdog, it appears.'

Art's patience runs out. 'It does seem so, doesn't it? Is that why you sneaked in here today, Lady? To remind me of how undeserving I am?'

Her eyes widen. 'No, of course not.'

'Then why?'

'To warn you.' She doesn't hesitate, as if she has been waiting for him to ask her outright.

'About what?'

'My family.'

'Forgive me,' he says, 'but your family is one of many who wanted the Sword. The Welyens aren't exactly the only people on my mind.'

'No,' Orcade says patiently, 'but they are the most dangerous.'

'I won,' Art retorts. 'That's it. There's nothing they can do about it.'

Once a dispute goes to the arena, it can never be brought forth again. A win is a win, whether as an indisputable mortal law or a sacred answer from the saints themselves. Caballaria is the final judge, the only wall against the winds of chaos.

'Yes, but you understand how it looks, don't you?' Orcade persists. 'It looks like corruption. It's a weak win, Sire. Even those against my brother are moved to stand in his corner on this. They see it as . . . unfair.'

'Your champion made his choice, and I had nothing to do with it. I've welcomed the scrutiny, the attempts to prove I paid off Borin, because I know it didn't happen. If I could, I'd ask him myself why in seven hells he did what he did, but I can't. By all accounts, he has retired to the ends of civilisation and refuses every communication.'

'Well, yes. Dead men aren't usually very talky,' says Orcade.

The skin on Art's neck crawls in response. 'What?'

'He's dead.' Orcade folds her arms against her chest, as if caught in a sudden chill. 'I saw his body myself.'

'How . . .?'

'Retribution.'

Art searches. 'No. It would be . . . the glows would be full of it. The bars would be packed in mourning for weeks on end.'

'Like you said, he refuses all communication. He was always famously capture-shy. It'll be discovered soon, I'm sure. A heart problem. Medical records produced to confirm it.' Orcade shifts from foot to foot. 'You have no idea what my brother is capable of. What he has done and will do for power. You should be afraid of him.' She hesitates. 'I am. Sometimes.'

Art feels a sudden, overwhelming urge to exit through the nearest window, keep running, and never look back.

'Agravain can't contest your win,' he hears her continue, 'so he's looking for more unofficial ways to bring you down. You are beginning your reign in a precarious position, overshadowed by the rumour of corruption. It won't take much to unseat you, especially if it comes quick. He'll find a way. And if he doesn't . . .'

Her silence says enough.

'Then I suppose he'll just have to try and make good on his promise to kill me,' Art says, his fear curdling into anger. 'Because I have nothing to hide.'

'How about the way you came into the world?'

Art stares at the painted lines of his ancestor's face.

'I am not a godchild,' he says. 'My mother was not a godchild. My father was not a godchild.'

'But he associated with one.' Orcade has a plaintive tone in her soft voice. 'And Edler's story about what he did for Uther—'

Art cuts her off. 'Is this really the best your family can come up with? That's ancient gossip-mongering that, need I remind you, Edler was banished from London for spreading. The truth is that no one will ever know what really happened to bring me into the world, because the three people who were involved are all dead, aren't they?'

He has become sharp and loud and just a little too undone. He can hear it.

So can Orcade. She inhales.

'I'm sorry, Sire,' she says, carefully. 'It was cruel of me to bring it up. You've lost both your parents, and . . . I can't imagine never even knowing either of them.'

Art concentrates on the fresco before him, not trusting the struggle going on in his chest.

'I have to go soon,' he says. 'Got to go and be Sworded. You know.'

'Yes,' Orcade replies softly. 'Yes.'

But she doesn't move.

'Lady,' Art says with the final reserves of his patience, 'did you come here today just to warn me about your murderous brother and do a little gloating over my origins, or is there something else you want?'

She speaks calmly. 'You need allies.'

Ah.

And now we have it.

'Allies,' Art responds equally calmly.

'You already know that the Welyens practically own Alaunitown. I can make sure at least one of the seven districts will always be on your side. I might be only a pawn, but I'm an important one.' She hesitates. 'You could put me on the Consilium. Make me the Lady of 'launitown.'

The Welyens might already control much of their district, but there is a big difference between controlling and ruling. In terms of power, the Consilium of the Seven are second only to the King.

'I hate to be obvious,' Art says slowly, 'but your brother is the current incumbent.'

'I know.' She drags in an unsteady breath. 'It's a difficult game to win, and it will take some time. But think about having a Welyen who'd be for you instead of against you. One who dearly wants to get out from her family's long shadow. I think you can understand that. I've been the move in their games long enough. I want to run my own game. I want to be free.'

There is more than a tinge of desperation to her. Art wonders what it must have been like growing up afraid of your own brother. How it would shape you. What does she want to escape so badly that she would propose an alliance with the one person she should not?

Art has always respected anyone who defies expectation. He

at least had a kind of freedom growing up at Si Hektor's country estate – everyone there knew perfectly well who he was, and even if he was inadvertently taught to be ashamed of it, at least they cared for him.

Before trust must come faith. One person always has to make the first move blind, without knowing whether the other will come to meet them or not. Orcade has made the first move. Now it is Art's turn.

'Then let's find a way to get us what we both want,' he says.

Even Orcade's admirable levels of self-control cannot stop the sudden hopeful gleam in her eyes.

'What about public opposition?' she asks.

Art ponders. 'From who? You're a Welyen, you know Alaunitown and its ways intimately. You've already spent years learning how to negotiate with a King. You know everyone in the palace. You're respected. It's an obvious choice.' He pauses. 'But what would your brother do about it?'

'That's just it,' Orcade says. 'The one thing that can protect me is if I have more power than him. It's the traditionalists you'll have a problem with. They'll say I'm too young and inexperienced.' She takes a deep breath. 'I was just a wife.'

'And I'm just a bastard, and apparently I don't know the first thing about how to rule.' He gives her a smile of steel. 'Isn't it fun that we're about to find out?'

They regard each other.

A knock comes on the door.

Rap, rap. Pause. Rap, rap.

Orcade is galvanised. 'They can't catch me in here.'

'Go,' he tells her. 'We'll talk again.'

She turns at the adjoining door, flashes him a look and disappears into his bedroom beyond. It is a hard look to read, but in it he feels the stirrings of hope. The first spinnings of the web of his rule.

A deal with a Welyen. Brune will be proud.

Some news glows are already calling him the Tricky King, in admiration of how an illegitimate scandal managed to snatch the throne from a nest of snakes, armed with nothing but an unknown champion and the evident favour of the saints.

The Tricky King. Art finds he likes it much better than the Bastard King.

He takes a deep breath. Opens the door. Steps outside the room.

CHAPTER 12

The Dungeons, Rhyfentown
Nine Months Ago

'Red and Kitani,' Frome calls, 'you're up.'

Today's mock fight is in a long, low room of black panelled wood. Sound in here is flat and muffled, the padded walls absorbing any ring or clash of metal. One end of the room is dominated by a weapons rig, a simple free-standing metal grid festooned with blunted training swords, maces, axes, knives.

Red and Kitani face each other, the rest of the group ringing them. Frome stands in his customary position to the side, arms folded, stance wide.

Athyen, a quiet trainee who favours a hammer-axe and never seems to run out of stamina, surprised the group last week by pointing out the training room's secret capturers while Frome was otherwise occupied. Tiny lenses are buried deep into the ceiling and the walls, barely even visible. Now Red feels them perpetually on her skin, itching her neck, her calves.

Kitani, opposite her, is entirely calm. A stocky, acrobatic boy with a wild mop of black hair like a dandelion, his fight dance is slow and controlled, chin often tilted downwards as if he feels a mild sadness for causing pain. He likes to goad his opponents closer by staying out of their reach and frustrating them.

'Begin,' Frome instructs.

Red and Kitani circle, eyeing each other up.

'I want to see you start to apply some of the techniques that we've been patiently attempting to insert into your eager minds,' Red hears Frome say. He likes to talk constantly throughout a fight, and he encourages the rest of the group to shout, shuffle, distract. 'You're nearly two months into your six-month holiday here in the Dungeons, my sweet pastries, and holidays don't come free. Show me you're swallowing my pearls of wisdom.'

Red tries to drown him out. Techniques. The parry and return footwork sequence that Si Jocasta hammered into them a few days ago. She can hear Sela laughing behind her left shoulder. Her mind immediately flashes back to their encounter in the bathroom, just as it has done every single day since it happened, and often at night as well.

The morning after the shower room, Sela came into the dining room at breakfast, sandwiched between Shannon and Hujo, laughing at some joke they were sharing, and walked right past Red without so much as a glance.

Then two nights afterwards, Red found a paper message that had been slipped under her door:

Meet me in the shower room at midnight

And three nights after that, another.

When Red thinks of the shower room now, she thinks of ache. Wetness. Slippery tiles echoing with her own panting. The drumming of water barely covering the mingled moans, awkwardness finally lost in their heat. During the day, however, Sela puts on an admirably convincing performance of pretending that Red does not even exist.

She shouldn't be so upset by it. Should she? It's not as if they've pledged to each other. Tension relief, that's all it is – but isn't she even worth a daytime glance? The smallest acknowledgement of the things they do to each other at night?

Concentrate, you idiot.

Peripheral vision barks a warning – a blur of movement to Red's right, a sense of shifting air – she has no time to think but she tries, tries to remember Jocasta's complicated footwork sequence, stumbles with indecision, reels back from Kitani's sword thrust.

'Sloppy,' calls Frome. 'Don't—'

The rest is lost in Kitani's follow-up, a fast press forwards that Red hurries to evade. The ground betrays her, shifting underneath her boots, and she goes down.

She feels the press of a sword edge at her collarbone and looks up into Kitani's calm gaze.

'SB hit,' calls Shannon, the trainee assigned to adjudicate their bout.

A Serious Blood hit might cost Red the fight unless she finds a way out of this, right now. She tries to get her frazzled mind together, flipping through exit routes, but there is no time to strategise and her body takes over, throwing her to one side at an angle too awkward for Kitani to follow through without overbalancing. It earns Red a shallow cut from Kitani's sword, but gets her away from a more serious one.

'Told you she looks good on her knees,' she hears someone say, their words clear and loud enough for everyone to hear.

Startled, Red looks around and into the face of a smiling Sela, whose diminutive stature makes her shoulder the perfect shelf for the towering Kay to lean his arm on as they stand together, watching the fight.

Kay, leaning on her shoulder. Casual as you please. Is that the intimacy of friends? Or lovers?

Are they screwing? No. She doesn't know. Why does it matter? *Focus*, Red—

'Final hit,' Shannon calls in a subdued voice.

Red looks back around to find Kitani's sword point pricking at her heart.

Back in her room, Red wrestles the boots off her feet and slings them into a corner, temper fraying.

After that initial message on her first day, the Sorcerer Knight has not sent her another. Officially, she has no place craving more attention from her benefactor. Officially, she is not supposed to be receiving any messages from the outside whatsoever, though the Sorcerer Knight clearly has the power to circumvent such rules.

She has run through all the possible reasons why there have been no more messages:

- the Scourge considers it too much of a distraction from her training
- Red is very low down on his list of priorities
- whatever rule he bent in the first place can no longer be bent
- he's already bored of her

Round and round the reasons go, until her brain, exhausted from its daily punishment, mercifully shuts down.

She has risked everything, *everything* to get close to the Scourge.

Now she is stuck in a dungeon, one step away from flunking her training and losing her chance forever.

The only light in the room comes from the glow screen embedded in the wall beside her bed. It takes a moment for Red to realise why it is lit.

There is a message waiting for her.

For one moment, she stands stock still. Then she pulls in a steadying breath.

When she opens it up, however, it is not from the Sorcerer Knight, and her racing heart crests in crushing disappointment.

The message doesn't seem to be from anyone – there is no sign-off and the sender's name is just a random jumble of numbers and letters.

red you are about to flunk out

Red stares at the message, runs her eyes over the words over and over.

She feels her anger surge, anger made of shame. She thought she had done something wrong. Some code or etiquette she hadn't understood. She had spent weeks agonising over it, trying to build up the courage to talk to Sela, apologise for her ignorance, for what she has or hasn't done right.

She replies to the message with one of her own.

don't worry sela, next training session I'm going to put you in the ground

The reply is immediate.

not sela

just someone who'd rather not see you lose

Whoever it is, is sitting in front of their glow screen right now.

tell me your name, then

Red writes.

no need

comes the reply.

just here to give you the warning

Glow-screen names are assigned to each trainee by whoever's job it is to do such things, and they are always the trainee's personal name. The tutors are the same. How did this person game the system to hide their name?

Red types a reply.

what warning

sela sees you as her main competitor
she has a strategy for everyone she thinks is better than her
she is a head fighter
a psycher

But Sela doesn't have to be the best. There is no official ranking. She just has to get through the six months of training without failing. Why try to take Red down?

you think people fail just because they give up or get injured
everyone has a weakness
naïveté is yours

Red's knuckles are tight. She tries to relax her hands. Her muscles flicker, urging.

why are you helping me

The anonymous reply takes a minute or two to come through.

i owe an old friend a favour
they want you to do well, so i want you to do well

who?!

But the messager has gone, shut down their end without replying.

Red sits back, mind working furiously. Whoever this old friend is, they seem to have a vested interest in seeing her succeed. The Sorcerer Knight, surely – but whoever his friend might be is a mystery for another time.

Red has learned to concentrate on the problem immediately before her. Looking too far ahead can be overwhelming; it feels like falling and never hitting ground. The current problem is that a wily head fighter has nearly cost her everything she has spent years working towards. She is close to losing her very first real battle.

Her eyes stray back to the message thread.

everyone has a weakness
naïveté is yours

And just like that, all the confusion of the past few weeks sloughs from her like dead skin. Saintsdamn. How has she been so preoccupied with something so meaningless? Sela is small in comparison to what lies ahead. Sela is nothing.

She is just in the way.

There are no more shower meetings with Sela.

Red stops responding to the midnight invitations she receives, and soon enough they stop coming. There are more attempts to throw her off in training, but they stop working so well. She fancies she can sense a kind of puzzlement and then a sullenness from Sela as she is thoroughly ignored.

Red is not blind to the looks between some of the other trainees. The significant tips of the chins. How quiet the group gets whenever she and Sela are paired in a fight. She simply no longer cares.

Every morning her alarm, now switched to the rather more soothing sound of hooting owls, wakes her from bone-deep sleep and into the thick velvet dark of her room. Every night she returns to bed, her battered body weeping piteously from the day's exertions, to open up the Code and try to force more of it into her buzzing, numbed mind.

Every trainee's room has its own copy of the awesomely heavy tome, the writings that serve as the intricate doctrinal spine of the Caballaria. A thousand pages of dense text in curling, cramped handwritten script on paper as thin as the skeletons of winter leaves, bound in thick leather the colour of dried blood. It would be a formidable weapon if it weren't so heavy to lift.

One day, they are told, if they make it through training, they will be presented with a freshly bound, blank-paged book of their very own to painstakingly fill in with their interpretations of the Code. The exercise will span their lifetime. It will become a form of meditation for them, something they are assured they will come to depend on, even crave, as a way to break from the world and remind themselves why they do what they do. It will ensure that they know the Code as intimately as their own hearts.

For now, it is only required that they read it from cover to cover, a section every night before sleep, no matter how tired they are, as they are tested on it the next day. They have all read pieces of it before, of course – it forms the moral and legal backbone of every education, no matter how rich or poor – but that was in the context of lessons and tutorials when they were young. Reading it in one go is much like trying to absorb a thousand stories at once, stories which illustrate every possible situation you could find yourself in and the four ways in which you could deal with said situation – well for you but badly for another, badly for you but well for another, well for both, or badly for both. In between all this are long, long, *long* philosophical meanderings on the nature of violence, of power, of morality and of existence.

The whole thing is several lifetimes' worth of contributions from hundreds of sources, a collective handbook to meaning and purpose. It is an extraordinary piece of work that has shaped a nation, venerated by the older generations and derided by the young, and undeniably a rich, deep part of each and every one of them – but its tone is so dry that it makes Red's eyes sting as she struggles to keep them open while reading in bed each night.

Three months into training and she has forgotten to be worried about disappearing so utterly from the world. Whenever she finds herself at the business end of her trainee opponent's weapon, she reaches a strange twilight place beyond normal fear. To win is to live. To lose is to die. Everyone loses, sooner or later. It is simply a question of how many good wins you can get in before then – but there is ultimately only one win that matters to Red.

Stillness lessons begin in month four.

'Fuck everything else,' Kay rasps, his head laid gently on the dinner table, the ends of his hair ruffling the rim of his stew bowl. 'Fuck the endless running circuits, fuck the fifth mock fight in a row when all I want to do is collapse, fuck the weights that make my muscles go into shock after five minutes, fuck even that damned philosophy class that makes my head feel like it's full of soup. Stillness is the hardest fucken thing I've ever had to fucken do.'

At its simple level, Stillness is just how it sounds – being still, in both body and mind. Body is the easiest part. Mind is where it gets complicated.

Being still is their mind's first break from the routine that has filled their inside wells to the brim. Being still invites review. They scroll through the last hours of their lives, looking for something to pick apart and examine. What they ate for breakfast. How they slept last night and the odd dream they had that they can still taste the edges of. Are they failing? Could they have done better in that last session? And back, further, sometimes unwillingly – stupid things said or done now surface, waiting patiently for another round of analysis. Snatches of old songs, bits of dialogue from half-remembered glow shows. Memories of anger or sadness come back to sting. Each time in their lives that they have felt powerless presents itself, ready for painful inspection.

The only task they have to complete in their Stillness sessions is to empty their minds completely for as long as possible. The sessions last an hour at a time. Red has so far managed up to one minute before conscious thought intrudes, and that full minute was hard won, a real victory. An hour of this and each one of them stumbles out, brains paralysed with exhaustion.

Weeks roll past with no markers to separate them. No days off, no respite from this relentless routine meant to break and remould them. There is no time to resent or rebel. To rebel is to fail. To submit is to pass.

Red receives her stats on her glow screen at the end of each week to review, noting with a disconnected kind of interest how lean she has grown at the same time as putting on weight. How muscle mass has taken over fat mass. She examines herself naked in her full-length mirror, free now to think of it as necessary. Her body is her tool, her power, her weapon, and she is cultivating it. The communal showers no longer incite blushes from even the shyest among them. A body is a body and they have seen each other's on a daily basis for months.

It happens gradually.

There is no climax to speak of, no epiphany. It is simply a feeling of fading, subsuming, each day's sharp edges filed soft by repetition. 'Training' is now thought of as 'life', something not to be endured, but instead to be experienced. Its simplicity is comforting and not confining, its monastic rhythm as quietly important as a heartbeat.

Until, one day, it is over.

Red is woken in the morning not by her hooting alarm, but by the soft chirrup of a new message. It blinks on her fuzzy glow screen, waiting for her.

She slides out of bed and crouches before the screen, opening it up.

The message is signed *Daedalas Caballarias Frome o'Rhyfentown*. It states:

you have passed training
attend breakfast at your leisure and await further information

Naked on her knees, the glow screen bathing the front of her body in cold blue light like a beatification, Red o'Rhyfentown becomes a knight of the Caballaria.

And she is another step closer to her revenge.

PART II

Sex and death – the oldest of lovers.

Traditional Seven Kingdoms saying

CHAPTER 13

Cair Lleon, Blackheart
Eighteen Years Ago

Loose, low laughter greets him as he opens the door.

The room beyond is one Art has not yet seen. There is very little time for him to go off exploring the brooding labyrinth of a palace he is supposed to know. Hundreds of years ago its construction began with a simple, enormous, lofty dome and a cluster of spindly, regimented turrets, their spires stabbing up into the sky like skeletal fingers covered in black rings. Over time it has been expanded in every possible direction, including down – there are whole networks of rooms below surface level, connected by quiet, dim wood-panelled corridors and echoing, rough-hewn stone hallways.

One of these days he needs to commission someone to map out the entire palace for him, secret places and all. For now, it is enough to know that he is underground, towards the – he hazards a hazy guess; saints, his sense of direction has always been miserable – western end of Cair Lleon.

This is the King of London's last appointment in a line of endless appointments at the end of a very long day. Art is struggling tired, but there are several unusual factors surrounding this meeting that are keeping him on high alert – not least of which is that he arrives unaccompanied by any of his constant retinue of advisors, all of whom have apparently retired for the night.

This is a first.

A silent vastos Art has never seen before brought him here via a bewildering series of descenders, corridors and antechambers and then left him by himself in front of a normal-looking door. When he asked where they were going, the vastos simply said, 'I'm taking you to the Green Room as instructed, Sire,' an answer at once both clear and obtuse. Further probing produced confessions of ignorance, expressed in such a way as made it clear that a King who didn't even know who he was meeting was a King to be pitied.

Which Art cannot really deny.

It is not that the meeting is blanketed in secrecy, exactly, which would at least be exciting. It is more as if it were an afterthought, left until the last minute, something almost no one knew about simply because it wasn't that important.

It was cleverly done, he would later realise.

He enters the room alone. Bathed in the warm light coming from the tall lamps set at each corner, he can see perhaps a dozen or fewer people, a mix of men and women of all ages. They sit on forest-green and buttercup-gold couches with thighs splayed, reaching forwards every so often to take a tiny pastry from the trays on the spindly tables in front of them, or to sip from cut-crystal tumblers. Clearly they at least have been prepared enough for a last-minute meeting to battle through lengthy district border controls to get here, security-cleared enough to have no trouble entering the palace at such an hour, and expected enough to have refreshments laid out for them.

One woman is showing off a projection on the wall next to

the door, and two others are clustered around it as if in study. The woman lowers the small glow torch in her hand as Art enters and snaps off the projection before he can see what it is.

Those sitting, rise.

Those standing, wait.

Then bows ripple out across the group, heads and torsos bending with various levels of grace. Art has found that most people are enthusiastic on first meeting him, some obsequiously so. He struggles with the latter, finding it hard to trust someone who hides their desires in flattery. Their visits are driven by want, after all. It is the nature of things. Why not meet and trade each other's wants as equals?

That, Brune often drily tells him, *is not how the game is played.*

So Art has become well used to the sense of want emanating in all its various guises from everyone he meets – but that feeling is lacking here. It is expectant, in fact, as if they are waiting for him to tell them what *he* wants – but he doesn't even know who they are, let alone what he might desire from them.

'Please, sit,' he says.

Some return to the couches. The rest stand or lean, careful to keep in his eyeline, as protocol demands. He casts around for his own seat. For weeks he has been led to chairs by various vastos, his path picked out for him with no need for his input. Embarrassingly, it is almost as if he has forgotten how to seat himself without help.

'Sire.' He is rescued by a nimble man in a fitted peacock-blue coat with a severe metal collar, who pulls out an empty chair from underneath his table. As Art takes it, the others at the table move away, relocating to stand behind divans or taking empty seats further off. He finds himself oddly sad at the loss of intimacy, even with strangers. No one sits close to him any more.

'Thank you,' he says.

'My pleasure, Sire. And yours, I hope,' the man in peacock blue says smoothly.

There is a ripple of laughter. A woman with bright blonde hair close by gives a snort.

'In there at the quick,' she says disparagingly.

The man in peacock blue affects to look modest. 'Ignore the lady, there. Professional jealousy can be an awful ugly thing, can it not? May I take the liberty of introductions?' His speech is lilting, with an affected vintage twang.

'Please,' Art replies in relief.

The man grins. 'I,' he pronounces grandly, and within his showy pause another ripple of amusement spreads among the group.

'Get on with it!' someone calls from the back, and Art, despite the mystery, begins to enjoy the scene.

Peacock man is undeterred. 'I,' he repeats, 'am Beaufort Pluma Clementine o'Iochitown, proprietor of the Fancy Feather.'

He has a grey metal brooch pinned to his shoulder – a pretty set of scales with a leaping fish just above them, the symbol of the district he calls home. He produces a stubby book from under his arm and places it carefully on Art's table. The very edge of each thick leaf of paper is brushed in silver, and etched on the book's black cover is a copper feather.

'The jealous lady to my left,' Beaufort continues, 'is Good Girl Tuesday, mistress of Shakes, Rhyfentown's most venerable establishment of grand times.'

Good Girl Tuesday looks like she acquired the name for her own amusement. She stands accompanied by the unmistakable creak of tightened leather and slides her own black book on to

Art's table. Printed on its cover in demure crimson letters is the word SHAKES.

Mystified, he stretches out a hand to it, but Beaufort is speaking again.

'The portly gentleman to my right—'

'Cheeky cock—' said gentleman exclaims comfortably.

'—is Lassither Joe of Doxie House, who keeps the finest selection of whiskies on this side of the river, but never, ever shares them, not even with his friends.'

'Well, you ought to see the import tax on 'em,' Lassither Joe begins, but he is cried down.

'Might that be the import tax colloquially known as "dealing direct at the docks on a dark night" so you don't have to *pay* the import tax?' calls someone from the back.

Laughter.

'Slanderers,' Lassither declares. He also has his own black book, and places it carefully on the growing stack.

This is the most relaxed – and puzzled – Art has been in a long time. The confidence of a group comfortable enough to make jokes about illegal activities in front of the King is infectious. He tries his best to look entirely up to speed as Beaufort introduces each of the remaining group. Establishments from every district are represented in the room, some districts more than once, and everyone has a book to give him.

A suspicion forms halfway through the ritual, but it isn't until a striking androgynous figure wrapped in red silk, introduced with the singular name of Dario Go, hands him a book printed with the title *THE NIGHT CARNIVAL* that he is finally sure.

There isn't a Londoner alive who hasn't heard of the Night

Carnival. The name is often used as a signal in everyday vernacular. Being 'tapped to join the Night Carnival' means that someone has expressed an interest in sleeping with you. 'Visiting the Night Carnival' is a term he heard often growing up but didn't fully understand until he was fourteen, when he realised that it meant losing your virginity. The Night Carnival is London's oldest and most famous bordel.

Acutely aware of the virginal ignorance that kept him from working out the situation until now, Art waits politely until everyone in the room is introduced, and until the stack of black books on the table in front of him has reached teetering point. He smiles and nods in the right places while his mind whirs. Now the clandestine tactics make sense. It has become increasingly clear since that black glass crown first touched his head that every aspect of a monarch's life is managed by the palace, so why not this, too?

Beaufort retakes his seat and an expectant hush settles over the room. Art pulls the book printed with *THE NIGHT CARNIVAL* towards him, running a fingertip over the embossed lettering. He opens it up.

It is a menu.

Each page has a name, an artfully done capture and a list of particular specialities. Art's eye catches the phrase 'highly skilled at rope play' and savagely fights a blush.

'How does this work, exactly?' he asks.

'You don't have to pick now, no, Sire, no,' Beaufort says. 'Take all the time you wish. You can place an order with us, day or night.'

'Place an order,' Art remarks. 'Like a steak at a restaurant.'

Beaufort laughs heartily, as do one or two others.

'Rest assured,' Lassither Joe speaks up, 'we have something

for every taste on the saints' good earth. Whoever – or whatever – you desire, Doxie House has someone on our books to suit you.'

The group grows bolder, crying Lassither down with their own promises of diversity and chiding him for his forwardness. Apparently it is bad form to try and influence in a group-pitching situation such as this one, rare though they are.

Only for the richest and most elite of new clients do the masters and mistresses of grand times gather together like this, each hoping to land the whale and ensure a nice new steady income for their house. The King, of course, is the biggest whale of all, because it is becoming apparent that this is a tradition that has passed down through the ages. Rulers have appetites, after all, just like everyone else.

Art waits until the camaraderie dies down enough for him to slip his knife in.

'Not for me, thank you,' he says, closing the Night Carnival's menu with a snap.

'Oh,' Beaufort says with the faintest slyness trying to take hold of his mouth, 'that's no problem, no problem at all, Sire. We shall leave you in peace to make your choices—'

'You're not quite understanding me,' Art cuts him off. 'I'm not interested. At all.'

The room falls silent.

'There's a special arrangement,' Beaufort begins. 'The utmost in discretion is guaranteed. Absolutely guaranteed.'

Grand times might be the world's oldest profession, and its services open to any citizen of London – as well as the millions of tourists who visit every year – but it is also a huge, carefully regulated industry that lives and dies by its discretion, especially concerning its more public-facing citizens. The saints only know the sorts of embarrassing secrets they have on half of upper society.

'I don't doubt your abilities there,' Art responds. 'I'm sure you've safeguarded the reputations of many Kings and Queens over the years. I'm simply not interested.'

Good Girl Tuesday speaks up. 'We understand, Sire, if there is someone already in your special regard.'

Art is stone. 'There isn't.'

A pause.

'Your father—' Lassither Joe tries.

'It should be abundantly clear by now that I'm not my father.'

'Absolutely not, absolutely not.' Beaufort hurries on. 'You are your own man, Sire, with your own particular tastes, and – I mean, there's nothing that we haven't seen, and also, if you'll note that your father had not one scandal of this kind in his whole life, what I'm saying about discretion, you can check all the news archives, not one report or anything.'

Art finds himself growing amused at how desperately fast the man is getting.

'But for you, well, any reports would be a trifle that would bother no one, anyway, as you are currently single, at least officially, and of course it's never harmed a ruler before, everyone understands the particular stresses of the Sword, it's really not—'

'Saintsfuck, Beau, take a breath.'

Dario Go's voice is a clean, sharp cut.

Beaufort stops mid-flow and Dario claps their hands once, a loud crack in the quiet.

'Esteemed colleagues,' they declare. 'It's late, our young King is exhausted and we all, I'm sure, have full nights ahead of us.'

Of course. This would be the first meeting of their working

day, not the last. It is a delicately thrown rope, and Art grabs it gratefully.

'Yes,' he says. 'I have a few busy days ahead, unfortunately. Perhaps when things are a little more settled, I can turn my attentions to' – he gropes – 'your wonderful selections.'

Diplomatic charm. There is an art to it, and Art is currently at stick-figure level.

It takes a while. They murmur among themselves as they gather to depart, swill down the last of their drinks, exchange soft anecdotes. Each of them bows to him as they pass his chair. He nods. He smiles. One of the first lessons taught to him – don't piss off powerful businessfolk.

It is not until the last of them has left the room that he realises Dario Go hasn't moved. The group had been careful to pull each other down whenever one of them tried to draw his attention more than the rest, careful to be equal – but they will let Dario be alone with him. Perhaps they, like everyone else, still defer to the Night Carnival.

Dario rises, red silks whispering, and plops into the chair in front of Art. He is surprised, and not a little pleased, at their boldness.

'May I ask you a question, Sire?' they ask. 'Now that we have a little more privacy.'

'In Cair Lleon?' he drily responds.

Dario withdraws a black sicalo from a thin metal case and offers it to him. He takes it gratefully. Dario lights it from the slender candelabra perched on the low table sat between them, and then lights their own. Their eyes, heavily painted in dark, secretive metallics, regard him keenly through the smoke.

'You are . . . romantic?'

Art fixes them with his own blank stare. 'I don't know.'

'You're monogamous?'

The word is said with care, as if it is a foreign word they are trying hard not to pronounce wrong for fear of causing offence.

He laughs. 'Is it really so strange to want to be with just one person? It's not that rare, is it, these days? Anyway, I'd like to think I could manage to find someone myself, the way most people do.'

'Oh. And how are you going to do that?'

'What do you mean?'

Dario shrugs. 'You imagine you can just . . . walk into a bar and find someone dancing underneath the pretty lights? A couple of drinks, a little flirting? Perhaps a dinner date is fixed, and when you meet, they're shy, you're nervous but you don't show it, and all the time through the lobster course you can't stop thinking about how they'd look on top of you. It's awkward, at first, of course. It often is. But not too soon after that, there in the darkness with them in your arms, you feel the first stirrings of love. Time moves on, and they become your reality. They meet your friends, your family, and you meet theirs. You begin to talk of your lives entwined instead of as separate threads . . . it's all so lovely, so normal. Right?'

Art wants to say yes.

'You're the King of London,' Dario continues. 'Haven't you realised that you will never, ever have such a relationship? You know that anyone you meet from now on until you die will either be too afraid or too in love with *what* you are instead of *who* you are to treat you as their equal? That anyone who shows an interest in you will always, always have their own reasons? That you'll never be able to tell, ever again, what anyone truly thinks of you because you are their symbol, a face and body on a pedestal?' Dario sits back, their wide mouth a concerned curve. 'Sire, no one wants the *reality* of you. You will only ever be used. Sometimes accidentally, but mostly with calculation. There are a few drawbacks to the kind of power you have. This is one of them.'

Art laughs, because there is no reasonable reaction to such a proclamation. It is ridiculous, of course. He watches Dario for signs of condescension or irritation at his laugh, but their eyes are on the table, the sicalo turning to ash between their thin fingers.

'That's an incredibly cynical viewpoint,' he says.

'I'd say realistic,' says Dario Go, and their smile moves slow. 'Your marriage will be arranged according to the rules of power, not love. But it's not so bad. You'll likely be paired with someone who has grown up under the weight of similar circumstances, someone who understands the kind of life you now have and will behave accordingly. You can continue with services such as ours, if your marriage dissatisfies, and your spouse can happily indulge their own tastes. That's all very normal, even expected—'

Art loses his patience. 'I have no intention of marrying someone I'm not in love with. Saints, why am I talking about this? I'm only eighteen, I haven't even *begun* to think about it—'

'I can guarantee you're the only one in Cair Lleon who hasn't,' Dario chides him gently, 'so perhaps you should start now, before you find that your hold on the decision has slipped from your grasp, and it's too late.'

They lock gazes. This feels like another lesson in politics, something that Brune would normally be trying to teach him. Perhaps she didn't have the stomach for this particular lesson, instead outsourcing to one whose livelihood depends on their intimate understanding of it.

Sex as a weapon and not a pleasure. The idea dismays him.

'In the meantime,' Dario says smoothly, 'you have this.' Their fingers brush the edges of the black book pile. 'Professional. Discreet. Your choice comes for one visit, or more if you take a shine to them. They don't speak to anyone of what transpires between you. We make absolutely sure of this. We pride ourselves on this. You'll already know what they want from you – to be well treated and well paid. In return they give you whatever you want, within the parameters that you set. Just think of them as another type of vastos. Their job is to serve you in a specific way.'

'I don't enjoy being served,' Art says.

Dario leans forwards, their hand spidering across the table and stopping just short of Art's wrist. They are not allowed to touch him without permission and they know this. They are playing with the boundary, testing its limits.

'Am I to take it that this might indicate your preference for *serving* instead?' they say.

Art feels himself stir, his treacherous body eagerly uncoiling. 'Don't flirt with me,' he says coldly.

Dario withdraws their hand.

There can be no trust between them. Just like any other meeting of the past few weeks, tonight's group have come because they want something from him. The only move left to him is to deny them what they want.

Dario gathers themself.

'When you're next desirous of a little relaxation,' they say, and Art notes the *when*, not the *if*, 'send a message to me. All you have to write is "dinner for two", with a date and time. Day or night, Sire. I've marked a suggestion in the book, someone I think might suit you very well.'

Dario rises. Art doesn't move. They tower over him, the moment growing awkward. They cannot go without his dismissal.

'What if I ask for you?' he says finally, forcing his gaze to meet theirs.

There is the merest flicker across their marble face. 'I'm not in the book, Sire. I'm in more of a managerial role these days.'

'Are you saying you're not an option?'

'I'm saying that you might want to start small and work your way up.' Dario dips their head in a concessionary bow. 'But if I'm your wish, then might I be so bold as to predict that your expectations would be more than fulfilled.'

'After the past few minutes in your company, Laerd Dario, my expectations are pretty high.'

Their eyes gleam in the candlelight. 'My King is too kind.'

Art rises from his chair and dips his own head in a bow. He has been curious in recent weeks to see what effect his habit of equalising himself in such a manner has on everyone he meets. Shock, sometimes. Amusement, others. Confusion, most often.

Perhaps inevitably, Dario betrays no emotion of any kind. It is easy to suppose that you don't earn a place in the Night Carnival, never mind come to run the whole establishment, without being one of the most gifted actors of your generation.

He watches Dario quietly exit the room, hears their murmuring to the waiting vastos outside. Once he has made sure that the door is closed and he is alone, Art sags back into his chair. Whatever he might have implied, he doesn't know if he's quite at the level to spar with Dario Go and come out unscathed.

His gaze settles on the books.

No one wants the reality of you. You will only ever be used.

CHAPTER 14

Riverside, Rhyfentown
Five Months Ago

The light has grown claws while she slept.

The morning sun (possibly, she has no idea what time it is) coming in through the bedroom window is attacking her. It rakes mercilessly against her closed eyes until she is forced, squinting, into consciousness.

No, no, no.

No, why must she be awake? No.

As Red sits up among the crumpled sheets of the narrow bed she managed to stumble into at the end of the night, memories come slowly trickling into her brain like the sour green cocktail they had finished the evening with. What had that drink been called?

Then the name arrives: *Dead from the Waist Up.*

Now she knows why.

Oh, the night. The night, the night, and their wild, neon-soaked ride across its endless terrain. Relief, it had mostly sprung from, and jubilation. A bunch of roaring cubs let loose for the first time in months.

★

It had begun with a gathering at a local bar, the designated meeting place for all trainees who were now newly made knights of the Caballaria.

There had been fifty-odd hopefuls at the start of this journey, a mix of those few picked up at challenger bouts and sponsored by the district, and the rest who had their training money from private means.

Only five of them had passed. Four faces turned to Red as she entered the bar; she stopped short of the table they clustered around as she saw who they were.

There was Kitani, whose dandelion mop of hair was uncharacteristically slicked back and his stocky frame strung with tension.

Then there was Danna, a curvaceous girl lethal with a mace, who had early on been renamed 'Six' in reference to Six Staffs, the incredibly exclusive ups area of Rhyfentown she hailed from.

Kay, hulking and brooding over a pewter cup. It looked like a child's in his meaty hand.

And Sela saintsdamned Delaney.

For one moment, Red considered turning and walking out of the bar rather than subject herself to an evening bathed in that irritating smirk, but she couldn't bear the satisfaction it would give Sela to know she was having such an effect.

One drink, Red promised herself. *For the ritual's sake. Then you can get out of here.*

The group was clustered around a long table they had claimed near the back of the cheerily lit bar, all their familiarity lost in the strangeness of the moment, this moment that they had taken pain and punishment for, had shut out the world and rewired their bodies and minds for.

'I always knew this determined fucker would make it,' Kay said, looking at her.

Well, some people hadn't suffered too much rewiring, it seemed.

'When I got a message saying to meet everyone in a place called the Knight's Passage,' Red said, 'I thought it was a joke.'

'Tradition,' Sela replied. 'Everyone comes here the first night after their passing-out, so a few years ago they renamed the place more appropriately. Don't worry, your passage is safe with us.'

Red didn't rise to it. Sela could taunt all she liked – now it was a shot from knight to knight.

'Sit your arse down, Pel,' Kay said affectionately, slapping the space on the bench beside him.

Red slid cautiously into the group, looking around the room. Low beams made of dark, warm timber gave the place a cosy, comforting feel. It was still early, and there weren't too many other patrons in the bar with them, but it felt crowded. The scuffed floorboards echoed people's footsteps loudly in her ears. The whole place had been done up with an old-world feel, dropped back to the wood and brick times before chrome and steel, trick and glow.

'It doesn't feel real, does it?' said Six. 'Like the outside world is a fake theatre stage laid on just for us, somehow.'

Red wrapped her hands around the polished copper cup offered to her. The sides were cold, beaded with moisture, a welcome sting on her fingers against the stuffy warmth of the air in here. Hot and cold. That was real enough.

'I feel like a monk who's just been let out of the monastery,' Kay grumbled, nursing his tankard.

'Randy?' Sela enquired.

'Raring?' supplied Kitani.

Six grinned. 'Tumescent?'

Kay scowled. 'Overwhelmed.'

The other four exchanged glances. Kay had effortlessly held his position in the group as the bluff, boisterous one, undeveloped in the department of nuance, perhaps, but admirably fearless. Everything was a challenge to be met, not to shy away from. Training had left its mark on him, after all.

'It goes away,' Sela said, eventually. 'So I've heard.' Her fingers skirted on Kay's back in awkward comfort. 'You just need to remind yourself of how it is to be in *this* world, instead of the one inside the Dungeons.'

'How?'

Sela raised her mug. 'You partake of this world's particular delights,' she said, with a smile.

So they did. They really, really did.

The Knight's Passage was soon abandoned for another bar suggested by Sela, deeper into the centre of Rhyfentown, and then another that Six favoured. They walked between their way stations if they were close enough, or caught a trag if it was too far.

London's electrical train network was the cheapest transport around. A good amount of trick was needed to keep a private quad running, so everyone used the trags, which ran through the night in most areas, as the city's famed after-hours life depended on them. Even the rich rode them – most often, as Sela scathingly supplied, when they were too in their cups to steer their own quads back to whatever safe ups area they called home. Six graciously chose not to rise to the bait.

When she first came to Rhyfentown, Red had been out of joint and dislocated by the dazzle, but now she felt herself stir at it, greedy and aroused. There was so much to feel on these streets, so much life, so much of every kind of thing. The sheer choice on offer had unnerved a younger, nervier her, but now it gave her joy. What an incredible thing to exist in this world, in this time, hearts beating strong.

They went to a little place accessed by an innocuous door with a snake painted on it, a bar called Serpentine, where all the drinks were black and green, where the servers' skins were painted with scales and their eyes were covered in slit-pupil lenses.

As the night deepened and made them bold, Kay took to telling every single person they came across, door staff and wait staff and random people on the streets, that they were newly trained Caballaria knights. At first Red found it embarrassing, but by their fourth round of free drinks, the attentiveness with which they were served, and the spontaneous whooping and clapping that Kay's pronouncements had elicited from complete strangers passing them by, even Red had to admit that it was, at its worst, useful currency.

At its best it was one long, hot buzz.

Careful. Don't get caught up in the glamour of this. It's just a means to an end. Don't you dare start to like *it*—

Red knocked back drink after drink, forgetting her earlier promise to leave after one, lured by the conversation and the dancing that pulled all her focus, until her brain was suffocated by the hazy clouds of alcohol and life, *this* life, *her* life, was a series of moments that existed only tonight and now, with no room for anything before or beyond it.

Her real purpose, lying in wait for her around future's corner, be damned.

Just for tonight. Just give me tonight.

Wilder they got as they went on, until suggestions turned to visiting the notorious Night Carnival, which was rumoured to offer an open house to newly trained knights. Inner Iochitown was its residence and it would be easy enough to reach via the newly built inter-district trags, but travel time might cut their evening into rags.

Kay said that Shakes, one of Rhyfentown's own famed establishments, offered mass orgies in their plush cellar rooms, but none of them could quite face so much performance involved in that kind of thing – and so, in casting around for something else provocative that might sate them, Sela spoke up.

'I think it might be time to wyrd.'

The others exchanged looks.

'To what?' Six asked.

'Wyrd.'

'What's that?'

Sela sneered. 'I suppose rich people don't need to get their fortunes told. Theirs are already taken care of.'

'T'chuss, Sela,' Kitani said impatiently. He glanced at Six. 'You never had your wyrd done?'

'You mean the thing with the soothsayers?' Six looked uncomfortable. 'That's illegal.'

Kitani flapped a vague hand. 'Not really. Everyone does it. Besides, it's a passing-out tradition. Every new knight gets their wyrd told. A harmless little peek at how much fame and glory the future holds.'

'Yes, but—' She hesitated. 'It's magic.'

'Got a problem with godchildren, Six Staffs?' Sela said, delighted at potential controversy. 'Remember who we're out with, now.'

Red, three drinks in and feeling far less inclined to hold down, snorted. 'Soothsayers. Cut your arm open and bleed trick just to get told that you'll "win many bouts and die fat and rich". They're not godchildren, just common con artists.'

'Not the one I'm thinking of. He's on the real. Rare as a blood moon and just as powerful.' Kitani gave a sidelong glance at Sela. 'My cousin Lina gave me the where. It's not far from here.'

The group had begun to buzz with a tense, mischievous air.

'Commons get turned away a lot, I've heard,' Sela said.

'From where?' Six asked, sounding nervous. 'Where are we going?'

Kitani gave a deliberately careless shrug. 'Godchild bar.'

Godchild bars did not officially exist. They belonged to the underworld, life underneath life, the night underneath the day. Much the same as Wardogs, London's notorious illegal underground fighting circuit, they were known of, occasionally shut down, and nevertheless by all accounts doing a healthy trade. They were hard to find and even harder to get into.

Unless you had a bona fide godchild in your group, of course.

'Red's our ticket inside,' Kay said with semi-drunk bravado, slinging a weighty arm around her shoulders. She leashed the sudden desire to shake him off. It was clear now that this had been a conspiracy from the beginning – they hadn't told her in case she had said no.

She could still say no.

The group's eyes were on her.

She shrugged. 'Don't blame me if they turn us away.'

Kay gave a calm-shattering whoop.

They made their way towards Hayken-eye, a quiet area of Rhyfentown that had once, in Sela's father's time, boasted the largest homeless encampment in all of London. The encampment had been razed a decade ago and a public Caballaria training ground open to street foxes newly built in its place.

Feelings were mixed on whether this had solved any kind of problem, but there was no denying the steady rate at which the area had been turning from downs to ups since then.

'Hey, Kitani,' Sela said, 'your cousin actually been inside this place we're going?'

'Oh yes. She said it was crazy, like being on Fever Dream.'

'I've journeyed on Fever Dream,' Sela said. 'It's weird.'

'You've done everything,' Six mocked nervously.

'Everything except you, my dear.'

'Keep fever dreaming.'

'What's Fever Dream?' asked Kay.

'It's a play drug for tech posers and angel chasers,' Six said dismissively. 'People take it to look good, but all that happens is that you hallucinate trees talking to you, or some such thing.'

Sela sounded amused. 'Have you ever actually taken it?'

'I don't need to take it.'

'Spoken like a true ignorant.'

'Stop flirting,' Kitani interrupted. 'We're here.'

The group looked up at the building.

'Kitani,' said Kay. 'This is a grocerie.'

The front awning was tattered, striped in desultory shades of yellow. Its flickering neon sign was shaped in the traditional grocer's rune. A board was sat underneath translating the sign into several more languages in thin, badly illuminated lettering.

'It's a grocerie,' Kitani agreed. 'And underneath it is a bar.'

'How do you get to the bar?'

'Through the grocerie.'

Red looked confused. 'That's stupid. How is anyone supposed to find it?'

'It's not supposed to be findable,' Sela said.

Kay tilted his head. 'It looks closed.'

'It's not,' Kitani responded confidently. He pushed on the door and a buzzer sounded from within the shop, announcing their arrival. They shuffled inwards.

A confusing mix of spices slapped Red on the nose as she entered – deep baskets of them were sat in untidy rows near the door, all dyed the red, orange and yellow colours of Rhyfentown. Strip lights buzzed tiredly overhead, illuminating corridors of metal racks filled with trays of fruit and vegetables piled high, interspersed with flecter-glass jars of the same offerings pickled, preserved, brined, salted, sweetened, flavoured, spiced, sauced and juiced.

'There's no one else here,' Red whispered to Kay as Kitani headed into the depths of the shop.

'I know,' Kay boomed back, shattering the silence. 'Place is a fucken tomb.'

Red winced.

'Friends.' Sela was nodding to a counter near the back.

Kitani was deep in conversation with a woman sporting a head of neatly piled grey hair and the tightly folded arms of the deeply suspicious.

'Red,' Kitani called in a clipped tone. 'I need you.'

Red made her way towards the counter. The woman's gaze lit on her appraisingly. Her expression changed.

'Maybe we should find somewhere else,' Red muttered to Kitani.

The woman spoke. 'No, no. Come in, come in. It's an honour to have you, Si. An honour.'

Her tone was edged in flutters. Her arms had dropped from their defensive position and now her hands floated on the air, fingers crooked and beckoning.

Red glanced uneasily at Kitani. He raised his eyebrows and said nothing.

'I saw the footage of your fight with the Scourge,' the woman went on in a sudden rush. 'So exciting. So exciting. So beautiful, you were. You are.' She pressed wrinkled fingers to her mouth. 'Pardons, I've never seen a godchild knight before. My husband, he goes to all the local bouts and he takes our daughters, oh they love it as much as he does, such a passion in our family, you know, but I've never seen one up close—'

Her hand reached out as if to touch Red, and she flinched back instinctively before she could control it.

'Thank you so much for letting us visit,' Kitani interrupted. 'It's a privilege.' He gestured to the others as he spoke, and they came trooping down to the counter.

'And to have met you on your passing-out, too,' the woman said, still gazing at Red. 'They've been speculating on the glow shows for weeks as to whether you'd make it through, but there's been no official announcement yet. Oh, I can't believe I'm the first to know. My husband will be so mad he missed this, when I tell him!'

With a rattle of cheap gold bracelets, she opened up a dirty grey door behind a haphazard stack of empty boxes.

'Down there?' Kitani asked.

The woman gestured to the stairs the open door had revealed. The stairwell beyond was lit with thick red lamps the colour of drying blood. A darkness loaded with thumping music and heavy with promise. With a triumphant look at the rest, Kitani led them on.

'Rhyfentown is behind you, Si!' the woman called as the group made their way down.

As the door closed behind them, Red spat out a tight, savage curse.

Sela barked a laugh in the dark. 'What's the matter? Your fame opens doors, quite literally. Lap it up. Rhyfentown is behind you!'

'I don't want anyone *behind me*,' she replied, ruffled by the jealousy she could hear in Sela's tone. 'I just want to be left alone.'

'My, my, you picked the wrong profession, didn't you?' Sela said. 'What's the matter, getting rope belly? There's plenty who'll take your place if you don't have the guts for it.'

Red stopped. Tension sang.

You don't know what I have to have the guts for, you carefree little fuck.

For one awful moment, she felt herself sinking into hollow, despairing envy. They would never know. They had their whole lives ahead of them, filled with successes and failures and the fight and all the love they would find. All those gorgeous, normal things that Red could not afford to want.

The eyes of the group were on her. The eyes of the whole world seemed to be on her right now. She would break under the weight of their scrutiny, and then they would see it – the reason she did all of this, the reason she lived. There was only one way to drown this panic and stop the desperate confession she could feel pressing in her throat.

'Get me a damn drink, then, if I'm so famous,' she said. 'I got you in here. Pay up.'

Sela whistled. 'Haughty haughty.'

They reached the bar. It was low lit and packed, its decoration rich with raw texture. Lamp brackets of intricately carved wood. Velvet chairs, fur-lined walls, thick candles of every colour dripping hot wax over every nook and alcove, bundles of claws and feathers and stones and long sprigs of dried plants strewn from the ceiling and twined around pillars with thin rope. It smelled hot, felt stifling. Felt like vibrant, desperate life, packed tightly into a box too small for it.

'Looks like a regular place to me,' Kay bellowed over the noise.

Kitani pointed to a corner festooned with sweeping silk curtains. 'Private section at the back. That's where the soothsayer is.'

'Excited to meet another godchild?' Kay asked Red.

He had delight written all over his face, and the others were straining with eager expectance. Red wanted to throw something. How could she tell them that she didn't give a rat's turd about meeting other godchildren?

The world liked nothing better than the tritest of stories. People believed that Red had deliberately gone after the Sorcerer Knight because of her desperation to meet another of her kind. It was annoying – if an undeniably useful subterfuge – and she had to play it.

She gave Kay a weak smile. 'Nervous, I think.'

'He'll adore you,' Kay declared.

'Is everyone in here a godchild?' she heard Six ask.

'What are you talking about?' Sela said scornfully, gesturing to the packed crowd. 'There aren't enough of them in the whole dis' to fill up this bar. All these idiots are nothing but common oglers. Just like us.' The last was muttered with a bitter edge. 'If you want a little magic up close, you have to pay for it.'

The curtains to the godchild's booth were guarded by a man and a woman who looked like they could make you pay as much as they wanted. There was, nevertheless, a discreet sign next to the curtains showing the cost.

'Shit on the floor,' Kay swore. 'That's an *outrageous* price. Fuck those guards, let's just rush 'em.'

'Kay, keep your voice down,' muttered Kitani. 'They're armed.'

The man and the woman did indeed have gun belts slung around their waists.

'Saints, that's illegal! No one can carry these days except knights, and they ain't no knights!'

Sela sounded impatient. 'Of course they're not, but the whole place is illegal, you think they care? Just hand over your trick and don't antagonise them.'

The group pooled their trick and approached the booth, Kay stewing in the rear. The guard man palmed it and begrudgingly pulled the curtain aside just enough of a sliver for someone to sidle through the gap.

'One at a time,' he said.

The group shuffled, but the guard man's gun had their drunken bravado temporarily cowed.

'Red gets first go, then,' Kitani said.

'What?' Red shook her head. 'No, someone else go.'

'She doesn't need her fortune told,' Sela said. 'She rides the tails of the famous: her future's already set.'

'Fuck you, Sela,' Red shot back. 'You have no idea what my future holds.'

With that she thrust past the curtain before Sela could whip out another bitter spike. The bar noise lowered to a muted roar as the curtain fell into place behind her.

Facing the curtain, with a small table between them, was an unremarkable-looking, curly-haired man. His clothes were too plain to say anything much under the dim lighting, and for a Londoner, the exposed stretches of his pale skin were curiously unadorned – which made his hands all the more obvious. Every finger was covered, from palm to tip, in jointed, burnished copper cuffs. So beautifully did they fit the length and shape of each finger that they must have been individually made.

In front of his hands, which were placed in a deliberately showy fashion on the table, were a tumble of flat, dull coins covered in runes: a cheap-looking fortune set, just like any back-alley soothsayer might have. A shallow bowl sat to one side, half full of some greasy-looking water.

'Sit, gorgeous,' the curly-haired man cooed mechanically.

His eyes flickered up at Red with a disinterested air as she took the chair opposite him. He caught her looking at his hands.

'Copper amplifies godchild talent,' he said in a bored tone, as if it were an explanation he had given a thousand times before.

Red snorted. 'Everyone knows that.'

His eyebrows rose. 'A temper. I like it. Very sexy. So what do you want to know, sweetlen?'

'It's my passing-out,' she began, and he interrupted.

'Ah, yes,' he said with a laugh. 'A newly pressed knight. I don't follow the Caballaria myself, but what an honour.'

His disdainful tone suggested that it was a lot less like an honour and a lot more like a waste of his time. He dipped a hand carefully into the bowl on the table and then extended it to her. The liquid inside the bowl clung to the surface of his copper cuffs in viscous, globbing beads, covering flesh and metal alike in a thick film. It wasn't water.

'Give me your hand,' he said.

'What is that?'

'It's just a kind of conductor. Calm down, it washes off.' He winked. 'What's the matter? Don't you like being slippery?'

Slowly, venomously, Red slid her hand into his. His fleshy, slicked palm closed over the top of her hand and his fingers tightened hard enough to cut the copper cuffs blunt against her skin. She felt a disgusted kind of fascination with its greasy intimacy, its thick intrusiveness.

'Now,' he said. 'Let's see.'

His eyes unfocused and lolled to the side. His free hand rolled listlessly over the rune coins, feather-touching their hard edges.

He breathed out. 'Tell me what you want, then.'

'I don't know,' Red said, already bored of his performance.

'*Lie*,' he snapped, and the word was so sharp that it punctured all his previous hazy lasciviousness. 'You want something very much. *So much*. And you're afraid of it, yes. Terrified. A cornered rat, scratching, scrabbling around.' He uttered a little laugh. 'Squeaking away.'

Red tried to pull her hand away, but he held her fingers too tight.

'Your hand is hot,' he said.

'It's boiling in here.'

'You're hot.'

'You're repulsive,' Red snarled.

His eyes were black and very wide. 'You're hot,' he murmured. 'You want to burn. You'll burn it all down because he took her from you. He'll never see it coming. He'll see you from far away, so pretty, twirling hair, twirling sword. Not 'til you get close that you hear the screaming.' His face twisted. 'Silly child. So your mammy died. So what? You think your hurt is so much greater than everyone else who's lost someone? You selfish bitch. Don't you ruin everything just because you're in pain. Don't you dare!'

He was staring at Red throughout this disjointed, blunt-cut speech, clearly furious and clearly frightened. It rolled off him like a stink. He had barely touched the runes. They were obviously nothing more than a ruse to get people's guard down. He was a real godchild, and a powerful one, because he could see things about her that she'd never told anyone. *Anyone.*

Could he see what she was here to do—?

The air was full of startled, flashing metal birds – no, coins. Rune coins, winging savagely from the table to ping against the curtain walls. The bowl full of viscous liquid lurched to the right and fell to the floor, splattering their legs with greasy globs. The soothsayer pitched backwards off his chair, his back hugging the wall as if pinned there by an invisible force.

Red had not moved, but she knew it was her doing it. Throwing whatever was in reach with magic – *illegal, illegal, you'll lose everything for this* – but it was already done. Her hands were screeching, itching, a thousand bugs crawling under her skin, each of their steps a needle-sting.

The soothsayer scrabbled uselessly, grunting and pushing. 'You're a pelleren,' he said.

He sounded almost angry, as if it had been the height of rudeness of her to say nothing of it. He hadn't been lying about not following the Caballaria, at least. He had no idea who she was.

Then he opened his mouth and screamed. 'Guns! Guns to table four! GUNS—'

His hands flew to his throat, winking copper as they went, scrabbling there. He was choking.

Red was the one choking him, crushing his windpipe from feet away.

I can't stop this, she thought dreamily. *It's coming out of me and there's no way to stop it.*

But a part of her, the part she tried so hard to leash, wanted to hear his bones crack. The screaming pain in her hands blended into a pleasing hum at the thought, a misplayed chord suddenly shifting into harmony. Her eyes fastened on his, greedy to extend the pleasure – but then she saw that he was crying. Tears were splashing down his cheeks as she crushed his throat.

The chord splintered. He was real. He was real, he was afraid, and he had done nothing to her.

He sagged as she let go, and dragged in a horrible, groaning breath.

Red felt hands grab her and pull her out of the booth. The magic left her, as always, feeling dazed and numb, and she could not more fight the hands that hauled her away than climb up to the sky.

'Thank you for getting us kicked out,' Sela said, as they wobbled their way up the street. 'I was having a terrible time. What did that poor boy do to you?'

'He was a hack,' Red muttered. 'I told you. He tried to fuck me over.'

The soothsayer had said nothing about taking her attack on him further, of course – he was unregistered and illegal. The whole place was illegal. Mutually assured destruction. The group had, however, been collectively banned from the bar.

'Ah, no one cares.' Six came up on Red's other side and slung an arm around her waist.

It appeared that no one did. Kay and Kitani led the way up the street, roaring some song together, howling like wolves up into the night sky.

'He must have upset you somehow,' Sela said, watching her.

'He propositioned me. I wasn't interested.'

Sela looked away.

Six hooted with pleased laughter.

'You're a Rhyfentown rat, all right,' she said agreeably. 'Why talk when you can punch? Ah, he likely deserved it. Let's get another drink.'

Red took this advice seriously. Each drink helped her to forget that she didn't know the soothsayer's name, and she didn't know how to find him, and even if she did, what would she do? Threaten him again over some vague play-acting about burning cities down?

He was a hack. He had played her, just as she had told the others. Before long she believed her own story, and carried on pretending she was nothing but a newly pressed knight on her passing-out, revelling in the moment and singing songs up to the sky with the rest of them.

At the lowest end of the night they found themselves in Six's part of Rhyfentown, ending up in a cavernous dockside apartment, apparently one of several owned by her family.

The metal ceiling was covered in huge, glittering lights echoing a thousand colours from the buildings below, while one wall of top-to-bottom glass afforded a spectacular view over the river, a gleaming black ribbon in the predawn. The water itself was suffused with a silvery glow, said to come, Six told them, from the old pretty but wasteful one-use trick coins, their silver casings tossed to lie discarded on the riverbed.

It felt just like a dream.

It was all just a dream.

Now, of course, that same glorious window is letting in the light currently busy raking Red's face into miserable reality.

On the daybed in the corner of the room is Kay, snoring the way he talks – loudly and confidently. Red vaguely remembers Six and Sela disappearing into the bedroom together, presumably to seal the night with a kiss, or more. They had lost Kitani somewhere before coming here – he had begged off soon after the godchild bar and had caught a night trag back to the Dungeons, where they technically all should be right now.

Unable to face sitting still and simply letting her hangover relentlessly happen to her, Red drags herself upwards and wobbles her way towards the back of the room, away from the accusatory morning light.

Along the wall is a modest kitchen with a sleek table and a set of angular chairs. On one of the chairs sits Sela, frowning down into a handheld glow screen.

She looks up.

'You're alive, then,' she says.

Red slumps into the chair opposite and huddles. 'Don't think so.'

'I told you not to have that pink thing you threw down your throat at the end, there.'

'It tasted like acid sunshine.'

The ghost of a smile touches Sela's mouth and then melts off.

'Listen,' she says, 'you should get back to the Dungeons.'

Red massages her forehead gently. 'How much trouble are we going to be in for not going back last night?'

'Please! They expect it every passing-out. My father woke up in a different Kingdom after his. It's *you* I'm talking about, Red.' Her voice has none of her usual playfulness.

Red frowns blearily. 'Why, what have I done?'

Sela leans back. 'You've been booked for your first official fight.'

Ice trickles down Red's insides, threatening her torpor. 'I only passed out yesterday.'

Sela's eyebrow rises. 'And yet. Someone's already booked you. The fight's in a couple of weeks.'

Red stares at her, searching for the hint of a joke in her eyes.

'I haven't even . . . no one's even . . . there's been no auction, no offers, nothing. I can't fight until I belong to a stable. That isn't even possible.'

Grim satisfaction marches across Sela's face. 'And yet,' she repeats.

'Where are you getting this from?'

She holds up the glow screen. 'Message just went round the Dungeons' trainers.'

'You're not a trainer.'

'Well, it so happens that Six's father and Frome are good friends, ever since they came up in training together. Also she left her personal glow screen lying around where anybody could take a little look at it.' Sela's eyes sparkle as she meaningfully wiggles the screen in her hand. She has been waiting for this moment, relaying the news so she could sit back and enjoy the effect.

Red swallows a sudden flash of temper. One day she will learn to stop reacting just as Sela wants her to. For a moment too long they stare at each other – then Red looks away, seceding.

'Fine,' she says thickly. 'It's a mistake. So I'm going to go back and get it corrected.'

Sela is all amusement, flush with the warmth of her win. 'Good luck with that, Pel.'

Red leaves her at the kitchen table, feeling the stab of a smirk at her back.

It is becoming deadly clear to Red that Si Finnavair was wrong. It is far too dangerous to try nurturing allies. It draws too much attention, invites too many eyes on her, and she has enough of those to contend with already. Forging friendships, even tentative ones, was a mistake. She has to cut them all loose.

She has to do what she came here to do alone.

Kay is still snoring on the daybed, Six is presumably still asleep in the bedroom and Sela has disappeared into the bathroom. Good. It makes things easier. Red leaves the apartment as quietly as she can and makes her way downstairs to street level.

As far as she knows, no Caballaria knight in history has ever been booked for their first fight the very day after they complete training. It is a mistake. It must be.

Her belly gives an uneasy roil.

Outside, a late spring day enfolds the district in the kind of warmth that promises new beginnings, and the sun climbs eagerly over the tallest buildings as Red rides the trags back to the Dungeons.

She is a speck of life in an indifferent city which has no idea of what danger it harbours in its midst.

CHAPTER 15

Cair Lleon, Blackheart
Eighteen Years Ago

Her name is Belisan.

To Art, she is gorgeous. She has glossy chestnut eyes that dominate her face, overshadowing a small, soft petal mouth and button nose. Her dark hair is wound into a coil at the nape of her neck, highlighting the soft angles of her cheeks and jawbone. Rich brown skin shows through sly folds of the barely-a-dress she wears. She is a dancer and an acrobat, which means that her list of skills is moulded around the ability to bend in all sorts of fascinating ways.

Perhaps that was what Dario was thinking of when they chose her for him. Even alone, he feels a blush creeping up his neck.

He tosses the black book aside. Picks it up again. Tosses it aside.

Garad and Lillath have just left his rooms. It has been a while since he has been able to see either of them properly, just them, just him, no retinue, no listening ears. They stayed far later than planned and it is now deep into the night – but instead of easing the restless itch inside him, their visit has only aggravated it.

He has spent all day in the Thorn, the venerated meeting hall on the banks of the river where the Consilium, the Lords and Ladies of all seven districts, a dizzying array of industry heads and policy theorists and vastos of various functions, gather to run the Kingdom in controlled chaos.

It is a ponderous, pressurised monthly ritual that makes Art more nervous, and more exhausted, than anything else day-to-day rule requires of him. Blowing off about it with Garad, however, earns him a chiding.

'You can't ever discuss all that in front of me, Art,' Garad says, their endless legs stretched out on a footstool.

'You're my saintsdamned champion,' Art protests. 'Who else am I supposed to trust more than you?'

'That's exactly why I'm the one person you can't tell. What if you talk to me about some law you're proposing and then next week I have to fight it for you in the arena?'

Art frowns. 'So? Caballaria knights always know who and what they're fighting for. That's just how it is.'

'That's not how it is in the Code,' Garad says stubbornly. 'Maybe we should go back to how it's supposed to be.'

'Purist.' Lillath rolls her eyes.

'You say that like it's an insult, but we'd do a lot better if the Caballaria got cleaned up.'

Art sighs, sinking further into the divan.

'You could make it better,' Garad carries on. 'You could make it a fair system again, instead of the play-acting it is right now. Everyone knows knights can be bought – and that's not justice. But if the knight doesn't know who or what they're fighting for, it preserves the integrity of the fight. It keeps them pure, focused only on the win. No distractions. No hidden agendas.'

'Isn't hidden agendas how *you* won?' Lillath murmurs.

Garad prickles. 'Sword tournaments are the exception to the rule, as you and everyone else in the entire world already knows. How are you supposed to be a potential King's champion without knowing about it beforehand?'

Art shoots Lillath a warning look. Her eyes crinkle apologetically at him over the rim of her cup. She often takes too much pleasure in goading Garad.

The King is currently under enormous pressure to revoke the Caballaria law that his father passed, rendering moves like Borin the Bloodless's outrageous forfeit illegal. Knights are not supposed to have the power to decide for themselves who rules a nation. The fight – and the saints – make that choice.

Even if he doesn't quite believe in the will of the ethereal Saith, Art finds himself reluctantly forced to agree with the logic. He is eaten up with dismay over how it makes him look – use the rule to win, then change it so no one else can win the way he did – but Brune bluntly told him to wrestle with his pride on his own time. The greater good must outweigh personal vanity.

Garad has been pushing these kinds of discussions harder of late. Their latest obsession is with the idea of a public Caballaria circuit, one that any London citizen can use to settle disputes without having to pay through the nose for the privilege. The cost to Blackheart of running and maintaining what would be, essentially, a free Caballaria would be laughed out of the Thorn, but the idea . . . the *idea* is a seductive one.

Garad's determination in cleaving so hard to honour and justice might irritate the more jaded – cue Lillath – but Art believes that the world needs people like them, acting as a moral counterweight: idealism on one side, cynicism on the other, balancing each other out.

Still, he can't help testing his friend, just a little.

'Wouldn't it ever bother you?' he asks Garad. 'Not knowing what you fight for every time?'

'No, Art,' Garad replies. 'I fight for you. I trust you.'

'That's a heavy burden,' Art mutters.

Garad nods. 'I know, but it astonishes me that you still don't see your worth, even now. It's been less than a year since you took the Sword and look at what you've already achieved.'

Art snorts. 'Oh, you count being constantly bent over and fucked by Agravain Welyen as an achievement?'

Fateful coincidence has Art's throne positioned directly opposite the Alaunitown seat, which means he has to spend every single monthly Consilium meet facing its current Lord.

When he even bothers to show up, Agravain normally spends his time lounging bonelessly on his chair and looking for all the world as if everyone in the room bores him beyond belief. In between that, his favourite hobby is to argue, decry, mock and flatly block every single proposal that Art makes. He has made it very clear what he thinks of London's 'child King', as he likes to call him.

Beyond that, all the Lord of Alaunitown contributes to matters is a litany of boasts on the achievements of other people that he espouses as his own. This time he did nothing but talk of an experimental type of capturer that one of his tech companies had produced, apparently no bigger than a hand. Typically, his first thought for its application was how it might be used to spy on his enemies.

'You're holding your own,' Lillath says. 'You managed to redirect half Alaunitown's weapons manufacturing budget towards building more war orphan hostels, didn't you? I'd've given anything to see the look on his face when that one passed.'

'If you call tricking the other districts into siding with me on it a win,' Art mutters.

Lillath shrugs. 'Anybody who believes in pure moral integrity has never had to live in the real world.'

Out of the corner of his eye, Art sees Garad bristle.

'That was risky,' they say. 'It might seem like you're using everyone else to personally attack him.'

'It was fabulous,' Lillath responds. 'It both seems exactly like that and also benefits people the Welyens couldn't give a shit about.'

Art says nothing. Every decision he makes is fraught with a million unknown consequences. Most nights have him going to bed with a head that feels filled with thick, gloopy soup.

Garad excuses themself not long after this to head home. Lillath stays a while longer, lying on the divan in Art's private receiving room with one arm folded behind her head, wine cup clutched in the other casual hand. Lillath at total relaxation is cat-like, stretched out and uncaring. She watches him through half-closed eyes.

Quietly he says, 'Where does tonight take you?'

She knows what he is asking. They have taken comfort in each other before, though it weighs nothing more than that on either of them. Lillath has a detached view to physical intimacy. It can be very useful – though for Art, not habit-forming. He understands just how close he can get to her before she starts to disentangle herself.

'I have a date,' she says, managing to sound regretful.

'Now?'

She grins. 'Art, it's still early.'

'It's close to midnight.'

'Sometimes I forget how much of an old man you can be.'

'Still, you don't have to go right now, do you?' he tries. 'Tell me more about your day.'

Listening to the minutiae of her life makes Art feel closer to the kind of reality he once used to know – because there is a wall between them, now, however much they pretend that it doesn't exist. His friends call him Sire when someone else is in the room, and they can't visit without a sanctioned appointment. They are busy living and he is busy ruling.

He is lonely.

Not that there haven't been attempts made in that direction. After Dario's pointed warning about the palace's determination to manage his personal life, he can see them coming a mile off. There are scheduled lunches where he inevitably gets sat next to a certain type of person. Dinners with various Saith-connected dignitaries who all happen to have at least one of their eligible progeny casually dangling in front of him like a worm to a fish. It is getting embarrassing.

There is still plenty of time to prove Dario wrong about his ability to get his own lover and on his terms, but in the meantime, he sits cushioned by the quietness of his room as the last of the day ebbs around him, distracting himself with books, with food, with papers that must be read, with his schedule, with all the things that must be done, but underneath it all—

—that surging, restless itch.

Once Lillath has gone, Art picks up the Night Carnival's black book and flips again to the page Dario marked for him.

Belisan.

He writes out a message, seals it with the palace emblem and arranges for it to be sent out with all possible discretion.

The message reads: *Dinner for two.* (Just *dinner.*)

★

It is the moonlight that Art notices first.

It streaks from his bedroom windows across the floorboards in stripes of cold, stark white. The black landscapes between each slat of light seem bottomless, each with a possible world hidden inside them. His drapes are open, he realises, pulled back to let in the soft air. The night is a warm one.

The heavy material shivers as a figure slides out from beside it.

They are long drapes, long enough to caress the floor. There is more than enough material to be wound around a body, and more than enough left to let them stretch out a few feet when the body the material is wound around moves forwards, but they come to the end of their length, eventually, and are let go.

The body, unclothed, continues on.

The face above the body is still in shadow, but the moonlight glints on a loose sheet of hair, on a slippery, lithe creature approaching him on noiseless bare feet. She stops just short of him, close enough for his hand to reach out to her skin if he so chooses, and now he can see the edges of her features, he knows exactly who she is.

'Lady Belisan.'

'Sire,' Belisan replies, barely above a whisper. She doesn't, he notices, dip into a bow.

Perhaps Dario told her that he doesn't enjoy deference.

'What are you . . . doing?' Art says, desperately coaxing out his voice.

'Your vastos let me in. I'm not late, am I?'

'But you're clothesless,' he blurts, and then, feeling odd, 'I asked for dinner. That's all.'

Belisan appears to consider this. 'I could be dinner.'

'With . . . food.'

'I am a kind of food, if you think about it.'

Art clamps down on a panicky laugh. Belisan steps forwards into his silence, and then again, and now his elbow wouldn't even have to straighten to touch her.

'Stop,' he says. 'Please.'

She does. 'You don't like what you see?'

Fuck you, Dario, Art thinks.

He refuses to answer. Guts tight, he puts his back to Belisan, walks over to his bed and drags off the thin silk throw that lies across its foot. Turning back, he shakes it out, its ends wafting gently back towards him in the breeze crawling in from his open windows. Belisan's face, her mouth now open in soft confusion, is the only thing he can see over the top of the silk divider.

'Please,' he says, gesturing. 'Take it. Please.'

After a long, painful moment, his hands feel a tug and she grabs hold of the silk to wrap it around herself.

'I'm sorry,' she mutters. 'I was told . . . I started this wrong, I'm so sorry.'

Oh saints. He has embarrassed her.

'It's not your fault,' Art says. 'It's a game, and you're the next move, but in here, I get to stop playing. This is my sanctuary, my only . . .' He realises his voice is getting louder and with some effort, he drops it. 'I didn't want . . . this.'

'Are you dismissing me?' she asks, quietly.

She holds the silk throw closed in her fists, only the tops of her shoulders showing. The thought of her gone and this place empty fills Art with sadness.

'No,' he says, but he doesn't know what else to say.

'Can I tell you something, then?' Belisan asks.

Curiosity lifts his chin. Her face is open.

'Of course,' Art says, uneasy.

She moves, walking past him to the foot of his bed. The bottom edge of the throw she clutches around her catches briefly on the edges of the flagstone as it passes over and Art sees a flash of smooth thigh, revealed and then hidden again.

Belisan sinks on to the bed, swaddled in silk.

'I've been . . . watching you,' she says carefully. 'We all have. I'm sure you know that. Everyone is wondering what your taste might turn out to be. Part of our job. Anyway, plenty of people wanted to be the first to land you – you might imagine. The new King. But I didn't. I was hoping you wouldn't pick me. I knew Dario had recommended me to you, but you've the whole of London to choose from, anyway, so I assumed I'd be fine. Then I get a summons from Dario – no details, no nothing, just a summons for a private discussion. And I know.'

Art trains his eyes on the wall. Utter mortification burns his face.

'Then it's my turn to apologise,' he says. 'I never meant to force anyone here against their will. I can't tell you how abhorrent the concept is to me.'

Fuck you, Dario, fuck you, fuck you.

To his astonishment, he hears Belisan laugh.

'You misunderstand,' she says, and her voice is kind. 'We usually get to choose, you know. Even when it's the King doing the asking.' She pulls the silk tight around her in what looks like an unconscious gesture. 'You could have insisted, and of course I'd have had to do it then – but Dario told me you don't like that at all. They told me, with you, I had the choice.' Her face is turned up to his, unreadable in shadow. 'I didn't want to come to you because . . . we're taught to avoid the ones we desire.'

The air seems to grow heavier, that light summer breeze now pregnant with unshed meaning.

'I thought I made it clear that I don't like games,' Art says calmly.

'I think about you,' she blurts. 'I see you on the glows and I think about what you . . . what you're really like, underneath. I just wonder. That's all. I came because I couldn't not, in the end. You're one of the loveliest men I've ever seen.' Her voice has the very tiniest of trembles in it.

Art stares at the wall. It is a performance. It means nothing.

Belisan is subdued. 'I'll go now. I just promised myself I'd tell you that, even if it cost me. I knew it'd cost me. I'm so sorry if I offended you, Sire. Laerd Dario will choose someone else, someone perfect for you. I can promise you that.'

He hears the creak of the bed as she stands, a rustling as she moves, and he turns suddenly, catching her midway across the room towards him. She stops.

'I left my clothes back beside the window,' she says, by way of explanation.

He doesn't know how to ask her not to go.

Talk. Say something.

But he can't.

He hears her indrawn breath over the quiet of his room.

'If you'd like me to leave,' she says, 'please stay where you are and I'll get my clothes and I'll be gone. But if you'd like me to stay, could you come a little closer to me, so that I know?'

After a moment, Art makes his body move one step closer.

With a glad, unfettered noise, Belisan opens her hands, letting the silk throw slide off her, and he wants, he wants, *he wants.*

As she walks across the floor to him he finds himself concentrating on the way the moonlight streaming in through the window falls across her body, accentuating the flare of her hip.

Her hands come up to his neck and begin to unbutton the collar at his throat. This close, her smell hits his nose and the warmth of her skin reaches him through his clothes.

Another body, this close to his. He had thought it was all he needed – and then she presses up against him, and it is not enough. Her fingertips skate his skin with deliberation as she moves down his chest, unbuttoning as she goes, completely silent and absorbed in her task. A hot, shamefully urgent tug flares in his groin as she dips her fingers in between his belt and his skin, pushing them downwards, teasing – and then she takes her fingers up, away, leaving him bereft.

Her hands take his and she pulls him back towards the foot of the bed, then pushes lightly, sitting him down. The silk throw she piles up on the flagstones between his feet, and then kneels gracefully on to the pile.

Art gives it an admirably heroic last-ditch effort.

'I promised you dinner,' he croaks. 'You're not hungry?'

Belisan crouches between his thighs, her fingers intent on his belt.

'Very,' she says, and her head dips.

Art feels a hot wetness engulf him and his brain promptly switches off, rendering any further protest impossible.

They do eventually, much later, get round to dinner.

CHAPTER 16

The Dungeons, Rhyfentown
Five Months Ago

Within minutes of Red arriving back at the Dungeons, the crows descend.

The front door opens and she steps into the dim hush of the building's hallway, marvelling at how it feels like passing back into another world, dark and warm and womb-like. But that cord has been broken now, severed by the outside's bright, hard knife-edge. She remembers what it feels like to live here, to be this, but it is already a memory. It no longer exists in her present, only in her past.

'Red.'

Frome appears, moving towards her before she can get much further inwards.

'Si,' Red says deferentially.

'Si,' Frome shoots back at her, folding his long arms and leaning his shoulder against the wall's dark panelling. 'How's your head?'

'Quite bad,' Red admits, expecting admonishment.

Frome just shrugs. 'Everyone fails that test. It's expected, neh?'

Red is silent. She has never enjoyed the sensation of behaving as expected.

'It should be a balance,' Frome is saying. 'Pleasure and work. Focus and freedom. When they're in harmony, then a knight is truly a knight.' His grin is crooked. 'Sadly, that perfect balance is a bit like Stillness – only achievable for short tides of time. What tides, though.' He studies Red. 'The circus is looking for you.'

The hallway's dark comfort shifts, feeling more like a trap.

'What circus?' Red says, guarded.

'Didn't Six tell you? You've been scheduled for your first fight.' Frome catches something in Red's face and laughs. 'Oh, please. I knew if I told her pere, it'd get to you quicker than a bull to a ready cow. I didn't know exactly where your jubilant wanderings had taken you all last night, but I knew you'd be out with her – it was the fastest way to reach you.'

Red's hangover surges, making her head throb.

'I can't be,' she grates out. 'I only passed training yesterday. The public announcement hasn't even gone out yet, has it?'

'Until you get an offer from another stable, you automatically belong to us, Rhyfentown Public,' Frome says quietly. 'That's how it goes. Is it really so bad working for the district, at least until you get a better deal?'

There is nothing to say to that.

Frome pushes off the wall. 'Come on. I need to take you upstairs. Time for the frimping.'

'Frimping,' Red says dubiously as she follows Frome to the black iron beast of the ascender, currently waiting on the ground floor to swallow up unsuspecting passengers.

Frome just smiles as he jerks the rattling cage closed, slides the door grille into place and presses a button. The beast rattles into life, pulling them up to the seventh floor.

Frimping awaits Red in a long, hot room full of clicking, clunking machinery. It reminds her of the measurements room. As she enters, a menagerie of five strangers stop exclaiming among themselves and turn their heads.

The tallest and most immediately eye-catching is a gorgeously voluptuous woman in an eye-punchingly yellow dress that bandages her body, tight against each sweep of her, setting off her dark skin. The short, pale, compact man with a crest of hair as glossy black as a crow's wing next to her is dressed in an immaculately tailored outfit. Two nervous, hen-like girls hover at their shoulders, and a quieter man, short and unremarkable next to his associates, hugs the wall behind them. Red notes the portable glow screens that everyone except the quiet man has tucked under one arm. These people are rich, or well-resourced at the least.

Frome dips his head to the group. 'May I present to you Si Red Caballarias o'Rhyfentown, a knight of the Caballaria.'

The words, absurd and overdone, nevertheless crawl up the skin of Red's arms like delicate spiders and set her itching in nervous delight. *Caballarias*, added to her name as the official designation of what shape her life now holds. It is a near mythic name to have as her own, and something in her wants to surrender even though she fights it – she wants to give herself over to it entirely, every facet and ideal.

All this fakeness and frippery means nothing. Remember what you came here to do.

'Good day to you all,' Red says politely.

The woman in the yellow bandage dress presses a hand to her chest.

'Oh my, she already has boxes of charm,' she flutes. 'I'm out of a job.'

The immaculately tailored man snorts. 'There'll be plenty of rough edges still to smooth, Blo,' he says. 'Innocence, perhaps, judging by the Si's youthful vigour?'

'Let's keep the innocence,' Blo argues. Her hands raise into the air and her palms curve as if she holds an invisible ball. She looks at Red through her hands. 'Yes,' she breathes. 'Too many jaded young knights knowing just how to work what they have. We all need to see something fresh. Provocative, but naïve.'

Red opens her mouth to protest, then loses her confidence – does *I'm neither provocative nor naïve* sound like something a provocative, naïve person would say? – and Frome rescues her.

'This is Blo DeCyng Gadaris o'Marvoltown,' he says, indicating the woman. She gives Red a generous smile.

'And they callian me Valiere DeCyng Fortesco o'Senzatown,' the short man introduces himself, breaking tradition. Valiere doesn't look like he ever cracks a smile, except possibly as a form of attack.

The DeCyng in their names is their career signifier, which means they work for who or whatever DeCyng is – a private stable, maybe. Red finds her interest unfurl at the mention of the Lady Blo being Marvoltown-born. It's a district she has never visited, the one with the most mystique attached to it.

The idea of growing up in an area dedicated to the Death Saint has always been a sure-fire indicator to the more prim Kingdoms outside London of just how depraved and strange the city-state is. The Lady Blo, however, looks disappointingly lacking in either depravity or strangeness, at least on the surface, although Red knows better than many that surfaces often don't reveal what lies beneath.

'Are you ready to start, maester?' Valiere enquires, looking over his shoulder.

The quiet, unremarkable man pushes off the wall he has been leaning against and comes forwards. His thick outline suggests muscle, and he wears a loose outfit in shades of dark, wet pebble. His fair hair is razored close to his skin, thick curls of wiry hair assuming a close-cropped and indifferent beard.

The room seems to wait.

It dawns on Red that there is no introduction because one has not been deemed necessary. She is supposed to know who this is.

'How does?' the man asks Red in a yawning Iochitown brogue.

'Well,' Red replies, aware of the rest watching them both like silent hawks. The man can't seem to meet Red's eyes. He begins to wander awkwardly around the room.

Blo claps her hands and the two nervous hens, who have been hovering all the while, bob over to the brooding sweeps of machinery that hug the walls of the room. They busy themselves with peering at screens and exclaiming at each other.

Red casts a helpless glance at Frome, who leans into her.

'That's Lee DeCyng o'Iochitown,' he says in a low voice, indicating the quiet man.

DeCyng.

'They all work for him?' Red whispers.

'Yes.'

'And what does he do?'

Frome gives her an odd look. 'He's a famed dresser. He wants to be the one to dress you.'

'I can't . . . dress myself?'

'Caballaria knights don't dress themselves.' Frome rubs the side of his face. 'You really don't know who DeCyng is?'

Red bites back the retort that she studied the fights, not the costumes.

Frome's gaze drifts to the far end of the room, where the group appears to be deep in the throes of lighting design, shining kaleidoscopic colours and textures of light down on to a large, empty space in the middle of the room.

'Anyone wanting DeCyng to dress them has to go on a waiting list of about two years,' Frome says, 'and throw down more trick than you or I have ever seen in one place. He dresses the Sorcerer Knight.'

Understanding dawns.

'Si Wyll paid for him,' Red says.

Frome looks at her, perhaps caught by her use of the familiar name.

'Yes, of course, and that's his right and privilege as your sponsor,' he replies. 'You think *we* could afford a dresser like Lee DeCyng? And by all accounts, Lee was the one who approached the Scourge to ask if he could dress you. It's a huge compliment. Lee does not often ask to dress people.' He folds his arms. 'Not only that, but we've been fielding requests for your services for a couple of weeks now – as soon as the news was leaked that you would almost certainly pass training.' He pauses. 'You're a curiosity, Red. Everything about you is unusual. You need to play that card for all it's worth. It's a good card, but it won't last long.'

'Si Red,' Blo calls across the room. 'Come into the light in the middle of the room, please.'

Frome touches her shoulder briefly, gives her a wry smile, then pushes her forwards.

'Look at that move,' Valiere declares from deep within a bank of machinery as Red approaches. Lee stands next to him, and their downturned faces are lit with screen glow as they stare at something together. 'That slide, there. I feel LIGHT. I feel SLICK.' He shouts each word.

Red stands exposed in the lit space, watching the group pay no attention to her whatsoever.

'She looks a little bit like Andra's *Dark Angel* paintings,' Blo murmurs over Valiere's shoulder. 'That figure standing in the background, flitting between the trees, neh? The one Andra always refused to explain. Perhaps dark, muted colours—'

'No, no – LIGHT,' Valiere insists. 'SLICK.'

'Wraithlike.'

'And look at that, play that again, the way she moves her foot as she turns into the attack—'

Finally, Red realises what they're doing. They are watching playback of her training fights. All their attention *is* on her, in fact, but a past her.

'Do I need to do anything right now?' she calls to the group, voice strangled with embarrassment.

Behind her she hears Frome bite off the end of a laugh and briefly wishes him dead.

'No, dear one,' Blo answers absently. 'Not yet, not yet, you just wait there, I see perhaps some transparent striping in between each colour, don't you, to get that ghostlike sense—'

And so continues one of the strangest days of Red's life. She is lit and blinded in an array of colours, given various weapons and asked to raise them above her head in a series of baffling attitudes – 'BRANDISH it,' Valiere shouts, 'MENACINGLY, yes! Now with an air of GRAVE NOBILITY, good, now with DETERMINATION' – or perform an attack on nothing but air – 'HATE the air, Si,' Valiere calls, 'you want it to SUFFER' – and, with obvious relish, told all about her signature move.

'Dear one, don't you know it yourself?' Blo purrs, clutching Red's shoulders joyfully with her hands. 'We shall *show* you.'

She leads Red to an embedded glow screen within the guts of the machine bank. 'We've watched hours and hours of your fights and it's definitely your highlight. An absolute killer, Si, absolute killer.'

The shadow of a smile hovers around Lee's mouth.

'It's a good finishing move,' he says. 'Really stands out from the ranks.'

Apparently, this is a compliment to die over. As he turns away, Blo manically widens her eyes at Red to convey the momentousness of what has just transpired. Weakened by Blo's relentlessly unflagging enthusiasm, Red finds herself, to her mild embarrassment, both amused and pleased.

Blo shows her the playback, slowing it down until Red is inching glacially across the screen.

'First you feint, then you dive forwards like a veritable *dolphin*, go into that tight roll, come to one knee, and *thrust* your weapon hand forwards' – she smacks her hands together, startling Red – '*into* the guts! You've got about a, what is it, Vali, a seventy-two per cent success rate?' – Valiere nods – 'a seventy-two per cent success rate with that move, which is beautiful odds, just *beautiful*.'

One of the two hens – 'Stelia,' she shyly tells Red when asked her name later on, as she is busy pinning a selection of metal ornaments into Red's hair – runs back into the room, whispering into Valiere's ear.

Valiere turns, raises his arms beatifically.

'Lee has the fabrics ready,' he says in a hushed voice.

Blo presses a hand to her chest.

And then come the outfits.

There are materials and colours Red has never even seen before, several of which she wasn't previously aware were in any way wearable – one thick, heavy tunic is apparently made from the outer treading of a bike wheel and another reminds her uncomfortably of intestines, though she is fairly sure that isn't what it's made from. She is wrapped in each and every one of them while Lee walks pensively around her, adjusting, pinning and loosening and re-draping.

After a while, Red begins to understand the maester's shorthand: a pronouncement of 'it's a bit lacking' is a disaster, necessitating the banishment of the offending material, whereas total silence is not necessarily bad. Only twice does Lee begrudgingly admire his own work with a cursory 'it's not terrible', and those approved materials are duly and reverently set aside, lovingly hung on the branches of the 'keeper tree', a steel apparatus standing in the corner of the room.

The evening is long by the time they are finished transforming her. The name under which she will fight, her appearance, her outfits – the fighter version of Red o'Rhyfentown that will 'transform your gorgeous raw materials into a sparkling artwork to bring the Caballaria to its knees in wonder', as Blo puts it – all this will be revealed before her first fight.

It's all subject entirely to her approval, of course, though she gets the impression that people do not really *approve* a Lee DeCyng creation so much as have it happen to them and be damned grateful about it.

The final fitting is scheduled for a few days' time and the team take their leave with extravagant affection. Blo clutches Red to her briefly before releasing her. Valiere's embrace is surprisingly warm, though his diminutive stature means he has to lift his chin to clear Red's shoulder in the hug. Lee gives her a nod, almost managing to hold her gaze, before departing.

Red collapses in a chair, clutching a cup of lemon tea sweetened with honey. Frome is sitting on the floor, his back against the wall. He has been in and out all day, organising regular supplies of food and drink from the kitchens, disappearing at intervals to attend to other matters – but mostly he has been there in the background, watching, ready to make himself useful.

'That was exhausting,' he croaks.

Red closes her eyes. 'I want to be dead.'

Frome tilts his head. 'Worse than my training?'

'. . . no.'

'You hesitated. I'm offended.'

'Your short weapons drills nearly ended me, if that helps.'

Frome grins. 'Somewhat.'

Red turns to look at the maddening, relentless, but above all patient tutor who has been a daily companion for the last six months of her life. She sees a man now, in a way that she couldn't have before: a man with his own life, his own desires, and an impressive well of quiet, subtle power.

'Shouldn't you have been tutoring today, Si?' she asks. 'I'm sorry if you've had to give it up for nursing me.'

Frome shrugs. 'We have six months until the next intake. In between times, I tutor privately. It's a welcome break, in honesty, because training you lot never gets any easier. You think it breaks you, but it breaks us too. We live through it with you. It hurts us when a good one craps out because of bad reasons, or when we can see you struggling.' He gives a tired smile. 'You had one or two moments, as I recall, where we started to get worried.'

Red stills.

'Will you tell me about them?' she says.

Frome is quiet.

'Your . . . friendship . . . with Sela,' he says eventually, 'took a toll on you.'

Of course. How could any of them have assumed that they managed to keep any moment of their lives over the last six months a secret? They have been relentlessly, necessarily, scrutinised, and Sela was never subtle in her personal attacks.

'How?' Red asks, dreading the answer.

'She affected your fight, Red,' Frome says. 'You became more unsure of yourself. Your stats took a deep dive. You started losing far more often – especially against her, but not only against her. She undermined you. That kind of opponent is the kind you must be most wary of. Their attack is far more insidious, far less noticeable, until the damage is done.'

Then it clicks, and perhaps because Frome meant it to.

'It was you who warned me against her,' says Red.

Frome's reply is smooth and too ready. 'I don't know what you're talking about.'

She studies him, wondering why he helped her – wondering if she will ever find out.

'There's no law against getting involved with another Caballaria knight, as you know,' he continues, 'but there's a reason why most relationships between fighters don't last. The ones that do, usually do at the cost of one of them giving up the Caballaria. Think about it. What if you find yourself up against someone you're emotionally tangled with in a real dispute, in the arena, where the pressure is a thousand times more, with all eyes on you, analysing your every move? What if your feelings for them weaken you, make you soften when you should press an advantage? What if they're clever enough to play that, like Sela did?' Frome stares into the middle distance. 'We allow your tangles during training, of course, because many of you need that outlet, but you should know that at least four of your fellow trainees failed precisely because they let those entanglements get too serious.'

Shit. She had had no idea.

'So sex and death aren't in fact the oldest of lovers?' she tries to joke.

'We don't deal in death. We deal in judgement.' He has a distant look on his face. 'But some knights, they have a hunger inside them. It is its own creature, and like all living things, it's driven by survival. Because if you're not hungry anymore, the hunger dies, neh? It'll deny you comfort just so it can go on living. So maybe you get your comfort and it'll be fine – for a while. But as soon as you think that's it, you're sated, it'll come a-creeping back.'

Even Frome looks surprised at how his speech went on, as if pulled from him unplanned and unwillingly. He laughs. 'I'm older than you.' As if that should explain it all. 'If you've that hunger, Red, and I think you have, then be wary of it. You need to learn to control it, not let it control you. And you did,' Frome continues. 'That's why you passed. Choose your lovers from outside the Caballaria. Best advice I can give you.'

Red cannot say anything to this, because all the things she could say will give away too much of herself. She doesn't want to control her hunger. She wants to be consumed by it. She has accepted that this might make her life short-lived, and there is precious little time to waste. Now she is a knight, she must find a way to get closer to Si Wyll.

The trouble is, she has no idea how.

'Ready to face your fate?' Frome asks, dusting off his hands.

Anxious, triumphant, determined, Red follows him into the unknown.

CHAPTER 17

Cair Lleon, Blackheart
Eighteen Years Ago

'I have this idea,' Art says to Belisan one day.

She is draped across him on the bed, her long hair spread across her back in a sheet, eating engorged grapes out of a bowl. Lazy afternoon light drifts in warm eddies across the room. They have the curtains open, but the windows closed. He has one hand on her flank, stroking absently, a part of him marvelling that he can do that with her and not think twice of it. During her time with him she is his to do that with, and she likes being touched, very much. Art has taken to calling her a nymph. Like those figures in antiquity paintings, she prefers being naked wherever possible. It is hard to picture her in clothes.

'My security guards are due to pick me up in an hour,' she says. 'Do we have enough time?'

'It's not a sex thing.'

'Oh. What is it?'

'Just this idea,' he probes. 'About how fear is formed. We're programmed to fear the unknown, itso? Survival instinct. But if you come to know something, your brain catalogues it, makes it familiar, and the fear goes away.'

Bel is frowning as her little tongue flickers over the side of a particularly bulbous grape.

'Exposure,' Art persists. 'Co-mingling. Making the foreign . . . less foreign.'

She seems no clearer.

He changes direction. 'How long did it take you to get here today?'

Belisan lives at the Night Carnival, of course, embedded deep into the historic Surwek area of Iochitown. Legend has it that the first-ever official bordels in all Seven Kingdoms were opened in Surwek.

'Two hours,' Bel says.

Art nods. 'Border control, right? How many people were they turning away?'

'Oh, most of 'em. The only reason I get through is because of that special bit of paper you gave me.'

'Well, what if we did away with border control?'

Belisan's frown deepens. 'That's crazy. Then anyone could go anywhere they liked.'

'I know,' Art says.

'Well, it'd make it a lot easier for us all to kill each other.'

Iochitown shares both a border with Alaunitown and some famously bloody historical clashes over its movable line.

'There's this theory that in the fullness of time,' Art says, 'it would prevent wars, rather than encourage more. People would start to mix in. Less tribalism, you see?'

'I think people *like* tribes,' Belisan replies. 'You want somewhere to belong, and you want somewhere to compare it to. Somewhere you can point to and say, "That's how not to do it." Human nature.'

'Yes, but—' Art searches for the words. 'If we'd never

successfully reshaped our natures, we'd still be scrabbling in the dirt and hitting each other with sticks.'

Belisan shrugs. 'We're still doing that. Just with better sticks.'

She sees Art's expression and lets loose a laugh. He has begun to understand her a little by now and knows the laugh isn't meant unkindly. It is the laugh she uses when he starts talking about something that she doesn't care to dissect further. Art finds this both attractive and frustrating. All he wants to do is please her.

'Never mind,' he says, giving up. 'I have another idea. Teach me how to do that thing you do, before you go.'

'Which thing?' she asks, cramming three grapes into her mouth at once.

'You know, when you . . .' Art stops, fighting the blush. Saints alive, after everything they've done together over the last few weeks, and he still cannot say any of them out loud. 'The thing with both your hands and your mouth at the same time.'

Belisan wriggles her hips, pressing her weight into his pelvis. She loves how it takes no time at all for him to spring to attention. She often teases him to do just that.

'You mean when I go down—'

Art cuts her off hastily. 'Yes.'

She turns her face to his with a mock hurt expression. 'Art, why do you want to know how to do that? Is there a boy rival for my affections? I demand his name.'

He has begun to insist that she call him Art. It is a breach of protocol, but there is no bearing the way the intimacy between them shatters every time she calls him 'Sire'. She recently asked him, quite boldly, why he enjoys the pretence of being equal to everyone so much. He said that it wasn't a pretence, and she laughed.

'Teach me to do the equivalent to you, I mean,' he says, secretly pleased at how his blush delights her. 'There's no one else, boy or otherwise. Only you.'

'Ah.' She picks another grape off the bunch and sucks on it. 'Now that's a skill. It's not something you can just pick up in one lesson; it takes time to learn.'

'I'm a quick study.'

Belisan smiles. 'Yes, you are,' she agrees. 'Very well. Shall we make a start?'

She rolls off him and lies expectantly on her back. What follows is one of the most pleasant lessons in power he has ever had.

Art knows he is young and inexperienced, and he also knows that Belisan is the one in control – most of those in her profession are. Their arrangement, ultimately, is down to him, but the nature of Belisan's services dictate what happens and how each time they meet. He can make requests, which Belisan will do her utmost to both meet and exceed – but if it is something that crosses the boundaries she has set, it is a no-go. And if a client crosses those boundaries, not only do they lose her, but they run the risk of being barred from everyone else in that establishment.

Of course, if they had the kind of arrangement that required a more obvious power game, things would play out slightly differently – but even then, no matter how much Belisan acted the part in their time together, one pre-arranged word from her and the act would stop. If the act did not stop the moment she wished it to – boundaries crossed, repercussions brought forth.

Her profession is as deeply embedded within the Code as the Caballaria, and the two industries have been closely intertwined for hundreds of years. Art knows that the lessons Belisan teaches him in their time together are valuable beyond their immediate pleasure. That afternoon, with his tongue and fingers buried in her and his eyes on her face, that lovely face so undone, her whole being subsumed into the sensation that he is producing in her, he learns about the intoxication of having someone, even for a moment, utterly and completely within his control.

Art gets his discretion, but complete secrecy is impossible. Soon enough the entire palace knows he has taken a lover. His habit of disappearing whenever he has a few hours spare, with a firm request not to be disturbed, does not go unnoticed by his closest advisors, though some are slower on the uptake as to the reason.

He is aware that many of them must know, as he is aware that they must tacitly approve of his choice in Belisan. If they didn't, he wryly assumes that he would have heard something about it by now. The Night Carnival is, after all, one of the very best establishments, and the attachment is of mutual benefit. They now count the King of London as a client and as such, their renown can only increase. In return, their reputation speaks favourably to the young new King's good taste.

As is his prerogative, Art is Belisan's only lover for however long this may last – and she is handsomely paid for the privilege – so she is usually available whenever he wants her, even at short notice. When he asks, she tells him that she is extremely happy with their situation. After all, though she never mentions it, he knows that to have been a King's meretrix will shoot her desirability through the roof. She will doubtless become one of the richest and most coveted women in the seven districts after their time together is over.

But he cannot think about that possibility. Right now, this feels endless.

She often calls him 'lovely' and 'beautiful'. She especially likes to run her hands down his stomach to his hips, over and over, and she tells him that the sight of his trousers straining against his slender colt thighs when he is sitting down drives her mad with desire. Their encounters often begin on his divan because of this – she will interrupt dinner and let their food go cold rather than wait for satisfaction.

Her gestures are so unconscious and her air is so unstudied that Art finds himself immediately besotted with her. She is exactly what he wants. Someone who doesn't make it feel like a game.

Night is in full swing when Lillath turns up unexpectedly at Art's suite. He is alone – and, he later realises, Lillath must have made sure of it before coming. Belisan paid her visit the evening before and she never comes over more than twice in one week.

He is at his desk perched underneath the window, trying to wrap his tired brain around the papers he has been given to go through before tomorrow's duties. The drapes are closed against the rising cold, which has taken its time coming this year, and his room feels comfortingly private.

He scans the same paragraph he just read three times in a row. His gaze keeps straying to the divan against the far wall where last night a sweat-streaked Belisan had wrapped her legs around his torso and said something that he could tell she hadn't meant to say.

'Art, I adore you,' she had murmured, then her eyes had widened and her mouth had curled into a quick smile to cover her reaction. Before he could reply, she had disentangled herself from him and suggested they finish up dessert.

He pushes the paper away with a sigh. Not a word of it has

registered. He will have to get up early and try to force it into his brain before the day begins.

As he stretches in his chair, a rapid knock comes from the door to the adjoining salon: Fortigo's knock, always recognisable from its staccato rhythm. A last-minute change to tomorrow's schedule, or some vital thing that Art has forgotten to do. Maybe, if he's lucky, it'll be some licoresse tea. Fortigo has an uncanny habit of anticipating his moods.

Art rises, crosses through the adjoining door that links the salon to his bedroom and calls for Fortigo to enter. He does, but he is followed into the room by Lillath, who peers around. Her gaze settles briefly on the door that leads to his bedroom before flickering away.

'Lil,' Art says in surprise.

'She requested a last-minute audience, Sire,' Fortigo begins. 'I had a message sent to you, although I naturally assumed you were too busy to see it, but she insisted on trying in person.'

Art throws a guilty glance at the message tray set into the wall by the salon door, in which currently lies a small, neatly folded note. There is a chance that he had seen the white rectangle lying there an hour or two ago, but hadn't yet found the energy to get up and check it.

'Saints, you make it sound so formal,' Lillath says, irritated. 'I don't want an *audience*, all I want to do is talk to one of my oldest friends – you know, like regular people do? Must we go through this farce every—?'

'When your friend is the King, my Lady,' Fortigo cuts in, his measured voice tinged with the merest sliver of acid, 'yes.'

'Oh, fuck *that*,' Lil declares. 'He's the least kingy King of all time and you know it.'

'The *palace*—'

'The palace serves the King, right? Shouldn't you all be, say, moulding yourselves to fit with his style? Isn't that what you're supposed to do with every ruler?'

Fortigo gives her a stone-cold stare.

'Sire,' he says eventually, and it sounds like a plea.

Art struggles, very badly, to hide his amusement. 'It's fine, Fortigo. I promise.'

Fortigo gives Art a short head bow. 'Please have a message sent to my room when the Lady is ready to leave.'

'I'm perfectly capable of finding my own way out,' Lillath retorts.

'I have absolutely no doubt of that,' Fortigo replies, looking past her ear at the wall. 'However, it is with sincere regret that I once again remind you that anyone found walking around the palace without an official escort tends to get shot by the guard.'

Lillath effects a puzzled face – and then her expression clears theatrically. 'Oh, *yes*, I remember now. Absolutely.'

Fortigo gives the merest of strained smiles, turns on his heel and closes the door behind him.

Art shakes his head. 'I think he hates you, Lil.'

'Oh, *I* think I'm in love with him,' Lillath declares. 'He's so deliciously stiff, and he has such gorgeous calves.'

'He has a girl.'

'Are they handfasted?'

'Not that I'm aware of.'

'Then he's still fair game.' Lil walks over to the salon's biggest divan and throws herself down on it with a contented sigh. Art takes the chair opposite and settles in, watching her. He knows

Lillath. She wouldn't put herself through all the rules and regulations the palace sees fit to build around him, and that she finds so irritating, just for a casual late-night catch-up.

It has been nearly four months since he last saw her, and yet she still has not come to the end of her advisory vastos training down by Permissos Park, training she had begun the year before he'd even taken the Sword. Most of her peers are Blackheart-born, but there are a few others like Lillath who hail from other districts. She has taken rooms at the training grounds, but Art suspects another reason, more than just avoiding a daily dose of border control. Hers is an impossibly close family who suffocate each other through sheer force of determined, relentless love, and Lillath likes her freedom.

'How's Henry?' Art asks her.

'Oh, I'm not seeing him any more,' Lillath says dismissively. 'He was fun for a while, but then he got all needy.'

'I remember that cousin of Lucan's you fooled with one summer,' Art ruminates. 'What was her name . . .?'

'Persivanne.'

'Didn't she start turning up at your school every day after you broke with her, weeping at you to take her back? And then she broke into the grounds one night and painted LILLATH DeHAVILLAND BROKE MY HEART, BEWARE THE BEAST across the front driveway—'

'Actually it was WARE THE BEAST THAT CALLS ITSELF LILLATH DeHAVILLAND,' Lillath says drily, 'but close enough. I know you've all dined out on that hilarity for years, but the fact is, I learned my lesson with her. From then on I've always made sure that I know precisely how far I can go with someone without causing such hurt – and I never,

ever lie to anyone about what I want from them. After that, it's on them if they choose me and get in too deep.'

Art subsides, catching the snap in her tone.

'I know, Lil,' he says. 'It's something I admire about you.'

She glances at him, surprised. They hold the gaze a moment too long, and then she drops her eyes.

'Speaking of lovers,' she says lightly, 'how's yours coming along?'

Art narrows his eyes at her. He'd lay trick down that she'd found out before almost anyone else in the palace. Lillath has always had a way of knowing things, though he has no idea how she does it.

'Fine, thank you,' he says stiffly.

Lillath laughs. 'Oh, come on, you needn't be so coy with me. She certainly wouldn't be. She's very good at what she does, so I've heard.'

'So you've heard?'

'Well, yes. I checked up on her.'

'Lil, there's a whole team of Cair Lleon golems whose entire job it is to do that sort of thing. I've no doubt she was thoroughly dissected and examined the moment I put in the fucken request for her.'

Lillath cants her head. 'You're angry,' she says. 'Why?'

'I'm not . . .' Art struggles to leash his sudden flare of temper. 'I'm not angry. I'm just . . . why can't my private life actually be private? Why don't I even get that?'

'Because who you fuck is just as important as who you marry, Art.' Lillath pauses, and then says, with delicacy unusual for her, 'You relax around her, maybe say things you shouldn't—'

'Saints, so now she's a spy?'

'All I'm saying is that you need to be careful.'

'And how would you know that I'm *not* being careful?' Art says, his voice thin with cold fury. 'Am I to suppose that I'm being watched in my rooms, too?'

Lillath's mouth drops open. She casts around, scrabbling for the right words underneath the weight of his stare.

'I wouldn't know anything about you being watched or not. What I'm saying is – she's your first, Art. It can be overwhelming, your first. It means something. It'll always mean something.'

Art stares at her strangely. 'She's not my first, Lil.'

Lillath sighs. 'You weren't like this with me. That's what I mean by first.'

'Like what? What am I like?'

'Distracted.'

'Oh my. Well then, we'd better throw her in prison, hadn't we?'

'Are you in love with her?' Lillath persists.

His hands are aching and he realises it is because he has them curled up tight against the sides of his chair. He tries to force them open. 'Why does it matter how I feel about her?'

Lillath just shakes her head. 'It matters.'

'My personal feelings are my business and no one else's.'

'Not any more.'

'Whether I am or I'm not,' Art says, 'why do you care? Why are you *here*, Lil?'

She sits up in a sudden rush, startling him. 'You know about the Night Carnival's strictest rule? If any of their performers feel that a client is getting too emotionally involved with them, they are to find a way to terminate their arrangement with that client as quickly and as smoothly as they can. You're not supposed to fall for them, Art. What they make you feel – it's carefully manufactured. It isn't *real.* You're paying them to give you exactly what you want, and it's only meant to be temporary, because fantasies aren't built to last. You realise that, right? She's a performer, and if she made it into the Night Carnival, she's a damn good one.'

Is everything he feels on display? Is the whole palace watching him and muttering behind their hands about his behaviour? Do they laugh at the silly boy King, do they wonder and worry if his flush is lust or love?

'You must think I'm a child,' he says.

Lillath's eyes widen. 'That's not what I'm saying at all—'

'No? What else could you have meant by that patronising warning?'

She is lost for words, staring at him.

Suddenly he is so tired of his cage – but even more, of her intrusion into it.

'Just . . .' Art bites his sentence in two, begins again. 'Just leave, Lil. Just go.'

She has turned to stone. 'Are you dismissing me, Sire?'

His laugh is furious, disbelieving. How dare she do that?

'That's fine,' he says. 'Yes, if you like. I'm dismissing you, Lady DeHavilland.'

In the yawning silence that follows, Lillath rises from the divan and turns her back on him, making for the door. In front of it she stops and he is suddenly glad – she will say something to make him laugh and they'll shake off this thick, choking air that has bloomed between them so sour, so sudden.

He hears her speak.

'You know, you used to be fearless about showing your true feelings. You never saw it as a weakness, and so it was always a strength. Now you dismiss me from your sight because you can't bear for me to see you be vulnerable. We're not the only ones putting up walls, Art.'

She doesn't even wrench open the door, like the loud, tempestuous Lil he knows would. She goes quietly, pulling it shut behind her with the softest of clicks.

They are neither of them who they once were, such a short time ago.

It makes his heart ache.

CHAPTER 18

The Dungeons, Rhyfentown
Five Months Ago

'Good day to you, Red Caballarias o'Rhyfentown.'

Red turns from the painting she has been gazing at to the sound of the voice behind her.

A man lingers in the doorway of the study, arms held straight by his sides. It is his study, his building, his family who own the training grounds on which it stands. He is descended from one of the knights' orders who served under Rhyfen's banner in the War of the Saith. Privilege and wealth hang around his neck like invisible jewels in Rhyfen's colours, sunstone and cat's eye.

This is the first time Red has met him. He is not the kind of man to be found wandering the corridors.

'Si Timor.' Red bows. 'Forgive me, they told me to wait in here for you.'

Si Timor Caballarias Merwic o'Rhyfentown just smiles. His hair is steel grey and tight to his head. He has become softly rotund in his later years, his visible skin unmarked, clothes the kind of understated plain that speaks of fine quality. He emits something of a disconcertingly huggable feel, and Red finds herself drawn towards him.

'Which one do you like best?' Timor nods at the wall. 'This one in front of you?'

The painting Red has been studying is an odd kind of landscape. Some of it is clearly recognisable. There is the unmistakable outline of Black Tom, and there, striping the Thames River, are several of the most famous parallel bridges – Lamhythe, Falkesall and the Blestern – each linking into a separate district as they radiate away from Blackheart. The skyline though, is all wrong. It is higher, jutting further up into the murky sky above it, and the buildings are all flat on top, like bricks dropped on their ends, with hardly a spike or spire in sight. Faint lines run across the bridges, with rectangular blobs of what look like overground trags – but none of those bridges have trag lines built across them.

'Is it supposed to be the future?' she asks at last.

Si Timor sounds pleased. 'Close. It's supposed to be an alternative version of London. One that might have existed, and might yet.'

He walks to the enormous desk dominating his study and lowers himself into the armchair behind it, gesturing to the empty chair opposite.

Red takes it.

'All these are by the same artist,' Timor says, gesturing across at the walls filled with paintings and sketches. Most are landscapes – street-level impressions of a city, rolling countryside, a wild, jagged coastline. There is only one portrait, of a pale man reclining in an armchair, the back reaching far above his head. He is dressed in severe clothes, his long black hair in a plaited rope draped over one shoulder, chin resting on his hand. He has been painted with some intensity, his angular face floating ghostlike against the dark background.

Timor has a misty smile on his face. 'This artist was preoccupied, shall we say, with the idea that our world exists in a dazzling array of alternatives, which we could travel between if we only knew how. She lived with them all in her head: many different Londons, with different skylines, different names. She often called it 'Capital'. 'Lud', she liked too – she said that name came up a few times. She was quite the extraordinary woman, with quite the extraordinary gift.'

'She was a godchild,' Red ventures.

'Yes.'

A strange seer of some sort, or maybe just mad. Had she been using magic to make these paintings? How would something like that be proved?

'What was her name?' Red asks.

'Rue,' Timor says simply, and offers no signifiers.

'She was your . . .?' She leaves the question hanging politely.

Timor holds up a hand. 'Oh, no. No, she was devoted to another. They were just passing through here together, really. I was lucky enough to know them for a time. She saw further than everyone else. While other people spent their days looking around at what other people had or didn't have, or inwards into their own lives, she always had her face turned outwards, towards what she said was an endless stretch of realities.'

'But . . . it was all made-up, in her head?'

'Yes, of course.' Timor seems faintly amused. 'That doesn't mean it's not real, though.'

'What?'

'Perhaps you should read up on some of the new theories being published right now. Expand your sight and your thought beyond what lies immediately ahead of you.'

Red tries to trace the point of the conversation.

'I'm not like her,' she ventures.

Timor snorts. 'Of course you're not. I don't believe in lumping godchildren all together like some vague homogeneous mass, Si Red. You are all of you different, just like everyone in this world.' His hand reaches out, fingers coming to rest lightly on a large black envelope lying on his desk.

'This is your Caballaria name,' he says. 'It was delivered this morning from the offices of Lee DeCyng. Would you like to open it?'

It appears that Red does not have to pretend emotion like she thought she would. The emotion is there without her permission, drying out the inside of her mouth. She reaches forwards and accepts the envelope, tearing it open as calmly as she can.

Inside is a bundle of thick woven paper, sewn together down one side like a home-made book. The top sheaf is printed with a simple name in the crimson of freshly drawn blood from the vein:

THE
RED
WRAITH

Each sheaf underneath this is covered in a gorgeous drawing of her, over and over, in different attitudes and poses, different outfits and weapons. In this lean, sketched version of her face, the artist has captured an elusive kind of beauty that suggests a wall between her and the viewer. This figure, this red wraith, has the kind of heart that cannot be known. Red can admire what the artist has done with her, but for some reason she does not love it.

She is a figure, now. A creation. The feeling is a strange one.

'How do you like them?' Timor asks.

Red places the bundle of sketches gently on the desk in front of her.

'They're lovely,' she says. 'They don't look like me, but they're lovely.'

Timor smiles. 'On the contrary. Lee has a wonderful eye for the detail hidden inside us.'

'He drew these himself?'

'He always does. What do you think of the name?'

'It's . . . whatever they want. It's just a name.'

'Ho,' Timor says. 'Names are important. Our names give us shape, purpose, family, origin. The Red Wraith. It's a little too . . . hmm, *obvious*, perhaps?'

'They said I move like a wraith in the fight. I wouldn't know.'

'No. One does not often get to see outside of oneself. But in the Caballaria, you'll be forced to learn how to do that very quickly. We try to prepare you in training by finding ways to separate the self you've always known and see it as an instrument. It's a strange profession, to be sure, especially nowadays. But still a noble one, at its core. Remember why it exists. Remember the Code.'

'My first fight—' Red hesitates. 'It's already been scheduled?'

'Yes.'

'That's not normal, is it?'

Timor inclines his head. 'It's unusual.'

Red is silent as she tries to work out how to ask what she wants to ask without giving herself away, but apparently Timor can read minds, or perhaps Red is far more transparent than she thinks – an unpleasant notion.

'Si Wyll was asked if his stable wanted to retain your services straight from training,' he says gently, 'but he indicated that they would rather you stayed with us for a while and gain some experience first. He – his stable – are still paying your way. It is a very generous favour to us, and the obligation he now has me under is not lost on me. And he is not the only benefactor you have attracted.'

'Not the only benefactor?' Red repeats. 'Who else could there possibly be?'

'Let us simply say that you are bringing a lot of attention to us, Si. It is, of course, an honour.' Timor's voice dries at the edges.

A weight of responsibility hangs in the spaces between his words. If Red fucks up, it is not just her own reputation she damages – now she has Rhyfentown Public stable on her shoulders too.

'It's an honour for me,' Red says.

'Mmm. Public stables can be tough and unforgiving. The messy sorts of disputes you'll have to fight for, and the prestige, by which of course I mean *lack of* . . . well, people are attracted to glamour, and there's very little glamour to be found here. Your ultimate goal has been clear from the beginning.'

'I'm sorry if I seem ungrateful . . .'

Timor laughs. 'Si, there's no need to be shy about it. Ambition and power, carefully managed and directed towards the greater good, are two of the most useful of tools in the advancement of civilisation.'

This is a direct quote from one of the most famous tenets of the Code. It is a well-known facet of Si Timor, his elevation of the Code above all else. Not all training grounds place such emphasis on it. He drums his fingers on the desk while staring at Red, who carefully freezes herself under the searching gaze.

'You might consider the possibility that Si Wyll is testing

you,' he says at last. 'He, for many understandable reasons, doesn't trust easily. You must find a way to earn that trust.'

Red is getting a little tired of being tested. She had thought once training was over that she would be free of that, but she is beginning to realise that from here on in, the scrutiny on her will only grow.

Red's gaze grazes the paper sheaf in front of her, the bold, stark lettering of her Caballaria name blazing out to the room.

The Red Wraith.

'How long do I get to prepare for my first fight?' she asks.

Timor gives her a faint, pleased smile.

CHAPTER 19

Cair Lleon, Blackheart
Eighteen Years Ago

Once she feels that Art is sated, Belisan always takes her leave.

She never sleeps at the palace. He has yet to see her lit by first light. Initially he feels embarrassed – is their time together so bad that she has to run away from him as soon as she can? – but soon he realises it is not staying with him that she dislikes, it is sleeping with him. She seems happy to spend hours lying in bed with him without any apparent desire to be elsewhere, but the moment one of them starts feeling tired, she is up and away.

It is something Art will come to regret not interrogating, because several months into their bed dancing, he discovers the reason why.

One night Belisan turns up much later than they had arranged, looking unusually tired as she arrives through the secret passage into his rooms. She apologises; Art asks her if she wants to postpone, she protests and eventually they fall into bed together, Art making sure to do most of the work. He is the student here, after all – though Belisan often says that he teaches her as much as she teaches him.

Afterwards, drowsy with satisfaction, Art turns to Belisan,

to find her eyes closed and her breaths deepening. Instead of waking her, he sinks down into the ruffled sheets and lets himself drift.

Then he wakes to find himself drowning.

His chest heaves. Wet heavy sea sucks at him, salt tang burns his throat. Something behind him is forcing his head down, dragging his lips under the surface. He opens his mouth and water greedily floods his insides. In the sea's soft, deceptive underworld he turns, forcing his eyes open to strain through the murk, trying to break free of what has him.

It is a monster with Belisan's face, a sleek, enormous seal-like thing, dragging him under with a look of intense concentration, the concentration of murderous purpose. It has her chestnut eyes, their glossy gleam murked by silt. A deadly selkie.

Art tries to scream, remembers too late that to open his throat here means death. He thrashes wildly, breaking free of the selkie monster's grip. His limbs pump, scrabbling him up to air and light and finding it for a brief, ecstatic moment.

The sky above is streaked a foreboding grey, grim clouds scuttling across it as if too scared to bear witness. There is a shore, impossibly close, a few strokes of the arm away, and yet underneath him the deep goes down and down for ever.

On the shore stands a figure, a human figure, their eyes closed.

It is Belisan.

'Bel!' Her name bubbles with water in his throat.

Her eyes open and she sees him.

He waves frantically.

A terrible weight grabs his foot and pulls.

'Bel—' he manages to scream before he goes under.

He feels rather than hears a muted splash from above, and the surface of the sea surges. The selkie has him, her arms iron bars around his body. His chest burns, burns. Horrified despair climbs over every inch of him, the likes of which he has never known. In mere seconds, he is going to die.

This is it, now

One last thought before you go

Make it a good one

Mama, he thinks with wondrous sadness, just before the human Belisan appears, reaching for him—

Darkness surrounds him. His throat swells, threatening to burst, clanging under his chest, and then he is vomiting. He curls on his side like a dying beetle as seawater spews from his mouth, launched out of him by the pressure of a fist in his belly, soaking the bedclothes under his head. It smells like the docklands: a sharp, tangy assault.

He drags in air – sweet, life-giving air – but it hurts, stinging his ravaged insides. He tries to suck it in, chokes, coughs a brine-sharp cough. His hands spasmodically clutch at damp sheets.

'Art.' He hears a panic-trembled voice behind him. 'Talk to me. Please say something. Art!'

A bed. His bed. He is not in the sea. He is in the palace, in his bedroom.

He feels the fist at his belly disappear, a hand flutter on his shoulder, his name called again.

Funny, he thinks, *I was drowning in water but my insides are burning like fire.*

He manages to lever himself up, flops back against his wet pillows.

Belisan is naked beside him. It was her fist in his belly. Her panic.

'I was in the sea,' he croaks. 'I was—'

'I was dreaming,' she says tearfully. 'I was dreaming – I'm so sorry, I'm so sorry.'

Dreaming? But the water is real. He can feel the bed sheet in wet folds against his skin. The smell of seaweed still hazes the air. Through the hanks of her hair, Belisan's gaze catches on his with a feverish gleam. She looks like feral prey. She looks like she has been caught.

And suddenly, Art understands why.

She must see it on his face, because she begins to move. Slow and fragile, she clambers naked off the bed and watches him, her shoulders hunched, her legs bent.

A moment where all is suspended in held breath and shivering form.

'What happened?' he says, or tries to, but the words are pulverised by a rack of wet coughing. His throat gives a menacing throb.

'A dream,' says Belisan. 'It was a dream.'

'It had your face.'

Belisan says nothing.

'The monster in the sea, it had your face.' Art can hear the wonder in his own voice. 'Did you just try to kill me?'

She shakes her head vehemently. 'No – *no*. I didn't realise. I didn't know what I was doing. Sometimes I pull people into my dreams, Art, I'm so sorry, I can't control it—'

Shock rushes at him in a sudden, savage wave. He very much wants to cry.

'Are you an assassin?' he asks.

'No. *No!*'

'You're a godchild.'

Belisan says nothing, but her face sparkles with raw misery.

'I was dying.' Art touches his chest. 'I can still feel it. I can—'

'I swear to you, I didn't—'

'But it was you. In the dream, it was you, pulling me under.'

Belisan just shakes her head, but she cannot drag up a denial. Tears spring from her eyes and track down her cheeks as she stares at him.

'Please,' she finally whispers. 'I didn't tell you because I didn't want you to hate me. It's why I don't sleep here; I was careful, I was so careful.'

'You lied to me.'

'I had to. I've had to do it all my life. If people knew—'

Yes. If people knew.

'I'll go,' she whispers. 'I'll go far away. You'll never see me again.'

'I can't let you do that,' he says, but shock has robbed him of conviction.

They both know what will happen if she stays.

'I'll disappear,' she pleads. 'No one ever has to know.'

'Bel.'

She is all anguish. 'Please. I never meant to hurt you.'

Art stares at her while his chest steadily burns with salt and betrayal.

Finally, he gives the smallest of nods.

Belisan works fast. She picks up her clothes and shoes. She doesn't stop to put them on but scrabbles across the room with her arms full of fabric and her hair flying behind her. Sconce lights stripe her fleeing form. She takes the secret passage out. The wall closes silently behind her.

Art waits. He pushes down on his panic and waits some more. His thoughts swing wildly, madly.

She didn't try to kill you – yes, she did, she's getting away – assassin – *just a panicked rabbit with a terrible talent – your lover, she loves you – no, you almost died, HUNT HER DOWN AND EXECUTE HER—*

Panic wins. He levers himself out of bed, takes wobbling steps to the door, opens it and screams for the guard.

CHAPTER 20

Corescent, Rhyfentown
Five Months Ago

'Nice form, but watch your back swipe. You're leaving your chest unguarded for too long, I could have scored a hit there.'

Frome crouches back down into a defensive stance as he talks, hollow cheeks flushed.

Red's sweat-slicked palms have been gradually greasing up the handle of the practice rapier sword during this training session. It twists and slides uneasily in her hands, threatening to slip right out of them.

'These stupid gloves,' she says through gritted teeth. 'They're about as practical as a chocolate cock.'

'Oh, but Si, you're wearing DeCyngs. They look amazing and that's what matters.' Frome grins, weaving his own sword tip gently in the space between them. 'Cut out the palms and wear a similar coloured grip tape underneath. No one will be able to tell, and you won't risk fumbling your weapon.'

Red straightens with a sigh, her hands drumming a dull throb. 'All the posturing.'

'All the posturing,' Frome agrees, straightening in tandem. 'Frimping and frooping.'

'I just want to fight the damn fight, preferably in private where no one can gawp at me.'

'Oh come on, you know the history. Private fights can be gamed so much easier than public ones. The circus around it all is the price paid for a fairer system.' Frome walks over to the weapons rack and slots his rapier back in, his bowed head lit by a ray of light streaming in through the high windows.

It is Red's third day in the Corescent monastery. Tomorrow will dawn with the promise of her first official fight.

As is typical in Caballaria monasteries, the room they are in is entirely panelled in wood. Rhyfentown's monasteries favour spiced wood, which lends the space a warmth that helps loosen muscles, and due to the colour, the light has a calming golden quality – but the sound, to Red's ears, is all wrong. There is no stone to echo back the clash of steel on steel, no high, clear, jingling tones as metal armour responds to movement. Each noise comes back flat and dry.

She used to find the concept of holing knights up in isolation for days before a bout a little strange, but now it is easy to see why it is done. Remove the outside world and all that is left is the fight. No distractions, nothing pulling them in different directions. Only one direction, only one focus.

It is a shorter, more extreme version of her Dungeons training. There, they all had other trainees to eat with and spar with, an array of trainers to see on the daily and a routine that involved encountering other bodies and minds in shared spaces. Here in the monastery, Red sees barely anyone. Caballaria monks are pleasant but silent, and they bring meals to her rooms instead of her attending a dining area. The bathroom next to the sleeping room is for her alone. She is allowed no visitors except for the trainer of her choice, who is admitted daily.

In the training rooms they are directed to use, too, they are always alone. If her upcoming opponent is here, as Red presumes they must be, they have never crossed paths. This is deliberate, and the law is strict. Contact between opponents before a fight can render that fight void, with both knights suffering disgrace as a consequence.

Red is glad of the law. She does not want to see her opponent. She does not even want to know their name until the moment she steps out into the arena, because at that point it will be too late to undermine herself by worrying about whether they are better than her, or their record, their stats, their weapon of choice, even how many fights they have won – which, no matter who they are, will be more than she has. The only fight that ever matters, the Code states, is the one immediately before you.

'I don't feel ready,' she hisses between her teeth.

'No one ever does. There's only so much you can prepare. After that, it's up to the saints.'

Red rears her head. Does anyone really still believe that the saints are the ultimate adjudicators of the Caballaria, or is Frome teasing her?

'Then why try at all,' she says, 'if the saints ultimately decide?'

'Because the saints choose based on desire and power, not based on a whim of their own. You must believe with everything you have that you fight for the right cause. *That's* what they feel. Your opponent can be stronger than you in all ways, but you'll still win if your desire is more powerful than theirs.'

'And if I don't believe in the cause I fight for, I lose?'

Frome gives a quiet laugh. 'Well, that's why fighters are forbidden from knowing anything about the dispute before the fight. Makes it easier. All you have to do is concentrate on winning.'

Frome is ex-Caballaria – most trainers are. He knows. He has lived it.

His advice is the only advice that matters right now.

It is a soft little slithering noise, barely registering, but it wakes her up.

The monastery is the quietest place Red has ever known. It is difficult to believe that she is in the middle of Rhyfentown right now, that out there the skyline is cluttered with clusters of spires and round domes and flat rooftops and the spindly, soaring webbing of conductors, the clouds above it all lit with flickering projections of a thousand ways to improve your life by spending all your trick, and for the latest glow shows filled with pretty, scowling faces.

She has been sleeping well the last couple of days, which she is grateful for, but this is the night before her first-ever fight. Frome had told her to expect little rest, and to factor in her wired tiredness by resting up in the hours before she is due at the arena. Tonight has been full of scattered, fitful bursts of sleep followed by long bouts of staring blindly out into the dark of her room, willing nothingness to take her.

At first Red assumes she dreamed the sound, an anxious tendril created by her mind, but as her eyes adjust to the murk of predawn, she spots a light rectangle on the floor by the door. She slides out of bed and cautiously approaches.

It is a small sheaf of papers, one corner pierced through with a curved, double-headed metal pin. Her first thought is that Lee DeCyng has sent her some more of his beautiful sketches – for what purpose at this late stage is hard to puzzle out – but the top sheaf is covered in dense text instead of sweeping lines.

There are no curtains in her room, nor is there any source of man-made light. Natural rhythms are important to the monks here, and they rise with the dawn. The outside world is still far away, though, as most rooms face into the huge, airy courtyard at the compound's centre. Red has been waking up to sunlight filtered through the vast canopy of the gnarled and sprawling oak tree dominating the middle of the courtyard, as if the monastery grew up around it. So she takes the sheaf of papers and lies back down on her bed, her head resting just under the window, waiting for the light to grow bright enough for her to read.

When it does, and she finally manages to work out just what it is she is holding, she drops it like it burns. The paper sheaf flutters as it falls off the side of the bed and hits the floor.

Red waits, heart pounding, for someone to come running. Someone must surely be poised to burst in here and catch her out, because that sheaf of papers holds every last detail of the dispute she is fighting for today: who is involved – what is at stake.

And if anyone catches her with it, it is going to ruin her.

She waits a good half-hour.

No one comes.

She will not look at it. This is a test. Has to be. The clock on her wall tells her that she has another hour until breakfast. She can wait until then. Easy.

The paper sheaf lies impossibly white against the warm wooden floor, drawing her eye.

Someone walked to her room in the dead of night and slid this under her door. If it is not a test, there is obviously something they want her to know.

No. It's a test.

But what if it's not?

Red cannot bear to be weak – weakness always costs too much – but surely there is no harm in her looking, because knowing what she fights for is not going to sway her. She is too strong for that. Too determined. She has risked too much to fuck everything up now.

Before she can change her mind she reaches out, scoops up the sheaf and begins to read.

Disputes are laid out in mind-bogglingly formal language, echoing the dusty, meandering parables of the Code, and it takes Red a while to sort through its dense text, but when she does, she finally understands the full weight of Frome's advice.

She is fighting for the wrong side.

The dispute is between a landlord named Mackeler and one of his tenants, Gedric. Mackeler owns the entire housing building that Gedric lives in, and several more scattered throughout the surrounding borough. Mackeler is rich. Gedric is not. He cannot pay his rent because he is too ill to work, and Mackeler's adjudicator claims he has been living rent-free for months, but Gedric's adjudicator's evidence is damning. The building he lives in has been confirmed as infested with black rot. Its toxic fingers run across almost every inner wall on every floor. Gedric has black rot lung. He cannot work to pay his rent to Mackeler because Mackeler's own housing has made him too ill to work.

Mackeler has refused to combat the black rot in the building. It is too widespread; it was discovered too late. He also claims that Gedric must have contracted the black rot from previous housing – not his. Perhaps there is no way of knowing for sure, but he would rather ruin a poor, sick man than help him.

Because Gedric is too poor to afford a private stable, the dispute has been brought to the public circuit. The canny Mackeler requested Red specifically as his fighter. He has that right, and presumably his influence got him to the top of the list. It would be reasonable to assume that he wants the newly trained knight who nearly beat the Scourge because of the prestige it will bring him, but unfortunately there is one more thing about this man that points to another reason: Mackeler is a registered godchild.

So the godchild landlord wants a godchild knight fighting for him. A risky game, and one that Red was never supposed to know she herself is playing.

This doesn't matter. None of it matters, because you're going to go in there and win, just like you're supposed to.

Aren't you, Red?

Two hours before the fight is due to begin, Red's only possessions are packed into one large bag, which sits ready by the door of her room.

Buried right at the bottom of the bag, underneath her few clothes and her weighty copy of the Code, are the sheaf of dispute papers she is not supposed to have. She is going to have to find a way to get rid of them at some point before the fight begins.

It's a rent dispute. It's not life or death.

Not for Mackeler, it isn't – but for someone like Gedric?

When Red is fetched to the monastery's entrance, she wonders for a brief moment whether it might be Finnavair come to collect her again – but instead, it is a stranger in guard leathers, an unsmiling woman with tight curls of muddy-brown hair and a hard stance, introduced as Si Hathawy. She gives Red a nod, a *how goes it*, and does not speak again.

Early evening streaks across the sky as they set out. Two more guard knights accompany them, one ahead and one behind.

Red's gaze strays to the bulging gun holster at Si Hathawy's hip. Guard knights are the only people allowed to even touch a gun. They exist mainly to protect valuable assets – whether people, objects or buildings – and to put down trouble of any kind. It must attract a certain kind to such a purpose.

The monastery is only a few minutes' ride away from the arena that shares its name and as soon as they reach the wide boulevard approach, everyone knows exactly where they are going, and who they must be. Echoes of incoherent shouting reach them as they slide past the foot traffic, the faces peering at Red a mix of curious and excited, eyes screwed up with the effort of trying to see if it is the young godchild who almost put down the Scourge underneath any of those helmets, or if it is her opponent.

The Corescent is one of Rhyfentown's biggest arenas, but it is still only half the size of Cair Stour, that renowned sunken beast nestled at the centre of London where only the most prestigious disputes are fought, that valve of the city through which its lifeblood seems to pour. Even so, the Corescent still towers above Red's eyeline on the approach, setting her stomach churning with nerves. That tattered little pit where she was discovered out in the dis' limits feels like a lifetime ago.

They circle the arena to the back, where a pair of tired-looking chain-link gates are all that separate the restricted areas from the public. They ride on through – no faces apparently need to be shown to the bored-looking guard knight who drags the gate open for them – and find themselves in a square of concrete scrubland leading to an innocuous door half-obscured by the towering waste bins squatting to its side. Burnt-out sicalo ends are scattered and squashed against the ground. The front of the arena is all polish and show. The back is all business.

The three bikes park close to the door. Red eases off, arm muscles strung tight. She had hoped the ride might calm her down, the buffeting wind she has dreamed of soothing her jangling body, but this is nothing like that first night ride with Finnavair – not long enough to get a real run going, too many eyes and faces turned to them like flowers to sunlight to get that mind-empty feeling, that stillness she often craves now.

Hathawy pulls off her helmet and swivels in her saddle.

'Never been on a bike before, ho, godchild?' she says.

'Once,' Red replies.

'Neh. I could tell by the way you clutched at my ass when we took that corner.'

Laughter.

'First official fight for you, isn't it?' another says companionably. He was briefly introduced outside the monastery as Si Griffid. He has a lumpy face, dwarfed by piercing green eyes that sparkle like gems. The question must be rhetorical – they know exactly who she is, after all – so Red says nothing.

'Such a burden,' the third comments, an older man called Castur whose notable visual characteristic is a thick, knotted scar that juts up from the leathers around his neck and curves around the back of his ear. 'Pratting about in an arena, swinging your glittery swords. You should try Wardogs one time, girl. My brother used to fight in Wardogs. That's a proper fight, I war'nt. No weapons, no rules, just fists and feet.'

'Wardogs doesn't exist any more,' Red ventures.

'Not since Utheran times,' Griffid adds.

Castur snorts. 'Just cos it got made illegal by that simpering idiot we have to call a King, don't mean it don't exist. Those mighty high Caballaria morals don't get you far in a real fight. We're all in the ground in the end, friend, so my advice is: break the rules and fight dirty, because it's the only way anyone ever wins.'

'Come on, I'll take you through,' Griffid says, rescuing her.

Red takes care to bow with scrupulous politeness to both Hathawy and Castur.

'It was an education to have knights like you as my first-ever escort,' she says in the most deadpan voice she can muster.

She has the momentary satisfaction of Castur's face creasing with the effort of trying to work out whether he is being mocked or not. Hathawy is more astute – her expression is cold.

'Don't listen to him,' Griffid says a moment later, as they walk together through a cold, narrow corridor on the other side of the door. 'He's trying to get you to screw your career before it's even begun.'

'Another godchild hater,' Red says. 'How novel.'

Griffid's eyebrows rise. 'Nothing like that. It's just regular guns and swords rivalry.'

'I'm not sure what you mean.'

'Never known any guard knights, neh?' Griffid sounds surprised. 'Well, let's just say that swords – Caballaria knights, Si, like you – tend to think that guns – guard knights like us – are a load of bloodthirsty trigger-happy charmless trolls, and guns tend to view swords as stuck-up pandering performing monkeys who wouldn't know a real fight until it skewered them in the guts.' The harsh strip lights overhead cast Griffin's lumpy face into stark relief. 'In an arena, no one wants you dead. Out there on the streets . . . well, sometimes they do. You think people clap and cheer and give free drinks to guns? It's a tough way to earn your trick, and it's swords that get all the fame and glory. Here we are.'

Griffid halts outside a black door. A thin strip of glow screen set into the door at rough eye-height displays, in cold, white letters:

PRIMUM ADVERSARIUM
THE RED WRAITH

Griffid turns to Red. 'This is your door. I'll be watching your fight.' He grins. 'Good luck.'

He leaves, striking back the way they have come.

Heart pounding, Red opens the door.

Inside is a small, well-lit dressing room. The far corner is tiled and the floor there dips into a drain, with a showerhead poking out from the wall and a free-standing smoked screen that offers only a vague sort of privacy. A large full-length mirror dominates the opposite wall and a suite of divan, low table and cabinet complete the set.

Perched on the divan is Stelia, the shyer of the two DeCyng hens. She looks up at Red. She seems nervous.

They stare at each other.

Abruptly she says, 'I'm here to put your clothes on.'

The total absurdity of it all strikes Red hard, and she bursts out laughing. After a moment, so does Stelia. Doubled over and giggling like a child with a girl she barely knows, but someone at least as bemused and overwhelmed as she is, something inside Red frays just enough to let her expand her chest and breathe.

Stelia takes her hand. She has touched her before – unconsciously, a body to position and drape and tug and hang things from – but this time it feels familiar and unexpectedly sweet.

'Ready to see your outfit?' she asks.

Red has been practising in a workmanlike version of her new Caballaria clothes all week, made for use when she is training, so nothing is a complete surprise – but the final show version of the Red Wraith is nothing short of breath-taking. Black and sleek, with accents of dried blood, it fits itself to her perfectly, following the lines of her body without compromising her range of movement.

The crowning jewel of the outfit is a clawed cestus, the unique battle glove that will be the Red Wraith's particular weapon. It has been created specifically to complement what the DeCyng team consider to be her finishing move. It extends in a half sheaf from elbow to wrist, connected there to the hand piece with a tightly woven lattice of tiny chains, a flexible mesh that allows full dexterity for her wrist.

The hand piece sits as a solid plate on top of her hand, connected underneath with a thick, flat sash of the same chain mesh, which her palm slots into like a glove. Each joint beyond the solid plate is articulated up to the second knuckle. Beyond that, the finger plates extend out into thin, wicked claws, sloping down into a gentle curve. The tips are razor-sharp, perfect for drawing blood across exposed skin.

The entire thing is both sturdier and more lightweight than Red dared think possible, made of a mix of black metals and what is apparently one of the most durable alloys in existence. Those claws are not going to snap. Thin silver strips act as piping, accentuating each line of the cestus, hinting at the skeletal structure of the arm and hand underneath it.

Once dressed, Stelia, with some ceremony, guides her to the mirror. Red stares at this strange new version of herself, moulded to others' visions of the character she will play out there in the arena. This Red is elegant, supple. Dangerous. Only now does she begin to fully appreciate the power in the eye of someone like Lee DeCyng.

'You look magnificent,' Stelia whispers.

She doesn't touch Red any more but stands further away, pulled back. The Red Wraith is to be admired from a distance, studied and judged like an artwork. She is no longer a person.

She is a Caballaria knight.

There is a knock on the door, and a pause. Red realises that the power to grant or deny now lies with her. There is no one else in the room who is accountable for her now.

'Enter,' she calls, hoping she sounds steady and in control.

A group of white-jackets crowd through the door, jostling and spilling their way into the dressing room. The Corescent arena team are the calm eye of the storm, the veins that carry the blood of the fight. They are *seen-it-all* unflappable – or so Red has been led to believe. They crowd around her like chickens to a cockerel, exclaiming at her boots, her mask, her clawed cestus. It must be rare for any of them to see a DeCyng outfit up close. Stelia hovers protectively nearby as their hands reach out to point and gesture, but like her, they don't touch.

When they have had their fill of their exclusive first look at the famous new knight, they take Red through procedure, making sure she understands the part she is about to play. She nods in all the right places, or at least she thinks she does. A dislocated haze has descended on her. She cannot be what she needs to be out there, but the Red Wraith can.

The time comes.

They lead Red out of the dressing room, back into the cold and draughty corridor. Stelia is left behind, her promises to watch every move from pit side, winning prayers on her lips offered fervently up to Rhyfen, patron saint of the fight.

As they wind their way through the bowels of the arena and approach the entrance to the pit, Red asks the head of the arena team the question that has been burning with guilty secrecy in her mind for days.

'Do you know who's in the stands today?' she asks.

The head, a sprightly veteran of the Caballaria circus, understands.

'There's a whole lot of your Dungeons people,' she says. 'Your trainer, Si Frome, of course. Your fellow trainees who passed with you.'

Red hesitates. 'Have you heard whether the Sorcerer Knight has come?'

The head looks baffled. 'Oh no, Si. No. If someone like that were . . . I'd have been informed days ago. Security, and such. You understand.'

Red understands all too well and her heart sinks into dark, fierce misery.

Before long, the noise of the crowd begins to filter down through the ceiling, swelling impossibly along the entrance to the pit. It is like being in the depths of a forest of fir trees on a stormy day, utterly surrounded by the sound of their swaying.

When the door opens and Red walks out into the pit, she is struck by solid, naked fear. They explained, they showed her a thousand captures of recent fights, they did everything they could – but nothing could prepare anyone for this.

Yet eclipsing it all is this thought, going round and round in her head:

He's not here. He's not fucken here.

It's all for nothing.

Underneath the cold metallic grip of the cestus on her left hand, she feels her palm give a warning, tingling itch.

Blinking against the lights that dazzle and confuse, her heart swelling in her throat and cutting off her air, her body numb, her mind a frozen blank, Red moves out on to the sanded arena floor, greeted by the crowd's rising roar.

CHAPTER 21

Cair Lleon, Blackheart
Eighteen Years Ago

'They're here, Sire.'

'Send them in,' Art replies without looking up.

Fortigo leaves the room with the barest rustle and swish.

It is the quietest moment before dawn. Art has chosen a room in the bowels of the palace for this meeting – the same room, in fact, where he had his first-ever encounter with his waiting appointment.

The door clicks open and in sweeps Dario Go, dressed in a severely cut white suit, stark against the room's muted, forest-coloured plush. A long indigo coat is folded neatly over one arm. They fold into a deep bow.

Art is leaning back in his chair, one arm extended on the table before him. Next to his hand rests a small silver bell. His eyes flicker to Dario's face, but he offers no greeting.

'I am flattered at my King's attention,' Dario says into the silence. 'I don't think I've ever been surprise-escorted anywhere by royal guns before. Am I to take it that you have learned all you need to from the lovely Belisan and would now like to sample a dish with a more complex flavour?'

Perhaps adrenalin has heightened his senses, because underneath Dario's smooth flirtations, Art swears he can hear nerves.

He still says nothing.

Lesser performers might be tempted to shift around, fumble with more words. Ask why they have been summoned to the palace in the middle of their work day with no notice or warning, picked up by two guard knights with demure sword sigils stitched on to their shoulders and guns hanging like deadly fruit at their hips as the only signs of their affiliation, and discreetly but insistently bundled into an unmarked quad.

Dario does not shift or speak again. They simply stand, holding Art's gaze.

'Did you know?' Art asks them.

'Know what, Sire?'

'That Belisan Meretrix D'Aroch o'Iochitown is a godchild. Did you know? Please remember that it is considered treason to lie to your King.' He gives deliberate emphasis to the last two words.

Dario is very still. 'May I ask what happened?'

Art hesitates. Some part of him wants it to be a mistake. He wants them to tell him that he has overreacted. So he plays along.

'She had a dream, and she brought it into the room,' he says simply.

That unmistakable salty, sharp tang of seawater. His bedclothes stinking like a fish market at the end of the day.

'Dremen,' Dario says softly. 'They're rare. There hasn't been a documented dremen for decades.'

'I know dremen are rare, but you and I both know just how many undocumented godchildren there could be out there. And I know what I saw.' Art wills his fingers to remain open.

They want very much to close into a fist. 'What concerns me is your complete lack of surprise at this revelation. Then again, what kind of Carnival master would you be if you were just. That. Unobservant?'

'A bad one. My King, I knew something of Belisan's . . . condition. That's to say, she's had a lifelong problem with nightmares, and we make special provisions for that. There was no reason to suspect that it was anything else. There's no evidence of godchildren in Belisan's family history. But even if there were . . .' Dario draws in a steady breath. 'Forgive me, I'm trying to understand where your anger comes from. Is it really so disgusting a concept to you to discover that you've been taking pleasure from a godchild? I know she's unregistered, and that's a crime, but hardly a huge—'

'How dare you,' Art cuts in pleasantly, so pleasantly that Dario takes a moment to understand what he has actually said. 'I know who was behind this, Dario. I know all about your connection to Agravain Welyen.'

Dario affects a look of surprise. 'I'm sorry, Sire, but I don't understand.'

'Before you joined the Night Carnival, were you not privately retained by the Welyen family?'

A flicker of shock, and then distaste, runs across Dario's face. 'That was a long time ago,' they say. Nothing more is offered.

'That doesn't mean you aren't still working for them,' Art pushes.

'No,' they reply, 'but I can assure you that I'm not.'

'Show me that you're not. Give me some definitive evidence.'

Dario is silent.

Art lets loose an angry sigh. 'You are moments away from being arrested. You should know that honesty is a gift I prize above all else. Tell me if this was part of a larger plan – tell me who you're working for, and I will be kinder than I should.'

'I work for the Night Carnival, Sire. We are for all, and owned by no one.'

'Pretty words,' Art says. 'Sadly, reality doesn't often measure up.'

'This was not some nefarious play of mine.' Dario's eyes are cat-cold. 'I have no reason to threaten your hold on the Sword. Investigate me. Investigate me and you'll—'

'Dario.' He watches them startle at his familiarity. 'I already am. There are people at your house as we speak.'

Dario regards him for a long, long moment. Their exquisitely carved face is a mask.

He sees it now so clearly: just as human as all the rest, just as fragile and complicated. They all learn the performance that serves as their attack and defence. They learn to survive.

Dario bows their head. 'I take it I am to sojourn indefinitely at your convenience.'

'Cair Lleon's clusterloc has rooms that are almost as luxurious as my own private suite,' Art replies. 'For a prison, it's a comfortable one.'

'I have a small request.'

'You may make as many arrangements as necessary for the continued care of the Night Carnival while you're away from it.' Art pauses. 'And the investigation will be extremely discreet – though not for your sake, of course. Nevertheless, perhaps you can take comfort in that, should things conclude in your favour.'

Dario inclines their head. 'Thank you. But that wasn't what I was going to ask for.'

'Then what?'

'I'd like to be the one to inform Belisan's family. I don't want them to find out that their girl is dead from some anonymous Cair Lleon official.'

Art manages to gather his shocked and scattered thoughts. 'You think I killed her,' he says.

Dario appears to sense his tone. 'An accident – in the heat of the moment.'

'Belisan escaped,' he says, as blankly as he can. 'She's gone.'

He watches Dario process this. Performance, perhaps, but they seem surprised. If they are hiding her, they're doing a good job of it.

Suddenly, he is very, very tired. Confused, tired and at the end of his strength. There are too many games, too many players, too many problems. He just needs this to be over.

'There is another way for you to avoid the clusterloc,' he says to Dario. 'Would you like to hear it?'

Dario gives him a wary nod.

Once Dario has gone, Art leans back in his chair and rubs his hands over his face.

'I know what you're going to say,' he tells the empty space in front of him. 'Be nice to me, I've had a hard fucken night.'

Lillath appears from her hiding place behind a floor-length screen, walking soft. Before he quite understands what she is doing, he feels her arms around him and her belly at the back of his head.

'I don't care about being right,' she murmurs above him as she strokes his hair. 'I just want you to be okay.'

He presses into her, feeling his shoulders lower.

'What did you think of Dario?' he says. 'Will they do what I asked?'

He feels her shrug against his back. 'If they don't, they go to prison.'

'We need evidence of their collusion with Agravain.'

'If there's any to find, we'll find it,' she replies. 'Either way, you can't afford to wait to make your countermove.'

Art wants to ask Lillath how she had known about Dario's connection to the Welyens, but he already knows what she will say. That there is and ever has been a healthy stock exchange for gossip among the elite, and that the powerful value few treasures more than collecting their rivals' secrets. Still, Lillath has always had a peculiar knack for finding them out. The DeHavillands are one of the most well-connected families across London, never mind their own district, and you don't attain that kind of power without being both very smart and very discreet.

Art has not yet appointed his Spymaster – or his Spider, as it's more commonly known. There has been a lot of speculation on who it might be. The title is an unofficial one, and the person who occupies it does so without any formal announcement.

Lillath has all the qualities necessary for the post. He wonders if she will say yes.

'Are you going to send God's Guns after her?' she asks him.

Art breathes out. 'No.'

'I know it's not the most savoury thing to do—'

'Correct,' he retorts, 'and I've done enough unsavoury things for one night.'

God's Guns don't officially exist. An old, secretive institution, created after the fall of the Lysander regime, they are employed for one sole purpose: to hunt down unregistered godchildren and turn them over to the law. In this case they would be a last resort, because in the darkest, most private part of his mind, Art can admit that he doesn't want Belisan caught.

'She did try to kill you,' Lillath says, 'which would be reason enough, but you do also happen to be, you know, the King.'

He hears the reproach in her voice. He wonders just how reproachful she might be if she knew that he intentionally let Belisan go.

'I don't know for sure if she meant to do that, Lil.'

'Is it worth taking the risk?' she asks.

He lets out a deep sigh. 'I just want to forget her.'

Lillath cuddles him.

Even if Belisan is guilty only of being a godchild and hiding that fact, it is all over between them. At some point Art will let himself feel the pain of losing her, but for now, there is too much to do. She is gone from his life as suddenly as she appeared and he assumes that she will never come back into it again.

He is wrong.

CHAPTER 22

Corescent Arena, Rhyfentown
Five Months Ago

'You threw the fight.'

Frome sounds even and calm, but not quite calm enough to hide his anger.

Up until now, Red has been sitting on the divan in her dressing room, feeling the sweat drying on her skin as she ignores the post-fight swirl around her, lost in the contemplation of her own bafflingly acute misery – what did she have to do to get Wyll to notice her, start swinging from the damn moon? – but Frome's staccato tone cuts right through the tail-chasing her brain is doing.

'I don't understand what you mean,' she says dully.

Frome folds his arms. 'Oh, well then, let me be clear. You deliberately lost the fight, Red. Somewhere along the way you decided that *you* should be the arbitrator of this dispute, because apparently you're under the laughable impression that you're well equipped to do so. You threw the Jesus-fucken fight.'

Red's head takes control of her mouth.

'You're a Christian?' she says in surprise. 'You never said.' She pauses. 'I haven't met too many of those. You don't really see their churches up north any more.'

Frome's smile is very, very slight. 'You don't even care, do you?'

She gathers her composure. 'I didn't throw the fight.'

'Red, you fool. You're good at hiding some things, like your fear, but there are other things that still show on you bright as glow, like your fake. You think after months of training you, *studying* you, at your side on the daily, I of all people couldn't see it? Don't lie to me. Do me that honour, at least.'

She does owe Frome that, and much more. As a knight, honour has become one of the cloaks she must wear. She thinks quickly, trying to calculate.

'The right person won,' she says.

Frome barks a laugh. 'That's not for you to decide. Haven't you learned *anything* over the last six months?'

'That landlord I was fighting for is a godchild. How would it have looked if a godchild won, with a godchild fighter? Knights aren't supposed to be political toys.'

'Don't be ridiculous, of course we are. That's the very reason you're kept in the dark.' Frome pushes his hands through his hair, hard. 'Christ, Red. Didn't you stop to think that if you'd won, it would mean that the saints favoured a godchild fighter – and a godchild claimant? That it could mean more legitimacy for godchildren? Isn't that something worth fighting for?'

Red is silent.

'Fights are always more complicated than you think,' Frome says. 'There are *always* more layers to consider, more than any one person could ever know about. Nothing is black and white. That is why, as a fighter, you have to keep it simple: there is nothing for you but the win or the lose. You are a tool. You are, and will always be, someone else's instrument. This is the life.

This is what we've tried to teach you. Your survival depends on understanding it, or you're going to drown. And if they know you've thrown your first-ever fight . . .'

'*Do* they know?' Red asks, trying for blandness and missing.

'The adjudicators?' Frome sighs, and his shoulders descend ever so slightly. 'Your friends, they knew straight away. Beyond that . . . it's hard to say. If there's any suspicion, the criteria for determining it depends on the bout, the fighters, the circumstances. It's more art than science.' He pauses. 'And as the trainer closest to you, I'd be called to give my opinion.' A sigh. 'It used to be easier than this. Just pay off all the adjudicators and have done. There was something to be said for the convenience of mass corruption, back in the day.' He glances at Red. 'I'm joking, of course.'

Red is too busy fighting nausea to listen. The notion of asking Frome to lie for her surges unpleasantly in her gut. Every step of this journey feels so precarious, so fragile. One small, emotional choice has jeopardised years of planning. She wants to be an implacable wall of ice, advancing on the enemy, so slowly that it could never alert them to the danger until they are crushed. Instead she is a silly, flickering fire, burning no one but herself.

'Why, Red?' Frome asks. 'I know how much you want this. The Caballaria is in your sinews. Why risk it all over your very first fight?'

Red thinks of the file pushed under her door. Yawning dismay threatens to overwhelm her.

'It was a test,' she says. 'And I failed.'

'What do you mean?'

Red tells Frome about the file, and watches his face change.

'Someone tried to game it,' he says, and his anger swerves

away from Red. 'Some cockless schemer. The file made you want the tenant to win, itso? How was it written?'

'It just read like the landlord was in the wrong.'

Frome is shaking his head rapidly, barely listening. 'Yes, yes. They gave you the version of it you needed to be swayed, the language all "poor victim tenant". Bet you a month's trick it was his adjudicator who wrote it and had it slipped under your door, or one of their lackeys. Big risk, mind. They'd have to take you for a thrower, and even I didn't suspect that of you. You strike everyone around you as the "swim to the win" kind. Very focused, is what I mean.' He eyes Red. 'Got a soft heart for the underdog, have we?'

It had felt more like common decency to Red, which, frankly, she is far more ashamed of. There has never been any room for common decency in her plan.

'This may just invalidate the fight,' Frome says, his expression alight. 'Not to mention the shit this'll kick up in the monastery, because there's no way they'd have been able to get that file to you without a monk's help. You still have it?'

Red nods mutely. In all the swirl of the pre-fight and Stelia never leaving her side, she hadn't had a chance to get rid of it.

Frome leans back. 'Then you might still get out of this all right.'

Frome is wrong.

Someone, whether it was due to the arena team's hawk eyes or the adjudicators' agenda games, suspects Red's throw and the suspicion is enough to lower the entire dispute into chaos. Not three hours after the bout has ended, Red finds herself in a small, airless room with two of the arena's own arbitrators. Frome is by her side as the official representative of Rhyfentown Public.

The bout's outcome is held off from being officially recorded, as is the mark of Red's first-ever loss on her own Caballaria record. All hangs suspended in limbo as they slowly argue their way through the mess. The landlord claimant who Red has screwed over by losing is, understandably, a little upset.

'He wants to *what*?' Frome thunders.

'Open a dispute against you,' the first arbitrator replies. 'It's his right, if the outcome is in question and one of your knights is the cause.'

'What about the file my knight got slipped?'

'That is a factor,' the first arbitrator says, carefully. 'Certainly a factor. But—'

'But nothing,' Frome thunders. 'That's the whole crux of this mess. Someone, highly likely to be on the tenant's team, got our fighter the details of the dispute. They're the cause of this, not us.'

'Certainly, certainly,' the first arbitrator replies. 'And what is procedure when a knight is confronted with forehand knowledge of a dispute?'

Frome hesitates.

'They either do all they can to learn nothing, or if it is too late for that, they withdraw from the bout and another knight is substituted. I'm not aware of a lack of knights that could have been provided on short notice from Rhyfentown Public stable, are you?'

Frome says nothing.

The arbitrator steeples his fingertips. 'Si Red had the choice. By her own admission, she was not forced to look at the file. She chose to. This all could have ended right there in the monastery, if she had simply not looked.'

'You know we'll contest this,' Frome said, his jaw tight.

'Yes. But I must advise you, as a public institution up against a private citizen, and in circumstances such as these . . . it might be a lot easier, faster and less expensive,' emphasis was placed so very delicately on those last two words, 'if you simply strip your knight of her rank, as has been requested.'

'She'll never work in the Caballaria again, and you know it. For one error, right at the start of her career.'

Silence hangs in the room, stiff and immovable as steel. Red knows what the silence means. In this case, one error is enough. She angered someone they cannot afford to anger. This is not about fairness or justice. It never was. It is about power. Some landlord called Mackeler has more than Frome, more than the arena adjudicators, and more than Rhyfentown Public.

Power always wins.

There comes a commotion outside the door, a rattling, and then it opens.

'In here, Si, but—' comes a voice through the widening gap, tinged with desperation.

'Thank you.'

Across from her, Red watches the two arbitrators' eyes widen at whoever has appeared at her back. There is a new weight, a gravitational pull that sucks everything in the room towards it.

'Si-Si-Si Wyll, what a completely unexpected pleasure,' stutters the first arbitrator. The second, unproven as much of a talker so far, has been rendered mute.

Red turns in her chair.

Standing in the doorway is her benefactor. The man she has craved to be near, to even hear one word from, for months. The Sorcerer Knight is too big to be contained by such a bland and regular arrangement of walls. He is dressed in anonymous leathers, the licoresse shades pronouncing him to be a Blackheart knight, and nothing more telling than that. Once the helmet comes off, however, there is no denying those famous hawkish planes, those liquid eyes rimmed in tell-tale gold.

'I apologise for interrupting,' he says.

His voice is softer than Red remembers. Maybe this is its cadence when it isn't being boomed across an arena.

'No, no, no,' the arbitrator continues to stutter, and then having exhausted the word, has apparently no more to offer.

'I understand there is an issue with the outcome of my investment's bout today.'

It is a casual reminder, played to great effect. Suddenly, the situation is far more serious – it involves the protégée of one of the most influential and powerful figures in the Caballaria.

'Not an issue,' the first arbitrator finds his voice. 'Not so much an issue as—'

'We're being fucked,' Frome cuts in curtly. He has turned round in his chair to face the Sorcerer Knight.

'By the landlord claimant, I presume.'

'You presume correctly. He wants to strip my knight and have her permanently booted from the Caballaria.'

My knight. Not *your* investment. Red begins to feel like a toy being squabbled over.

'An overblown countermove,' the Sorcerer Knight replies. 'He knows that wouldn't pass, not with such a famous new face. He just wants to draw attention.'

'Quite,' Frome says acidly. 'And I'd rather not give it to him, but being a public servant, I don't really have the resources to stop it, do I?'

'No, you don't,' the Sorcerer Knight agrees, either missing the sharp parts of that sentence or choosing to ignore them. 'So let's fuck him over in turn before it gets to that, shall we? We pull Si Red from Rhyfentown Public and start her over in a private Blackheart stable. No more bouts, not until her new trainers deem her ready. Could be years. Could be months. It's up to her, isn't it?'

Frome's eyes slide to Red. She sits stock-still in her chair, trying her hardest not to speak, move, do anything that could derail this.

'A private Blackheart stable,' Frome says slowly. 'You mean, yours? The Royal stable!'

'Of course not,' the Sorcerer Knight replies. 'Another of lesser stature, unaffiliated with the palace.'

For one incredulous second, Red watches her heart's desire dangled in front of her, only to have it snatched away in the next moment. She manages to mollify herself with the thought that any Blackheart stable gets her closer to her goal.

'You're promoting her,' Frome says.

'It's not a promotion, it's a demotion.'

'You're well aware that private Blackheart stables are seen as the cream. What kind of punishment is that? What kind of *message* is that?'

The Sorcerer Knight regards him patiently. 'She re-enters training. She'll be back on probation, which she'd have to be anyway, for a Blackheart stable. There's huge shame attached to this move and you know it. She goes from being a full knight on the circuit back down to a knight-in-training. You were too eager to use her shiny celebrity and you pushed her out there too fast. The blame for that lies with you.'

Frome gives him a look of pure contempt. 'We don't have the luxury of coddling our trainees on the public circuit,' he says. 'We need the bodies.'

'You have plenty of bodies. She was a publicity stunt.'

Frome flushes an ugly shade and says no more.

For the first time since he has arrived, the Sorcerer Knight turns his gaze to Red.

'Well?' he asks. 'Do you accept this punishment, or would you rather fight for your honour?'

Honour means screwing over not only Rhyfentown Public and draining its resources, but also Frome and Si Timor, and potentially jeopardising a dozen other pending bouts because they can no longer provide the knights necessary to see those disputes through.

Honour can go fuck itself.

'I accept the punishment, Si,' Red says.

She knows she doesn't sound meek enough.

The Sorcerer Knight nods. 'Then I will have a short conversation with you outside before I release you back into Si Frome's care.'

In all this time, neither arbitrator has said a word. It is as if their part in the whole thing ceased the moment he stepped into the room.

Red is led outside and down the corridor a little way, her gaze fastened on the leathered back before her. They stop in a nothing alcove next to an unremarkable door. They are far into the bowels of the arena, the adjudicators' domain. Most of the arena team are topside, busy with the next scheduled bout. It is quiet, and they are alone.

It is the first time she has ever been alone with him.

He leans his shoulder against the wall and folds his arms. 'You're turning out to be quite the risk-taker,' he says.

Red, unsure, keeps silent.

'I can see why. It seems to keep working out for you.'

This stings a little too much.

'I didn't expect you to come riding in to rescue me,' Red responds, 'if that's what you mean.'

'Well, how could I not, when I set you up in the first place?'

It takes a moment, but when the realisation comes, it feels like falling.

Red searches the impassive face before her. '*You* got me that dispute file.'

'Faster in the body than the mind, I see,' the Sorcerer Knight murmurs.

'Why? You could have . . . I could have . . . you were testing me. What *for*?'

'I was curious.'

Strangled mute by a sudden surge of helpless fury, Red can only stare at him.

'I wanted to see what path you would take,' the Sorcerer Knight continues. 'Who you would side with, and whether you'd have the courage to see your choice through. I wanted to see what kind of person you are.'

'There are easier ways to get to know people. Like, I don't know, say, *talking*.'

The Sorcerer Knight's head cocks slightly, as if to indicate what an odd notion that is.

'Talking is second nature to humans,' he says. 'We're good at talking. Good at saying one thing, meaning another. Talking hides – but actions don't, especially under duress. Put someone in a situation with hard choices and their actions will speak louder than words ever could. It's a good test.'

'And did I pass?' Red spits.

'If you hadn't, do you think we'd be standing here together right now?'

The word *together* rolls its way through Red's stomach, leaving a hard knot in its wake.

'You wanted me to throw the bout,' she says.

'I wanted you to care about the person with no power.'

'I went against the . . . the godchild.'

'You think we're supposed to feel a kinship with every godchild who exists, as if some automatic bond is made between us the moment we're born?' The Sorcerer Knight snorts. 'Mackeler is a vulture. He also happens to be a godchild. So what?'

'I broke Caballaria law. I did the worst possible thing.'

To Red's astonishment, the Sorcerer Knight laughs.

'Caballaria law,' he says contemptuously. '*The worst possible thing.* Why do they never arm new knights with the dirty truth as well as the shiny weapons? The Caballaria is a circus of hypocrites, political manoeuvrers and power-grubbers. Bouts are thrown all the time. Disputes are decided before they ever get to the arena. Just because the penalties for being found out are a lot harsher nowadays, doesn't mean people have stopped trying to game it.' He pauses. 'The public circuits were created to negate corruption and strengthen equality. It's supposed to be a place where those with no power can be heard as loudly as those with too much.' His voice dries. 'It was a nice idea, but you may have noticed that we're not quite there yet.'

'What about honour?' Red ventures.

'People like Frome still want to believe in a world where honour can not only exist but actually guide collective hearts, but I'll tell you this – throughout all of humanity's history, all those times where progress has been made, it only happened because the ones fighting for it made choices every bit as cold-blooded and underhanded as the people on the other side.' The

Sorcerer Knight gives Red a bland smile. 'Fairness is never achieved by playing fair.'

'Mackeler will still open a dispute with Rhyfentown Public,' Red says. 'He'll get his revenge.'

'No, he won't. You think Blackheart will allow it? The public circuit was a creation dreamed up between Si Garad Gaheris and the King himself, and they made a lot of people very unhappy in its forging. They had to fight hard for it, and for many years. Neither of them are about to let some little *landowner* screw it up.'

Landowner seems to hold a similar meaning for the Sorcerer Knight as *cockroach*.

'So,' he continues, 'you'll take your punishment and train hard at your new stable. Then we'll see how we can next move you.'

'Will you be training me?' Red asks.

'Me? No.'

'Why not?'

The Sorcerer Knight stares at her, apparently struck dumb by the suggestion.

There is no use in holding back. It is the only card she has, and there will never be a better time to play it. Red takes a breath and jumps.

'Si, there's something you should know,' she says.

He waits.

'I threw the bout because of Mackeler, but there was another reason, too.'

He waits some more.

'I . . . I nearly lost control,' she says. 'In the arena.'

Of my magic, she wants to say, but she doesn't need to. He understands at once.

'What was the kick?' he asks.

Red hesitates. 'I'm not sure.'

'There would have been an emotional kick that made the magic come out. You should know this. What was it?'

When I realised you weren't there and all my plans went swirling down the drain.

'I just couldn't face winning for him, with everyone watching me,' Red says. 'And my palms began to itch and get hot. It took everything I had to hold it inside. I was scared the bracelet monitor might explode, so I threw the bout too early. It was fine in training – the magic. It never came out. But in the arena . . .' She doesn't have to fake the shame on her face. 'I've no parents. I've never known any other godchildren. There's never been anyone who could explain it to me. Teach me how to control it.'

She hates the desperation she can hear in her own voice, but there is no other way. The lack of control over her magic is not a lie – between the nightmares and that con-artist soothsayer, there have been enough close calls recently – but it is an excuse. She needs to get closer to the Sorcerer Knight by any means necessary. She needs to get him alone.

'I can find you someone who can teach you how to control it,' he says.

Red steels herself. 'I want you to do it.'

She waits for the why, assembling reasons he might go for, so what he says next takes the wind right out of her.

'All right. But I'm touring for a couple of weeks. It'll have to be when I get back.' In someone else, someone less powerful, his pause might almost feel shy. 'Is that all right?'

Red tries to hide her shocked triumph. 'Yes. Yes, of course.'

The Sorcerer Knight regards her for a moment more. Then he nods, pushes off the wall and turns back to the room where a presumably highly irritated Frome still waits for them both.

Red follows in a daze. Just a moment ago, her entire life was in the hands of a landlord who, in comparison to this knight, is barely a gnat in the sprawling spiderweb of power.

She was afraid of a boulder. Now she is in the shadow of a mountain range, and it is getting dark as hell.

CHAPTER 23

Fickledunn, Alaunitown
Eighteen Years Ago

He is not supposed to be here tonight.

The house guards make that clear – at first. When they realise who he is they step back, shock on their faces. The front door of Fickledunn, the Lord of Alaunitown's private estate, is not on their mental list of 'places where the King of London could reasonably be right now'.

'Sire,' flusters the head footman, a tall pole of a man with a proud, eagle-beak nose. 'My King. Unexpected. Pleasure.'

He bows deep. Art, ten months into his reign, is still learning how to keep hidden his embarrassed squiggling at the automatic deference. He manages a nod.

'I do apologise for turning up like this,' he says. 'It was a last-minute decision. Urgent business. One day we'll have some sort of glow-screen communication tech that will make this in-person necessity a thing of the past, neh?'

'Neh,' the head footman repeats, and then adds, 'I mean, yes, Sire. Yes, my King. I mean, you've come to the right place if that's what you want to discuss, standing as we are in the heart of tech city. I mean, Alaunitown will provide.'

'Is Lord Welyen available?' Art gently nudges.

'My Lord is entertaining another guest,' the head footman says. 'But I will send word that you are here at once.'

Art and two of his personal guard are ushered inside while the rest of his retinue wait within visual of the house, astraddle their bikes, silent, and watchful. His guard are temporarily divested of their weapons, as private-residence law dictates.

The head footman has disappeared into the quiet, lofty depths of the house beyond. The King is deposited in a tasteful receiving room and furnished with a splendour of refreshments, none of which he touches. His guards stand behind him, hugging the walls and monitoring the doors.

A short while later another servant appears and obsequiously beckons him upstairs.

Art ascends the sweeping staircase, one guard in front and one behind. An array of past Welyens frown down at the small retinue from their projections, painting the walls with hard-edged luminescence. He is led along a dark-panelled corridor, boot heels emitting clunks against the concrete floor.

They pause at a vaulted doorway. The servant knocks, waits for a muffled tone of encouragement from beyond the door and then bows deeply as it opens, inviting Art inside.

He leaves his guards stationed in the hallway and ventures inwards, prepared to see another sitting room of some kind, lit by warm lamps set to demure evening levels. He is not at all prepared to walk into a starkly lit room dominated by an enormous bed, upon which two naked figures are contorting. One is a man with a shape like a pale, wet rat. The other is the unmistakable figure of Dario Go.

Art stops dead.

They rut a few moments more. Art is compelled to watch,

paralysed with agonising indecision, until Dario turns their head towards him as if his entrance has only just caught their notice.

'My Lord,' they pant.

Agravain stops his grunting and follows their gaze, twisting round in his awkward position.

'I'm so sorry,' Art blurts. 'Your servant . . . he told me to come straight in.'

'Oh, don't worry,' Agravain says. 'I'm almost finished.'

His rounded body jerks under the bedclothes and Dario gives an unkempt gasp.

'I'll wait in the—' Art reverses course. 'I'll wait outside.'

'Suit yourself,' he hears Agravain say as he closes the door on them and waits in the hallway, horrified shame flaring across his face and down every limb.

He looks for something to kick, then clamps down on the impulse. The cursed servant has disappeared, but his own guards are there, wary eyes on him.

A performance. A deliberate power play. *Look who I can fuck.*

Art shudders, despising himself for his own reaction, and gropes blindly for composure while flashes of what he has just seen run unheedingly through his brain.

It is only a minute or two more before the door opens again. Standing in its frame is Dario, their hair dishevelled from its usual styled slickness, a thin robe now dripping off their angular frame. Other than the hair and the merest tinge of flush on their cheeks, they are entirely composed.

'Sire,' they say formally. 'Won't you come inside?'

Art tries to catch their gaze, tries, unsuccessfully, to ascertain whether they are all right, or upset, or . . . But nothing shows at all.

'You forgot your things,' Agravain calls from the inside the room. He has, mercifully, put on a pair of stiff breeches and a pale yellow shirt, left flapping open to display his belly. He indicates an elegant bag on the dressing table and a familiar long indigo coat draped across the back of a chair.

'I'll come back for them after my bath,' Dario says.

Agravain snorts. 'You haven't changed, I see.' With queasily manufactured intimacy, he looks sidelong at Art. 'They always love taking an after-bath here – don't ask me to explain it.'

'It's no great mystery,' Dario says mildly. 'Your bath is set pleasingly deep; it's like being in a little swimming pool.' Their gaze flickers briefly across Art's face and their head bows low. 'If my King consents to release me.'

'By all means,' Art manages to say.

They glide out of the room, muttering something under their breath as they pass him. The door shuts behind them.

In the ensuing silence, Art turns to face the man who wants him dead.

Agravain's mouth has a sour little pucker to it. Evidently he found Dario's parting deference to Art a little bitter for his taste. He rallies tolerably, however, perhaps too pleased to dwell long in the mire. After all, he currently has the upper hand.

'So,' he says. 'This is a surprise, Sire.'

'No doubt,' Art stiffly replies.

'Can I offer you refreshment? You have a taste for Pollidori, do you not? I have a particularly excellent and rather rare vintage in my cellar.'

'You do? Well, how can I refuse that?' Art says, with no intention of touching a drop.

Agravain rings for a servant to take the order and then indicates one of two plush chairs set around a low table, its glass surface spun as thin as a spiderweb in the latest, typically innovative 'launitown style.

'Actually I'll take this one, if you don't mind,' Art says, moving to the nearest chair.

Agravain takes the other set against the back wall, slumping into it and extending his bare feet across the rug. 'Not at all – you've given me the seat I prefer: no air behind it and a clear view across the room.'

'The classic position of strength,' Art remarks. 'Still, the view is mostly of your dressing table.'

Agravain shrugs. 'It's a nice dressing table. I take it your urgent business couldn't wait until the next Consilium meet?'

No mention is made of the scene with Dario just a moment ago, as if to reinforce the point that the only person it was embarrassing for was Art. Agravain appears to be cocksure comfortable about being alone with the object of his two day-old assassination attempt.

He is not even remotely afraid of you.

'No,' says Art. 'It couldn't wait. I want to talk with you.' He hesitates. 'In an environment where we might be free to say whatever we like.'

Agravain smirks. 'Our boy King wants to be controversial, does he? Well, he can here, with my utmost assurances. My house is private and secure and my servants are the most loyal to be found, because they know what happens if they're not. The only way to ensure loyalty, in this sad day and age. Not like the palace, eh? More leaks than a rusting bath tub.'

'Agravain,' Art says, and the use of his familiar name begets a gratifying startle. 'I must know: what is it about me that you hate so much?'

'Hate?' Agravain affects a kindly chuckle. 'Whatever makes you think I hate you?'

Every word that comes out of his mouth sounds greased.

'Many people expected you to win the Sword – and then Borin betrayed you . . .'

'Oh, please,' Agravain says dismissively. 'That's all in the past.'

Art thinks of the death threat Agravain signalled at him across the arena. He thinks of the hundred different ways the man before him has undermined, counteracted or downright mutinied against him in every Consilium meet. He allows himself a toe dip into the freezing cold water of Belisan.

All in the past.

He screws his anger tightly inwards.

'Still,' he says, hoping he sounds a little anxious, a little hesitant. 'I'm getting the impression that you might be holding a grudge.'

Agravain tuts, growing more comfortable the more that Art appears not to be. 'If I were to hold a grudge against anyone, it'd be your father.'

'My father? Why?'

'Leaving his mess to come back and bite us all on the flanks? I'd have dealt with the matter a little more cleanly.'

'Meaning you'd have had me throttled in my crib?' Art says it as light as a joke.

Agravain smiles. 'Not at all; I'd have had done it while you were still in the womb. Oh now, don't look so worried. All in the past, like I said. As is Uther himself.'

'I'm glad to hear you say that,' Art says. 'Relieved, really. What I want more than anything is to come to a peace with you, for the good of London. Infighting only weakens our collective power. With Alaunitown and Blackheart aligned, I think together we could make extraordinary changes—'

'You know what we need?' Agravain interrupts, as if Art hadn't spoken at all. 'A war. Haven't had one in decades. Does *wonders* for the economy. Jump-starts its flagging heart. If you think of a country like a man, with a man's biological system, a resting heartbeat doesn't get much done, does it? It's good for maintaining a plodding equilibrium, keeps everything ticking along, but it doesn't push a man to greater heights, does it? No, a racing pulse does that. An injection of new energy. Fight or flight. Gets the blood going, a war. Peacetime makes babies of the general population. It has everyone far too used to handouts and coddling. Detrimental, in the long run. We're not teaching them to stand on their own two feet, see? They'll suck on the teat their whole lives and milk us all dry.'

Art waits a moment, digesting everything he just heard.

'You're . . . serious,' he says.

Agravain shrugs. 'It's not a publicly popular opinion, to be sure, but you study your history and you'll see the sense it makes.' His brows rise at Art's expression. 'Oh, come on. You're acting like war is the absolute worst possible thing that could happen. You're not really as naïve as you appear to be, are you? You should really take a positive attitude towards adversity. Find the opportunities within.'

'What opportunities are there in lots of dead Londoners?' Art asks, unable to keep the astonishment from his voice.

'To the funeral business, an extraordinary amount. It's all about perspective.'

'You're not in the funeral business.'

Agravain crosses his feet at the ankles. 'No, but I am in the weapons business, and it's bad for business when no one wants to fight.'

'The Welyens are in tech,' Art says.

'You think *tech* is where the trick is?' Agravain laughs. 'Dear saints.' He gives Art an appraising look. 'Come, come, Sire. You were the one who wanted to talk freely. Say whatever we like. Well, I think I've just proved this a safe space, have I not? So let's *really* talk.'

Art says nothing.

An undaunted Agravain continues, 'Let me tell you what goes on in every single elite's head in London, no matter what protests and philanthropy they do for the show of it. They're rolling along safe inside their quads, they're going through a downs area, they look out at the dirty world sliding past their tinted windows, they see all those oblivious little pigs swilling around outside, rootling in the rubble, and they feel . . . repulsion.' He shrugs.

Art clears his throat. 'You think poverty is like being a pig?'

Agravain spreads his hands. 'Listen, I'm not saying it's their fault. I'm just saying what everybody thinks and doesn't have the guts to say out loud. I'm tired of people squawking any time anyone speaks a little truth. This is a free world: freedom should mean being able to say whatever you like.' He reflects. 'It did used to, once. It's about time we made our way back to those days. But really, what all these equality fetishists don't like to confront is the fact that the world is structured around an innate hierarchy. There was, is and always has been an order to things. It's built into the very fabric of reality. And this current order just happens to have you and me at the top. Now, there's nothing bad nor good about that. It just is. But mess with the order, and—' He smacks his fist into his palm. 'Chaos. Death. Misery.

History has taught us this time and time again. It just baffles me how we never learn from the past.'

'I was taught,' says Art, 'that everyone deserves the chance to be healthier, cleverer, better off. It shouldn't be about who you're born as. That's not fair.'

'*Life* is not fair. Anyone who believes differently has no business trying to survive.' Agravain seems to realise how fierce his tone has become and relaxes. 'Listen, cubling, I'm a lot older than you. I've seen much more of the world than you have. I've been listening to your heartfelt little Consilium speeches – I have. And I admire your idealism, I do. Used to have some of that myself, once upon a time. But then I grew out of it. I stopped being a child and became a man. It's really past time for you to do the same. I'm telling you, London will suffer under a soft-hearted King.' He shakes his head. 'It always does.'

Art swallows. 'What if I disagree with that viewpoint?'

Agravain gives an expansive shrug. 'London is good at making new Kings.'

An awful, ugly worm of fear wraps itself around Art's heart and gives it a sickly squeeze.

'Generally speaking,' he forces himself to say, 'the old King has to die first.'

He won't possibly admit to it, will he?

'We're good at killing Kings too.' Agravain smiles. 'Uther being a case in point.'

That is the second time he has steered the conversation to Art's father. Clearly he has something on his mind that he wants to share.

'The King-in-the-Ground died of heart problems,' Art ventures.

Agravain grins. 'Yes, of course. And poor Borin the Bloodless, as well. Did you hear about that? A real shock. It makes you think, doesn't it? If two such strong bulls can have such weak hearts – well. Any one of us could go at any time.'

Art feels like he might be going now.

'Anyway,' continues Agravain, 'as much as I mourn Uther's untimely end, I have to confess that I'm a little relieved, for Orcade's sake.' He tuts. 'Not a happy marriage, I'm sorry to say.'

'No?'

'He was a violent man. Men like that usually are, don't you find? Every time she came to me with bruises and broken bones, I wanted to snap his neck. No one touches my fucken sister like that.' An ugly expression passes across Agravain's face. He means it. 'But she always talked me out of it,' he continues. 'She suffers a lot for others, Orcade. Always has.'

Art tries his best to sound hypothetical. 'Would you really kill someone just because of Orcade?'

'You say it like it's such a strange notion. I forgot, you don't have a sister, do you? You wouldn't understand that kind of bond. It's very special.' Agravain has a peculiarly adoring expression on his face.

Art represses a twitch of disgust.

'Are you implying that you murdered the King of London for your sister?' he tries again.

Agravain lets loose an uproarious laugh. 'Naughty boy, trying to have me say something so treasonous.'

Art hears Brune in his mind's ear, her lessons to him on diplomacy.

There is always, always common ground to be found, even with those you despise.

Think of what you dislike about yourself. It could be what they hold most dear.

'You think I'd be upset with you?' he blurts. 'Marvol knows I'd thank you for it. If it were true, of course.'

Agravain just looks at him.

Art swallows. 'Well. Perhaps that was too rash. I wouldn't want such an opinion repeated.'

An impish smile curls Agravain's thick lips. 'You have nothing to worry about. I had this room well soundproofed a long time ago. Some of the things I like to do in here – well, it became a necessity, really.' He winks. 'You know what I mean.'

Has Orcade ever been trapped in this soundproofed room with him? Don't think about that. Don't, *don't*.

'I've never hated a man so much as my father,' Art says. 'I'm glad he's dead.' He tips his head back. 'Saints, that feels good to get off my chest.'

Agravain gives a beneficent chuckle. 'Glad to be of service. I can't imagine having to grow up under the shadow of such a scandal. Tough. Very tough. Yet here you are.'

'Here I am,' Art agrees. 'Somehow.'

'Don't sell yourself short. You could be a great King, Dracones. You just need to learn a little ruthlessness, that's all. You can't think of people as people. You have to think of London as one organism. If a man's diseased kidney starts to fail, it gets cut out, right?' Agravain spreads his hands. 'Everyone dies. This is the inevitable point. You might get to decide how and when many of them will, but they die regardless, right? And maybe some of those deaths are the kidney.' Agravain stares off into the distance. 'That's what it takes. The necessary sacrifice for the survival of the body. Sometimes we must be ruthless in service to the greater good.' He glances sidelong at Art. 'You look surprised.'

'I just . . .' Art pauses. 'The greater good. It's my focus too, of course. Well, it's more than a focus. I'm not religious, but if we had a god of the greater good, it'd be the only deity I'd ever bend the knee to.'

Agravain chuckles. 'Well said.'

Art contemplates the older man. 'I'm really glad you're being this honest with me,' he says at last. 'I like honesty. I hold it in the highest esteem.'

Agravain inclines his head. 'As do I, Sire. As do I. Perhaps we are more alike than you think.'

A knock on the door interrupts them. A servant enters, carrying a crystalline bottle of amber liquid and two thick glasses.

Agravain turns to Art and winks. 'Gentlemen make deals over drinks. Now let's go back to your mention of Blackheart and Alaunitown working together. To the greater good, eh?'

'To the greater good,' Art echoes as they clink glasses.

CHAPTER 24

The Thorn, Blackheart
Eighteen Years Ago

The Thorn is a beautiful, imposing marbled room that echoes with long-tempered violence.

Its seats are gracefully carved, but their backs end in the tapered, jagged spikework common to Blackheart architecture. The candelabra fixed in long rows down the length of the ceiling were made of human bone, until they were quietly replaced by copies in silver and iron. Many of the wall stones famously date back to antiquity, when the chiefs of warring tribes would meet to settle their differences with words or blood.

It's not so different now, Art thinks. *We still go for the blood, but we do it with the drapery of civilised debate.*

The throne of the Sword-in-Parlement – Art's throne – presides on a raised dais above the rest of the room's seating. The throne curls forwards towards the throng below like a bird of prey.

Immediately before the King, arranged around a round oak table, are the Saints-on-Earth, the seven district leaders of London. Behind each of the Saints-on-Earth sit their coterie of vastos and representatives from every major industry, culture and religion, spreading out from the round table like spokes on a wheel, poetically echoing London's layout.

Orcade is in her usual position near the front of the Alaunitown coterie. She has chosen a tight blue outfit today and looks darkly magnificent among the drab plumage in her section.

Her brother lounges in his place at the round table, dressed head to toe in Alaunitown pale yellow with charcoal accents. He talks and laughs with a dignitary just behind him – his uncle, current head of the Welyens' biggest manufacturing company. As the Consilium is called to order, Agravain turns in his seat and gives an open nod to Art, the first time he has ever shown the slightest deference to the King since the start of his reign. Art fancies he can see people's surprised reactions at the sudden reconciliation.

Facing the throne from across the room is the Maeder, a traditionally non-partisan adjudicator, there to keep order and ensure that all voices are heard in equal capacity. More often than not, however, the Consilium descends into mild chaos, reminding Art of a clutch of squabbling hens with their claws firmly around their own eggs.

The current Maeder's voice has a soothingly soporific quality that has unfortunately more than once lulled a number of attendants into unwitting repose. It is, however, the beginning of the session, and therefore most people are awake when the walls of the chamber begin to echo with faint shouts. The noise cuts through the Maeder's long-winded rumblings and he halts in confusion.

The Thorn's doors are always locked by the Master of the Key once a session begins, and guarded from the outside. Once the doors are closed and the meet begins, no one from the outside is granted access, not even those who should already be inside.

The shouts grow louder. The doors give a great shudder, as if from a sudden blow.

A frightened voice speaks into the ensuing quiet. 'Impossible,' the Lord of Evrontown says. 'No one can even get near this *building*, it's *impossible*—'

This room has seen its fair share of bloodshed, even in recent times. Consilium meets are the perfect opportunity for a coup, seeing as how the entire Saith is there for the killing, which is why the building is normally extremely well guarded—

The doors slam open.

The Master of the Key stumbles through, rights himself and stares at the Consilium. 'I'm so sorry for interrupting,' he babbles. 'I couldn't stop them.'

'Stop *who*, Edward?' the Maeder roars.

In answer, knights begin to flood through the door past the luckless Edward and flow into the room. They have the sword emblem on their shoulders and guns at their hips.

Blackheart knights.

Royal knights.

Some break off to line the doors, preventing anyone from leaving. Some line the back wall behind their King. Three peel away towards the opposite end of the round table.

Art waits for the panicked noises to die down.

'My apologies, everyone,' he says. 'I didn't mean to startle you.'

'Sire, what is the meaning of this?' the Maeder says. 'We do not have begunned knights in the Thorn's inner chamber! Ever!'

Art nods. 'There is one exception to that rule.' He steadies himself. 'Agravain Welyen, Lord of Alaunitown. You are under arrest for high treason.'

Mouths fall open.

Silence.

Then:

'Is this a joke?'

Agravain has a puzzled smile on his face. He half-rises out of his seat, but the three knights standing next to him touch the heels of their hands to the tops of their guns – a warning, a readiness – and he sinks back down.

Art takes a moment. His voice must carry. His voice must be his authority.

'No,' he says. 'It is not. We have evidence that you assassinated my father, Uther Dracones.' He calls over echoing shouts, 'And that you tried to do the same to me.'

The Maeder screams for order, but he does not get it for some time. Art's knights stand impassively, watching for signs of trouble.

Agravain bellows panicked laughter. 'You are in*sane*. How can you possibly have conjured up such drama out of nothing?'

'I captured you,' says Art simply. 'I have the footage.'

The older man blinks. 'What? When?'

'At your house. Our "frank discussion".'

He snorts. 'Impossible.'

The Maeder is fixed on Art. 'Illegal. No one may use a capture made on private property for any kind of public viewing.'

Art holds up a hand. 'I know, and I will take sanction for breaking the law on that, but I hope it will be considered against Lord Welyen's far greater crimes.'

Agravain turns in his seat, searching. His gaze lights on his sister, as if for help, but Orcade's eyes are lowered to the ground in front of her. She looks rigid with shock.

'You . . .' Agravain flounders for the right adjective. 'There's no possible . . . I said nothing, *nothing*, to prove—'

'I'm sorry, I definitely took it as confession. But if you think that's the only evidence I have against you, you're a fool.' Art pauses. 'I also notice that you haven't yet refuted the charge of trying to kill me.'

'Because it's insane; you've lost your mind!'

'The girl, Agravain. The girl you picked out for me, in collusion with Laerd Dario of the Night Carnival. Haven't you been wondering where she's disappeared to?'

Agravain stares at him.

All now turns on this. For one moment, Art thinks it isn't enough. That he might not break.

Then he does.

He turns to the rest of the round table, facing their open mouths, their foreboding silence.

'I have evidence,' he says wildly, 'unequivocal evidence that our King has been consorting with a godchild! Dear saints, don't you all remember the last time a King did that – his own *father*, with Edler? The product of which is sitting right in front of me now? That alone should be enough to cost him the Sword, saintsdamn it. He's been bedding a godchild spy!'

For one horrifying moment, Art sees himself pulling a gun from the guard knight standing next to him and shooting the awful bastard in the forehead. For one moment, he even fancies he can see the first trickle of blood running down that pale, baby smooth skin.

Stop, he tells himself.

'I had no idea she was a godchild,' he tells the room. 'Do you think I would have allowed such a person into my bed, a person with the express intention of killing me?'

Agravain's face is twisted tight. 'You . . . this is all a ridiculous lie!'

'No, it's an operation. Cut out the diseased kidney.' Art pauses. 'Thank you for the lesson.'

That one strikes home.

'Now I can only assume,' Art continues, 'you thought that telling me you murdered my father in the same way that you did your ex-champion would scare me enough to become your biddable little puppet, perhaps. But you didn't scare me, Welyen. What you did was make me angry.'

Agravain looks around wildly. 'You can't be serious, I didn't have anything to *do*—'

Art cuts him off. 'I'm currently within my rights to invoke moldra lagha for my father's death. An attempt on your life for the one you took.' He stares Agravain down. 'Tell me, do you think the saints will favour my champion to win against yours a second time?'

Agravain flushes. 'How dare you, you spineless kambion-fucker!'

The room echoes with hisses at the shocking godchild slur.

Art resists the viciously happy smile he can feel threatening to break across his face.

'Get him out of here,' he tells his knights. 'Just . . . get him out of here, please.'

Agravain is manhandled out of his seat and marched across the floor in silence. His face is a naked picture of disbelief at what has been done to him by a soft-hearted child King. He twists his head round as he is moved, trying with everything he has to catch his sister's eye.

'Orcade,' he pleads finally. 'Did you know about this? What are you doing? Why don't you say something?'

She has not once looked up. She will not look up. She hunches in her seat, small and frightened.

Agravain recovers his panic at the door and begins to shout. 'He's destroying our industries! He wants to ban every Londoner from carrying guns – except his own guard, of course! He'll take away your personal freedoms one by one! He's a *unificationist*! He'll rip down the district borders! It'll be war!'

Funny, Art thinks, *I thought that was what you wanted.*

'Congratulations, Sire,' says Orcade.

Art tilts his head in acknowledgement.

It is long into the evening as they sit together in his private salon. The hours since the Consilium meet this morning have proved rather interesting, and Art is beginning to feel the pull of exhaustion, the crash after the victory high.

'I'm impressed.' Orcade takes a steadying sip from her wine glass. Her hand shakes, just a little. Residual nerves. 'Particularly on all the evidence you have against him. I did suspect him of . . . of Uther, but I was never able to come up with anything definitive.'

Art says nothing. The trouble is, all the evidence they have against Agravain amounts to nothing more than a vaguely veiled confession over drinks in his bedroom.

The recording itself was cleverly done. Dario's bag – just large enough to conceal the Welyens' own prototype mini-capturer – was deliberately left in the room. Dario's whispered instructions to Art as they passed ensured Agravain took the chair facing the dressing table, the better to get him in full, uninhibited view of the hidden capturer's eye.

But the capture is all they have. So far, no substantial evidence has been found to tie Agravain to either Uther or Borin's death. Poisoners can conjecture what he might have used to induce a heart attack in both men (and they have, enthusiastically and at length) but that is all they can do. Post-death examinations turned up nothing concrete.

And Belisan? Dario admits to being employed to foist her on Art, but claims total ignorance of assassination plans, and they gave up Agravain quickly enough. Still, threats of prison can make anyone eager. None of it amounts to much at all.

Orcade should know the truth.

Art exhales. 'Apart from the capture I have, there's no evidence.'

She looks startled. 'What?'

'I had to play my hand fast. There's nothing else – so far. That's the reason it will be exile for your brother instead of Caballaria death.'

He watches this sink in.

'Sire, you bluff magnificently,' she says. Is that *admiration* on her face?

'I'm learning,' Art replies, feeling more than a little grim about it.

He watches her roll the stubby stem of her wine glass in her fingers, her face pensive.

'Exile is less of a scandal for your family,' he says gently.

She shakes her head. 'This might ruin us for some time, either way. He has a lot of enemies. We. *We* do. They've been waiting for a chance like this.'

'I'm sorry.'

She drags in a deep breath. 'This is the game, Sire. Never apologise for winning it.' The look she gives him is steadier. 'And at least now I'll be free of him.'

Art fancies he can almost see the weight lifting from her shoulders. There is a new lightness to her form, perhaps absent since childhood.

'Thank you for your trust,' she says quietly. 'It means a lot to me.'

Art shrugs. 'Without trust, the world goes to shit.'

'I was never taught that. I'd like to believe it.' She gives him an encouraging smile. 'You really are nothing like your father.'

'I feel a little more like him today,' Art says.

'Compassion can be a weakness, Sire. My brother killed your father, my husband, and tried to kill you. I'd say you were a little too kind to him.'

Perhaps time would tell on that one.

'He demonstrated an extraordinary amount of affection for you in our private talk,' Art carefully suggests.

Orcade's mouth thins.

'I had a horse as a child,' she says. 'Strada, I called him. I loved him more than anything. One day he tossed me – not on purpose; he was spooked by a squirrel or some such thing – and I broke my arm in the fall. Once I'd recovered, the first thing I did was go to see him, but he wasn't in his stall. It was the head groomsman who told me that Agravain had had him shot.' She sounds distant. 'That's what my brother's affection is like.'

Art feels his residual guilt drain away.

'How does it feel to be the new Lady of 'launitown?' he asks.

Orcade thinks for a moment. Then she gives him a small, uncertain smile. 'Terrifying,' she says. 'And wonderful.'

Art raises his glass. 'Isn't it? To the terror and the wonder.'

Their wine glasses ring with the toast.

CHAPTER 25

Unknown Location
Four Months Ago

By the time the helmet comes off, Red has had enough.

It was already late and the day far over when she got the message to prepare herself for an unscheduled pick-up in two hours' time. When the quad arrived to fetch her, Red was already outside the building waiting for it, rolling impatiently from foot to foot in misty rain.

The outside of the quad was just battered and unpolished enough to look used and averagely maintained. She clambered into the back seat, the door auto-locking behind her, and only then did she realise that she couldn't see outside. Not even a whisper of street light got through this quad's windows. The front half was entirely separated from the back by a solid divide, so Red had no idea what the driver even looked like. When they spoke, their voice came floating out of a glow screen's speaker grid fixed to the divide, low and amicable and unfailingly polite.

Red asked for their name.

'Evil Bastard was my fighting name back when I was in Wardogs, Si,' the driver responded, 'but most people call me Ford, if you prefer.'

Red, not entirely sure which she preferred, lapsed into a nervous silence.

Her request for the window screens to be cleared so she could at least see where they were going was met with Ford's regretful and polite refusal. There were frequent stops – presumably for traffic – and leisurely rolling in-between times, the quad eating up the road with the quietest of purrs, and no tell-tale sounds to tell her what kind of area they might be riding through.

When the quad finally came to a stop, Ford cheerfully informed Red that the helmet on the seat opposite should now be placed on her head. The helmet had its own smoked screen that began at her forehead and came all the way down to her chin. She wasn't able to see a thing through it. When she refused, Ford just as cheerfully informed her that she wouldn't be going anywhere until she did.

Red put on the helmet.

Now, in the muffled darkness that her world has shrunk to, she hears the far-off whine of an opening door, and then a hand wrapping around her upper arm with a vice-like grip, pulling her slowly but firmly out of the quad. She hears Ford warn her that she is about to be searched. She stands stiff until it is complete.

Apparently satisfied, the vice grip on her arm pulls away and she is led across unsteady ground, walking on dirt and weed, that much her feet can tell her, but it is the only – entirely uselessly generic – clue she is able to pick up, as the rest of her concentration goes on not falling over.

She has never been blinded before. She feels weak, wobbly as a day-old calf. The hand on her arm tightens and relaxes as it guides her. They pass into a building – that much she senses, as the night breeze she hadn't realised was there is cut off and the sound of footsteps comes back to her instead of being carried away.

Not one word has yet been said.

'Fuck this,' she mutters at last and stops abruptly, pulling away from the hand on her and tugging off the helmet, half-expecting to be tackled to the ground before she can get her eyes uncovered.

Echoing space surrounds her on all sides. She is standing inside a vast, strange edifice. Walkways and gantries loom far above her head, bulging out around hulking machinery, whose massive drum shapes are rendered strange and ghostly in the half lighting that suffuses the guts of the building.

'I take it you didn't get on with Ford,' says a voice.

Red turns to find the Sorcerer Knight standing close beside her. It had been his hand on Red's arm outside the quad, his hand guiding Red into the building.

She swallows, feeling suddenly lost and small.

'What is this place?' she asks.

The knight arches a brow. 'Not even a "good evening, Si" for me?'

'You don't seem to be the kind who enjoys the politeness dance.'

The faintest smile threatens the knight's mouth. He shifts, leaning against an ornate octagonal pillar that rears up to the high ceiling above.

'It's an old Liessan-era power station,' he says. 'Out of action now, as the world moves on. The tech is clunky, but they still use it as an emergency back-up. It got used several times during the last inter-dis' war, decades ago. Pulse bombings took out the main power stations in this whole area, but this tech is too old to be affected by them. Sometimes old is useful.'

What area? Red wants to ask, but stops herself. No one goes to the trouble of sending a quad pick-up with smoked windows and a blinding helmet if they want her to know where she is.

She looks around again. The emptiness is beginning to take on structure: tall, fluted pillars support soaring archways, each decorated with intricate symbols and patterns carved in bas-relief. Everywhere is curve and grace.

'It's . . . pretty,' she says.

'You should see it in daylight. The brickwork has starburst patterns and the ceilings underneath each archway are covered in stone latticework. It's extraordinary.'

Red dares to turn and fully contemplate her enigmatic sponsor.

The knight is dressed in soft, tight clothes made for ease of movement. In deference to the mild chill in the air, his wrap coat looks fur-lined. The drape-hood clinging to his head only adds to the sense of fluid menace he is well known for exuding. He has a timeless, weighty presence that belies his twenty-three years, although without his arena costuming, his youth shines through a little more.

'Why all the secrecy?' Red asks.

'I like privacy.' He shoots her a look.

'I'm not going to tell anyone about this place,' she protests.

I couldn't even if I wanted to. I've no idea where the merry fuck I am.

'No,' he agrees, 'because if you do, you're never coming here again. What happens here today could get us both landed in prison, as if you need the reminder. Don't speak of this to anyone. Ever.'

She fixes him with what she hopes is a righteously injured glare. 'I won't.'

He nods, pushes off the pillar and wanders off into the gloom.

'What do you think of your new stable?' His voice drifts back to her.

Red has been living in Spittelgrounds, the Blackheart stable she now calls home, for two weeks. Its speciality is providing fighter knights for the private Caballaria circuits and guard knights as protectors for hire. Its main building is an intimidatingly lovely manor house nestled into a rich, quiet outer borough of the district. It has a salt-water pool, a colossal armoury, scores of training rooms replete with every practice weapon known to humankind, and two enormous outdoor gun ranges for the guard knights. It is an oppressively serene oasis in the heart of London.

Spittelgrounds does not house many trainees, as a rule – Red is one of only three, and the other two follow their own schedules, largely ignoring her. The rest of the knights attached to the stable visit every so often. They all look seasoned, impressive, sure of themselves. She is by far the youngest – even the other trainees are several years older than her.

She has begun to recognise the subtle shift in body language when someone realises who she is. They all know, from the trainers to the kitchen staff, but Spittelgrounds is the kind of place that considers fame and celebrity a rather trashy aspect of society – even as it takes full advantage – and so everyone there is exceptionally good at making no reference to it whatsoever, or at least not around her.

Training at Spittelgrounds is vastly different from the Dungeons. Red had thought the whole point of this new phase would be to realign herself properly with the rules of the Caballaria, since it was flouting those rules that landed her in trouble in the first place, but her new trainers place less emphasis on honour and more emphasis on show.

They work to finesse her signature move, to show her how to use certain angles of her body to best advantage. They refine her footwork and breathing, and while they do it they often enjoy making jokes about the 'rough-hewn' nature of public circuit training. She is a badly moulded lump of clay and they wish to make a rippling statue out of her, one worthy of the honour of belonging to a Blackheart stable.

They coach her in interview technique, how to give almost enough and not too much away. They teach her to speak less than she thinks she should. To arch a brow just so instead of answering. To steer her default 'fuck you' expression into one that is more 'I'm simply far too enigmatic to answer that'.

She is getting bored of the polishing. She is beginning to itch. She wants to get dirty, to feel grime and sweat and passion surging in her blood.

She wants to *fight*.

'Um,' Red says. 'It's going well.'

'Well,' the knight flatly echoes.

This man is the key to everything you want.

Be. More. Grateful.

'It's an amazing place,' Red quickly adds. 'I'm indebted to you for the opportunity you've given me.'

The knight snorts. 'You're a terrible liar. Presumably, they're teaching you how to be a better one.'

Red tries not to grind her teeth. 'They seem to prioritise that over teaching me how to fight.'

'Well, they assume you already know how to fight. Their goal is to teach you how to be a Caballaria knight.'

She has followed him to an area further in, this one cleared of hulking shapes and surrounded by a tall array of strips and bulbs that light up a large, bare square of sanded concrete. Off to one side sits a long weapons rig, a jutting skyline of handles and blades.

'Places like Spittelgrounds offer glamour,' says the Sorcerer Knight, 'but the glamour is like the lies they teach you to tell. It can rub off.' He pauses. 'Just be careful that your background doesn't make you focus on it too much.'

He switches his disconcerting focus back to Red. 'You have the privilege of being able to shape your life around meaning as well as comfort. We're all in the dirt in the end, neh? All you've got is a bit of time to make yourself unequal before the great equaliser.'

'Via the gloriously meaningful pursuit of fighting for money?' Red drawls before she can stop herself.

The knight's gaze speaks of the disbelief that the slim body before him has enough room to contain so much dumb.

'Via power. The only currency worth anything in this world.' He pauses. 'You are advantaged, Red. You've begun with more power than most others.'

'Someone told me the exact opposite,' Red says, the craggy face of Faraday drifting into her mind. 'That what I am would be a disadvantage, because no one would ever trust me.'

'Power is also perspective. If you believe it's an advantage, you'll use it as such. If you believe it's a handicap, you'll allow it to be so. Never listen to how others tell you to think.'

'Logically,' Red responds, 'wouldn't that include you?'

She is rewarded with a faint smile and feels a flash of annoyance at how happy it makes her to have provoked it.

'Logically,' the knight agrees. 'Take all learnings given, but then make up your own mind. You may well decide that I'm full of shit—'

Si, thinks Red, *I'm already there.*

'—but right now, you're mine to teach. That's what you wanted, isn't it?'

In the pit of Red's stomach, a slick black feeling flutters its wings. This is her next test, and she will not fail.

'Yes,' she says.

The knight nods. 'Tell me about the first time your magic kicked.'

Red pauses, assembling the story in her mind. 'I was twelve. I got into a fight with another cub at the hostel I was living in.'

'What about?'

She hesitates.

'What's wrong?' asks the Sorcerer Knight. He sounds a little softer.

'Nothing. It's just . . . you're the first person to ask me that. I was expecting to have to talk about it in the registration interview, but they never asked.'

'Of course not. They don't care *how* we work, they just care about controlling us.' He pauses. 'If it's too painful, you don't have to tell me.'

It is, but she doesn't want him knowing that.

'It was about my parents,' she says. 'It was the one thing we all had in common there, having none, so it was the easiest way to hurt each other. Anyway, the other cub called my mother a bad word and I told him to take it back, but he wouldn't. He kept saying it, over and over, in a louder and louder voice. All I remember about what happened next was feeling hot and itchy, and then the next thing I knew he was lying underneath an upended table, howling about his arm being broken. I remember wondering how he'd managed to get a table on top of him like that. It was really heavy, that table, it took two adults to even lift it. He said I'd thrown the table at him, but I hadn't even moved.' She gives an uncomfortable shrug. 'I worked it out pretty quickly after that.'

A plausible story, worn smooth by repeated practise in front of a mirror – but this is the first time she has had to tell the lie to another godchild. She keeps her gaze down. Let him think it hurts to tell, if he likes.

'Do you notice why it comes out when it does?' she hears him ask.

'I don't know. It's happened so rarely – three times in my whole life.'

Lies come out easier the more of them you tell. Oily tongue.

'That's unusual,' the knight comments. 'It's very hard for us to keep our emotions inside.'

'You mean our magic.'

He shrugs. 'We are our magic. It is ourselves: body, mind, feeling. It's all the same set of interconnected systems. You can't think of it as separate – if you do, you'll never understand it, and so you'll never control it.'

Is that why you are the way you are? You control yourself so hard you can barely crack a smile?

Red decides to keep that bright little opinion behind her teeth.

'Let's see what we have, then,' the knight says. 'Defend yourself.'

He makes no move towards the rack. A weaponless session? Well, fine. Red tightens into a quick, solid fighting stance, but the knight, still two lengths away from her, doesn't move.

She sees the white-fire tongue of an electric whip lash out low towards her legs, hears the mosquito whine of the path it cuts in the air – out of nowhere it comes and there is no time to get away, a microsecond of a decision gets her into the air, jumping high – but the whip is no longer underneath her and she lands awkwardly, stumbling, her legs uncertain and afraid of feeling the lash.

'Your defence is to hop like a frog?' he says.

Red looks back up at the knight, who still hasn't moved – and has no whip in his hand. No whip anywhere. Where did it go?

'The whip—' she says, feeling stupid.

'The whip was an illusion.'

Red stares at nothing as she replays the moment the whip came for her. She has never seen his magic before. She had no idea it would seem so real.

'Your first instinct,' the knight says, 'should have been to push the lash away from your legs before it could get near you. Fear from threat is usually the first emotion that kicks out a magical response. We often reach for the magic before we reach for anything else.'

'But I need you to teach me how to *banish* my magic, not use it.'

'First we need to set it free,' the knight says distantly. 'Only then we can learn how to control it.'

Red frowns. This doesn't make a lot of sense to her, but then again, her grasp of magic is dismal at best. Up until now, the only godchild she has ever known is herself.

'How do I push away an illusion?' she asks. 'Is it touchable?'

'No, but as a pelleren, you use the air around other bodies to cause physical change, pressure, damage. You should be able to dissipate my illusions with just a thought, before they can ever reach you. After all, they're only manipulated light. Touch, taste and smell are the three senses I can't mimic. You should remember that.' The knight's tone grows acerbic. 'Might come in handy.' He nods. 'Again.'

Before Red can gather herself the air sizzles and glows and the whip comes for her, too fast to decide or think about it, forcing her instinct to kick. She jumps again, already knowing halfway through the movement that she went wrong.

'No. Again.'

She wants to say 'wait', ask for a moment, just a second to think, prepare – but clemency is weakness and no weakness can be shown in front of the man who has none. The whip comes again. And again. She jumps, she dodges, she flaps her hands at it, cutting the air fruitlessly with her palms. One hour slides into the next. The tall lighting rig that sentries their play area renders everything beyond a black nothingness, until Red starts to fancy that it has simply ceased to exist. Her world has shrunk to the ragged breathing in her ears, the echo of her mentor's voice on the stone, the succession of illusory weapons thrown at her – axes, swords, knives, fake razor beams from a fake razor-beam gun that nevertheless look so real that her stomach clenches hard every time the beam lands a hit on her body.

'Stop hiding,' the Sorcerer Knight calls, safely hidden behind his illusions. 'I want to *see* you.'

Red grits her teeth, levers herself up from the floor. 'I'm trying—'

'No,' he cuts in, 'you're not. You're holding back.'

No matter how many illusions he throws at her, no matter that she knows what they are, it never gets any less real. Each one is as convincing as the last. Over and over Red tells her eyes not to trust, her ears not to hear, but it does nothing. Her sweat has the tang of fear. Facing down maiming or death over and over without pause is exhausting. She falls again and again.

'Wait,' she says, calves trembling with the effort of keeping her upright. This place is cold, forcing movement just to keep warm.

'No,' she hears the knight say.

'WAIT—'

He is there suddenly, the space between them gone in an instant. Up close, Red can clearly see the toll the hours of magic have taken on her opponent. His outline trembles, his skin is greasy grey. Her surprise undoes her – the knight flashes past her guard to pin her by her neck.

'Fear's too easy a kick, but we have to bring you out somehow.' His words are ragged with effort.

'Get off me,' she hisses, straining against his grip, her fury swelling. He has her pinned with the same move that made her submit the first time they met, but she does *not* submit, she brings others to *their* knees in front of *her*, screaming sorry for all the wrong they've done—

'Where's your magic, Red?' he says. 'Where is *you*?'

He searches her face, she his – and then within a heartbeat, the game switches on her. His gaze drops to her mouth, then back up to her eyes in a speedy flicker.

And for one lurching, swooping moment, it stops feeling like a fight.

Then her hands come up and she hits the flat of her palms in a hard double tap against the knight's ears. It is enough – the disorienting sound shock loosens the grip around her throat and she breaks it with her forearms, delivering a shoulder push to the solar plexus in front of it and reeling the body before her backwards, away.

Adrenalin screams at her to go forwards and destroy the thing that hurt her, but she is too exhausted to deliver. She only has enough to keep herself upright.

The knight straightens, and they stare at each other as Red drags in one straggling breath after another.

'Your body reacts, at least,' the knight says, but his tone

suggests that this is no good, no good at all. 'I thought you said you had trouble controlling your magic in a fight? You're giving me nothing. I might as well be attacking a corpse.'

'All you're doing is torturing me!' Red spits.

It is the only thing she can say, because she certainly cannot say that she lied to him and that she is not here to learn how to control her magic.

The knight releases an unsteady sigh, drags a hand over his face. 'We're done for today.' He points to the darkness beyond the square of light.

Red leans forwards, trying to catch her breath. The sweat running down her back is cold now, adding to her mounting sense of failure.

'I'm sorry,' she says. 'We can keep going.'

The marble-cut creature before her shakes his head. 'You're too tired to continue. We'll try again in a few weeks' time. Ford is outside. He'll take you back to Spittelgrounds.'

A few *weeks*? Red tries to protest, but she has been drained to exhaustion. Furious and defeated, she stumbles back to the outside world with her mind in a desperate whirl.

His physical talent for the fight is extraordinary, perhaps impossible for her to defeat. Add in those illusions and he becomes overwhelming. His magic is far more powerful than the public has ever dared to contemplate. She doubts if the people around him have any idea. How can they? If they knew, surely they would have locked him up by now. No wonder he keeps the world at arm's length.

So how in seven *hells* is she ever going to get close enough to kill him?

CHAPTER 26

Cair Lleon, Blackheart
Ten Years Ago

The air in the vast, echoing ballroom glitters silver.

Tiny sparkles shift and wink in slow, rolling eddies, dispersed slowly and gently around the hall by a circulatory system of air grilles embedded into the walls and at regular points in the endless floor. By the end of the night, all the guests will have caught the motes of glitter on their exposed skin, trapped within their hair, winking on the folds of their clothes. They bring with them multitudes of languages, styles of dress, colours, passions and allegiances – but above it all is silver, the colour of trick, the colour of London, covering every persona alike in its binding gleam.

High above the heads of the crowd soar the famed black iron chandeliers of Cair Lleon. There are twenty spread across the ceiling, each holding hundreds of candles apiece. A sturdy pulley system lowers each chandelier carefully to the ground when the candles need to be replaced. The ballroom isn't used very often. When it is and the candles are all lit and thousands of sparkling flames float above the crowd, the sight remakes the world into a dream.

This is the annual Caballaria Ball, the biggest occasion of the year. It is a resplendent menagerie of pomp and show, and the eighth such occasion during the Artorian era, the now well-established reign of the so-called Tricky King.

A large area has been cleared at one end of the ballroom, right in front of the royal dais. The knights who fight there tonight are chosen for their blossoming fame as well as their prowess. It is considered the mark of great things to come for each chosen fighter, and no less so for Finnavair Caballarias o'Rhyfentown, who now takes her position, ready to perform.

The knight known as the Fair Fae has only been fighting in Rhyfentown's fledgling public circuit for a few months, but already she is a favourite of the glows and has a burgeoning cultdom among the general populace. Walk through almost any part of Rhyfentown on a fight night and see her face and sigils among the crammed and jumbled wall projections in every Caballaria bar.

She has been cited for beginning the fashion trend among younger Londoners of wearing synthetic overlays. The translucent, sliver-thin material moulds to the contours of the face and fuzzes the features underneath, suggesting instead anything ranging from temporary tattoo patterns to animal faces to creatures that exist only in stories. Whatever you can think of, you can buy it as an overlay. The cheaper ones are available from every corner market, a throwaway party costume, but if you pay enough, you can even wear a more famous face over your own, though they are never particularly realistic.

Overlays have been a part of Si Finnavair's fighter garb since the beginning, and tonight is no exception. She fights with the face of a fox in deference to her street origins, its vulpine planes rendering her unknowable.

The only problem with that is that Art would very much like to know her.

The knight ends her performance with a spectacular move that involves deftly cutting her opponent's hat into three pieces and skewering them all on the end of her sword. The ballroom explodes with applause, closed fists hitting palms in rhythmic pounding, and Art enthusiastically joins in.

Lillath, on the royal dais at Art's right-hand side, leans in. 'She's fabulous, isn't she?'

She is watching him speculatively.

'Yes,' he replies as casually as he can. 'Very'– he searches for the right word – beautiful, no, arousing, *no* – 'impressive.'

'Mm,' Lillath replies.

'What?'

'Nothing.'

Art levels a gaze at her. 'I don't know what it is you're not saying. I just know that you're not saying something.'

'No, nothing,' Lillath says again, annoyingly stoic. 'Maybe you should ask her to dance.'

'I should not,' Art replies.

Lillath sits back. 'Get Lucan to ask her. He is your communications advisor now, after all.'

'What are we, twelve?' Art says. He hesitates. 'Anyway, Lucan is busy.'

The man in question is below them, mingling and glad-handing important guests. Always a better talker than a fighter, his decision to drop out of knights' training and move into a career as an advisory vastos surprised precisely no one. Lucan can talk his way both into and out of anything, but his job is to help run palace communications, not Art's love life – or current lack thereof.

'Are you going to do that thing where you're too cowardly to ask her until the last minute,' Lillath says, 'and though she'll probably have a whole host of offers lined up, she'll have to shake them all off for you, and then you'll feel so awful about encroaching on everyone else's plans that you'll withdraw your offer, and it will look like she's offended the King of London, and her entire night will be ruined and it'll be all across tomorrow's glows—'

'I swear on Rhyfen's own sword,' Art says pleasantly, 'if you don't stop needling your beloved sovereign, he will make it look like *you* offended him, and *you* can enjoy being the subject of all the gossip for the next week solid.'

Lillath adopts a lofty tone. 'I'm used to it. Do your worst.'

'What do you want, DeHavilland?'

'I was just wondering why you haven't talked to her yet, considering you've been pining after her for months.'

'I have done nothing of the kind,' Art retorts, fighting a sudden blush.

'You've been watching her recent bouts.'

'Who *told* you—?' He bites it off. He knows exactly who. Fortigo Balanchine, his supposedly loyal personal vastos. He and Lillath have had more than one bedroom encounter over the years, developing quite the roller-coaster of a friendship along the way.

You're in the shit, Balanchine, Art promises silently.

Garad, in the champion's place at Art's left side, leans in. 'Art, I didn't know you were a fan of the Fair Fae!' they say with marked enthusiasm.

'I—' Art hesitates. 'Not a fan, exactly. The only bouts I really watch are yours.'

Garad laughs. 'Well, I'm glad you're following the Caballaria a little more closely these days.'

'Yes, apparently there's finally something worth looking at,' Lillath murmurs.

In Art's head, Lillath dies a thousand terrible deaths.

‘Have you met her before?’ Garad asks.

‘When would I have had the time for that, Garad?’ Art shoots back, nettled.

Garad shrugs. ‘Time is made, not spent.’

Art likes to think he knows his champion and oldest friend better than anyone, but there is a well inside them, a deep reservoir that they keep closed off from the world. They often say that it is a necessary defence against the intrusion of the public into their life, but the truth is that even Art doesn’t get access to that reservoir.

It also means that sometimes Garad does things that catch people completely off guard, like opening their mouth and bellowing ‘FINNAVAIR!’ across the ballroom, making every single head turn their way.

The lady in question looks up like a startled cat. When she catches sight of Garad and realises the noise came from them, a smile paints her face. With a few murmured words to the small crowd surrounding her, she detaches herself and begins to move towards the royal dais.

Art waits patiently for his spiking heart to subside back down to normal levels.

‘What,’ he says in his calmest voice, the voice he reserves for the very deepest of emergency situations, ‘are you doing?’

‘Introducing you,’ Garad replies.

‘This is not. The way. People. Get introduced. To the King. Of London.’

‘Art,’ Lillath chides reproachfully, ‘you always whine about wanting to cut out all that dull ceremony and act like a normal person for once.’

‘No, this is wonderful, really,’ Art says through a smile as he watches the Fair Fae approach out of the corner of his eye. ‘It’ll feed the gossip machines for a month.’

'Si Finnavair,' Garad says. 'It's a pleasure to cross swords once again.'

'Only in conversation, sadly,' the knight says, having arrived in front of them. 'One day I would love to actually meet you in the arena, Si Garad.'

Her voice undulates with a deep Rhyfentown lilt. Now her performance is done, she has changed out of her show armour and sports a tight black waistcoat that lays bare all the curved muscles of her arms. Her trousers are tucked into thigh boots that hug her flesh. The overlay is gone, leaving behind a sparkling, animated face and her trademark mass of tight, colour-tipped curls, tonight a vibrant shade of coral. Her eyes dart briefly in the direction of Art's face, then lower quickly to the floor.

Art gives his champion the merest flicker of his gaze. Garad is the only one who can break the protocol deadlock. The King does not introduce himself, and absolutely no one can introduce themselves to the King.

Worlds die and stars collide and an eternal second later, Garad picks up the reins. Their hand extends.

'Sire,' they say, 'please allow me to introduce Si Finnavair Caballarias o'Rhyfentown. Si Fin, please allow me to introduce Artorias Dracones, first of his name, the King of London, Ruler of Blackheart and the London Saith of the Seven Kingdoms, Regent of the—'

'Please,' Art cuts in. 'Stop.' He takes in what he hopes is a steadying breath. 'Si, it's an honour to meet you. Your performance was superb.'

The poised woman before him looks unmoored by his compliment.

'You really thought so?' she says, sounding nervous. 'Oh, I understand it's part of your duty to be kind to everyone—'

'No,' Art cuts in with haste, 'no, I mean, yes, that's part of it, but that's not what I . . . I genuinely meant it, with you. Not to say that I'm always lying, with others.' The pause is excruciating to all parties. 'Of course,' he continues brightly, 'now we're in a bind. Nothing I say henceforth will sound at all true. How can I convince you?'

Finnavair lets loose a wild, graceless and utterly charming laugh. 'I don't think I know anyone who uses the word "henceforth" in actual speech.'

'Well,' Art replies, 'now you do.'

'Now I do.' Her forehead wrinkles in a frown.

'Is there something wrong?'

'Well, you complimented me, so I should compliment you back. I was just trying to think of one.'

'By all means, take your time,' Art says. 'There must be so many to choose from; I understand it might be overwhelming.'

She brightens. 'Wait, I know. You're quite a good King.'

Art's mouth opens, then shuts. 'Just . . . quite good?' he manages to say.

'Well, you've only had the Sword a few years now, and you're still young. You've got plenty of time to become great, don't worry.' Si Fin beams him a smile.

'Well, let's hope I last a little longer then,' he says. 'Henceforth, my only ambition as King is to finally get you to call me "great".'

She lets loose another wild laugh.

He finds himself desperate for new ways to provoke it.

'I apologise, Sire,' she says. 'Can I tell you something that isn't a joke, to make up for it?'

'If you like.'

Blood tinges the knight's cheeks. 'Being a knight is my life's purpose. It means everything to me. I owe you a debt.'

Art blinks. 'I don't—'

'I'm an orphan,' she says. 'If you hadn't changed the law on Caballaria entry requirements, I wouldn't have even been able to trial for it.'

'Ah.' Art squirms. 'Well.'

His awareness of other people only now surfaces. He can practically feel Lillath's grin.

'Si,' he says, 'would you like to dance?'

Finnavair looks positively shocked. 'With you? Sire,' she adds in haste.

'Well, we could try it separately, but I worry I'll find it much less interesting.'

She considers him. 'What a thing to be worried about.'

'Oh, I live a dull life. I only have to worry about the small things.'

'Aren't you supposed to be bagging a Lady?' she asks.

'It's a dance, not a marriage proposal.'

Finnavair regards him with a fascinated smile. After a moment, she places her hand on top of his. Her palm is soft and warm and damp – from sweat, he realises. A celebrated knight who has recently fought to victory in one of the biggest arenas in the world, a crowd of millions hanging on her every move. The sheer pressure, the charged air . . . But it is a dance with a King that brings out her nerves. The arena is a world she knows, but this is uncharted territory.

Still, they manage to navigate it together well enough.

'Funny,' Fin says, a few hours later. 'I heard you don't really like violence.'

Art lies on his back as still as he can, trying to remember how breathing goes.

'That kind of violence,' he says eventually, 'I seem to have a taste for.'

Her laugh vibrates through his chest. She nestles into his side, her legs thrust through his bed sheets like daggers.

It has, Art reflects, been an interesting evening. He waits for his heart rate to settle into a less medically worrying rhythm.

Then he says, 'I'd like to see you again.'

'For this? Are you sure you can handle it, Sire? If you turn up to greet dignitaries with broken bones, there may be questions.'

Art laughs. 'You're not so tough.'

Fin is quiet. The quiet stretches on.

'I'd like to see you again too,' she says eventually. 'But I can't.'

His heart dries into dust. 'You've a promise to someone else?'

'No, nothing like that.'

He searches. 'Then what is it? Can you tell me?'

He feels her sigh tickle the soft, thin skin over his ribs.

'I just . . . can't. Caballaria is my one true love. It's the only love I have space for in my life.'

'Plenty of people manage to have both.'

Fin sounds subdued. 'Not well. One always suffers, I think. I haven't had much luck there. Have you?'

He wants to sling a cut retort. He wants to lay out her argument and point out every one of its flaws.

Then he thinks of Garad, always alone.

Then he thinks of himself.

'No,' he says finally. 'I'm starting to wonder if I ever will.'

'You will.' Fin pauses. 'Of course, if you ever want some more . . . exercise . . . in the meantime?'

She leaves it hanging.

'I'm sorry,' Art says. 'It tends to mean a little more than that to me, as much as I'd rather it didn't.'

She lifts her head and gazes at him solemnly. 'Know thyself,' she says. 'That's a very useful trait.'

He tries to smile.

Not long after that, Fin disentangles herself and takes her leave.

Art lets himself wallow for a while. Why does he keep wanting people he can't have? There are plenty he *could* have. Saints know they get dangled in front of him with wearying regularity. What is wrong with him?

His gaze strays to his desk, which is festooned with papers. Finnavair is not the only one whose heart has already been claimed. He lets out a resigned sigh, sits up, sends for coffee and turns his attention back to the Kingdom. Stooping to his private message plate, he sweeps up the missives that have gathered there since this morning.

The one on top is new. It must have arrived during his rather bruising time with Fin. It's from Lillath – he recognises the handwriting. He is well used to regular private updates from his Spider, so it takes a moment for this one to fully register. When it does, it sucks all the air from his lungs.

We've had a message from B. She's in trouble.
– L

After eight years, Belisan is back.

CHAPTER 27

Surwek, Iochitown
Three Months Ago

Spittelgrounds rears into the sky, gloriously haloed by the setting sun behind it.

The clouds are mottled in rich blue and thick, creamy gold, impossible colours and shapes that make it easy to believe in sky gods – or at the very least, the kind of evening that drops jaws open with its opulence.

Red doesn't care about any of it. She trudges across the wide, pearl-white stone-scattered boulevard that serves as the entrance to the beautiful manor house she now calls home. Her thoughts are so a-whirl that she doesn't even notice who waits for her at its front.

Then comes the sudden snarl of a bike, purring directly her way. Familiarity surges. There is no mistaking those Rhyfentown leathers, those patches and badges and charms.

Finnavair. A casual grin is slung across her mouth as she pulls up.

'I just saw you,' Red says, puzzled.

Fin cocks her head. 'Where?'

'I caught the end of the bout you just fought today on the glows. Didn't it only finish an hour ago?'

She laughs at Red's quizzical expression. 'Even the miraculous Fair Fae can't be in two places at once. More importantly, where have *you* been?' She jerks her head towards the house. 'They said you were due back this afternoon.'

'Nowhere.'

'You're going to have to come up with a better lie than that,' she says firmly. 'Stables don't much like it when their prize horses wander off. Come on, you can practise on me.'

Red sighs. 'I was at Wendelsworde.'

Fin looks baffled. 'Saints, you were in another dis'? That's far. What's in Wendelsworde for you?'

She hasn't the energy to lie. 'I went to see the Merewīowing.'

Fin bursts out laughing. 'The Sorcerer Knight museum? Damn, Red.'

'I didn't realise it had been turned into a gawk gallery for thirsty tourists,' Red says sourly.

'You're one of the few people in the Seven Kingdoms who can lay claim to an in-person connection with the Sorcerer Knight. Why in the hells would you feel the need to visit his childhood home?'

For clues. Insights. Something, *something* that could get her closer to him, prise him open like a ripe mussel.

Instead, all she found was a ticket-seller perched on a sturdy metal stool at the door to the Merewīowing, a grizzled man who barely looked at her as she handed over her trick, muttering 'one hour inside only' in a bored litany.

Inside the house-turned-museum, the walls were painted a uniform white, the better to showcase steady wide-beamed projections of the original wallpaper, patterned in vintage Alfrenan style. On the floor, when she peered hard enough, Red saw the original faded tiles underneath the patterned light, worn and smoothed down to stop their cracked and broken surfaces catching on visitors' feet.

In the house's cellar, she saw the infamous long iron chains fixed to the wall by a thick iron circlet that jutted out of the brick like a bull's nose ring. The iron chains the Sorcerer Knight had used to keep himself tethered to this little room as a young teen, trying to keep his magic contained, just the way his notorious father had taught him to do. *Hide yourself. Don't let the neighbours see.* Across from the chains sat a dank little roller bed, beside it, a small, forlorn chest of drawers: recreations of the Sorcerer Knight's meagre childhood possessions. Ghosts of his old pain. Small wonder that he keeps everyone at bay, offering nothing of himself but his fight, when his life is on display like this.

What if he knew that she had spent her afternoon gawping at his past like the snake of tourists that wound itself through his childhood's guts?

'I was just curious,' Red says out loud, and then, with an effort, pushes the talk on. 'You're waiting on someone in Spitelgrounds, then?'

'Yes, you, idiot.'

'Me?' Red frowns. 'Why are you waiting for me?'

'I'm taking you out to a party. You can't say no. Anyway, you need the distraction.'

The look on Fin's face suggests that any of Red's possible reactions to this would amuse.

'I'm in training tomorrow,' she says.

Fin shakes her head. 'You don't start until past lunchtime. I asked about your schedule.'

'But . . .' Red struggles to come up with a valid reason not to go. 'Where is this party? Who's there? We might get recognised.'

'Don't worry, we go anonymous.' Fin holds up a sparkly overlay in her fist.

Red frowns at her. 'You've thought of everything, haven't you?'

'I try to.' Fin bounces on the balls of her feet. 'Coming, Si? Or would you rather spend your evening researching the Sorcerer Knight's favourite foods?'

From the outside, it looks like an abandoned warehouse in the middle of Iochitown's vast commercial storage sector.

Fin tells Red that things are never as they seem. They skirt across the scrubland and stop at the fencing that rears before them, twice as high as the average man, that cages a huge square of sparse, rubble-strewn land with the warehouse squatting at its centre like a discarded box. Slits of light spill out from its tall, thin windows, pulsing and searching across broken rubble and flat, packed-dirt ground.

Fin bends down, her fingers searching in the gathering dusk.

'It's here somewhere,' Red hears her mutter, followed by a pleased, 'win.'

She pulls aside a section of the fencing and scrabbles through the hole she has made. 'Come on then, pup,' she says.

Red hesitates. 'Is this . . . legal?'

'Absolutely not. If you hear guard-bike engines, run like hell out the back exit.'

The face overlay Fin has chosen to wear tonight is that of a snake, an incredibly disconcerting meld with her own features. Her cheeks and forehead are patterned with tiny emerald scales, her eyes are twin black pools and her mouth has been reduced to a grinning slash. She has hidden her mass of curls under a short-bobbed white wig. When she goes out, she likes no one knowing who she is. It is the only time nowadays, so she says, that she gets to feel free.

They walk towards the warehouse, Red's heart beating a nervous rhythm. Sound increases as they approach, a thumping burr that makes the building seem like a rumbling, growling dog with its belly low to the ground.

'It's a good crowd at these things,' Fin is saying, her voice pitched loud over the music. 'Artists, usually. The people who run it are all sorts of mischief. And they're so creative. One time they threw a party that was almost in the dark. You couldn't see a thing, except when the walls would glow this kind of sick flesh colour every so often, and the music was this weird wailing that set your teeth on edge. The name of the party was *In the Womb of a Dying Animal*. Isn't that genius?'

'Amazing,' Red says weakly.

When they arrive at the front door, it is padlocked shut. Fin presses a rigged-up switch that hangs from the wall. After a moment, a tall window a little further along creaks open. A girl with a mass of ginger hair and ouroboros patterns tattooed across every inch of her face appears beyond its grimy glass pane.

'Password?' she yells over the pounding behind her.

'*She devours the weak*,' Fin yells back.

'Come on in.'

Red clambers awkwardly through the window's opening.

'Nice password,' she says to Fin as they follow the ginger-haired girl through a narrow corridor. Above their heads swing rows of rusting, industrial-sized metal hooks.

'It's the title of a Flowers for Kane song.' She laughs at Red's quizzical expression. 'Music?'

'I don't know much music,' Red admits.

'You will if you bike with me for any length of time.'

Then the doors at the end of the corridor open and as Red emerges into the main space, sheer sensory input shuts all else down.

The place is vast, the ceiling lost to time and space. A sea of bodies is surrounded on all sides by undulating ribbons of pinprick lights, swirling and receding and pulsing. It feels like the entire room is falling.

'They've rigged up wide-beam projectors that cover the walls and floor,' Fin shouts into Red's ear. 'They say it's supposed to be like being in the inside of a black well. You know. Up in space?'

'No one knows what that's like,' Red protests. 'No one knows if they even exist!'

'Imagination!' Fin shouts, and raises her arms, twirling. 'What does it feel like?'

'Like dying!'

'Good! Then consider this night your rebirth!'

The snake girl in front of them laughs.

'Listen, I know I cajoled you here, but you still could have said no. Why'd you come?'

Red looks around at the sea of humanity before them. Slippery bodies everywhere, every shape and size, covered in every kind of identity imaginable – black- and metal-clad space-hoppers, angels with curling wings and painted skin, animal-embodying gewenden with their feathers and fur, glass-clothed machinettes, flashing mutineer pilots.

She has never been to anything like this in her life.

'To forget,' she says. 'For a little while.'

'I have just the thing.' Fin takes her hand. 'Don't be afraid, Red. I'll look after you while you lose yourself.'

So she does. And so does Fin.

It is much later, so late it could be early, when the machinette approaches Red.

Tiny runs of electric lights have been sewn underneath his skin. They glow faintly through his arms, made pink through the thin covering of his flesh. On his bare chest, small nubs of polished metal poke through carefully cut and healed holes in his skin. Machinettes do extreme things to their bodies, Red knows, but seeing it in a capture and seeing it in the real is an entirely different thing. As her eyes run over his body, her belly gives a queasy lurch.

'I heard you came here with Fin,' the machinette says over the music. 'I'm a friend of hers.'

Red regards him. He is small and young, and has a disarmingly cheerful air.

'They callian me Perfectly.' He holds his hand out.

'That's really your name?' Red says dubiously as they touch fists.

'Yep. Picked it my own self. I know yours, of course.' He tips her a wink. 'Don't worry, no one else here knows who you are. I'm very discreet. People tend to prefer that of me. My line of business. I sell access to other dimensions. Dreams. Altered states of being. General fun. Don't you think it's amazing that there are people in the world who are so scared of having fun, they try to stop everyone doing it? Then again, it's only worth doing something if there's someone in the world who'd much rather you didn't, itso?' He lays a cold, glass-gloved hand on her arm. 'I've got something you'll like.'

'I don't think so,' Red says, taking his hand from her arm and turning away. Saints, he talks a lot.

Undeterred, Perfectly follows her. 'Don't you like having fun?'

'I'm already having it.'

'I've got useful things too, very useful to people like yourself. You know Tidal?'

'No. Go away.' Red looks across the crowd for Fin.

'You should,' Perfectly says, persisting. 'Oh, you should. You of all people. It enhances your talents, if you know what I mean.'

'I've got good trainers, thanks.'

'No, not *that*. Your *magic*.' He hisses the last word.

Red stops, caught despite herself. 'Why would I want something like that?' she asks. 'I don't use my magic. I can't.'

Perfectly smiles. 'There's a client of mine,' he says, 'very famous meretrix. I'm not telling you who it is – I said I was discreet, didn't I? Well, he's a godchild – unregistered, you understand – and he uses Tidal to amplify the, er, the experience of being with him. At significantly climactic moments, you might say. Most of you don't have a handle on your assets, but he's got real good with it, so I've heard.' Perfectly lets out a stuttering laugh. 'He makes so much trick he doesn't even know how to spend it all.'

'Really?' Red says disbelievingly. 'People pay for that?'

'Grand times with a godchild? Highest paid in the industry. Any amount you can think of, triple it and you're close. The more illegal an activity, the more trick to be made, neh?' He sighs. 'Wish I was a godchild. It'd be amazing. You're so exotic.'

Red swallows an impulse to knock him to the floor.

'How much is it?' she asks. 'This Tidal?'

'Oh, I can get you a great deal on it. You tell me how much you want, I'll get it for you.'

'You don't have it here?'

'No,' Perfectly admits. 'But there's only one place you can get it. And you'll only be able to get it on my word, I can promise you that. The seller's a nervy one, understandably.' He leans in, places a sliver of etched glass in her hand. 'Access to my personal glow channel. Any time you want some, you call me up.'

Red pockets the glass. Perfectly might be full of shit, but if there's even a chance that Tidal actually works the way he says, then it could be enough to give her the edge over Wyll. Get him under a killing blow.

She'll need all the help she can get.

'Thank you, I might,' she says, and then walks away.

'Aren't you going to buy anything from me?' she hears Perfectly's outraged cry.

Red ignores him, letting the crowd swallow her up.

CHAPTER 28

Surwek, Iochitown
Ten Years Ago

The Night Carnival's sprawling welcome hall looks, at first, chaotic.

Small tables perch on top of deep, spread-eagled rugs. Electric light chains suspended from the ceiling hover over each table and swing above the stage, where allurements of every possible kind and shape use the platform to entice, invite and intoxicate.

Figures walk, talk, sprawl across divans, all lit in cream, pink, gold, bronze, toffee, chocolate and umber. Fingers trail on exposed flesh. Disguises are common here, as part of the game you begin to play when you walk in the door. Cats, bears, insects, vipers, demons, wrapped in leather, muslin, silk, rope and glass. Shifting, laughing, whispering, cooing.

Art hates it on sight. It reminds him of Belisan.

Tonight he wears a synthetic overlay of his own – a metallic gold mask that covers his face – and his distinctive blond hair has been slicked with a mute, silvery grey. His leathers are Blackheart black, the patches fake. He plays at being a knight, a banally common enough costume in places like these. He deliberately does not stand out.

She is at a table in the corner, furthest from the door. Her back is to the wall. Her eyes roam the crowd. Eight years of a faded pain memory, in the corner of a room full of lives being lived.

She is not supposed to be so lovely. Everyone has it the wrong way round, he thinks. They pinhead fantasy as a glowing, oversaturated realm that reality cannot possibly measure up to, and yet nothing he has conjured in his mind compares to the visceral realness of her. Still that sheet of dark hair, still those huge eyes.

The same eyes silted blank as she pulls him under, drowning him in a dream.

He shoves the memory away as he draws near her table.

They stare at each other.

'I didn't think you'd come,' Belisan says at last.

Art lowers himself into the seat across from her. 'How could I not, after the message you sent? You said you were in trouble.'

Instead of answering, she gestures behind him. 'You brought reinforcements.'

His guards, currently taking surreptitious positions at his back, are in as much disguise as he is. It makes him uneasy to think they stand out so easily.

'And you didn't?' he asks.

'Of course not. Who associates with someone on the run?'

Art stifles a tight reply. In the eight years since they last laid eyes on each other, Cair Lleon has expended considerable secretive effort and resource in trying to find her, but to no avail. She has had help. She'd be a fool to meet him now without it.

He has the crawling sensation of being watched. It feels like more than just his own with eyes on them both. Like all good rulers, Dario Go knows most everything that goes on in their own Kingdom, even if they choose not to show their hand about it.

He always suspected Dario to be Belisan's true ally, though like so many other things about Belisan, it has gone unproven. It is an amazing, and dismaying, lesson of his reign so far – just how many unjust and underhand dealings remain hidden, how many secrets and lies go undiscovered and unpunished. His favourite stories growing up taught him the opposite. He is beginning to hate them for all the ways in which they differ from real life.

'I told you it was too dangerous to bring anyone else,' says Belisan.

'Someone who once nearly killed me asks to meet me in a crowded place, in secret, refusing to explain why unless I come in person and alone,' Art retorts. 'How did you think it would go?'

Her lips thin.

'So if you're just going to arrest me,' she says, 'what's the point of even having a conversation? Why the pretence?'

He frowns. 'Don't be ridiculous. They're for my protection, not your arrest.'

Belisan's expression drops. What it drops into, he cannot possibly say. He can't read her. The lines of her face – he can't read her. Saints, did they ever really know each other? How much has time changed her? So much time, so much change.

He wonders how different he seems to her. He was a child when he knew her, their boundaries well set from the first night. How are they supposed to talk to each other now? What the fuck are the rules here? He has swum for so long within the neat borders of etiquette and protocol, this unknown feels like drowning in an endless sea.

No, *no*, not like drowning. Push that reminder away.

'Are you so scared of me, Sire?' Belisan asks.

Whatever doors he might have begun to tentatively open for her slam closed.

'After all these years of hiding,' he says, 'why show up now, Bel? What is so damn urgent that you'd risk so much just to see me?'

She sits, poised. A moment's silence. Then:

'I want you to give Agravain Welyen a pardon.'

Art takes a moment. Lets the surprise run its course.

'Say that again?' he asks.

She won't meet his eye. 'Give Agravain a pardon. Lift the moldra lagha on him and let him come back to London, to his family.'

It has been a long time since that name has been spoken aloud in his presence.

Agravain's exile from London these last few years has been a balm, a gift that keeps on giving. In his absence, the malice of his family appears at last to have been tempered. Orcade has been a steady, willing and agreeable Lady of Alaunitown, a rock Art has come to depend on.

Her brother was a poisoned thorn removed from London's foot. There is no possible scenario in which Art would willingly stick it back in and lame his city again.

He swallows the bile clawing up his throat. 'So you *were* working for him,' he says. 'You were his from the beginning.'

Belisan looks away. 'Does it matter?'

'Does it matter? Does it *matter*?' He wants to break something, hear it snap. 'He tried to assassinate me, Bel. It matters.'

She gives a shake of her head. 'He didn't try to assassinate you.'

'Come on. He had Dario put you on the menu – and how, *how* in seven hells did I pick you?' Art marvels. 'How did I pick the one person working for my enemy?'

'You'll believe whatever you need to believe,' Bel says in a terrible, hopeless voice.

'The truth. That's what I need to believe. Am I finally going to get it?'

'The truth?' Her face is a challenge. 'Dario put together a menu of nothing but godchildren to offer you. It didn't matter who you picked – one of them would have been a godchild.'

Art struggles. 'That's . . . that's ridiculous. Why? A common meretrix with a bit of skill would have had as much chance of killing me.'

Belisan vibrates with impatience. 'Aren't you listening to me? Because that wasn't the play. They didn't want to *kill* you, they just wanted to set you up as a kambion-fucker.'

It shocks him to hear the slur out of the mouth of a so-called kambion, even if it is delivered in syllables of pure acid.

'They hoped it would be a big enough scandal to lose you the Sword,' Belisan continues. 'It was about humiliation, not death.'

'You're expecting me to believe that every performer in the Night Carnival's menu was a godchild?' He tosses her a scornful look. 'Come on, Bel, there were dozens of them. There aren't that many godchildren in all of Surwek.'

Belisan just looks at him.

In absence of any other sane reaction, Art laughs. 'Paranoia? That's a weak play.'

'Oh, I think it's got you going,' she replies. 'Is it so strange a thought, that there are so many more of us than you know?'

'You're trying to frighten me now.'

'If that thought frightens you,' Belisan says, 'then maybe you're more like your daddy than you care to think.'

He blows out a winded breath. 'I didn't deserve that.'

Her eyes drop and she says no more.

'Bel,' he tries, 'this isn't you. This . . . cynicism.'

'No,' she agrees. 'You never saw that. You only got the acceptable parts of me, the parts that flattered you. You know: the cooing, coy slut. I hid all my jagged edges. I had to.'

His mouth falls open. 'Did I mistreat you so badly?'

She sounds softer. 'You were very good to me. And I played my part willingly.'

'Saints.' He reflects. 'Your acting skills and my naïveté . What a winning combination for him.'

Belisan's mouth opens and then shuts, words unspilled.

He is almost glad. A platitude from her now might snap his last thread.

'When I let you go, it was because I thought you had people you could go to,' he continues. 'Don't tell me you've been hiding out with Agravain fucken Welyen all this time?'

'I didn't have a lot of choice. I had a family who needed me . . .' She pauses, and then continues in a strained tone, 'I have a family who needs me.'

Her eyes are soft and hurting, and he softens in response. He can't help it.

'You don't have to go to him, not any more,' he says. 'Not ever again. I can help your family now. I can protect them.'

The naked hope in his voice. Years of ruling millions and he'll still drop to his knees in front of his first love like the eighteen-year-old boy he was. He sees her hesitate, feels his hope swell – and then she closes her eyes.

'I have my own way of protecting them,' she says.

'Is he forcing you? What does he have over you?'

She has been holding on to herself too tightly. A tear seeps out and crawls down her face.

'Nothing,' she says. 'I'm just loyal to him. Understand?'

'I don't believe that,' Art insists. 'He's threatening you, isn't he?'

Belisan shakes her head. 'Stop trying to save me, Art. I don't need to be saved.'

Her eyes stay closed – but her hand snakes out across the table, palm up, fingers loosely curled. There it stays, waiting. Art looks at it, longing, suddenly, to touch her again. If he could just touch her, everything would make sense again. They wouldn't need to use words to communicate, awkward, stupid words that can never convey all the shifting, complicated layers of this thing between them.

Art extends his own hand across to hers. Their skin connects and—

He still sits in the hall of the Night Carnival, people shoaling around him, but his perspective has suddenly and inexplicably changed. Now he has his back to the wall, where Belisan was a moment before. From here he has an unobstructed view of most of the hall, so when Belisan enters the room, he sees her immediately.

She weaves through the space, dancing alone.

No – not quite alone. A man has followed her in, walking behind her with a proprietary air.

—somewhere else, somewhere back in the real world, Art can feel Belisan's hand tighten against his own as he tries to pull his fingers away—

The man is Agravain. He wears a Kembrish cap that wings forwards over the sides of his face and covers most of his hair, but the set of his face is unmistakable. The lines around his mouth are more crevice than dent, these days. This is Agravain now, marked by years of exile.

'Brown leather jacket,' says a voice in Art's ear and he turns towards it, catching Belisan's face now impossibly next to his, watching him intently. 'Black cap. Back and to my left.'

—this isn't quite real. He can feel reality underneath this, the reality in which he and Belisan sit at a table holding hands like lovers. Overlaid is this, a dream of a memory—

What is this, dream-Art tries to say, what are you doing to me, but as in the drowning dream she shared with him all those years ago, he is utterly helpless. She has pulled him into her world, and in her world she is the one with all the power.

The gun in his hand, for example, was definitely not there before.

'He's here, Art,' dream-Belisan says. 'Agravain is here, in the Night Carnival, and you can kill him right now.'

But Agravain can't be here. Agravain is too much of a coward to come and face Art himself, so he forces someone with as much to lose to go in his place and bargain for his life.

'You're going to wake up now,' dream-Belisan tells him. 'You're going to have a gun in your hand. You're going to see him, back and to my left. And you're going to kill him, before he can kill you. Do you understand what I'm saying? He didn't come here for a pardon. He came here for revenge.'

There is a shift from blur to focus, as if the two realities – Belisan's thought-world and Art's sense-world – finally harmonise. Art is back on the opposite side of the table, Belisan's entwined hand in his, Belisan's eyes on his own.

Only now there is a gun in Art's free hand.

It rests in his lap under the table, pushing his palm against his thigh with its weight. He drops his eyes and stares at it. It isn't a kind of gun he has ever seen before. The nose is very short and the tail plain, not ornately curled like the long grips of the guard guns he knows. It is heavy and strange against his fingers.

Art grasps the gun. His hand knows what to do even as his brain tries desperately to cut in and stop this. Despite his protestations, palace security insisted long ago that the King receive guns training. Art has touched them, fired them and proved to be a surprisingly decent shot. It wasn't supposed to be a skill he would ever need to call on.

It is not possible that he now holds a gun in his hand. Then again, it is not possible for someone to dream of drowning in seawater and wake up vomiting the real thing across his bedclothes, either. All this time, and he still remembers the salt stink.

Belisan inclines her head just a little, drawing Art's gaze to her left, and Art sees him immediately. A hunched figure sat two tables away, in the same brown leather jacket and the same black Kembrish cap from the dream version, his head tilted downwards and his eyes hidden. Art can see his mouth, though, the creviced skin.

That bastard. He's right here. He's been here the whole time. If she hadn't shown him what to look for, he never would have known.

'Art' – and he can feel her cool fingers tight on his – *'I can't kill him, but you can. Moldra lagha. Marvol's Law says you can.'*

'No, Bel—' he begins.

'Don't talk out loud, he can hear us.'

What does she mean? Agravain is too far away, and the welcoming hall too noisy, to hear a word they are saying.

'Please, if you have ever cared for me, don't talk and just listen. Please.'

Despite everything, he does.

'We don't have much time,' dream-Belisan says. 'He'll be getting suspicious, and he's not here alone.'

Art feels a tremor of foreboding sluice through his veins. He has allies?

'I never wanted to hurt you,' pleads dream-Belisan. 'I know you have no reason to ever believe me, but I want you to remember that I said that. I want you to remember. Please remember.

'He's just over your shoulder, Art. Take the gun and kill him before he kills you.

'He came here to kill you.'

But there are people here. Agravain hides behind innocents. He doesn't care who else might get hurt for him. He never has. He deserves to die for all that he has done, and for all that he could still do. Art has never felt this kind of savagery before. It is wild and desperate and relentless.

It isn't his. It is Belisan's.

'Kill him,' he feels her say somewhere inside. *'End this. You can kill him. You have to. Art, he has a gun on you, he's going to shoot—'*

Enough, he thinks with furious petulance. *I'm the fucken* King. *I've had* enough.

His arm, the gun, rises. He can feel Belisan pulling at it like a hungry child. He tries to shake her off, but he was the one who let her in. He let her in and she is everywhere now, filling up every corner of him with a fury terrifying in its simplicity, its need for one thing only, and with the horror of a realisation that comes far too late, he can see now just how powerful Belisan is, just how completely she could have owned him and never tried.

Until now.

It is as if Fria Lysander herself has come back to punish him, punish them all, and her fury meets a rising tide of his abject fear.

Behind Belisan he can see the man in the brown leather jacket moving, rising from his seat—

'Kill him,' Belisan screams in his mind, *'BEFORE HE KILLS US BOTH—'*

Then comes a scream, as high-pitched as a child's. Belisan's head whips around. Her fingers slacken their tight hold on Art's. The tide of her fury stutters, not much but just enough, and his fear pushes back and overwhelms him. *Kambion*, he thinks with utter repulsion, and there is no unfolding of choice and then choice and then choice, instead everything is all at once, a crowd, a mob of confused, screaming emotions. Art wrenches his hand from Belisan's and then points the gun towards her. She shrinks back in her seat.

'You don't understand,' she wails out loud, 'he has my—'

Art hears a flat clap tear up the air. The gun in his hand kicks in response. Belisan stops talking and swings violently backwards, rag-dolled off her seat. There is movement, people around them shouting or screaming, or both.

Agravain is fumbling, turning to run, so Art swings the gun and stands up and strides forwards and shoots him in the back. He has to pull the trigger twice before Agravain has the grace to fall to the ground. Art reaches his body, stands over it and shoots him four more times.

He pauses, waits for movement.

None is forthcoming, but he shoots twice more anyway, just to make sure.

CHAPTER 29

Unknown Location
Three Months Ago

Red stands at the door, one hand bunched into a fist.

She has had a mad, dangerous idea about how to get closer to the Sorcerer Knight, how to worm past his guard, maybe enough to take him down. The trouble is, if she is wrong, she could lose everything on this one play.

Risk and reward. A constant striving for the perfect balance between the two. Arguments rage in her head. She might get no further than tonight, but she's been on the flirt with death for years. Why draw back now? She's no coquette.

Her hand rises to knock on the door, but before she can, it opens in a sudden yawn. The Sorcerer Knight stands in its black square, dressed in his usual muted training clothes.

'You're on time,' he says. 'Good. Come inside.'

She waits to be searched the way she was last time, but instead he simply steps back, giving her space to enter. The room beyond is set up as before. The towering lighting rig cuts a square of white on to the bare, swept ground. The weapons rack bristles.

'Something wrong?' the knight says behind her.

Red shifts. 'No.'

'We'll begin when you're ready.'

'Wait.' She turns to him, surprised.

'What?'

She searches. There is something in the set of his form, his terse replies. He is on edge.

'It doesn't matter,' she says.

He stares at her. She stares back. She will give nothing away.

After a moment that stretches tensely on, he drops his gaze.

'Let's make a start,' he says.

Red feels something shamefully eager in her unfurling, wanting him close, closer, close enough to hurt – but as before, he stands feet away, all nuance and clue stripped away from the distance. His skin takes on a hard, bright cast under the rigged overhead light. He shifts in his stance. His hands are loose by his side.

And then come the illusions.

As before, Red tries her best to fight them, but for some saintsdamned reason she can convince neither her body nor her mind that they are nothing more than light. Her mind screams warnings, her body angles her away from each danger. Her opponent gives no quarter. He is restless, twitch-filled. There is no wall tonight, no impassive face and careful movements. Something in him jumps like crickets on hot concrete. He wants to punish her, or punish himself – she can't land on which it is. It might be both.

A lion appears in the corner of her vision, its bulk terrifyingly massive and riotous in gold underneath the lighting rig they fight within. Its claws click at the ground, each one bigger than a human finger, and its jaws begin to stretch open . . .

A burst of pain in her side forces Red down to one knee.

'Is there really a lion in an abandoned power station?' the

Sorcerer Knight asks, withdrawing his own training stave from the vicious swipe he just dealt her.

'No.' Red tries to think through the savage throbbing her body is currently communicating to her with all urgency. 'I know that, but it's—'

'A distraction,' the knight cuts in. 'It's not real.'

'I *know*, but . . .'

'You don't know, or you'd be able to ignore it.'

'This is *pointless*!' Red explodes. 'Why are we doing this? I'll never be up against illusions in an arena, I don't need to know how to fight them!'

'You're a godchild,' he says. 'Magic is in your blood.'

She straightens, pins her mouth shut. She has to keep control. She has to keep her head.

The knight steps back. 'Once more. Same attack.'

'No – you'll just smack me down again. What's the point?'

'The point is to *learn*,' he barks. 'We keep doing it until you show me your magic. Again.'

Red draws up the staff. Exhaustion makes brittle sticks of her bones. She will not show weakness. She will not lose.

The knight turns, savagery in his every line.

'I'm going to kill you, Red,' he says.

Before she can even think, he attacks.

His speed, his *speed*. They dance, but not long enough for Red to save face. A beautiful swipe cuts her legs out from under her and she lands on her back, the unforgiving ground pushing the breath from her.

She lies there, wheezing. The knight appears, crouching over her.

'Emotions distract,' he says. 'Provoke them in your opponent and watch them open up like a flower.'

I'm going to kill you, Red.

'You think I'm afraid of you,' she pants, 'but I'm not.'

He searches her face. Something he sees apparently surprises him.

'Maybe that's it.' His tone has something of a childlike perplexity. Then his expression drops. 'Well, pain works too.'

A hand reaches out to Red's arm and grips it, giving it a sharp twist. A clenched scream forces its way from her mouth. She can see the bare muscle of the knight's forearm skipping with the effort he drives into it.

He strains. 'Yield.'

'Fuck you.'

'Frome was right about you. You're self-destructive. You don't know when to stop.'

She pants a short, wild laugh. 'Maybe that's how I win.'

The Sorcerer Knight frowns with that same wonder in his face.

His eyes flicker down to Red's mouth – just a flicker, just like last time – but it is enough of a tell for her. She feels her eager hunger surge. He is close, so close, *now's your chance, take him* – there, she can feel his breath on her lips – who knew he could breathe so fast; is it adrenalin, or is he scared?

The thought thrills her, urging her upwards until their mouths meet. Her kiss is a bite. He gives a sharp, inward hiss and his lips fall open, unguarded. The inside of his mouth is hot and wet, and the sensation squirms inside her.

She feels the edge of his tongue slide eagerly against her own. Hard, knotted elation pulses through her veins. He grips her shoulders, twin aches; pain signals confuse and become pleasure. His tongue is inside her mouth and his lips pull at her lips and his breath comes in short, hard bursts against her skin.

After a long, agonising tangle, he pulls his head away. His forearms drop against the floor on either side of Red's head and he levers himself upwards, giving them both a hand's width of breathing space.

'What are you doing?' he murmurs, his gold-rimmed eyes wide.

'Emotions distract,' Red shoots back.

She taps her hand against the knight's groin. In it is a short knife she had concealed in her boot. Its point rests against the thick, straining bulge there.

The Sorcerer Knight explodes. Red laughs as he rolls enough to catch her wrist and wrench the knife from her hand, hurling it far away. They scrabble like rats, scratching off each other's clothes in hard, awkward jerks. The hard stone ground takes bites out of her naked back. She pushes a knee into his side and rolls him over, pinning him down with her thighs. His eyes plead. She lets loose another laugh, giddy.

'Yield,' she tells him.

'No,' he snaps.

She goes for his throat and his hands catch hers and he wrenches against her grip, pushes, fights. She presses her body down into his with weight and thigh, muscles clenched hard. He frees a hand and worms it in between them, then prises her open and impales her with his finger.

Her whole body clenches in a paralysing throb.

'Yield,' he pants.

She fights a helpless shudder.

'Yield,' he insists.

Her hand yearns outwards and she *pulls*. There is a sudden skittering sound. The knife he threw, her knife, slithers across the floor with frightening speed and the grip bangs into her leg. She picks it up and aims the point at the hollow of his throat.

He goes still, eyes wide, mouth open, staring up at her with the hungriest expression she has ever seen.

She keeps the knife steady at his skin, close enough to leave a scratch if he breathes too hard. With her other hand she reaches down in between them and carefully pulls his hand away. Then she braces her palm against his stomach, lifts her hips, grips him tightly and pushes him into her, all the way to the hilt. He gives a great groan, latching his hands on to her flanks.

They grab feverishly at each other underneath the lamps. She *has* him, she has him arching his back, stomach taut as a drum, her hands and body and throat full of young, hungry man. Scarred, soft flesh and heated, sweat-slicked skin shudder underneath her.

They fight to exhaustion, but neither yields.

CHAPTER 30

Alfren's Crypt, Cair Lleon, Blackheart
Ten Years Ago

The crypt is heavy with gathered, undisturbed darkness.

Wall torches cast light in huddled batches, pooling in the hollows of the skulls they are carved from and spilling over their bone bowl lips. On the ceiling overhead is a huge, stark painting of Marvol the Death Saint, a close-up of his face as it watches over the room, long hair splaying from his head like tentacles.

The far wall is covered in another painting, this of Marvol and Gwanhara the Fair Saint, his reputed lover. They are intertwined in a close embrace. His hand is on her back, pinning her close to him, and her fingers are closed around fistfuls of his hair, keeping his head in the crook of her neck.

Levels above is the height of a particularly blistering summer and despite the numerous free-standing fans stationed at the corners of rooms and ice in constant supply, the palace swells and swelters. The crypt's temperature change is startling and welcome, its cool air sliding slow across exposed skin.

Even so, no one will be coming down here to take advantage. Cair Lleon's famous crypts house the decaying bodies of all the

Kings- and Queens-in-the-Ground. The interment ceremony of a former London monarch happens above ground at far more impressive and official surroundings, and then the bodies are brought down here to rot gently in perpetuity, timeless markers of historical death. The tunnels that interconnect the crypts are long, winding and hard to navigate. No one pays a casual visit.

Today is no exception.

Art leans against the longways lip of a raised stone coffin. It is carved in typical Alfrenan style, bulbous and organically ornate. Arranged to his left and right in a crescent moon shape are Garad, Lucan, Brune, Fortigo and Lillath. His champion, two of his closest advisors, his personal vastos and his Spider.

He used to think it a groundless superstition, that rulers create their own version of the Saith with their inner circle. Past rulers went so far as to officially rename six of their most trusted people after each saint, claiming embodiment or resurrection, but that tradition fell out of fashion decades ago and Art has no desire to resurrect it. He doesn't believe the saints work through anyone. He doesn't believe in creating his own version of the symbolic long dead.

Yet somehow, unconsciously, he has.

Fortigo is Evron the Gentle, saint of humility, competence, compassion. Anyone in a service career has Evron as their chosen icon.

Lucan is Alaunis the Canny, saint of innovation and intelligence. Curious, clever Lucan can think his way around anything.

Lillath is Iochi the Slippery, saint of performers and spies – those drawn to secrets and games and disguise.

Brune is Senza the Just, the ultimate adjudicator, weighing right and wrong and creating law.

Garad is Rhyfen the Fierce, the warrior, the fighter, saint of courage, determination and violence.

That just leaves two. Art's lover, Belisan, is dead – he is the one who killed her – which makes her Gwanhara the Fair Saint, the artist, recorder of the world's story, saint of creativity and passion.

Which means he is Marvol the Death Saint.

The neat, awful rightness of it all makes him feel dizzy.

Footsteps echo in the hallway outside the crypt. The door, a heavy, ponderous slab, has been left open for the newcomer, who slips through it with the barest whisper of sound.

The Lady Orcade stops at the mouth of the crypt and runs her eyes over the crescent moon of people before her. Despite her famous reserve, there is something about the birdlike set of her shoulders that suggests nerves.

Lillath stirs. Orcade's attention flicks speedily to her.

'Lady,' Lillath says, 'thank you for coming.'

Orcade doesn't immediately respond. The formality in Lillath's voice seems to unnerve her further.

'When my King summons me to talk in private,' she replies eventually, 'I obey.'

Lillath is smooth. 'It was a request, not a summons.'

Orcade's gaze floats across the group in a manner that suggests her disagreement. She moves down the steps and into the crypt proper. Her gait is stiff, as if she is in pain.

She stops before Art and folds her hands demurely at her hips.

'You caught my curiosity with our choice of meeting place,' she says. 'I've only ever been down to the crypts once before, for your father's interment.'

She waits for Art to respond.

'We asked to meet in Alfren's crypt for good reason,' Lillath says. 'He was a technophobe, as you may recall.'

Orcade nods. 'Quite famously.'

'There's not a whole lot of eyes down here,' Lillath continues in an easy, offhand tone. 'Even less so in this particular crypt. The masonry's too thick to support capturer tech. This meeting will not be officially recorded in any way.'

Art watches the implication register on Orcade's face. No one will ever know what was said or done down here today, save the people who walk out of this place alive.

The air grows thick with gathering menace.

'Am I to be executed the same way my brother was?' she asks.

There is no defiance to her. She is as closed and demure as ever.

'No,' Brune says. Orcade switches to her. 'This is not an execution, Lady. Nor is it a trial.'

'Then what is it?'

'A conversation between allies.'

Orcade digests this. She glances at Art again. He knows that his face is shadowed, he knows she can't see his expression, but he still looks away.

'It has not been long since the death of your brother Agravain,' Brune says. Her voice echoes forcefully along the crypt's stone walls. 'We regret that we had to publicly announce the details of the events at the Night Carnival so quickly, and without informing his family, but our first priority is and always will be London. Steps had to be taken to alleviate any burgeoning panic among its citizens. We hope you understand.'

Orcade's chin lifts in the merest hint of a flinch.

'He was lawfully killed under moldra lagha,' she replies. 'We understand perfectly.'

They all understand perfectly: whoever gets their version out first controls the tide. The palace had no choice but to announce the news as soon as they could.

'Nevertheless, in case any confusion remains as to the particulars, we are keen to put your mind at rest,' Brune says.

Orcade's head bows under their combined scrutiny. It must be quite the weight.

'It was always clear that Agravain's insistence on pursuing his awful, groundless vengeance would lead to tragedy,' she replies. 'I'm ashamed that we share a name, and so some of the responsibility. If I had known of his plan, I would have done everything in my power to stop it.'

'Your hip seems to be paining you,' Lillath observes.

Orcade flashes her a surprised look. 'I . . . yes. An old injury that flares up from time to time.'

'I'm sorry to hear that. How did you get it?'

There is a pause that lasts a little too long.

'My brother,' Orcade says finally, 'was the cause of it.'

Don't, Lil, Art silently thinks. *She wasn't at the Night Carnival. A dozen people have sworn to her being elsewhere. Don't make her tell you about the things he did to her. It's cruel.*

As if Lillath can hear his thoughts, she simply nods and says no more.

Brune smoothly cuts in, 'Understandably keen as you are to distance yourself from Lord Agravain's actions, we have so far found precious little reassurance that the Welyens feel sufficiently removed from his viewpoints to accept the justice that was meted out to him.'

'Then let me reassure you that there will be no pursuit of moldra lagha for his death,' Orcade says. 'Not by any one of us. Ever.'

'Is the word of a Welyen worth that much?'

It is Lucan who spoke. His usual bright energy is nowhere to be felt. He is all edge.

Orcade's fingers twist together. She huddles. 'I have served on the Consilium for many years now, Sire,' she says, addressing Art directly. 'Have I disappointed you somehow? Have I betrayed you?'

'On the contrary,' Brune cuts in. 'Alaunitown is lucky to have you representing it.'

'Sire?' Orcade asks quietly. 'Won't you talk to me?'

Art's jaw is wired shut.

Orcade clears her throat. 'Despite the King's faith and generosity towards me, the Artorian era has so far not been too kind to my family,' she says. 'Agravain's actions over the years have had disastrous consequences for us. We're suffering. We've lost too much too quickly. We're scared.'

Art notes the ripple of surprise that spreads through his Saith. The reversal of Welyen fortunes has been unofficially known for some time, but Orcade's admission startles in its risk.

'I mean no disrespect, Sire, but we are not a Rhyfen family, we're an Alaunis family,' she continues. 'We are businesspeople. We calculate risk and reward. There's precious little reward in vengeance.'

'We share your viewpoint,' Brune says. 'So we have a proposal for you. You will blood-sign an immunity agreement between you and the King, stating that no Welyen will be allowed to pursue moldra lagha in perpetuity for the death of Agravain. This agreement will be kept private, only to be revealed should a Welyen try to break it.'

A sample of Orcade's blood will be kept preserved to test against the blood sealed in the document, to confirm its veracity. It is next to impossible to wriggle out of the irrefutable evidence of a blood-sign.

She stands and thinks electric-fast thoughts.

'I've never heard of an immunity agreement,' she says cautiously.

'You will have by the end of the week,' Brune replies. 'The law to bring it into being will be fought in three days' time, on the same day as several other proposed laws, hopefully lessening the attention on it.'

'But . . . you might not win.'

'I'll win,' Garad says. Their arms are folded. They lean casually against their portion of the coffin lid.

Orcade holds their gaze for a moment or two, then drops it.

'If you sign the agreement,' Brune continues, 'Blackheart will begin negotiations with whichever Welyen businesses you deem suitable for some very lucrative inter-district contracts. The King himself has particular interest in common-use applications for communications tech. "A glow screen in every home" is the idea put forth by one of your biggest innovation companies, isn't it?'

Orcade gives a wary nod.

'Such open favour from Blackheart will surely lead to the fast restoration of the Welyen name and the improvement of your fortunes,' Brune says. She fixes Orcade with a cool stare. 'No one ever heard of a Saith made of six. London suffers the loss of a limb. It needs your family doing well. It needs its Alaunis back.'

Orcade is still, deciding fate. 'Then I'll sign,' she says.

A descendant of Alaunis through and through. The Canny Saint has his hand on her, as they say.

Art stirs. 'I thought you'd ask for more time to consider,' he says.

She looks at him. 'Would you have let me out of here to do so?'

His silence is all the answer she needs.

'Then I don't have much choice,' she says, and quickly adds, 'Agravain made sure of that.'

Memories of his Swording day surface briefly in Art's mind. He sees a younger Orcade in dove grey, standing coiled and tense before him as she bargains her way out of her brother's shadow. Now her brother is dead, and it has all led to this.

He feels numb. He is grateful, as it is currently the only thing he'd like to feel.

Orcade is looking at him. 'Sire, I . . . I have a question.'

He inclines his head. 'Please.'

'I have heard,' she says carefully, 'there was someone else involved in the attack on you?' She looks to the floor. 'Your official statement said that she was my brother's long-time accomplice, but none of our family know anything about this woman. For all we know, she could have been manipulating Agravain from the beginning. Apparently she was a godchild with some peculiar talents?'

She is careful to present it as a bargaining chip and not a threat. Everyone in this room is all too aware of the twisting the palace has had to do to paint the picture they prefer. Agravain was clever enough to hide any real evidence of his hand all the way to the end, and Belisan really had been so much more powerful than anyone could ever have guessed.

Cair Lleon has been ruthless in severing any possible ties between Art and Belisan. As far as the world knows her, she was a godchild assassin working with Agravain in an evil conspiracy to behead London with the murder of its King.

Remember that I never meant to hurt you.

Art does remember. He remembers too much detail from

that night that he would rather forget. He remembers how her body bucked as his bullets punctured her. He remembers the high-pitched screech that sounded like a child but was probably her, the last noise she ever made. He also remembers the flood of her rage in his head, pushing him to an act he had never believed himself capable of.

The state of the hall afterwards, the tables overturned and the rugs littered with glass from every smashed wine cup. The panicked, mindless crowd around him, the shouts of his guard. There were too many witnesses to keep this one private, so Belisan is hidden no longer. The world knows her now, and the world has made its judgement.

'We will make sure to highlight her influence on your brother,' Lucan says. 'She didn't have much family to speak of, so there's small danger of a counter-statement.'

Orcade inclines her head. 'Thank you. Such a kind gesture would be much appreciated.'

Lucan nods. 'Please, allow me the honour of accompanying you upstairs and we'll get the necessary documentation begun.'

Brightly brittle practicality sweeps them from the crypt. As she stiffly mounts the steps, Orcade turns her head back to Art. He swears he sees a look of pity on her face before she disappears.

He can feel the anxious eyes of his remaining Saith rove over his every expression, his every gesture, looking for clues to his thoughts. But he has none to give them.

She had the potential to be a new Fria Lysander, they said.

You did the right thing, they said.

Art, they would have killed you, they said.

For the greater good, they said.

He had agreed, because it was either that or collapse under the weight of what he has done.

He turns away from them all, walks towards the steps, mounts them and leaves the crypt wreathed in silence. There is nothing to say. Enemy or lover, the result is always the same. They lost and he won. He won, and winning is the only thing he has now.

He moves along a soothingly cool corridor, making sure to avoid the exit Lucan and Orcade would have taken. He has little idea of where he is going. He'd like to wander aimlessly in the dark for a while. He might even get lost down here. The thought comforts him.

'Sire. Wait.'

He quickens his pace. His brain is too tired to even form a cogent thought of 'leave me alone', but his body knows what he wants.

'Artorias.'

His full name, and in such a forceful tone, stops his forced march. Only one person in the world ever says his full name. Besides, he can hear the muted tocks of her bladed feet on the dusty stone ground.

He has had nine years of Brune at his side, guiding his eye through the thorny, bewildering viewpoint that is London politics from its very top. Despite knowing that she was his father's closest vastos advisor, or perhaps because of it, trusting Brune has come easy. Her allegiance is to the Kingdom above whatever sovereign it might currently glorify. She is calm, controlled, frightening when her rare anger is provoked. He respects her perhaps more than anyone else in his life. For her, he stops.

'Where are you stalking off to in such a huff?' she says, puffing a little.

Art just looks at her, waiting for whatever it is she needs to get off her chest. Once she is done, he can be alone again.

Brune cants her head. 'It worked out well. Better than we could have hoped.'

'And all I had to do was kill anyone who stood in my way,' Art agrees.

'Indeed,' Brune replies without a trace of sarcasm. 'I'm glad you've finally found your ruthlessness, Sire. It took a man like Agravain to tip you just a little more that way, just enough. We have that to thank him for, at least.'

'Thank him,' Art flatly echoes. 'Yes. Every day I thank him.'

'You can have your grief, for a while. I know you loved her.' This is said with a touch of brisk impatience.

'And now she's dead because of it,' he retorts.

'What a silly thing to say,' Brune observes.

Art just waits. There have been a number of speeches like this from his friends over the past few days, ranging from sorrowful to kindly to puzzled to irritated. He knows they all mean well.

'So,' Brune continues, 'your plan is to mope dramatically along the dark halls of the dead for a while, wondering whether it wouldn't be better if you joined them?'

Of course, no one else has dared to be quite as blunt as that.

'Do you hate yourself because your survival instinct had you kill her before she killed you?'

'She didn't want to kill me,' Art mutters.

'Who says?' Brune evenly replies. 'The woman who lied to you from day one? Your enemy's willing game piece? The hard truth is, you'll never know what she really wanted. You can agonise over it for the rest of your life, if you like, but it seems like a sorry waste of time to me. And believe me, when you get to my age, wasting time will be your biggest regret. That's the one that'll eat you up at night. She made her choices, Sire. She made 'em, and she didn't make 'em with your happiness in mind, but her own. That's what people do.'

'Her death is still my fault.'

Brune laughs. 'No, it's not. Dear saints, how did you get all the way there? Are you a total idiot?'

For a moment Art's disbelief at her mockery stuns him into silence.

'Let's see,' she says to herself, and in the exact same way she used to lesson him: teacherly, motherly, irritatingly condescending. 'What is it you truly believe about being King? That you are responsible for every decision you make?'

'I have the Consilium, I have you, I have advisors coming out of my backside,' he replies, nettled. 'But at the end of it all, I make the final choice and I bear the responsibility for that choice. I always have, ever since I took the Sword.'

Brune actually looks annoyed. 'You, take the Sword? You barely had a hand in it.'

Art gives a short sigh. 'Yes, fine, I'm very aware I wouldn't be King without Garad and Borin playing their parts too, but you're being pedantic.'

'I'm not talking about *them*,' Brune shoots back. 'I'm talking about me and Hektor.'

Something about the way she says it, with an added weight, gives him pause.

'Hektor? My childhood guardian, Hektor?' he says dubiously.

'Well, who else, Artorias? It's not a common name. We were supposed to marry, once upon a time.' Brune gives a curt nod at his surprise. 'Yes. Back a million years ago, when we were both young.'

Art tries to picture his old guardian: a gruff but kindly knight with a huge handlebar moustache, the grey hairs around his upper lip stained yellow from years of smoking. A man utterly incapable of speaking at normal volume, everything said at a booming shout. His servants loved him dearly, often showing their affection by bellowing 'PASS THE SALT' and 'IT'S COLD TODAY, ISN'T IT' at each other whenever he was out of earshot.

Si Hektor, unabashed adorer of dogs and horses, but often barely capable of acknowledging another human's existence. A lifelong bachelor, Art would have sworn to the ground, and he would have sworn the same for Brune. He cannot imagine them together.

'What happened?' he asks, his curiosity aroused.

Brune dismisses the question. 'Life. But we remained friends – bound together by the way we saw the world, I suppose. We were young enough to be idealistic, and therefore all the more crushingly disillusioned when those ideals were tested past breaking point. So we made our own play.' She looks at him. 'Didn't you ever wonder why Hektor stepped forwards to claim you when no one else would touch you? He has a tremendously kind heart, but even so.'

Art studies her cool expression. 'What are you saying?'

'That you were a strategy. We had several, of course. You were simply the one which, against all the odds, paid off. It depended on so many ungovernable things. Keeping you alive and safe as a child, because we couldn't guarantee that Uther wouldn't change his mind and try to wipe out his mistake, or even that Ingerna's family might not try for some misguided vengeance of their own. Educating you the way we wanted, which didn't necessarily mean you would end up sharing our values.' She pauses. 'And then Uther dying once you were of an age to actually take the Sword, of course.'

In the face of it, all Art can do is laugh. 'You can't be serious.'

'I'm perfectly serious,' Brune admonishes him.

'Are you trying to tell me that it was you who had Uther killed?'

'Don't be silly,' Brune says impatiently. 'I don't go around murdering rulers; it's far too destabilising. That's the move of a petty, amateur player like Agravain. I will admit that I had something to do with Borin forfeiting in the arena, however.'

Art's mouth falls open. 'What in seven hells did you have over him?'

Brune just shrugs. 'Moves and countermoves. Most of them you'll never even know about. Most of them *I* will never even know about. So many players in the game, so many influences, so many moving parts, so many stakes, so many differing desires pulling the world in a million directions, shaping it in a million ways. It isn't just wilful stupidity convincing you that you make any of your choices alone. It's downright arrogance.'

Art stares at her. It stings, and more than it would from anyone else.

'I love you, Artorias,' she says stiffly, 'as if you were my own son, and more than I ever suspected I could. Now up there' – she points vaguely to the ceiling – 'the world still turns, and there are still choices that you must make. But you never make them alone. You're never alone.'

At this his heart gives a great, glad shudder, and entirely without his consent.

Brune looks away.

'Kembrish ambassadorial meeting first thing in the morning,' she reminds him, and then clicks off into the darkness.

PART III

Marvol comes for us all.

Traditional Saith prayer

CHAPTER 31

Wendelsworde, Gwanharatown
Six Years Ago

'Art, this is the worst idea you've ever had.'

Garad Gaheris, the Silver Angel – twelve years the King's own champion, famed for their ability to face down opponents that would turn most other knights' bowels to water – actually looks nervous.

'Surely not,' Art says, employing his most reasonable tone. 'Remember that time I persuaded you all to explore that abandoned water tower in the middle of the night and part of the roof collapsed on top of Lucan's—'

'This is worse,' snaps Garad, their uneasy gaze trained on the dilapidated townhouse currently rearing before them.

The journey to get here took a two-hour burrow into the southwestern depths of Gwanharatown. They came together on a bike, with Art covered up in what has, over the years, become his favourite incognito outfit – battered, generic Blackheart leathers with a dark smoked helmet to match, obscuring his face and hair. Garad is in muted blues, betraying their Evrontown roots, but their patches are fake un-affiliations.

'He is just a man, Garad,' Art says, even as his pulse skips in response. 'To treat him as anything else would be to disrespect him.'

Garad snorts. 'Somehow I'll cope. Art, listen to me. Edler Feverfew is long dead, no matter what the glows say.'

That name, even now, carries a sickly weight.

For the last few months, rumours have been circulating that the notorious thwimoren and disgraced former King's pet is not only alive, but back in London and openly flaunting his exile.

It began with an excitable report of a sighting near Edler's old neighbourhood in Gwanharatown, then *sighting* became plural, and soon enough the rumour trickle turned into a flood. Soothsayers began sprouting varying proclamations of Edler's intentions. He wants a pardon. He wants to offer his services to the son of his old master. He wants to kill the current King, whom he helped create. Hysteria has its buzzing fingers around London's throat, and the palace has begun to feel the squeeze.

It has been four years since the deaths of Agravain and Belisan. In all that time, Art has barely left the sprawling fortress he calls home. His security won't allow it. Their sovereign must never be placed in such danger again, no matter what the situation – and in any case, it can't be counted a hardship when his place of confinement is such an embarrassment of riches. No one could ever want for anything in Cair Lleon.

Yet Art does. He *wants*. He has spent the last four years feeling half dead himself, numb to every kind of strong feeling. Hearing the Edler rumours is like climbing out of a cold, dark well to feel the first prickliness of heat and light on his skin again, kindling him back into painful life.

This time, he will get some answers to his past. By the saints, he will.

'I just want to talk to him,' he says.

Garad tries again. 'I know the last few years have been hard for you, but sneaking out of the palace alone like this is . . . it's self-destructive. You need to go out with protection.'

'Why d'you think I asked you to come with me?' Art replies. 'Garad, I trust you with my life.'

'Don't flatter me just so you can get away with this,' Garad says, close to losing the battle and fully aware of it. 'If Jaksen finds out that I helped you with this, I'm dead.'

'We both are,' Art retorts. 'You think being the King will save me?'

Garad gives a resigned sigh.

Jaksen is the head of the King's personal security, a terrifying woman who appears to have had her sense of humour surgically removed at birth. She was the one who insisted on teaching Art how to shoot a gun, and in his uglier private moments, she has shared the blame for the consequences of that.

'I don't even know why I'm being so nervy,' Garad grumbles as they pick their way forwards. 'There's nothing here to find. Look at it, it's been abandoned for years.'

The townhouse looms over them both like an omen from a nightmare as they reach its rusting gate, which is already unlocked and listing gently on its hinges. It gives out a sad squeal as it moves back to let them in, the metal scraping against the ground. Weeds line the stone path, poking up through cracks in the cobble. The front garden is a bristling tangle of vegetation, damp and dark and crawling. The crumpled, blackened front wheel of a pushbike lies forgotten among the tall grass.

Art fancies he can feel eyes on both his front and his back as they climb the steps and pass under the porch overhang. The cracked marble echoes with their footsteps. As Art raises his hand to knock he senses Garad move beside him, a subtle shift into a defensive stance.

'You hear that?' they murmur.

'What?'

'Music.'

Art cocks his head. The strains drift through the door, soft and high. Layered stringed instruments with a strangely thin, veering kind of tune.

'What was that about nothing to find here?' Art asks, raising his hand – but before his fingers touch the bell button, the front door unlocks and slowly swings open by itself.

Instead of the fear he knows he is expected to feel, the fear rolling off Garad like a palpable smell, Art finds himself getting annoyed.

This feels like showmanship.

The place is spotless. The hallway floor beyond is tiled in black and white, with a deep red carpet running down the middle. The tiles are scrupulously clean, as if newly laid. Dully gleaming brass brackets line the white walls, holding electric candle lamps running light upwards to pool on the ceiling. Threading through it all is that quivering ethereal music. Despite outside appearances, someone definitely lives here.

In the gloom beyond the hallway lights, Art sees something move. He steps over the threshold, ignoring Garad's warning hand on his arm.

The voice, when it comes, is melodiously male and pitched low. 'You going to tell me what you want?'

Art halts, his heart scattering its beats across the floor.

'I'm looking for someone who knew Edler Feverfew,' he calls back.

A pause.

'I knew him,' says the voice.

Art searches for the source of the voice in vain. Edler had a family, didn't he? A wife and son. It's not the wife talking, and the son would be too young for this voice, which rolls with the gravel of mid-age.

'I mean you no harm,' Art calls. 'I just want to talk.'

'About the rumours of him being alive? I saw the statement the palace put out yesterday. All cock-hard denial.' The voice takes on a childishly mocking whine. '*Edler Feverfew died several years ago overseas. There is no truth whatsoever to any talk of his return. And even if there were, London is barred to him. King-in-the-Ground Uther's sentence still stands. He was an exile, and an exile he remains, even after death.*'

The voice has a knack for memorising speeches, it seems.

'I just want to talk,' Art repeats.

'Come on in,' the voice says at last. 'Come see me, and I'll tell you all about him.'

'Where?'

'First door on the left.'

'Stay here,' Art whispers to Garad.

'Don't be stupid,' they hiss back. 'I'm going first.'

Art does not protest. Garad moves ahead, their fight hand resting on the short scabbard buckled at their hip, fingers caressing its catch. The Night Carnival incident prompted a long, difficult review of the laws on personal weaponry. Guns are now illegal for any non-knight citizen to carry, and other weapons may follow suit. Reliably reactionary glows networks have warned the law will soon extend to knights, but Garad has made their feelings pointedly clear on that possibility. In all his life, Art has never once seen them without some kind of sword attached to their side.

Art steps on to the crimson carpet. It sucks stickily at his feet as he walks, even though it looks new and freshly brushed. He watches Garad reach the first door on the left and push it open.

Beyond is a little parlour. The fireplace dominating the room is framed by a white stone mantelpiece that draws the eye. Charcoal symbols have been drawn on the surrounding walls, and in the flickering light coming from the candelabra on the mantelpiece they look alive. There is a plush emerald-green daybed and two high-backed armchairs.

In the armchair closest to the fireplace sits a man. He is grizzled but neat, a wispy white beard tumbling from his chin and resting against the purple velvet topcoat he wears. Small black eyes in a leathered face above long, steepled fingers. The glossed tips of shined shoes, the kind you might wear to a ball, catch the light. Altogether he looks about ready to hold a party, albeit of a kind that regretfully sacrifices hapless victims in the cellar before congregating in the parlour to sip molasses-laced tea and nibble on hors d'oeuvres among pleasant conversation.

'Why, it's the Tricky King,' says the man, with dramatically feigned surprise. 'What are you doing here? Where's your retinue?'

The man his father Uther had once called both the greatest friend and the greatest enemy he had ever had sits blithely before Art, and he doesn't appear to have aged a day since he left everything he had ever known in disgrace.

The rumours are true. Edler Feverfew is alive.

Art finally manages to speak. 'You're supposed to be dead.'

Edler regards him cautiously. 'Well, maybe I am. Maybe you're looking at a ghost.'

They stare each other down.

'You wanted to talk,' Edler says at last. 'Didn't you?'

Art gives a weak nod of his head.

'Well, won't you sit down, Sire?' Edler indicates the daybed opposite his armchair with elegant fingers. 'I've no refreshments fit for the King of London, but you didn't send word you were coming.' There is a note of reproach in his tone.

Art crosses to the daybed in a daze and sinks downwards. It sags underneath him, catching him off-guard. He sees Garad take up position in the open doorway, blocking the only exit with his short sword stiff-ready in his hand, which makes him feel a little safer.

From this position, Edler's profile barely protrudes beyond the curve of his chair back. It is impossible to tell what he is thinking.

'You look like Uther, you know,' he muses. 'In the face. Not in the body, of course.'

Art is an insect in comparison to his huge mammalian father, all knobbly waving arms and legs. The question comes out of his mouth before he can think to stop it.

'Why did you help him rape my mother?'

The music, which has been winding its way through the background all the while, abruptly stops. In the screeching silence, Art forces his hands and his posture to remain relaxed.

'That's not what happened!' All trace of decorum is gone in a snap. Edler's profile turns a little, sensuous lips pulled angry-thin. 'Where d'you get that lie from? The gossips?'

'From my guardian family.'

'Who, though? Who?' Edler's voice drops to a furious, petulant mutter. 'Not the pious Si Hektor. Not him. He'd have protected you from all that.'

Pious is said with the slant of a slur to it.

'Si Hektor did protect me,' Art replies sharply. 'It was someone else.'

There is a shuffling sound from Edler's chair. Propping one thin elbow comfortably on the chair's plush arm, he turns in his seat to face Art. It must be the candlelight reflecting in his eyes to turn their edges bright gold like that. It must be the candlelight throwing those thin shadows up the walls like that.

'Do you want the truth of what happened between them?' Edler asks. 'That's what you came all this way for, isn't it? It must hurt not to know.'

'Yes,' Art murmurs.

'I can show you, if you like?'

This is a straining need in Edler's tone that makes him sound unexpectedly puppyish and young.

'How?' Art asks.

'Art,' Garad warns, sounding nervous. 'Don't. Let's go, now.'

'It's just magic,' Edler says, almost pleading. 'It's just a show. Illusions can't hurt you, can they?'

Art does not agree, but he can no more walk away from this than he can voluntarily stop breathing.

'Please,' he says. 'Please show me.'

Edler's smile widens, the smile of a child eager to show off his talents.

The light brightens and darkens around him at the same time—

—and then, suddenly, Uther Dracones is standing in the corner of the room. Alive, tall and real and there, filling out the air. He is handsome. Art had forgotten that. Sharp, roving eyes. Hair razored close to his scalp at the sides. Legs spread wide, hands clasped behind his back . . .

No. King Uther is dead. He is King-in-the-Ground now, and besides, this is not him as Art knew him. This is a younger version, beard barely showing a thread of silver. His gaze passes over Art and Edler alike, unseeing, but Art cannot stop watching his father. It is all there. The way he would always walk slowly and purposefully, as if he owned every bit of space he was moving through. The way he would look at people full in the face, as if he owned them too.

Only now does Art begin to appreciate just how dangerous Edler is. He has never heard of any godchild with a talent as unbelievable as this. It is more than illusion, more than mere projection. It *is* Uther. Living, breathing, seemingly touchable.

A woman blinks into existence in front of Uther. No slow materialisation – she is just there, and so fast it takes a moment for Art's brain to remember that she wasn't always.

One physical trait Art actually shares with his father is that pale, unruly hair. Otherwise he is all his mother: tall, slender as a tombestere – though he himself shares none of the grace those tumbling dancers are famed for – with green-glass eyes, currently cast to the ground as she listens to Uther murmuring into her ear.

Ingerna Gorlais, as real as you feel.

Art drinks her in greedily. It still disturbs him how desperately he needs to feel something about her. It is not pain that he feels but the absence of it, which is somehow worse. At least pain is undeniable. Hollowness is so endless, so nebulous.

She is not as studied as she looked in all the official captures of her. She would always have her head tilted up from below, the better to accentuate her jawline, polished even further by the sharply cut hair just grazing her throat in the style she favoured back then. Here, now, in this room, her cheeks are flushed and her chin is up. The hair is more dishevelled, strands of it falling in rumpled waves. She pushes it back from her face absentmindedly.

Art cannot hear what is being said into her ear, but her response to it is quite clear. It is in the way she keeps exposing the line of her neck to Uther and the way Uther's eyes drink her up. His hands are by his sides, but one keeps lifting as if to touch her, then dropping back down.

They are flirting.

Art's stomach drops. This is not right. This is not how it was.

'How do you know?' comes Edler's soft whisper, and Art realises that he must have spoken his thought aloud. 'I was there. You weren't even born yet.'

Art is frozen, locked in horror. Now he realises what he is being shown. This is not a recreation of his parents randomly dancing to Edler's tune like puppets made of light and air.

This is a memory.

They are watching the first step in the conception of Artorias Dracones, recreated through an illusion more magnificently artful than the very latest in glow tech. Art's father takes his mother's hand, pulling her into a dance while she makes pretty little protests. Uther is laughing. He looks sweet, and young. They begin to move silently to music that Art cannot hear, clearly delighted with each other.

'This is a lie,' he says. 'She was another man's wife and she rejected him. So he used you and your illusion magic to make himself look like Gorlais, and then he went to her, and she thought he was her husband so she—'

'Why are all commons so ignorant about how these things work?' Edler sounds aggrieved. 'An illusion might be able to fool the eyes and ears, but not the smell and certainly not the touch. What kind of miracle do you think it would take for a woman to lie with a man who only *looks* like her husband, but doesn't smell or feel like him? Never mind the different body shape, underneath the illusion—'

'He raped her,' Art says, his throat dry.

'They had an affair, Sire. It only lasted the week he was staying at the Kernowyen court, but it was every night of that week. My role was to fool onlookers, that was all. Couldn't have the King of London going into a married woman's room every night, could they? Servants and guards, they can be such terrible gossips. So I made him look like her husband.' He gives a soft snort. 'Anyway, Gorlais deserved it. He liked nothing better than to sit up all night getting methwern on beer 'til he could barely speak, then stumble to bed half blind in the small hours. Of course, there wasn't supposed to be a child out of it. But you know what your saints-fearing, fight-loving pere did when he found out your mere was pregnant?'

Art does not have to ask, for it is being played out before his very eyes. He watches Uther, his arms folded, his face a terrifyingly blank void as a swollen Ingerna screams at him, her mouth stretched comically wide.

She has come all the way to London, to Cair Lleon itself, to confront him and demand that he acknowledge the child. He refuses, and then has her exiled from ever setting foot in London again. She defies his orders, risking prison to give birth to Art in a private Blackheart bone house.

Then she dies.

'Why did she have me?' Art whispers, and here it is, finally, the truth he has been seeking. The question that has squatted inside him his whole life, leaking into his guts. Why have the unwanted child of a sordid, week-long festival fuck?

'Well, it may have something to do with the soothsayer she saw before you were born.' Edler rises from the armchair, moving to the mantelpiece and leaning a shoulder against it. In the background, Art's dead father looks stonily on.

'What soothsayer?' Art asks.

'She had one come to do your birth wyrd.' Edler gives him a sidelong glance. 'Do you even know what that is?'

'Of course I do,' Art snaps.

'Touchy! Commons can be rather ignorant about our culture, I've found,' he says. 'Well, the soothsayer comes along and pronounces your wyrd, and guess what he tells her. He says that despite everything stacked against you, when you came of age you'd take the Sword of London. He foresaw your glorious ascension.' Edler snorts. 'I suppose it heartened her enough to decide to go through with you. P'raps it was her final vengeance against your pere. Who can say for sure, apart from her, and we can't ask her now, can we?'

Art can feel his fists trying to clench.

'How the fuck do you know so much about it?' he says.

'Who do you think she asked to get her a soothsayer?' Edler replies. 'I was the only godchild she knew.'

Art wants to rip out his lying tongue. His mother would never have gone to the man responsible for her assault for help. This has all been cut to make Edler look good and his own mother look bad.

'He was right to break with you,' Art says. 'You're poison.'

'Poison?' Edler looks incensed. 'Me? Your father was nothing but a bully braggart and your mother was an ambitious little cu—'

Art snaps.

He leaps to his feet and surges towards Edler, his fist lashing out at the man's thin jaw. At first he doesn't realise why it goes wrong so fast, why he keeps going forwards instead of connecting, why he sees his fist pass *through* Edler's face before it swings him down on sudden water legs.

He stumbles, dropping to his knees, and then looks up from the ground.

Edler has disappeared, gone in the space of a breath. Behind him is a boy Art has never seen before. He is dressed in old, stiff trousers and an old, stiff jacket, both curiously out of style. He stands still and shocked. His head cocks like a bird's as he regards Art with wide, wary eyes.

Holy fuck. Edler was an *illusion*.

Before Art can draw another breath, the boy breaks, fleeing to the back of the parlour, wrenching open a door there and disappearing beyond it.

Art hears a bark of anger from Garad, the sound of running feet, the bang of another door. After a moment, he pulls himself unsteadily to his feet. He is too dazed to follow. His mind is a mad whir, trying to sort through everything he has just seen and felt.

That boy – not only did he make Uther and Ingerna, but he overlaid himself with Edler and inhabited him like a puppet – just the way Uther must have inhabited Gorlais. He made them all out of his own head. No wonder the Edler illusion sounded so young in his manner of speech. That boy couldn't be more than sixteen or seventeen years old.

Illegal magic is the least of their problems here. The sheer *realness* of those illusions makes Art feel dizzy. That had been a walking, talking trio of people, full of visceral life and expression. It is almost impossible to believe that he has been interacting with nothing more than bent light and manipulated sound. Is any of this real? Is the boy himself real . . .?

Art checks the thought before it can run him all the way into madtown. Illusions can't open doors, no matter how good they are.

Garad appears in the parlour doorway, breathing hard. 'He just ran down into the cellar and locked himself in. There isn't another way out of there, so I'm not sure what he's playing at. Who is he? Where did Edler go?'

'Edler wasn't real,' Art says in an absent, *do try to keep up* voice. 'That must be his son.'

Garad's mouth falls open.

'He didn't try to leave the house?' Art asks.

'I was blocking the front door.'

Art considers. 'Perhaps he found you so intimidating that he panicked.'

'A godchild with that kind of magic? I should be frightened of *him*, not the other way around. Art, we need to contain this.' Garad sounds dangerously close to panic themself.

'Child is the right word. God*child*.'

'What?'

'He's just a cub.' Art regards the panting Garad. 'And he went into the cellar instead of escaping.'

Garad stares at him uncomprehendingly as Art walks out of the room, moves down the hallway and heads straight to the closed cellar door.

He knocks.

Silence.

Art talks through the door. 'That was incredible. Making my parents like that. Making your father like that.'

Silence.

'You're Edler's son, aren't you? They callian you Wyll, as I recall.'

Silence.

'Why did you pretend to be your father?'

Silence.

'Scare you away,' mutters Wyll at last.

He sounds thin and young, nothing like the melodious tones of the conjured Edler.

Art considers this. Recreating both their fathers and playing out an elaborate, emotional conversation between them is a strange method of trying to scare someone away.

It feels more like a clumsy attempt to impress him.

'Why would you want to scare me away?' he asks.

'I'm dangerous, right.' Wyll's voice has a tremble to it.

'Why are you dangerous?'

'You saw why.'

'Yes, and it was one of the most impressive things I've ever seen. You should feel good about that. People try to impress me all the time. They rarely succeed the way you just did. Can I come in? I don't want to talk to you through a door.'

A long, long silence.

Wait. Just wait.

A scrabble.

A click.

The door swings open.

'Art, let me go first—' he hears Garad say behind him, but instead of waiting he moves slowly down the steps, giving the boy before him enough time to scramble back down to the bottom and retreat around the corner.

The cellar is dingy. A naked bulb dangles from the ceiling, pooling in a weak circle on the centre of the floor. There is an old roller bed. A table with a half-empty glass of water on it. Several plates on the floor, smeared with the remnants of food. The curled edges of an old, well-thumbed book on a nightstand. More books fill the tall bookcase in the corner and rear in teetering piles at its foot. Heavy furniture dominates, hundreds of years old in style. There is just one source of natural light, a small grille of iron bars set high into one wall. The bars are set far too closely for anything larger than a cat to wriggle through.

Art turns his attention back to Wyll, who has pressed himself into the furthest corner of the room.

'You live down here?' Art asks, bewildered.

'It's the safest room,' Wyll croaks. 'Cos of the iron.'

'The iron?'

His eyes dart sideways and Art follows his glance. Piled like snakes on the ground are a set of thick chains, pulled through a ring set into the wall. On the end of each chain is a metal bracelet.

An ugly, rancid feeling unfurls in the pit of Art's stomach. 'You chain yourself up in the cellar,' he says.

Wyll hesitates. 'Pere told me I must.'

'Edler? Why?'

'He said . . . he said my magic was too big. It had to be contained, or we'd get in trouble.'

Iron is supposed to render godchild magic harmless. London boasts a long history of selling iron trinkets and junk to commons. Apparently godchildren can be as superstitious as everyone else.

'I'm sorry about all the things I said upstairs,' Wyll says suddenly. 'Pere used to teach me to pull his memories out and make them real. It's how I used to practise. And after he died, I just . . . kept on practising.'

So that is how he can conjure Art's parents so well, despite having never met them. Art has heard of past illusionists who could perfectly recreate people and images they had seen with their own eyes – but from other people's memories?

'Edler's dead?' asks Art gently.

Wyll looks away. 'Few months ago.'

'How did he die?'

'Been ill a long time. Something in the bones.' Wyll gives a sullen shrug. 'They never told me much about it.'

'Where's the rest of your family?'

He hesitates. 'Overseas. They've kept to the exile, even after Pere died.'

'So you're here by yourself?'

For a moment, a touch of defiance skates across Wyll's slender features, then it sinks away just as quickly. He ran away. To be self-sufficient at his age is both a source of enormous pride and enormous shame. A common sixteen-year-old might find it almost impossible to do without raising suspicion – but a thwimoren? He could make himself look like anyone. He could make a house look dilapidated and abandoned so no one would ever think to come knocking.

Until Art did.

'You seem to know a lot about me,' he tells Wyll.

'You're the King. You're . . . I've watched all the glows on you.' The boy hesitates. 'I'm sorry, I didn't mean to hurt you. I just like things to be real. I used to make the things in my head real, so I'd have someone to play with. But people didn't like it when I did that. They always got afraid.' He speaks eager-fast, but his voice is flaky and crackled as if with disuse.

Art keeps his concentration locked on Wyll. 'I'm not afraid.'

Wyll just looks down into the ground, head bent. He has the tense set of a kicked dog.

'So you're alone here,' Art prods.

He gives a wary shrug. 'It's better if I'm kept away from everyone.'

'I respectfully disagree,' Art replies, looking around the cellar. 'Will you tell me why you came back to London? This isn't your home.'

When the word comes, it comes whispered-soft. 'Clemency.'

Art frowns. 'What?'

'We're not our fathers,' Wyll says. 'Maybe . . . maybe we can break the vengeance chain with us.'

He looks frightened.

'You think I'd have come after you?' Art asks curiously.

Wyll shivers. 'My father could have helped your mother, Sire. She did ask him. I saw it in his memories. He only came forwards after she died, and only because he hated the King and wanted to punish him.' Wyll swallows. 'My pere killed her, Sire, as much as anyone. You've the right to moldra lagha. You've the right to take your vengeance on me.'

But, Art wants to say, *you didn't kill my mother.* I *did.*

Held up to the mirror of Wyll's illogical guilt, Art suddenly realises how strange that sounds, what a foolish burden he has been carrying all this time. He is no more responsible for his mother's death than Wyll is. They have inherited the sins of their fathers and it is past time to set them down.

He cannot walk away from this boy. Somehow, he thinks Wyll knew that, might have even been counting on it.

Art rubs his face, thinking fast. 'Would you come with me, if I asked you to?' he asks.

Wyll watches him. 'What do you mean, come with you?'

'Live somewhere else. Somewhere you could be safe. Somewhere you wouldn't hurt anyone.'

Wyll's sudden look of painful hope is electrifying, excruciating – then his face shuts down again.

'This is my home,' he says, uncertainly.

Art says, in a tone painfully raw with sincerity, 'Home is where you're happy. Not necessarily where you're from, or where you live. Are you happy here?'

'No,' whispers Wyll.

'So, then.'

He watches the reality of his offer dawn on Wyll's face. Watches him rapidly, precociously adjust.

'Is there a lot of iron, where we're going?' he asks. 'It keeps me contained. If you take the iron away, I'll be capable of anything.'

Art shrugs. 'Isn't that the point of life? What you *actually* do versus what you're capable of, though – that's the real test of a person.'

Wyll just looks at him. His irises are encircled with a colour so bright they look set with rings of gold.

In the creamy murk of a dead winter's day, the boy's bronze skin shows pale and uneven. He picks at the loose threads of his jumper, pushing the sleeves back from his wrists and then pulling them down again, back up and then back down, as he sits on the back of Art's bike.

Garad's expression as they look at Wyll is akin to them watching a fuse burning down. They pull Art off to the side.

'Are we having him arrested?'

'We can't leave him here,' Art replies.

'Well, of course not,' Garad says. 'He's far too dangerous to be left loose.'

'He's spent the last few months locked up in a cellar, do you really think I'm about to exchange one prison for another?' Art's tone shows knives. Garad looks startled. 'His father is dead. The rest of his family evidently doesn't give a damn about him or they'd have dragged him back by now. He's all alone. Are we also going to abandon him? What would that make us?'

Garad stares at him for a moment too long. He can see it all in their eyes.

Identifying a little too hard, Art?

Art moves over to Wyll, who looks up.

'You're really going to take me away,' he says.

'Only if you want it. We can contact your family—'

'They won't care.'

There's still a chance they might, and Art does not want a scandal on his hands. He will have the palace open up discreet talks.

'Am I to stay with you?' asks Wyll.

Art hesitates. 'We need to find a good home for you.'

'You said home is where I'm happy.'

Art nods. 'I did.'

'What if I'm happy with you?'

Art opens his mouth and then pauses, at a momentary loss.

'I know it sounds fun, to stay with a King,' he says eventually. 'But it's not, really. You'd be much better off with someone else.'

Wyll is silent.

'We'll see,' he says finally, and suddenly he doesn't sound sixteen any more.

Garad is standing straddling their bike, helmet balanced in their hands, watching them both. Art knows what they are thinking, because he is thinking it too.

Just what are you planning to do with Edler's son? he hears them asking him.

I have no fucken idea, he silently replies.

CHAPTER 32

Iochitown
Three Months Ago

Red stares at the grimy machines arrayed before them in a radiating wheel.

'Pedaloes,' she says, unimpressed.

'Oh,' Fin scoffs. 'You thought we were going to go roaring through the streets on bikes shouting, "Look at us, sirrahs, look at the knights!" Anyway, you don't even have your own bike yet.'

'But,' she protests, 'these things are unsafe.'

'Thousands of people use pedaloes on the daily – and the trags, of course.' Fin pauses. 'Well, apart from the idiots who still think sitting in quad jams are a good way to get around, and the businesses who need bigger transport.'

'I know all that,' Red says, stung. 'I'm not a complete idiot.'

'Then you know how to ride one.'

Red stares at the pedalo. It looks simple enough. If you can ride a bike, you can surely ride one of these toys. Trouble is, she *can't* ride a bike. Not yet.

'Help me,' she says, giving up.

Fin doesn't hesitate. She sits Red astride the pedalo and shows her how to go fast and slow, how to ride uphill and down. Then they set off, Fin leading the way, Red wobbling along behind.

It was Red, this time, who sought out Fin for company. It has only been a week since her encounter with the Sorcerer Knight, but it tortures her. Training eats up most of the day, but the rest of it is spent in constant contemplation of his body, his voice. The exact sound of his moan. Sleep slips further out of reach the harder she makes the grab for it when she thinks of his moan.

Red wonders if he shows on her, as if his hands were covered in paint that only reveals itself hours later, marked and smeared on her skin in every place he touched her. He hasn't yet sent her a message, and she has no way of contacting him. Thinking of him maddens and frustrates her, but her brain refuses to do anything else. She can give herself temporary relief – and she does, has to, before her body will even let her do anything else as difficult as getting out of bed – but temporary is all it is. The ache comes crawling back soon enough.

You should have killed him, not fucked him, her mind argues with her. *You're being a coward.*

It was too dangerous to try, she argues back. *I need more time. I need him to trust me.*

So she waits, scratching up the walls. Company takes her mind off the torture, at least for a little while.

She and Fin have taken pains to dress patchless and leatherless and wear hats, though somehow the pedaloes render them invisible. After all, what kind of Caballaria knight would be seen dead on such transport? It's easier to understand their appeal as people's gazes slide right off her like they're greased. After a few minutes Red's riding smooths out and her confidence swells.

This is easy, she thinks.

As they ride alongside the canal, a duck wanders nonchalantly into the path of Red's pedalo. The only way to not squash it is to either ride straight into the canal or straight into the path of a young woman with a baby perched on her back in a high sling. Red chooses the third option, which is to veer off wildly to the left and completely lose control, coming off the pedalo and landing in a heap on the – as it turns out – incredibly hard and unforgiving ground.

'Red!' she hears Fin call, and then moments later she zooms into her vision, leaping off her own pedalo with the ease of a cat. 'Are you all right? Are you hurt?' She crouches down, looking anxious. 'Was it that fight I saw going on back there? Did one of 'em knock you off? I swear, I'll go knock 'em right back—'

Red holds up a hand to stop her gathering heat. 'It was a duck.'

Fin stares at her. 'What?'

'There was a duck,' she says. 'A fucken duck cut me off, and I had nowhere to go—'

Fin begins to laugh. She rocks back on her haunches and tips her chin up to the sky, hooting. 'A duck?' she manages to gasp. 'You fell off because of a duck?'

Then she begins to howl.

'Shut up,' Red says, desperately trying to hold on to her anger. 'It just sat there. It was almost like it wanted me to ride straight into the canal.'

'A fowl deed,' Fin proclaims, and out bursts a fresh gale of laughter.

'Fuck you.' Red begins to laugh.

They sit on the ground together, people side-stepping them with a mixture of determined ignorance and the bare minimum of irritated grunts, while they giggle like kids until every belly muscle hurts.

'It was evil,' Red manages to say eventually as they subside.

Fin wipes her eyes. 'Oh, Iochitown ducks are demons. Everyone knows it.'

'Thanks for the warning.'

'Sometimes,' she proclaims solemnly, 'the only way to really understand something is to live through it yourself.'

'So this was some kind of lesson for me?' Red says as they pick themselves up.

Fin just grins at her, then points to her elbow. 'Does that hurt?'

Her skin is skidded pink and red where the ground took a loving bite out of it.

'Starting to sting like a trick shock now I've noticed it,' she says. 'But I'll live.'

'Your first proper city scar,' Fin tells her, straddling her pedalo. 'Congratulations, Si!'

She rides off and Red, wobbling a little again, follows.

They trace the canal bank for a few miles, using the narrow strips of path. As she grows used to the pedalo Red relaxes and begins to notice the world within a world they move through. The canal is stuffed full of life. Long, brightly painted boats are moored up along the banks, wallowing comfortably in their watery support. Some are growing gardens on their roofs. She sees leafy vegetable plants, thick spindles of longreach, bushes of rosemary and creeping tangles of Knight's Passion, the bitter-tasting herb they turn into the brain-buzzingly strong tinctures drunk in all the Caballaria bars.

Along the decking of the boats they pass come flashes from tiny mirrors fixed to thin fishnet rope, scarves fluttering in the breeze, posters advertising theatre nights, book collections, trinket sales, antiques, fresh fruit. There are boat bars, boat bookshops and tea shops, boat 'everything that exists on land, we have too'.

They hold a panoply of people stretching, sitting on decks, hanging out of tiny cubbyhole windows. Two children, no more than nine or ten, fish off the canal-side while someone hollers at them from across the water to come and have their lunch *right now*, the leaf trout will still be there later. More than once Red notices a symbol fixed on a door or hanging in a window like a charm or a chime, in wood or metal or glass or thick weave. The symbol is a circle, one side broken open by a waving line bisecting it.

Clustered along the edges are the bankside folk, living over and next to the water but never on it. They occupy untidy, narrow jumbles of houses or stark, elegant buildings with riverside walls of glass that loom over the canal ribbon. Red thinks of Six's dockside place. Presumably they paid handsomely for that view. Willow trees droop down to the water, which mirrors their greenery with soft, thin carpets of algae furring its surface. Narrow house moves into warehouse moves into dock moves into clusters of bars and eateries, their tables perched right at the water's edge.

'They say to throw your cutlery into the water, for good luck,' Fin tells her when they leave the canal behind and take a pause. 'The canallers will find it. The trinket-sellers dredge the thing all the time, don't you know, looking for other people's crap to polish up and mend and sell on again.'

'What's the circle with the wavy line mean?' Red asks.

'That's the symbol of Ephas. They hang it up or paint it everywhere to call on his protection.'

'Who's Ephas?'

'River god. Or gods, rather. He's the big one, the leader. There's a few more. Belisama, Dorin, Hefaster.'

'The canallers have their own religion? I thought . . . I mean, they're Iochitown. They're London.'

Fin gives her a puzzled look. 'Neh, but they also have their own things as well as those. Identity comes from places within places. Places in your heart as well as your feet. You look confused.'

Red frowns. 'This city is complicated.'

'It's made up of millions of people boasting several allegiances each. The most complicated dance there is. It bothers you?'

'How am I ever supposed to understand it?' Red says.

Fin considers. 'Why do you need to? Besides, it's hard to get bored of something that will always have more to uncover, hard to tire of something that keeps changing on you. It takes so much, but it gives so much back, too. It's an exchange. You have relationships with places as well as people.'

'Who made you so wise?'

For just a moment Fin's sparkle dims, greyed by the clouds rolling across the sky of her face.

'I spent my childhood running up and down London's veins,' she replies. 'She's my mother and my father.'

Over the next few hours, they make their way across a good portion of Iochitown. There is a calmness to the pedalo, a lightness. Where a bike is a roaring lion of freedom, a pedalo is a bird, gliding across the world rather than muscling through it. Crossing a bridge, Red catches sight of words painted on to the dark stone in stark, white letters, phrases in fat or curling or barely legible scripts:

FROM SHITHOUSE TO GRANDHOUSE
THE CHILD RETURNS AND NIGHTMARES FOLLOW
ALL BOW BEFORE TERMINAS

She has no idea what any of it means.

Quiet brick streets. Lantern-strung alleyways. Flashy night areas, sleepy in the daylight. Cramped apartment blocks, winding house snakes, and then gradually the view streamlines, simplifies, familiar trappings left scattered in their wake. They follow enormous fences past huge, functional buildings squatting in stretches of nothing landscape and barely roads that seem to lead to nowhere much. She never knew that a Kingdom filled with twenty-four million people could have so much emptiness inside it.

Fin stops them both next to a magnificently strange construction behind a set of gates next to a wide dirt track. A limbo place of scrub and skyline.

'Know what this building is for?' Fin asks.

Red looks up at it. It is a deep, rusty red, with cream bricks in pretty patterns around its tall, somehow sad windows. Spires and turrets jut into the sky, suffusing it with grandeur and mystery. It is all by itself, and beautiful in its aloneness.

'Some sort of abandoned castle?' Red hazards, mystified.

'It's a sewage plant.'

She tosses Fin a look of utter disbelief.

'Serious,' Fin says, unmoved. 'The biggest sewer network in the whole dis' running underneath our feet, right here.'

'But . . . it looks like a *church*.'

Fin throws her arms wide. 'A church to the Saint of Sewage.'

'Holy shit,' Red says.

The look Fin gives her is one of pure, unfettered delight.

'You made a good joke!' she crows. 'I can't believe it. Why didn't we capture it?'

'I'm funny.'

'You are,' she agrees, 'but almost never intentionally.'

'You don't know me that well,' Red insists, somehow not even remotely offended.

'No. That's what today is all about, itso?' Fin grins. 'Come on. There's something else I want to show you.'

They ride along the wastelands, flitting past concrete and steel, criss-crossing girders making stark patterns against the endless sky. Humans are creatures of patterns, creatures of nature, for nature loves a pattern. They imprint themselves desperately against the earth. If they control something they think that means they own it – but maybe the beauty and the pain and the life comes in the things they don't control.

Fin leads them to a series of strange sunken metal constructions set deep into the hollowed-out ground. Sheets of water sluice through a giant steel gate, glistening and roaring and sprinkled with sunlight. Sentrying each side of the gate is a gantry way housing the gate's mechanism, which looks something like a giant's version of a flick switch. Each switch looks almost as tall as Red.

Each gantry way rises up from a sturdy concrete block, speckled with its own unique pattern of stains left by the water. Old dark rings bisect the block, the levels rising and falling over months and years and decades, rising and falling, over and over. Everything changes, it says. Even things that seem to have such permanence in the world, like concrete, are changed by the world around it.

This was all here before Red was alive and will be here after she is dead, and someone like her made it. A lot of someones, fragile and fleeting humans building things who last far beyond them, who transform the lives of yet more fleeting humans, rippling out across time.

'What is it all for?' Red asks, curiosity on fire.

'Something to do with water power.'

'But what does that mean? What happens, exactly?'

Fin shrugs.

A kind of magic, but made of concrete and steel. A slower bending of the elements to fit a purpose.

'Let's sit for a little while and catch our breath,' Fin says. 'I brought drinks.'

They select a gantry and dangle their legs out over the roar of the water below. Fin hands Red an open sip tank and she takes a grateful swill of beer.

Fin sighs. 'So you finally got your heart's desire.'

Red shoots her a startled look.

'Becoming a knight,' Fin explains.

'Oh.' Red attempts nonchalance while the memory of Wyll's warm, wet tongue douses her brain. 'I suppose so.'

'What comes next?' she asks.

Red shrugs. 'The next thing you want.'

Fin huffs a little laugh. 'Mm. What's that, for you?'

'I don't know. I've never been able to think that far along.'

'Careful. It might sneak up on you.' Fin tips her tank and takes a pull.

'Is that mirror talk?'

'Ha! Too sharp, too sharp.' Her glance is scarcely less. 'What's today all about, then? Why did you want to come out with me?'

Red nurses her tank. 'I just needed some time away.'

Fin nods. 'I understand that. Our gloriously privileged lives come with a certain weight.' Her head tips. 'Or is it something else? You can trust me, if you need it. We have no one in common, who'm I going to tell?'

'We have one in common.'

'Who?'

'You know' – Red swallows his familiar name away before it gets out – 'the Sorcerer Knight, don't you?'

Fin waves a dismissive hand. 'Ah, his secrets are the most closely guarded in Blackheart, and he despises gossip. I've known him a little while, but I don't feel I really *know* him. For such a darling of the Caballaria, he's curiously averse to its world. I'm not sure he has any close friends at court, either.'

'He has the King,' Red says distantly.

Fin suddenly and obviously drops into guard. 'Neh, he does at that.'

'I've heard no one gets close to the King without going through his champion first.'

'That's so,' she agrees.

'Is it true the King hasn't left Cair Lleon in years?'

'I'll tell you something,' Fin says suddenly. 'I'll tell you it first if you answer the same question afterwards, true as you dare. That's the game.'

Her eyes are full of challenge.

'I'll play,' Red warily responds.

'If you could have anything you wanted, right now, with no consequences, no obligations standing in your way, no nothing – what would it be?'

'You first, then.'

Fin raises her sip tank to the rushing water beyond. 'The ability to be absolutely unable to fall in love.'

Red gives a whistle of surprise. 'That's a big one.'

'But undeniably useful.' She winks, a pleasureless gesture.

'Who is it?'

'That you're not getting,' Fin says. 'Your turn.'

Red stares out across the gantry monsters before them. 'I'd like to disappear,' she says.

Hard to tell whether it is Fin or the beer that kicks out such an honest response.

Fin's gaze turns on her like a searchlight. 'You've come to the right city for that.'

Red keeps silent.

'People who want to disappear don't often choose to be the focus of a million eyes in the arena.'

'Violence is the only thing I'm good at,' Red says.

'I saw you dance at that party we went to. You were pretty good at that. For someone methwern on party dust, I mean.' Fin laughs at the expression on her face.

'I wasn't methwern,' Red protests.

'You mean you move like that when you're sober?'

'Taunter.'

Fin sucks in a breath. 'Easy with the insults, now.'

'Just giving back what I was thrown.'

'Ho, I only insult those who I want to like me,' she says, disarming Red with another flick of honesty. 'Me and London. You have to like London too, Northerner.'

Red shakes her head. 'I don't belong here.'

'That's not how it works. You're here now, so you're London. Anyway, no one who ain't London looks at it the way you've been looking at it all day.'

'How have I been looking at it?' Red says.

'Like you can't get enough of it. You're already half in love. Go all the way.'

'And what does going all the way involve?'

Fin smiles. 'Seeing its guts and not just its skirts. Most people don't bother trying to find the hidden layers. The streets they walk every day, the places they work, the buildings they eat and sleep in: that's all life becomes, for most. That's all they've learned to see – and that's a tragedy. They miss out on this wonder all round them. If they'd just take the time to look . . .'

Fin isn't looking at Red. She is looking at somewhere beyond here.

'It's all about risk,' she says dreamily. 'Risk is in our blood, yours and mine. It keeps us breathing. If I spent my life playing it safe, I'd never find all that wonder. Go after what you want, Red, and don't be afraid about it. You've only got the one life, and tomorrow you might be dead.'

'Marvol comes,' Red murmurs.

'Marvol comes for us all,' Fin agrees.

As the clink of their bottles echoes across the rush of the water below their feet, Red comes to a decision. She will play things out a little longer, just to see what comes of it. She is no longer so sure of what she wants, but she does know what she doesn't want. She doesn't want Wyll to die.

Not yet. Not yet.

CHAPTER 33

Si Hektor's Estate, Senzatown
Six Years Ago

The lawn is the right side of manicured, enough to keep the unpretty parts of the wilderness at bay.

It sweeps downwards in a gentle slope, melting into a haphazard treeline at the far bottom. Berry bushes dot the periphery, scattering fruit on to the grass. Through the little wooden gate off to the side sits a vegetable patch, currently buried under an embarrassment of fat yellow squash and wolf peach vines. The air is soft and warm with the last dregs of summer. Mykke birds call from the treetops, content with the day. It is a place to believe in the quality of human beings again. A place that gently pours quietness into the mind.

As Art leans back into his chair, he hears the approaching swish of footsteps across the lawn.

'T'chores, Wyllt Ambrosias,' he says out into the gathering dusk and indicates the empty seat opposite him. 'Come and sit with me?'

He has filled out even more since they last saw each other, Art notes with approval, though when all the growing is done there may still be hollows left underneath the cheekbones, making sharp, sweeping planes of his face.

'How d'you get my full name?' Wyll says as he takes the empty seat.

'Your family told me,' Art replies.

Wyll watches him. 'You've been talking to them?'

'Yes. And they have finally agreed that it's in your best interests to stay here, rather than go back to live with them.'

The *finally* is a small, kind lie. Wyll's family were only too glad to hand him over to the Gwanharatown district officials they were contacted by. They have no idea who is really behind it all. The news glows would near faint with jubilation if they ever got wind of the King's involvement in Wyll's well-being, but all possible steps have been taken to make sure that they won't.

The boy is well hidden here at Si Hektor's estate. Art's old guardian has proven adept at defending lives from prying eyes, and well he should, having had enough practise with Art.

Wyll looks out across the lawn and says nothing.

'Only if that's all right with you,' Art prompts. 'To continue staying here.'

Wyll shrugs.

'I know it's a little bit quiet, in the countryside.'

Wyll shrugs again. 'Quiet is nice.'

Si Hektor's estate is in the very outer borders of Senzatown, a long ride out from the centre. Out here is all farmland, rolling hills, woods and pastures and paddocks.

'You don't miss the city?' Art asks him.

'They take me in for day trips, sometimes.' Wyll hesitates. 'I like the theatre.'

Art raises a brow. 'Yes, I heard about that.'

A few weeks ago, Wyll had been taken by Hektor's coterie to

see his first live show. During the interval, he had expressed bafflement at the lack of realism in the painted set design on the stage and was given a quick crash course in suspension of disbelief.

The second half of the play had really come alive.

'It was stupid,' Wyll says, a touch of sulkiness in his voice. 'Everyone sat there cooing and gasping at this sagging wooden thing they wheeled on to the stage. It didn't look anything like a horse.'

'So you made it into a real horse,' Art says as calmly as he can.

'I thought people might like it better,' Wyll protests.

His illusion had been so convincing that it had caused a sensation. The local glows had been full of baffled praise for the play that had managed to get a real stallion onto its tiny stage, even if they weren't quite sure how on earth it had been done.

He had been lucky. There was enough confusion and doubt to cover his tracks.

'People don't go to the theatre for reality,' Art says. 'They go to get away from it.'

Wyll digests this. 'It's been a while since your last visit,' he says.

There is something surprisingly direct about his manner. He is quiet but not unsure. Reserved but not shy. In only a few months he has come a long way from the cowed boy Art met in the cellar of a dying house.

'I know, and I'm sorry,' Art replies.

Wyll gives a wry smile. 'You're the King. You're busy. That's not why I said it.' He looks out across the lawn. 'It's nice, here. It's nice.'

Art feels it coming.

'But?' he says.

'When I'm eighteen, I'll be an adult. I'll be able to do whatever I want.'

Art nods. 'Yes.'

Instead of elaborating, Wyll rises from his chair. He takes a few steps away on to the lawn, his back to a puzzled Art. He stands, unmoving, looking down into the treeline. Just as Art opens his mouth, movement catches his eye. Long, spindly legs pick their way out from the brush. Glossy fire fur burns under the dwindling sunlight.

The deer steps on to the lawn, one ear twitching back and forth.

There is something heartbreakingly perfect about its placement here, in this place, at this time, something that makes Art ache for all the beauty in the world. It moves forwards, delicate hooves lost in the grass.

Wyll raises his hand and crooks a finger in a gesture of beckoning.

The deer approaches them fearlessly. Its white throat glows. Muscles slide and ripple as it moves. Wyll reaches out. It is close enough to touch. Astonishingly, the deer dips its head into his palm. Even more astonishingly, its muzzle passes right through his hand.

'There's a whole family of them in the woods back there,' Wyll says softly. 'I studied them for days to get it perfect.' He lowers his palm and smiles. 'The real deer are too stupid to be fooled by my deer, though. Or maybe they're too smart. It doesn't smell, see, my fake one. It's only bent light, after all, made to fool human eyes.'

He claps his hands and the deer disappears.

It takes a moment for Art's brain to catch up with his eyes, to understand that it has really gone.

Wyll turns towards him, arms folded defensively against his body. His face is a mix of sheepish and defiant. 'I don't really need to clap or anything,' he says, 'but people find it less weird if I do. They don't like it when I just think things into appearing or disappearing.'

'Can't imagine why,' Art murmurs, his heart in his mouth. Somehow he had managed to forget just how extraordinarily, utterly convincing this boy's talent is. And how easily he conjures it. 'Wyll . . . I know you're under-age, but magic is still illegal. If you get caught—'

'Did you realise the deer was a fake?'

'No.' Art finds it hard not to be honest around Wyll. 'But that's not the point.'

'I know, Sire,' Wyll says. 'I just wanted to show you that I can make good things with it. Beautiful things. But . . . I can make bad things, too.'

'Don't call me Sire,' Art says automatically. 'Wyll, I've told you before. I'm not afraid of you.' He gazes at the coltish boy-man standing before him. 'Everyone has the power to make bad things. It's a choice. Make that choice, and become a certain kind of person.'

'The kind of person you hate,' Wyll murmurs.

Art raises a brow. Just who has he been talking to?

He sits back. 'In my view, there's only one way in the universe to ensure anyone's loyalty.'

'Give them a ton of trick,' goads Wyll.

'Trick can run out, or someone else can give them more.'

'Be more powerful than them.'

'Power is finite, and fosters resentment,' Art responds.

'Then how?'

Art shrugs. 'By being the kind of person they want to be loyal to.'

Wyll says nothing. Art thinks of the horse, and the deer, and wonders if this place feels like just another cage to him.

'I think I know something of how you feel right now,' Art offers.

He is met with disbelieving silence.

'You have this . . . thing inside you. It won't leave you alone. It tugs relentlessly, making everything you do and everything you are not enough. It's not enough for you to just be alive. You have to be *more*. You have to do *more*. Every day that you spend not pushing for the *more* is a day wasted, until you wake up with a sick feeling in your heart, a sick, heavy feeling that drags you down and makes you wonder why you even exist at all.'

Wyll is staring at him with his mouth open. 'How did you know that?' he says.

Art smiles. 'Trust me, you're not the only one who feels it. It's the curse of a brain that has evolved beyond the preoccupation of survival. We did it to ourselves. We wished to be different to animals. Now we have to live with the consequences of that wish.'

Wyll hunches in his chair. 'Sometimes I wonder if it wouldn't be better to be the deer,' he says.

'Sounds boring,' Art says lightly. 'But your life is yours to choose what to do with.'

Wyll lets loose a sudden, wild laugh. 'No, it isn't! You own it!'

Art stares at him in astonishment.

'*Own?*' he repeats. 'One human being can't own another. Where did you get such a stupid idea?'

'You think it's stupid, what I feel?' Wyll says, thumping his chest. 'Don't you understand? You've given me everything. It's worse than the hold Pere had over me, because I'm *grateful* to you for it. I'm not free until I fulfil it.'

'Fulfil what?' Art demands, taken aback.

'My *debt*. I was rotting away in that cellar. I would have been something . . . something like him. I know it. I had no way out. But you came and you gave me a way out. You saved my life, so now I'll have to save yours.' Wyll throws his hands up in the air. The gesture is so dramatic, so unlike the calm, poised boy Art has up until now known him to be, that it is almost funny.

'You see a prophecy, soothsayer?' he says before he can stop himself.

It is a phrase with a double meaning, meant as a sarcastic retort when a know-it-all declares an opinion. In this case, he supposes that it could be taken a little more literally.

Wyll lowers his arms and flops back into his chair.

'I'm no soothsayer,' he says at last. 'But you're the King. People often want you dead, right? Stands to reason your life is going to need saving.'

'Your optimism is cheering,' Art drily replies. 'Wyll, why don't you tell me what it is you want?'

'To come to Cair Lleon,' Wyll says in a rush. 'To . . . to serve you, as best I can.'

Art stares out across the lawn, struggling with an unpleasant falling sensation. It is the feeling he always gets when he sees the choices before him narrow down and down, until the only thing left is inevitability.

'Why?' he asks. 'Because of a debt you think you owe?'

'Not just that. You're the first ruler with . . . with sympathies.' Wyll rushes on, apparently aware of the dangerous ground he treads on. 'After my father . . . things got so much worse for us. Uther created godchild registration, didn't he? It was said to be done to legitimise us, but all it did was make us become so much more illegitimate. And the hunters they send after us – God's Guns?' He takes a breath. 'It was a punishment, Sire.'

What, Art thinks, *has he been reading, and who,* who *let him read it?*

'I understand the history,' Wyll says. 'I know all about it. But it was a long time ago, and we've paid for it now. We've *paid* for it. It's not fair to make us keep suffering for hundreds-years-old sins that we had no part in. To get spat on and beat down and kept away from any path to success, just because of the way we're born. I didn't have a choice. I didn't ask to be a godchild, did I? It just is. It's just who I am. And I have to live with that and find a way to love it, or spend my life hating my own skin. Why should I be asked to do that? Why can't I be – be *useful*? Why can't I be good? You said it. *You* said I could.'

Art closes his eyes.

Wyll is aflame with all the urgent passion of his idealistic youth, his raw pain. 'I know you're not one of us, but you could change things! It could be different; it could be better. And I could help you.'

'No,' Art says.

Silence.

'But—' Wyll tries.

'No. Never. You hear me? That's never going to happen.' Art unclenches his jaw and grapples for calm. 'Your father and mine – together they created a legacy that I've been doing my damnedest to unmake. What do you think it would look like if you appeared at my side?'

History repeating. That is what it would look like.

'Not at your side,' Wyll says doggedly. 'Just around. In the background. Protecting you, helping you.'

Is that how it had begun between Uther and Edler? Protection? Help? Good intentions?

'No,' Art repeats. 'I want you to stay away from court.'

I want you to stay away from me.

Wyll's mouth thins and his expression grows stormy.

Art hardens. 'It's not a request, Wyll.'

'Then let me learn how to fight,' he quickly responds.

Art blinks at the sudden turn in conversation. 'What for?'

'I want to go into the Caballaria.'

Art hesitates. There is technically nothing stopping a godchild from becoming a fighter knight, but it is so unheard of that he might as well try to mount the sun. No fighter would ever go up against someone capable of magic.

'That would be very hard for you to achieve,' Art says carefully.

Wyll shrugs. 'You're the King. You could make it easier, couldn't you?'

Art laughs. 'You overestimate the power I actually have.'

'Is it because you hate us?'

'What?'

'I wouldn't blame you,' Wyll says, rushing on. 'Not after what my father did. I really wouldn't. But I'm not him. I'm *not*.'

He stops, unshed tears clotting up his throat.

He is Art's ghost, a mirror, a reminder.

'It's complicated, Wyll,' Art says gently. 'It might take a long time to even try.'

Wyll sniffs, swallows his tears down. 'I can't apply to the Caballaria until I'm eighteen anyway, can I? You've got well over a year.'

Art laughs, a rueful laugh.

There *is* time, he consoles himself. Time for Wyll to grow and change and lose all interest in imaginary debts. No one has to know who he is, after all. He has the choice of shedding his past that Art never did. He has no idea of the wealth of possibilities for his life, because he has never been shown. By the time Art is done showing him, Wyll won't even want to set foot in London ever again, never mind come anywhere near court.

It is time to send him away. Away from the people who might use him as a weapon, away from the King who feels a dark and awful itch to do the same.

This is protection. This is the right thing to do.

Art clears his throat. 'Have you ever wanted to go travelling?'

CHAPTER 34

Stredforthe, Marvoltown
One Week Ago

'Eventide, Si Red.'

'Eventide, Ford.' Red shuts the quad's door with a dull snap.

'The pass into Marvoltown'll be a bit clogged, what with the autumn festival going on in the dis' tonight,' Ford says, as he pulls along Spittelgrounds Boulevard.

'Itso?' Red responds, puzzled at the significance.

'So enough. I've let Si Wyll know you might be a little later than usual.'

The quad turns on to dark streets.

'So it's in Marvoltown,' Red says after a pause. 'Where you take me.'

'Stredforthe, to be more exact,' Ford replies. 'Bit of a bare downs around there, for my taste; I prefer a more family-friendly area these days. Still, I can see why Si Wyll chose it.'

'Mm,' Red agrees.

Ford isn't stupid. He wouldn't break the Sorcerer Knight's privacy by so unconsciously letting the location of his secret training ground slip. He must have been told that he could.

But why?

They drive for a little while before Ford trips another alarm during an enthusiastic exploration of his plans to join in Marvoltown's revelry. His schedule sounds so outrageous that it prompts Red to jokingly wonder if he'll have time to come back for her.

'Oh, I'm not picking you up tonight, Si,' Ford replies. 'I was told you wouldn't be needing it.'

Red battles a nervous flush. Because it is assumed that she'd be staying the night, or because she won't be leaving at all?

Dead people don't need pick-ups, whispers her paranoia.

For the rest of the ride, Red uses Stillness to try and undo her tension knots. By the time she arrives at the Sorcerer Knight's private training ground, she is calmer. She is ready.

Then he opens the door to her and she lays eyes on him for the first time in several weeks.

Fuck, he's beautiful. Fuck, fuck, *fuck*.

'Come in,' he says.

She walks over the threshold. She feels him in the darkness behind. Her mind treacherously replays a flash of him uncovered and panting beneath her.

The front door shuts with a very final click.

'We're going to try something different today,' he tells her. 'Follow me.'

He walks into the gloom ahead, coiled inwards, all openings guarded, leading her to one side of the cavernous room. Machinery sits silent, waiting for purpose. Come too close and those hulking beasts might feed off her, their pistons brought back to life with her meat. Beyond their blocky shapes, a draped sheet is covering the vast brick wall behind. The Sorcerer Knight stands at one end of it. Beside his shoulder dangles a long metal winch.

'Have you ever seen a galdor wall before?' he asks.

Red shakes her head.

He reaches up and begins to work the winch. Metal hands extend down from their fixes at the wall's top, gathering the sheet at its dusky skirt in their grasping claws and hauling it slowly back up the wall, waves of material bunched in their steel fists.

As the sheet ascends, a riotous mess of colour blazes out from the brick behind it. The entire wall is covered in paint. Tiny scribbled phrases in ghostly white. Sprawling poetry. Snatches of song. Strings of nonsensical sentences. Fat rainbowed words as big as a horse. There are yellow and green mice maybe nine feet high dancing around a fire, caricatures of knights squabbling over swords, slender-hipped guard girls with guns gripped in their fists, monkey-headed boys and cats with seven legs and wise eyes. Faces. Sunsets. Blood. Swords. Skulls. Flowers. Boots. Skylines. Suns and moons. Names and numbers, over and over, cramped into every tiny space between artworks.

Galdor walls can be found throughout every district of London. Bare stretches of brick or metal or cement or glass – the sides of alleyways and docks tunnels, the walls of houses, abandoned storehouses, trag stations, and even often the ground – are covered in paintings and messages. Some walls are historical, left preserved as a window into the past. Some are active, with sections regularly painted over to make room for new messages, or older paintings embellished and added to by other artists. No active wall stays the same from month to month.

Supposedly, the only person who can paint a galdor wall is a godchild. They claim they can tell if anything has been written or drawn by a common – it gets immediately erased. Some commons declare the walls are dangerous coded information points, and rage for their destruction. Some call them prophecy or art, and argue for their protection. Many assume them to be nothing more than the ramblings of bored creatives and half-mad soothsayers. Either way, destroying them doesn't do much as more always spring up elsewhere. There are no end of surfaces to paint in London.

Red stares at the wall, entranced. It would take hours just to see it all.

'It's an old one,' she hears the Sorcerer Knight say in a soft voice. 'They stopped adding to it decades ago. A more secretive one as well, presumably, since it's inside an abandoned building.'

'Do you know what any of it means?'

He leaves the winch and steps back to regard the wall. The moment he comes closer to her, Red feels her belly give an eager, yearning roll.

'That one.' He points. 'Apparently it was painted by Lailoken himself. You've heard of him? One of the most powerful soothsayers of the last hundred years, so they say. Some scholars think it's a prophecy made about our current King.' He gives a derisive snort.

Red traces the words he indicates.

THE FORGOTTEN CHILD
WILL COME TO CLAIM THE SWORD
AND LONDON WILL BLEED

'Galdor walls are slowing down,' the knight says, his gaze on the brick. 'Fewer and fewer active walls are changing, and the ones that are don't get updated half so often.'

'Why?' asks Red.

He folds his arms. 'Because godchild numbers are dwindling. They have been for a long time now. Fewer of us born. Magic is being bred out of the world. We're becoming a fucken endangered species.' His fury, normally so tightly controlled it can barely be seen, startles in its plain view. 'They'd rather have a world without magic than a world that contains something they don't own. They're like spoiled toddlers who want all the best toys so no one else gets to have them. We must be kept on a leash. It makes pets of us all.'

Red watches him warily. It made no sense before, why he would want to give her control of the one thing that would make her more of a threat, but it is starting to now.

'You don't want to teach me to control my magic,' she says. 'You want to weaponise me.'

The knight frowns. 'I just want to do something – *something* – to push back against our own decay. What you can do, it should be encouraged, not forced behind walls where all it does is rot. Another loss of talent, of, of *life*. And for what? So we can all be more banal? More common?'

'I'm not interested in being part of some political uprising, or whatever it is you're doing.' She resists the urge to step away from him. 'I'm just here for one thing.'

The knight finally turns to look at her. 'And what's that?'

Death.

'Knighthood,' she says out loud.

'Being a knight is not everything, Red.'

'Easy for you to say,' she rejoins. 'You already have what you want.'

'It's a lonely way to live,' he says. 'Don't you realise that? Everyone either worships or hates you. It's boring.'

'Right,' Red scoffs. 'But there's a part of you that likes it. The hate and the worship, both. Makes things easier, in some ways, doesn't it? At the very least, it keeps them all away.'

He says nothing, but his face tells her she scored a hit.

Perhaps the reason he goes searching for other godchildren has nothing to do with the paranoids' theories of him building an army of magic, or eventually taking control of London. Perhaps what he is looking for is the opposite of control.

'Why are you really here, Red?' he asks of a sudden.

'To learn from you—'

'No.' The Sorcerer Knight cuts her off. 'You've risked a lot to get here. More than anyone knows, I've no doubt. Why? Just to get noticed and make your showy debut?'

'No, I—'

'I'm not the only one's been keeping secrets. Why are you *here*?' he demands. 'Why are you invading my life?'

The full weight of his attention is so heavy that she feels it like a snake tightening around her chest, cracking her ribs.

She snaps. 'I don't know, I don't know!'

'You want to use my fame to get some for yourself, is that it?'

'I don't care about that! They said that local challenger bouts don't get recorded. I didn't want to end up on the damn glows being paraded across the damn sky. You told me not to speak of these training sessions, and I haven't told a soul. I just want . . .'

'What do you want?' says the man, because he is a man, and all Red's fantasies feel childish now in the starkness of the living, breathing human before her.

'To prove to you that I was worth your attention. Not anyone else, just you. I'd have fought you alone, if I could, but the challenger bout was the only chance I was ever going to get.' Red waits a beat. 'You can laugh at me now, if you like. You can call me an arrogant little cub and dismiss me.'

The Sorcerer Knight contemplates her.

'What if I said that you'd have to promise me, swear on

whatever is most precious to you, that you'll never even mention my name to anyone, no matter how much you trust them?'

'I'd say yes.'

The knight's reply is entirely flat. 'I don't believe you.'

'I'd say yes because I'm losing this fight,' Red snaps, her temper fraying. 'Because I've tried not to, see, but thinking about you makes my insides tie up like dock knots. Because that one message from you at the end of my first day in the Dungeons sent me wild, but then you didn't message me again, not once, and I didn't understand why I needed another one so badly. Because when I realised you weren't at my first bout it cut me to the bone, and I didn't understand why then either. I hated you for saving my arse when I threw that bout. I humiliated myself in front of everyone, but it was you I cared about seeing that. And I should have told you not to save me, I should have done the honourable thing and taken the fall, but I couldn't, because it would have meant that I'd lost my chance to be near you again. So I became a coward because of you, and I hate myself for it. And I hate that I came here tonight wanting something more than training, and I hate that I'm talking to you like this now, because all I do is humiliate myself in front of you, and all you do is stand there and watch me do it, and I don't even know if you want me at all, or if this is some game you're playing. And even then I'll let you play it, because it means that maybe you'll let me get close to you—'

She stops. The pressure in her chest is incredible, agonising. She has never felt anything like it before. What in seven hells is she doing to herself?

'Don't tell me not to come after you,' she says. 'I don't know how.'

It feels like truth, and the pain eases.

'Red.'

Her name in his mouth makes her insides give a delicious squirm.

'I just . . . don't want you to use me.'

He sounds unsure, and a little lost.

'I don't want you to use me, either,' she says, and that, also, feels like truth. Perhaps just in this moment. Perhaps that is enough.

'Come closer,' she says, to see if he will.

He gives a little shiver, and then he does. This time not to defeat her, but something so nearby that it twins with the same pure, single-minded desire. It feels unsteadying. It feels like falling.

They stand still, close, without touching.

'Tell me not to give in to this,' says the Sorcerer Knight.

'Tell me to go, then,' Red goads.

'It's too late for that. I've been craving you every night since we met.'

The words curl around her like the tip of a tongue. She tries to swallow but her throat is so dry she might as well have drunk a cup of dust. The knight waits in front of her, straining against his leash. Red looks down. Saints, quite literally straining, rock-hard.

'Will you tell me what you want?' he asks, and Red can hear a thread of soft, hesitant nervousness running underneath all that careful reserve.

'You,' she says.

'Tell me that again.'

'I want you.'

'Now that you have me, what do you want me to do?'

It is getting harder to breathe like a normal human being and not a rabbit – fast, fast, fast.

'To kiss me, Si,' she says.

The knight surges forwards, then stops himself. 'Please, don't call me that. It's Wyll.'

She tests his name out on her tongue. 'Wyll.'

Wyll's next words set her on fire. 'Where should I kiss you?'

Red reaches out and takes Wyll's hand in her own, pressing it against the throbbing ache currently trying to rip its way out from between her thighs.

'Here,' she says. 'Kiss me here.'

She has never imagined it possible that two people could stand unmoving, wanting each other so much that it pours out of them, all coyness and shame abandoned, breathing so hard that passing out is surely nearby. They haven't even taken their clothes off yet.

Saints, saints, saints.

Wyll sinks to his knees. He takes his time. He settles himself, vulnerable as a pet, at Red's feet. She reaches down, desperate to see his skin, and together they tug his shirt upwards and off while he kneels. His hands come up and sinewy fingers grasp Red's belt, pulling it out of its secure loop, leaving both ends wagging open and free. The fingers then move on to Red's trousers, unfastening, focused on their task. He has a constellation of freckles on his shoulder, she notices hazily, a sign to guide her on, but to where?

He tips his head up, catching Red in a liquid gaze that at this angle seems to plead steadfastly with her as his mouth opens and his tongue unfurls and he presses the flat of it entirely up against her. She feels her knees buckle with absolutely no agreement from her brain. For a moment she struggles, nothing to balance with, and then feels herself pushed gently backwards.

'The wall is just behind you,' Wyll murmurs. 'Just there.'

Her palms go out and she feels it, leaning herself on cool solidity from her tail bone all the way to the back of her head. As soon as she has it behind her she feels the tongue again, rasping through her wetness in thorough, even, licks.

He takes his time. His tongue explores every crevice, agonisingly. She shifts on its tip, rising urgently on her toes when he gets close to undoing her too fast, sinking back down when he relents. His left arm braces against her hip, nudging a thigh to one side to make room for his full attention, and his fingers spread her wide. He might be on his knees before her, but he makes her the helpless one.

Before he can undo her completely, she tugs him up to her and kisses him, tasting herself in his mouth. Her head ducks, pushes hard into his chest. Her forehead brushes against the skin there as she tips her chin up, burrowing her face into his neck.

'Will you tell me what you want, now?' she asks the skin at her lips.

She feels the hands on her shoulders tighten and the body against her presses into hers, crushing her into the wall behind.

'Tell me,' she says again, and takes the skin of his neck in her mouth as her hands crawl down his sides and grip him to her.

'Just keep touching me.' The words come tumbling down on her. 'Please just keep touching me. I'll tell you what I want.'

'Promise,' Red says. Her teeth clamp around the flesh of the neck before her, and the neck buzzes with a groan.

'I promise,' Wyll manages to say.

They strip each other fully. He has dammed his eagerness, made a longer, softer, surging wave of it. When she grips him in her hand and urges him into her he won't. He teases until her temper flares. Then he pushes in slowly, slowly, digging further in until he can burrow no more and a spike of pain makes her gasp and bite him.

Their fucking is languid against the galdor wall. They pause often, rhythms building and ebbing. Red is lost, all consumed by the simple feel of him inside her hands and inside her body and behind her and up against her.

Only once does she climb back out, just for a moment. She has him clamped between her thighs on the floor. She stretches upwards as she sits on him, her eyes rise, and she realises they are right underneath Lailoken's prophecy. It seems to lunge out of the wall at her, *the forgotten child* and *London will bleed.*

Everything bleeds. Tomorrow waits death, the only sure thing. That's where she is going. That's where the constellation leads her.

'What's wrong?' Wyll asks her in a breathless whisper.

'Nothing,' she says. 'Nothing.'

And she dives back into him, his flushed skin, the sweat streaking the hollow of his collarbone, his lovely, insistent, urgent hands.

Wyll has a bed here. It is a simple thing, hidden behind a half wall that bisects the room. He told her that despite the splendid suite of rooms he has at the Royal stable of Cair Lleon, he often sleeps here. He likes the quiet.

Drenched hours slide past unnoticed. Time is divided into binary sections of locked bodies and unlocked bodies. During an infrequent unlocked period, Red lies on her side and watches the way Wyll presses his back into the bed to stretch out his spine like a contented cat, lingers on each visible rib pushing gently against his skin.

'Do you have any other lovers?' she asks him.

Wyll stops stretching. 'Would you prefer it if I didn't?'

Red thinks. 'I don't know.' She hesitates, looks away. 'Maybe you'd like me less if I said yes.'

She feels the bed shift as Wyll moves to touch her face.

'I'd like you the same either way,' he says. 'But since you asked, I'll tell you. I don't have any other lovers.'

'Oh,' Red says casually. 'Not even the King?'

Wyll makes a choking noise.

'Art?' he says, eventually. 'You must be joking.'

The King of all London gets called Art. Such a short and sweet little name for such a man.

'You and he are close . . .' Red trails off.

'He's like my older brother,' Wyll says gently. 'Not my lover. You shouldn't listen to gossip.'

'I don't,' Red protests. 'I just thought . . . well. He's still unmarried.'

'His choice.' Wyll shrugs. 'I don't really know why. Anyway, he's not alone, he has someone.'

'Does he?' Red says, surprised. 'Who?'

'That would be his business, Red.'

She plucks at the sheets underneath her hand. 'I've always wondered what he's like.'

'He's a great King,' Wyll replies. 'That's all people really need to know.'

'You love him,' Red says.

Wyll shoots her an amused look. 'You sound surprised.'

'I just . . . I don't know. I've heard bad things.'

Wyll snorts. 'He's the best ruler London's had for centuries. They've no idea how good they have it.'

'Well, if he's that impressive to you, I'd like to meet him,' Red says lightly. 'But I've heard no one gets near him nowadays.'

'Not if I can help it.'

Red laughs. 'But you're his champion, not his gun. He has a thousand knights to guard him.'

'And if they fail, there I'll be.'

'Like you were at Mafelon.'

Wyll is silent.

'You can't huff about that,' Red says. 'It's one of the most famous stories about you.'

'Stories are one thing,' Wyll says, 'reality another.'

He closes his eyes and Red knows that line of conversation is done. She rolls on to her stomach.

'Have you ever heard your nickname?' she asks in a teasing tone.

Wyll slides his hands underneath his head and stares up at the faint steel girder-criss-crossed darkness just visible beyond the lamplight. 'I've heard many nicknames, and I despise all of them.'

Red grins. 'Yes, but this one comes from one of those late-night glows that likes to spend hours discussing what each Caballaria knight is like in bed and if they use their weapons as *tools of pleasure*—'

'Please tell me you don't watch that atrocious shit—'

'—and their favourite name for you is *pulchra belua*.'

Beautiful monster, it means in Caballaria-speak.

'Oh, that one,' Wyll says, his voice flat. 'Well, I'm neither beautiful nor a monster, so it's a stupid name.'

'Well, you are beautiful. Even if people are afraid of you, they still find you beautiful. Up close, even more,' Red muses. 'You'd think it would be the other way around. I've seen the paint they trowel on to some fighters to make them look good on screen, but you're even better without anything on you.'

Wyll annoyingly decides to ignore the compliment. 'Are you satisfied, right now?'

Red frowns. 'What do you mean?'

'What I just did with you. Did it please you?'

She manages to turn her laugh into a cough. 'You couldn't tell? I made some noises I . . . didn't even know I could make.'

'Then it's the satisfaction talking,' Wyll informs the ceiling, 'and nothing more.'

Red replays the conversation back in her head.

'Let me get this right,' she says eventually. 'You're saying that you aren't beautiful.'

'No, I'm saying that your viewpoint is tarnished by what you just felt.'

Red stretches out a hand and touches Wyll's flank, running her fingertips along the warm flesh. He does not respond, but his eyes half-close in obvious pleasure.

'I think you're the most exquisite clothesless man I've ever seen,' Red says matter-of-factly.

Wyll gives a short sigh.

Red's fingers crawl further in, skating. 'Magnificent.'

'Stop that, long-word-girl.'

'Spectacular body.'

Red feels the bedclothes stretch and wrinkle as Wyll rolls on to his side and pulls Red underneath him.

'If you won't stop your mouth, I will stop it for you,' he promises.

'Ma*jest*ic, even—'

Red's words are cut off as threatened, a bite on her lip temporarily silencing her. Wyll's tongue soon follows, and then, further down, an unfurling that presses hard against her inner thigh.

'That part, though,' Red mutters as her breath shortens, 'that part of you is my *favourite*—'

'You talk too much,' her lover tells her, and then proceeds to silence her for a good hour.

Afterwards, he curls himself, sweetly childlike, into her side. One of his hands rests across her stomach. Hands that stroke her into a frenzy, that grip a sword, that touch his lips when he talks, a bare brush of a gesture he makes more often than he appears to realise.

His whisper drifts up to her. 'I'm very glad you came after me, Red.'

She stares up into the tall dark.

After a long while, Wyll's breathing deepens, stretching, pulling him into sleep. If she concentrates, she can feel his neck pulsing, pumping his blood. Humans are nothing much more than bags of liquid, and so easily punctured. Make enough of a hole and they drain to their end. It's so easy. So why hasn't she done it yet?

Inch by slow inch she unwinds from their tangle. Wyll shifts a little, nestling into the warmth she leaves behind on the sheets. She picks her clothes up from the floor, pulls them on as silently as she can. He doesn't stir.

All this would be fine if he meant nothing. All she has to do is decide that he means nothing.

The galdor wall glows balefully at her back as she watches him sleep.

Now is her chance. Now, while he is vulnerable, and she safely out of his reach. So what if she wonders whether she could fall for him, fall in a way that makes her feel a dizzying kind of elation? So what? Did she think she could have that? Did she let herself think that she was built for that? She exists for one purpose only, and he stands in the way of it.

But her hands do not tingle, and the surge is not there.

Saintsfuck, is the reason she can't end him just because he screws her well and he's nicely formed? Does that make him more deserving of life than anyone else? Fair is a fairy tale.

Kill him, you fucken coward—

Kill him, you snivelly, cowardly—

She searches, but nothing happens. It does not come.

She can feel the wall. All those messages, all those faces, the hundreds of hands that have touched it, imprinted the brick with their magic, their emotions, themselves, a want, a hunger, to reach across divides and speak. And what will they tell about her? What do they see? They see her weakness.

Because saints damn everything, she *likes* it here.

It's not just Wyll. It's this city. This baffling, glamoured, bright, hard, beautiful city and its maddening, stupid, wonderful life. The sheer vivacity of it turns her on. Its wild improbability. It feels like discovering that there are fifteen more dimensions than the four she was told are absolutely all that exist. She is not the seducer, she is the seduced. Faraday warned her. *Curiosity doesn't kill here*, he had said, *it saves*, and she is curious, so curious it hurts.

But there wasn't supposed to be anything else! She wasn't supposed to have anything more!

And with that thought, *now* the pain, *now* the surge – but still he sleeps on, untouched, while the world around Red begins to flake and crack, sloughing off to reveal the ugliness underneath—

'How in seven hells did you do that?'

Wyll speaks from the direction of the bed. He is sat up with the sheets pooled at his groin. His voice is suffused in sleepy shock and his gaze goes beyond her.

The galdor wall is in ruins. Decades-old paint lies in useless flakes at its feet, mixed with puffs of brick dust that flash-streak the ground like earthed lightning. Poems are cracked, missing whole lines. Faces torn open. Words have become useless floating letters, their neighbours gone.

She turns back to Wyll, her mouth open and her heart wild.

'There's something wrong, isn't there?' he says, and his voice is very soft. 'Something you're hiding. Please tell me. Let me help you.'

Such compassion. Passion of every kind. She sees it now, all the passion in him. No wonder he guards it with every ounce of control he has – he'd overwhelm anyone with it.

She catches herself pulling towards it hungrily, and wrenches away.

'Red,' she hears him plead as she leaves.

She does not stop. If she stops, she will make the wrong choice.

CHAPTER 35

Mafelon, Blackheart
Three Years Ago

The second time Art watches someone die, he is thirty-three years old.

He is at an ambassadorial dinner, an elaborate affair bringing together diplomats from across the Seven Kingdoms. Lillath is across from him, entertaining the Eiran dignitary next to her. Art remembers wondering what the Eiran might say if he knew she was the King's Spider, that the woman giggling at him with blue duck sauce smeared across her lips has held the most secretive and notorious post in the country for the past fifteen years. He remembers laughing at her antics, so perhaps that is why when the first shot goes off, he doesn't immediately register it.

The next shot makes Lillath cock her head, which is the first alert Art gets that something is wrong. Violent events are always so much more scattered and confused than it feels like they should be, he thinks afterwards. Why is it never clear what is actually going on until it is almost over, and so too late to do anything, anything at all, to prevent it?

It will take at least a day after it has happened to pin down the order of events, a badly fitting jigsaw made of many jumbled witness testimonials, but this is, as Art later comes to understand it, roughly how it goes:

The first spray of bullets hits the table next to his. The setting for this ambassadorial dinner is a beautifully preserved historic dining hall in Blackheart's Mafelon area. These days it is not often that Art gets to leave the confines of Cair Lleon – and after this, it will never officially happen again.

Several bullets embed themselves harmlessly into the wood and explode nothing but pieces of tableware, splattering people with uneaten food and splashes of rotaflower wine. Three hit an Alban knight, who dies almost immediately. The sounds of the shots are so flat and small that in that first moment, not one person is yet able to understand what just happened.

A woman has stood up from her place at a table near the door. A woman holding a gun.

She screams into the air:

'FREE US FROM FRIA'S FRY!'

It is heard clearly over the waning dining noises.

The woman moves at a run, weaving from her seat and heading straight for Art's table at the other end of the room. She keeps shooting as she goes. The emissary to Queen Hafa of Ingoland, a jovial man called Kolé who is often at Cair Lleon and who Art has had placed next to him, not only because of current politicking necessities but because he very much enjoys his company, is hit with two bullets in the side of his neck. He dies twenty-three hours later in Cair Lleon's own bone house, with the best medics in the country at his side trying to save him.

It is then that several people realise there are no guard knights in the dining room. There is normally no need for guard knights in a secured dining room. They are outside, seconds away – but seconds are long enough for death.

The woman's mouth is moving, but Art now cannot hear her over the screams and shouts, which began at some indefinable point in the last few seconds and are climbing in scattered bursts. He imagines all sorts of things during the moment that he watches her approach him – is it a prayer in her mouth, or an apology, or maybe a song? – but most likely it's a repeat of that alliterative slogan associated with one of the most notorious common supremacist groups, *FREE US FROM FRIA'S FRY* – and he feels someone grab hold of him and begin to pull him down to the floor.

The dining room doors are open now, he realises, because there is a panther in the room. He definitely does not recall there being a panther in the room at the start of the dinner, so it must have got in through the open doors.

The impossible panther is right in front of Art's table, right in front of him, feet from the woman who is feet from him, filling his vision from top to bottom. It is glossy black and *monstrous*, rearing as high as a man's shoulder. It springs straight for the woman.

The woman turns as it moves in her peripheral vision. Her mouth stretches wide when she sees it, like a snake preparing to devour an animal twice its size, only she is the one being devoured. She crashes reflexively to the floor.

There is a strange, stomach-rolling moment as the panther disappears. Art's brain seems to buzz unpleasantly as it adjusts to the empty space it has left behind.

The woman is on the ground, cowering on her back. Standing in front of her instead of a panther is a tall figure with a half-shaved head, dressed in travelling leathers. The figure says something, but the room is filled with the sound of people fleeing and shouting, and it is lost.

The woman raises her gun up in one unsteady hand and points it at the figure in front of her. The gun bursts into flames, smoke pouring off her fingers in thick streams and billowing up to the ceiling. Her arm jerks and throws it before her brain seems to intervene.

The gun fetches up close to the shaven-headed figure, who crouches and picks it up, apparently possessed of flame-retardant skin. It dangles from their hand as if they have never touched one before, and the fire winks out as if it was never there at all.

The room is considerably quieter – most of the guests have escaped – so Art can hear the shaven-headed figure's voice quite clearly as they address the blank-faced woman on the floor.

'It's a coward's weapon. You should be ashamed.'

Don't let any of the guard hear you say that, Art thinks, and swallows a manic laugh.

The King's private study room desk is strewn with books, with papers, with the food detritus from the exceptionally late hour that Art had worked to the night before. A half-eaten twist of cheese pastry and an air-browned apple core sit on silver plates, while next to them a silver cup bears the dregs of ruby wine, the late-night sugary pick-me-up he defaults to when his head begins to creak in protest at the strain he puts it through.

Silver, silver, everywhere. Silver city, glittering and sparkling and draining, fostering murderers and innocents alike. Giver of life and of death.

Tears of frustration and grief claw their way into Art's eyes and slip out of him until he feels like a leaking balloon. His rage is the escaping air. It goes, rolling out into the night and taking the last of his energy with it. He cracks his fist on his desk, making papers scatter and the silverware jump. As soon as it's done, he is ashamed. Violence, even where no one can see it, is an empty reaction. He understands it as a weapon, but he is still, always, afraid of becoming the kind of person who defaults to it.

The fire in his room snaps. Over by the far corner, the bottom of his long window curtains shiver in no wind. The nights are long and cold in London's winters, and every window is shut tight. The curtains should not be moving.

Art feels his skin prickle.

'I have no time for ghosts,' he says under his breath.

'Not a ghost,' comes a voice from nowhere.

Art sits perfectly still, trying to get his skyrocketing pulse under control.

'I'm sorry.' The voice hesitates. 'I can come back another time.'

'Come out where I can see you,' Art says.

Not that it matters – he knows exactly who it is – but it is harder to talk to a disembodied voice. Besides, he'd like to get a good look at the person who saved his life today.

The void by the curtains shimmers, and a man steps out of it.

Only just a man, on closer inspection. People who can conjure black panthers out of nothing in life-threatening situations might very well appear older than they actually are. Art has seen him only a handful of times over the last four years, and each time he does he marvels at how much he has changed. Time shapes the young so much more quickly, speeding over their forms in hurricane clouds.

'You've definitely got better at giving orders,' Wyll says.

'Well,' Art replies, 'I think you can understand my being a little tense at the moment, especially when people turn up where they aren't expected.'

Wyll's face is more sculpted than ever, and strange in its

familiarity. He has shorn his head on one side, exposing scalp, while on the other side his hair hangs down to his shoulder. His clothes are practical and mute, built for moving around in, and his boots are dirty.

Art takes in Edler's son. Definitely no longer sixteen years old.

'You broke a dozen laws getting in here,' Art says. 'I should have you arrested.'

Wyll just inclines his head at this, waiting and watching.

He wants you to know that he isn't tame.

Art inclines his own head. 'How *did* you get in here?'

Wyll gives him a faint smile. 'Your security really isn't as good as you think it is. You should get that seen to.'

'Well, I suppose they hadn't considered having to protect me against master thwimoren, which is understandable. You are rather rare.'

'Will you lock me up?'

'Is there a prison that can hold you?' Art asks.

'Of course. Just bind me in iron chains.' Wyll's face breaks into a wry grin, running cracks across his heavy words and shattering them like glass.

Art snorts. 'I forgot how melodramatic children can be.'

'Better that than being a tired old man.'

'Well, I'd expect such an opinion from a baby.'

Wyll laughs. Oh yes, how things have changed. The ground has levelled between them. The gulf has narrowed.

'No one bothered to inform me that you were back in London,' Art says, managing to keep his accusatory tone mild.

Wyll hesitates. 'Only just. Did you get my last letter?'

'I'm not sure. Which one was it?'

'Doesn't matter.'

Art relents. 'I read all your letters, Wyll. I'm sorry if it sometimes takes a while to respond.'

'You're busy,' Wyll says with a carefully careless shrug.

'Busy getting shot at,' Art agrees.

Wyll tosses him a swift, surprised look, while Art suppresses a tremble that threatens to run right through to his bones. Marvol was at his door tonight, but right now is not the time to deal with that dumb, creeping horror of a feeling.

'How long will you be in London this time?' Art asks. 'A few days?'

Wyll shifts on his feet. 'Actually . . . I was hoping to be here indefinitely now.'

Not even a hint of that plan in his last letter. It is so infuriatingly like him to spring such a decision on Art without any warning.

'Nothing new to learn out there in the world?' Art says, all calm.

Wyll expects him to be angry, but he can at least derive some small satisfaction from defying his expectations.

'It's much the same as the one I came from,' Wyll replies with studied cynicism. 'Pain and happiness and injustice and loveliness everywhere you go – just in different packaging. I thought I could learn those things here just as well.' He hesitates. 'But I've not come here to ask anything of you. I've got a place I can go, things I can do.'

For a moment Art struggles, caught in that age-old 'only if you want', 'no, only if *you* want' back and forth between two people who care about each other enough to feel the need to be shy about the truth.

'I'm glad you're staying,' he says at last.

Wyll's shoulders come down and he seems to sink from the

high, tense place he has been holding himself in. 'I thought maybe you were glad I was gone.'

Art shakes his head. 'I was afraid that you weren't ever going to come back.'

He indicates the two high-backed armchairs beside the fire, feeling the disconcerting sensation of watching a stranger move into the flame light. It isn't until Wyll sinks down, settling in, and then gives an unexpected wide yawn that softens his face up that Art sees the boy he knew again.

He moves to the cabinet behind his desk, opens it up and withdraws a green bottle. His other hand snags two small cups. He crosses to Wyll and places everything on a spindly drinks table between them.

'What's that?' Wyll asks.

'It's a kind of grape liqueur. You look like you could do with the sugar hit.'

Art pours out two small measures and they reach in to touch cups.

'You've done a lot to the trags network,' Wyll says after a long swallow. 'Those new inter-dis' connections are pretty good.'

'Pretty good' is a fantastic way to sum up the result of two years of disruptive, extortionately expensive work – and it is not done, not nearly.

'The outer burbs are still too out of reach,' Art grumbles. 'They keep giving us the run-around about how long it will take. Two years means three, and then it means five, and oh, because we've taken so long, now the pricing on the materials has all changed, yes, we know we said it would cost that much but we're sorry, actually it's going to be three times that by the time we've finished screwing you—'

Wyll gives a rich, unexpected laugh. 'Who knew being King would be so much fun?'

'Infrastructure,' Art says drily. 'No one warned me about infrastructure.'

'Don't you have whole networks of people taking care of this for you?'

Art pauses. 'I might have been accused of being "too involved" once or twice.'

'Can't imagine why.' Wyll's gaze slides meaningfully over to Art's overfull desk. 'You don't have much of a life, do you?'

'Well, don't worry, it's not all infrastructure.'

'No, sometimes it's attempted assassination.'

Art gives him a level gaze.

'How many times have they tried to kill you now?' Wyll asks in a blithe tone.

'Don't tell me you're one of those anxious conspiracy-makers.'

'How many?'

'Who are *they*?' Art retorts.

'Whoever is trying to kill you, Sire. Now, how many times? From where I'm sitting, it looks like you could do with better protection.'

'I am constantly surrounded by hundreds of extremely well-trained guard knights whose job it is to protect me on a daily basis.'

'And they're doing very well at it.'

'They've kept me alive so far.'

'Until today.' Wyll stares at him. 'If I hadn't been there, you might have died. Sire.'

Art ignores the fearful surge in his chest.

'And what exactly were you doing there, Wyll?' he says. 'I don't recall seeing your name on the guest list.'

'You were the one who had me set up with the Barochian Ambassador's retinue. He has a thing for employing godchildren, remember?'

Art does now vaguely recall the suggestion being put to him by the small group of trusted people who have been in charge of Wyll's well-being over the years.

'Well, there is no possible instance in which I would not have been made aware of your presence at that dinner,' he retorts.

'Maybe I asked to have my name kept off the official list. Your *security* knew,' Wyll says distastefully.

Art spreads his hands. 'So you hide away at a very long formal dinner without even once announcing yourself. Were you even going to tell me you were back in London, never mind sitting at a table in the same damn room as me?'

'Yes, of course I was!' Wyll sounds anguished. 'I just . . . *you sent me away!* You banished me from London!'

'Wyll, no—'

'You made it perfectly clear that you wanted me nowhere near you.' He rises from the armchair as he talks, and turning his back on Art, goes on, 'And I understand, believe me. I'm a danger to you. I know that. I'm nothing but a scandal waiting to happen. I knew you'd be angry if you thought I wanted to come back. I knew you'd look to keep me away. So I didn't tell you. And I'm sorry. I'm sorry, but I'm not going anywhere. London is my home, too. I belong here as much as anyone.'

Art puts down his cup.

The damage you've done, he thinks to himself sadly. *Art, you idiot.*

'I would have come to you. I would have. I just didn't know what the right moment was. In between the duck and the cheese course? After wine but before the digestifs?' Wyll slumps. 'And then that woman stood up and started shooting, and I didn't think. I just . . . reacted. I'm sorry.'

Art watches him. At that moment, it's easy to remember just how young he still is. Despite all his power he is only twenty, still unsure of his place, his permissions, his welcome. Small wonder with what happened today. So powerful, but still so vulnerable.

Art realises several things, suddenly. He has missed Wyll. He has been worried about him. He wants to protect him. And he wants to use him. It is that desire that he has been running away from for the last four years, perhaps more than any other.

'Conjuring a panther was a little dramatic,' he says.

He hears Wyll give a faintly shuddery laugh. 'Well, I've always been an attention-seeker.'

'You've seen a panther in the flesh, I take it?'

'Yes.'

'I never have. I'm jealous.' Art pauses. 'I hear you've been keeping up your fighting studies.'

Wyll is silent in acknowledgement. From what Art hears, it has gone beyond study and developed into a passionate obsession.

'Is the Caballaria still something you want to pursue?' he asks.

Wyll half-turns, all restrained eagerness. 'More than anything. But I don't expect any favours. I want to be treated just like everyone else.'

'Don't be ridiculous,' Art snorts. 'I can't treat you like everyone else. An entire roomful of ambassadors just saw you save the King of London from attempted assassination. You think you can be ordinary after that?'

Wyll opens his mouth and then wisely shuts it again.

Art ponders. 'We have to be careful in how we handle this – for your sake as much as mine.'

'So you think I should try out for it?' Wyll sounds unbearably hopeful.

'The Caballaria will be a very hard path for you, Wyll. I hoped you'd have an easier life.'

'You once told me that it's my life to choose what to do with.'

Art sighs. 'I wish your memory wasn't so good.'

A godchild in the public eye, working to better the country for all and not just for his own kind. A godchild with his immense power lit by bright lights, not blanketed in the dark as his father was, where secrets and suspicion grow like mould. A godchild fighting for justice, and doing it without magic.

It is a powerful symbol.

Art looks up into the eyes of the grown-up boy before him, his irises circled in gold, picked up by the firelight playing on his face. He seems to understand the part he will have to play. He looks calm about it. But perhaps that is only the lie Art needs to tell himself in order to go through with this.

For the greater good, Art tells himself. *Always for the greater good.*

CHAPTER 36

Fitzroy Market, Blackheart
Two Days Ago

Housed in an old fishery, Fitzroy's market ground is permanently stained with hundreds of years of scales and blood, giving the whole place a faintly metallic smell.

Its main entrance bisects an artery of a Blackheart street that runs all the way to the gates of Cair Lleon. The market sells almost anything that can be sold, from hair oils to machine parts – but it is the very back area, furthest away from the main street, that it is known for, because that area deals in protection against magic.

There are stalls there selling preventatives, cures and wardings. Tonics that, when drunk, are supposed to make you impervious to any magical manipulation. Certain shaped stones with natural dark veins running through their bodies apparently mimic the dark veins of a thwimoren, rendering their illusions invisible to you as long as you hold the stone. Headbands that, when worn, prevent your thoughts being seen by a wearden. Bed webs, ranging from plain knotted spreads to beautiful, intricately woven canopies, which, when hung over your bed, will catch bad dreams sent from a dremen before they can enter your mind.

Red passes a stall boasting huge trays of decrepit, filthy parts from old petroleum mechanicals where two excitable children are exclaiming over a tiny piston they're passing back and forth between their hands, covering their skin with black grease in the process. She pulls her hat more firmly down, reassured by the way the brim shades her eyes, and makes her way through the market, stopping to check the maps at every major intersection, the directions glowing faintly on the wall columns. The machinette from the warehouse party had told her to look for a small stall with a sparse, innocuous display, but it takes her a while to find it.

The seller behind the stall is a diminutive man wearing a traditional doctor's outfit, a deep blood-red coat with the familiar snake knot symbol as a patch fixed on at the shoulder. He purports to sell tonics. Mostly. He also sells things that are not on display, if you know how to ask.

He watches Red approach.

'T'chores,' he says. 'Looking for anything in particular?'

Red hesitates. This is definitely the place. The description fits.

'Something from the coast,' she says.

It is a pre-ordained password phrase, and Red is here at a pre-ordained time.

The man's expression does not change in the slightest. 'Ah yes,' he replies, butter-smooth. 'Sea air is good for the soul.'

The man is balding, his hair close-shaved to better disguise it. His demeanour is neat, friendly and unthreatening. He could be anyone, and no one.

He shifts. 'Buy a tonic.'

'What?' Red says. She didn't come here for bullshit tonics.

'Buy a tonic,' the man repeats pleasantly.

'Which one?'

'It doesn't really matter, does it?'

Red scans the seller's table. At its front is a long metal rack sporting a row of transparent stoppered tubes. Each tube is neatly labelled in Laeden, the ancient language familiar from her Caballaria training.

The seller points to the sickly green coloured tonic on the far left. '*Troubled Hearts*,' he says. 'For those with an anxious turn of mind. Nice and calming, in the correct dose.' His finger moves to its neighbour. '*Baby Bloom*. A fertility enhancer. This one is *Blood Quickening*. Improves circulation, boosts strength. A favourite with fighters.'

'*Troubled Hearts*,' Red says. 'I've a friend who could do with relaxing.'

'Good choice. Now, it's a rather experimental . . . tonic. It can have some interesting side-effects, but it kicks in quick.'

His eyes lift to hers. Now it sounds as if he is talking about the thing Red actually came to buy today.

'How does it work?' Red asks.

'It's a carefully synthesised combination of ingredients based on the latest research into brain chemistry and body waves,' the man says, his voice still quiet, calm. 'See, every person has a unique set of energy waves. What this does – and very effectively, I might add – is magnify the wave signal you give out, so to speak.'

'Magnify by how much?'

'Tenfold, with a triple dose.' The seller leans in. 'But it's not recommended to take that much in one go. Things are very hard to control when it gets that powerful. They might happen whether you want them to or not.'

This is just what Red needs: to be forced, if necessary, to do what she should already have done. Her body will unleash ten times its power without any pesky interference from her mind.

She nods to the seller, who selects the tube labelled *Troubled Hearts* and packages it up. At the last minute he deftly slips a small packet filled with pills in with the tube. He charges Red three times the tube's marked price, then drops the package into her hand.

Red feels a surge of misgiving. But she has gone through with it. She has taken the risk, paid her trick. She takes the package, thanks the seller and turns to leave.

'Best of luck in getting back on the circuit, Si,' he says.

Fuck. He recognises her.

So that was what the pointed look over the fighter tonic was about. The odds were low enough – she's hardly fresh news; the glows don't care about fighters who aren't actually fighting and she looks blandly different out of costume and make-up, with her tell-tale dark sheet of hair covered up. Sharp-eyed bastard.

'I'm not a knight,' she says.

Kick me and I kick you. That's the deal with the black market, isn't it? If he exposes Red, he goes down too.

He inclines his head. 'My mistake.'

She gives him what she hopes is a puzzled look and walks away, heart beating fast.

It doesn't matter if he outs her about the damn drug, anyway – soon enough she'll be gone and the career she shouldn't even care about will be in shreds behind her. Becoming a knight was only ever a means to an end.

She reaches the outside avenue. The crowds move blanketed in evening drizzle, hunched underneath their rain shields, crowds of transparent flecter-glass mushrooms gleaming wet colours under the neon shop signs.

She has one hour before Ford arrives to pick her up for tonight's meeting with Wyll and it will take her almost that long to get back to Spittelgrounds from here. She'll have to take the Tidal now to give it the chance to be working at full tilt before she finds herself in front of Wyll. Three doses, the maximum amount, has to be enough to overpower even him.

She ducks off into a side street. There are a few people clustered at the far end, but this section is quiet. As the rain slides down she fumbles in her pocket, opening up the package, feeling the cool glass sides of the tonic tube, and then – *there it is* – a bumpy plastic square holding dowdy coloured pellets.

Red pinches three between her fingers and brings them up to her mouth, places them on her tongue. Then she takes in a long, calming breath and begins the walk back to Spittelgrounds.

The pills have a sharp, buzzing tang, as if she's just eaten mouldy orange peel, but it takes a good few minutes before she notices the kick. It begins with a tingle that spreads downwards from her tongue, lighting up the inside of her throat. Then it goes prickling along each nerve ending, pooling at the hollows of her collarbones, trickling down her breastplate and sparking in the space between each rib. Bright fingers reach into her belly, push downwards, gather at the tops of her thighs, flashing in the muscles there, before racing down to her feet.

The sensation is so preoccupying that she walks into the back of someone, bumping them and stumbling on her feet. 'Hoi!' the someone exclaims, a woman with a severe haircut and pastel-pink eyebrows.

'Sorry,' Red mutters. 'Sorry.'

She turns and walks away fast. Her legs are going too fast. Why don't they slow down? Who is controlling them? Is she even here? Is there another her? At the lowest dose, the machinette had said, you barely even notice the fun part of Tidal – it just gives you a feeling of supreme power and control.

Red does not feel in control.

Up ahead, a vertical light sign catches her gaze, spelling out TRAITOR in flashing violet. Red stares at it and blinks hard. It doesn't change. TRAITOR. Just one word. What kind of shop or bar calls itself TRAITOR?

She veers away from the sign, swerving blindly across the street. Someone on a pedalo shouts at her, but she keeps going, jostled by giant mushrooms that brush against her with wet squeaks. Her feet are made of toffee. They soften and cling alarmingly to the ground when she tries to lift them.

This is not right. This is not how it should be, surely. Did that fucken seller give her the wrong drug? She is alone, all alone, in this, panicking and careening from side to side in her own head. The walls of her head are made of mirrors and all they reflect is her, and each her screams about how stupid she is, how evil, how worthless.

In among the chaos, a small, rational part of her has time to wryly observe what astronomically poor judgement it was to take an experimental drug and assume it would turn out all right. She feels wide open, a walking wound bleeding her poisonous magical blood out on to the streets, and where it drips, the ground hisses and melts underneath it. The city can feel her bleeding on it, and its silent alarms are screaming a warning.

She has to get off the streets, but she can't go to Spittelgrounds for help – they'll kick her out for doing this – and there is no way in seven hells that she can go to Wyll. She can barely walk straight, never mind kill him.

There is only one person who can help her now.

Red stumbles into a brightly lit station. Every edge she sees is too hard, too sharp. The floor is too smooth. She catches a mercifully near-empty trag and begins the long journey to Fin. As it slides its way between tall building blocks, their lights rearrange themselves, spelling out her long-kept secret for the whole world to see.

'Red!'

Fin stands in the doorway to the private apartment at her stables, looking visibly alarmed at the sight of her.

That should have been the first warning.

For now, though, Red assumes that Fin's shock is in reaction to how terrible she looks, and this makes her panic even more.

'I need help,' Red says. 'I took something. I don't think it's working right.'

She has no idea how that came out. Did she slur, lose words? She can't hear herself properly. She feels disconnected from her own body, floating above it on a thin, fragile tether that could snap at any time. Evidently Fin understood enough of what she just said because she drops a saint name and softens enough to let Red move inwards.

Panic pushes at her shoulder blades. She has to get inside quickly and shut the door and block out all the alarms the city is ringing before Fin can hear them. If she can just get deeper inside and away from the alarms—

She hears Fin behind her: 'Not that way, to the right!'

But it's too late. Red barrels down the short hallway and walks through the first door she sees. Her brain is on lag. Yes, it exists now in an alternative version of this reality where the only difference is that time runs a second or two behind. Her brain is in the slower universe and her body is in the faster universe. This explains why it takes her a moment to understand what it is that she sees in the room she has just walked into.

Her secret, the one she has spent a lifetime nursing, is written across the wall of the room.

In big letters.

Right across the wall.

It is nestled in between a crazy mass of clashing art, bleeding on to the ceiling above and the ground below. There are patches of frenetic, explosive colour jumbles, lines of script and rune and indecipherable scribbles. The colours seem to pulse, oddly fluid, oddly alive.

Fin has a galdor wall in her apartment. Why does Fin have a galdor wall in her apartment?

Sitting cross-legged in front of the wall, so dull in comparison that at first she hadn't even noticed him, is a figure with curly hair and copper cuffs on his fingers. He looks up.

For a moment, they just stare at each other.

Then slow-universe clicks into fast-universe and Red's brain catches up.

It happens when the curly-haired soothsayer leaps up from the floor and says, 'Fuck. FUCK. What the fuck are *you* doing here?'

He backs away, pressing himself into the corner of the room, tangled art exploding from behind his back. His fingers wink as the copper cuffs catch the light. One hand clutches a paint pen. He is the one who wrote her secret on the wall.

'What is this?' Red hears herself say.

She turns. Fin has come into the room behind her, and now stands between Red and the door. Her gaze flicks briefly to the soothsayer.

'You two have met before, then,' Fin says, and her voice is subdued. Not puzzled. Subdued.

That should have been the second warning.

The soothsayer opens his mouth. 'Get her away from me. Why did you bring her here? What is wrong with you?'

'*I* didn't bring her,' Fin says. 'She just showed up, just now.'

'You know him,' Red cuts in.

Fin contemplates her. 'Yes, I know him. But it's not what you think.'

'Not what I think?' Red gives a juddering laugh. 'Not what I think? What do I think? I don't even know what I think.'

'You need to calm down.'

'Get her out,' pipes the soothsayer. 'She's a fucken murderer.'

'T'chuss, Roben,' Fin says, and her hands rise in placation. 'Everyone needs to calm down. Red, just listen to me for a minute.' She sucks in a breath. 'What did you take?'

On the wall, Red's secret surges, pumping steadily like blood through a vein.

'This is real, right?' she says. 'I might be high right now, but this is real, isn't it? That little rat is really here, and he's painted your wall.'

'He sees things,' Fin begins.

'He's a faker.' Red rounds on Roben, who looks as panicked as she feels. 'What have you been saying to her about me?'

Fin's voice comes out slow, too slow. 'Red, I need you to tell me who you really are.'

'What? *What?* You know who I am.' Red struggles to control her panic. 'He's a liar. You believe some ratshit jackster? He's just trying to game you for trick!'

'I've known Roben since I was six years old,' Fin says steadily. 'And he's never wrong.'

Dread, somehow both hot and cold. The swooping, falling feeling of betrayal. The disappointment of its total inevitability. This is, after all, the way the world is. Fair is a fairy tale, and friendship doesn't come for free. How could she have ever thought any different?

'It was a set-up, wasn't it?' Red says. 'You pretending to be my friend – wasn't it? You were watching me.'

'Who are you?' Fin asks. 'Really?'

'Fin,' Roben whimpers. 'You said it. I'm never wrong. I told you. I told you what she came here to do.'

Red takes a step towards Fin, who tenses.

'What did he tell you?' Red asks. Suddenly, she feels very calm. So calm that when Fin licks her lips, opens her mouth and says her darkest secret out loud, she doesn't even react.

There, she sighs to herself. *There it is, out in the open. All out now. All over now. Doesn't that feel better?*

The secret hangs in air between them all, a ponderous toxic cloud.

'Kill her!' Roben shrieks suddenly. 'Fin, you have to kill her before she can—'

The rest of his sentence gets mangled in the gargling noise he makes. His hands come up, winking copper. There is a flat little tinkling sound as his finger cuffs bang uselessly against the hilt of the blade protruding from his throat.

Red doesn't even remember throwing it, but her arm is outstretched.

Roben's body shakes. One foot kicks at nothing. He slides to the floor.

It's amazing, Red thinks, *how easy it is to know when someone is dead. It's the eyes. The eyes go so flat, as if they just lost dimensions and now only exist in one. I could almost believe in the myth of a soul, if I was so sure that I don't have one. Maybe godchildren are born without. They should test us for that instead of the magic.*

Fin is silent.

Red sees the decision the moment it is made, opening up like a flower on her face.

'Don't,' Red says. 'Please don't.'

But Fin isn't listening. She turns to the door, opens it up and runs.

CHAPTER 37

Cair Lleon, Blackheart
Two Years Ago

Wyll stands as if lost in thought, his head bowed.

He appears to be unaware that he is being watched by some of the most powerful people in the Caballaria. Warm candle-light bathes his neck and runs its bright fingers down the length of the curved crescent-moon knife held loosely in one hand.

He is still.

Then he begins to move: slow, deliberate, water-fluid, never a jerk or a snap or a savage thrust. It's like a dance much more than a fight, courtly and controlled. His arm rises, the crescent-moon knife arced over his skull. He stands, balanced on one foot, paused, staring off into the distance.

Then he begins to *move*.

The crowd ripples with delighted gasps.

'Gwanhara's face,' Art breathes, a soft oath.

Garad leans in from their seat to whisper in Art's ear, 'I told you. You really should watch more of his fights.'

'You keep me updated,' Art absently replies, his gaze on Wyll. 'How does he . . .? Where has he got that style from?'

'He calls it "air pushing". He practises that slow dance routine every morning and every evening. He says it flows naturally into the fight.'

The word, Art thinks, is *ferocious*.

'You asked me to judge if he truly has the makings of a Caballaria knight,' Garad says quietly. 'What do you think?'

'You're the expert.' Art taps his fingers against his chair. 'But you told me that his last three bouts were voided.'

Garad snorts. 'Suspected magic, my arse. The arena capturers work fine and every moment of his fights are scrutinised by an array of adjudicators. It's his opponents crying foul because they're embarrassed they got beaten so badly. We'll get those voids overturned.'

Art becomes aware of a thundering silence. Then, slowly at first, gathering quick, comes tumultuous thunderous approval that sets the chandeliers shivering.

It has been long work getting Wyllt Caballarias Ambrosias o'Gwanharatown to anything approaching acceptance. Tonight's display, and its rapturous reception, is the latest move in an arduous line of move after move – some of which furthered their cause, and some of which were vehemently screamed down. Throughout every setback, Garad has been there, the diligent spine of it all.

'No trouble from his crowds?' Art says under the noise.

'Some, in the beginning, but it's dying down now. He's getting too popular. You can see how he has them all by the throat. That's what matters. Everything else is just bureaucracy. Hate him, love him, London will fall for him.' Garad pauses. 'You've done it. You have a godchild in the Caballaria.'

'Perhaps they'll call it my biggest win, after I'm gone,' Art says absently. 'And I've had precious little to do with it. If it's anyone's win, it's yours. You've trained him, supported him.' He hesitates. 'Despite your doubts.'

Garad gives a soft snort. 'He's a thwimoren with immense power who doesn't even believe in the Code. Did you know that? He feels no greater being or purpose than himself. It's difficult to trust someone like that.'

Art rubs his forehead. 'Garad, godchildren are humans, same as everyone else.'

'You're not creating a human. You're creating a Caballaria knight. I just think you should be on your guard around him, that's all.'

'If you feel that strongly about it, why help him?'

'I serve the Sword,' Garad says.

'Yes, but . . . I'd like you to believe in what you're doing, and that you're not just doing it because the prick wearing the crown tells you to.'

'For the greater good, remember? Always for the greater good.'

Art turns to face his champion. It has been a while since they have been in such close proximity to each other. The first thing he notices is how much older Garad is looking, especially around the eyes. Their features still resemble the picture he has in his head, but the visceral truth of seeing and feeling a thing in front of him adds depth, layers and disappointment – the disappointment of something less perfect than memory, and more complicated.

'Thank you,' he says simply.

After a moment, Garad dips his head. 'I think the world might be ready for the idea of him as your champion. I wouldn't have said so in the beginning, but now . . . yes.'

Art frowns. 'What are you talking about?'

Garad is still for a moment, their pale eyes cast to an elsewhere.

'I'm going to retire soon,' they say.

Art nearly chokes on his wine.

They offer up a ghost of a smile. 'You knew it would happen eventually.' Their head inclines towards Wyll. 'Besides, wasn't that your plan all along?'

Art feels a little shame. It has never been openly discussed between them, but the right moment would have come along. Eventually. One day.

'Yes,' he concedes. 'But . . . a long time from now. A long, long time, Garad!'

'It's been nineteen years since I became your champion,' Garad replies. 'By all reckonings, I've had a longer career than most could ever dream of. And I'm getting old.'

'You're a year younger than me,' Art retorts in a highly offended tone.

'But physically I feel twice my age. The Caballaria is no friend to the body.' They sound carefully distant. 'And I'd like to have more time for other passions in life.'

Lillath once called Garad the Monk, and unfortunately the name latched on like a limpet. They guard their personal life with ferocity. There have been people, over the years. Some people, Art is sure. Several. Three or four.

One or two, at the very least.

'By passions, do you mean love?' Art says, unable to resist.

Garad opens their mouth.

'What's this about love?' Lucan has appeared before them, boisterously drunk. 'Who's in love? Oh, that's right. ME.'

Garad eyes him. 'I don't think I've seen you sober since before your wedding.'

'That's because I haven't been. Not once.'

'It was more than a month ago, Lux.'

'Really? That long?' Lucan looks at the glass in his hand. 'The time, it disappears.'

'Does your husband maintain some moral stability, at least?' Art enquires.

'He's the head of a glows network, of course not.' Lucan lets out a genteel burp.

'Saints,' Garad says. 'You're like a toddler.'

Lucan spreads his hands. 'Love makes children of us. It's very freeing, Gar, you should try it.'

Garad rolls their eyes.

Lucan whisks a finger over to Art. 'And *you* should be on my side here, Sire King, considering.' Realisation crawls cartoonishly slow across his features. 'Ohhh, wait. We're not talking about that, are we? Very secret.' He drags his finger towards his mouth, but misses completely.

Art fixes him with a stony stare. 'You know, for my head of communications, you are curiously prone to spreading gossip.'

'Ah, that's where you have it all wrong. Communications, as in "to communicate". As in, communication must happen in order for communication to be happening.' Lucan waves an airy hand. 'Lillath is the secrets master, not I.'

Garad frowns between them. 'Whoever Art is choosing to spend his personal time with shouldn't be a matter of gossip.'

'Except,' Lucan says, 'when they're *famous*. Furthermore, it's not gossip when it's between friends, it's sharing.'

'I can have you exiled, Lucan,' Art says with a smile devoid of good humour.

Garad raises a brow, caught despite themself. 'Wait. Caballaria-famous?'

Lucan grins delightedly. 'The champion scores first blood!'

'Lux, I swear—'

'Guess who it is, Garad,' Lucan cuts in. 'Guess. You'll never guess.'

Garad taps a finger on their teeth. 'Hester Blood. No? I always thought he had a thing for her. The Iochitown Twins. No? Who's that cute one with the oversized axe?'

'Fuck's sake,' Art mutters.

'There's a reason everyone's talking about this knight moving to a Blackheart stable,' Lucan trills. 'What they don't know is the reason is sitting riiiight in front of me—'

'That's not true,' Art protests. 'She's been wanting to go private for a long time.'

Garad lets loose a snort. 'You *cannot* be talking about Finnavair.'

'SB hit,' Lucan calls. 'The Silver Angel wins!'

Art massages his face.

'What?' Garad's mouth hits the floor. 'Fin?'

'I know you two are friends,' Art begins.

Garad looks flustered. 'No, I mean, yes, but – that's not – that shouldn't have anything to do with anything. Anyway, you met her almost the same time as I did.'

'That was a long time ago.'

His friends are both wreathed in demanding silence. He is not going to get out of this.

He resignedly folds his arms. 'I hadn't seen her in years. Then a few months ago, Wyll brought her to the palace for some Caballaria dinner or other – saints, there seems to be one of those every damn week.' He tries not to shift around in his chair. 'Anyway. We caught up, and we talked.'

'And then you *fucked*,' Lucan puts in.

'Will you shut your mouth?' Art pleads.

Lucan looks chastened the only way a drunk man can.

'Anyway, we've been . . . catching up . . . for a couple of months, now. It's nice.' Art looks defensive. 'That's all.'

'Then why so secret?' Lucan asks.

'You know why. The glows have a party every time I even look at someone. She gets enough scrutiny as it is.'

Lucan scoffs. 'She's well used to it. That's not why. You only ever get secretive about someone when you're in love with them.'

'I'm not.'

'Yes, you are.'

'I'm *not*,' Art insists, even though Lucan is totally and utterly correct.

'Come on.' Lucan throws his arms open. 'What's frightening you about it?'

'It's temporary. It can't possibly work.'

'Listen, you shouldn't want to hide it. You shouldn't care if it's embarrassing, or if it doesn't work out. Need I remind you that no one can predict the future, not even you, Sire King of us all.'

Garad folds their arms, looking uncomfortable with the whole conversation. An oblivious Lucan plops himself down between them.

'Let's at least discuss the *theory* of snaring the rabbit,' he says. 'You know, just for fun. No harm in that, eh?'

Their silence is enough to give Lucan the win.

'Would you like to hear my proposed strategy?' he asks cheerfully, beer slopping over the side of his glass. 'It is extremely charming and unbelievably clever.'

'Knowing you, this proposed strategy will also risk my total humiliation.'

'How dare you,' Lucan says. 'And yes.'

Art snorts. 'Then no. I told you, it's too soon for grand gestures. It's only been a couple of months.'

'So?'

'It needs more time, Lux.'

Lucan holds up his favourite tutorial finger. 'Fine, fine. I'll make you a deal. If she's still your *special friend* a year from now, then you have to do it. A year to the day, if you like.'

'Two years,' Art says.

Lucan is outraged. '*Two*? Why two?'

'Because that makes it less likely to happen?'

'Two years is for ever!'

'Weren't you courting your beau for three before it got serious?' Art says.

Lucan opens his mouth, but nothing comes out.

Art looks triumphant.

'All right,' Lucan says, momentarily defeated. 'Two years. But we're making it an official bet. Garad, you'll be witness, right?'

'I'm having nothing to do with this,' Garad says.

Lucan tuts. 'You're so grumpy. What's the matter, got a secret thing for the Fair Fae yourself?'

'Saints alive. Fine, fine! I bear witness to a childish bet made about a woman who deserves more respect than to be gamed with.'

'Love *is* a game,' Lucan declares. 'You heard, though!' He rounds on Art. 'With Garad as witness that makes it official. Two years from now you have to implement my plan, or forfeit your honour.'

'You,' Art says through gritted teeth, 'are having too much fun.'

'You,' Lucan happily replies, 'haven't even heard the plan yet.'

Two years? No lover Art has ever had has lasted much past one. As they seal it with a hand clasp, he consoles himself with the knowledge that this is one bet he is sure to win.

CHAPTER 38

Terminal, Marvoltown
Two Days Ago

Boots clatter against stairs.

That is the sound that snaps Red out of her momentary torpor, the fascinated contemplation of her own monstery. Fin is getting away. She can't. If she gets away, if she warns anyone, it is all over: everything Red has worked for. The meaning of her existence. The years of obsession. This is all she is, all she has, and Fin is about to take it away from her.

Red wrenches open the door. She leaves Roben's body behind, where it may stay, haunting her for the rest of her no doubt short life. She will probably die tonight.

The exhilaration that comes chasing on the heels of that thought is better than any stimulant. Red spies stairs through an open door – the cellar. She runs downwards, reaching a floodlit space with one wall open to the night. The hind of a bike flashes at her as it purrs outwards, escaping into the darkness beyond with a small, hunched figure clenched around it.

Cascading realisations hit her in dizzying succession:

Fin is on a bike. There is no way Red can catch her now.

There is another bike at her feet. Fin has two bikes, and probably more somewhere; she's machine-obsessed.

A silver coin winks at Red from the plain ground beneath the second bike. The power key. Fin must have tossed it there.

Fin is not escaping to warn anyone.

Fin wants Red to follow her.

Red drags the bike upright, arm muscles skipping from its weight, fumbles the coin into the slot, nestles the machine between her thighs, upkicks the engine and skids unsteadily out into the night.

At first, as she pushes into the crowded roads, it feels impossible – she'll never find Fin in all this mess of people and machines – but the ride serves as a fast reminder of the power she has underneath her. The traffic organism parts before the bike like flesh around a surgeon's knife.

And Fin is easy to follow – too easy. There are barely any bikes out on the streets, so few knights abroad tonight. Fin is going fast, but not fast enough to shake Red. For more than an hour, she leads her through the veins and arteries of London. The city feels it, lets it happen. No more alarms. It waits, now, waits and watches for the winner.

They move across the border into Marvoltown, slipping towards Daeccanham. The traffic thins, sputters, all but disappears. The streets quieten, draw close together like a predator pack. Down here, with tall building blocks rearing up in every direction, dusk must always come early.

There.

Fin's bike sits quiet and still and riderless in front of a tall fence. The fence surrounds a little courtyard nestled among a cluster of dirty white-brick buildings set back from the main drag. The bustle of life is only moments away.

Red rolls to a stop, leaving her bike a distance from Fin's. She withdraws a needle knife from the inside of her boot, tugging it free of its sheath, her eyes searching.

There: movement beyond the fence.

As Red cautiously approaches, she sees Fin's shape crouched right in the middle of the courtyard, intent on something at her feet. There is a clink, a scraping, and then she is hauling up a thick square of grating. A dark hole gapes at her feet. She is too far away to stop or attack and the ringed metal fence that separates them might as well be a stone wall.

The buildings behind Fin's back look like dark, hungry, open mouths as she climbs down into the hole.

She looks up at Red. Then she disappears into the darkness below.

Red does not hesitate. She moves towards the fence and scales it as quickly and as quietly as she can, a mantis clinging to the giant chain-links, swaying in the wind. If Fin wanted her dead, or to escape her, she would have had plenty of chances on the bike ride – she's a superb rider, and Red can barely steer right. No. Fin wants to fight, and she wants to do it on her terms.

Red has no choice about seceding the ground. She cannot let Fin escape, so she must follow. There is a beautiful clarity in having only one clear path to take, a kind of freedom in having no freedom at all. Still, descending into darkness makes every nerve give off a warning buzz. Her hindbrain kicks, drenching her with new adrenalin.

You are the hunter, not the prey.

Her mind repeats this as she climbs into the hole, taking rough-hewn steps carved into bare dirt rock, sloping down into a gut-wrenchingly small but walkable tunnel. Coin-shaped lights have been embedded into the walls at regular intervals, striping the ground yellow and black, light and dark. Barely a minute later and Red comes across a tumble of dirt and stone and a gaping hole in the tunnel wall. Some careful wriggling and she is through.

Beyond is a plain, square room, dotted with pillars, its corners black with shadow. At the foot of each wall are mounds of broken tile shards patterned with simple coiling designs. The air is still and full of dust. The needle knife is cold and thin in Red's hand.

'You know where we are?' comes a voice.

Fin's voice.

Red's mind races as her eyes search the dimness. She begins to glide backwards, her shoulder blades searching for a wall to put her back against.

'No,' she says.

'You know about Beconthree Trag Station?'

Red nods. 'Terminal.'

Terminal was a long-abandoned trag station of near-mythical status belonging to a time near a century ago when most of the network was still below street level, and the thousand-year-old catacombs of London had been harnessed as connecting tunnels for the trags to run through.

Over time and multiple savage civil wars, after too many tunnels collapsed, killing too many people, the trags network was painstakingly elevated to street level and higher, its tunnels sealed off. Terminal had the distinction of having not only its underground line but its entire station abandoned to the darkness below.

'It was just Beconthree, for a long time,' Fin says. 'People only started calling it Terminal more recently. You know why?'

Red shakes her head. Her eyes are adjusting. Distinct shapes begin, agonisingly slowly, to present themselves. If Fin so much as twitches—

'About fifty years ago,' Fin continues, 'a couple of kids found a sewer entrance that led down into the abandoned station – only passable if you were small and could squeeze through the rubble. A local Wardogs syndicate got to hear about it. They widened up the access and set up an illegal fight venue down here. They called it the Dead Line. Now, if you managed to score a ticket to ride the Dead Line, you'd find yourself on a hundred-year-old underground trag, running the tunnel back and forth between Beconthree and Daeccanham, watching two disgraced former Caballaria knights, now clearly very much down on their luck, fighting to the death.'

A pause.

'There are no yields on the Dead Line. One fighter would not come out of there alive. But the winner could make a lot of trick, maybe turn that bad luck into good. Beconthree Station was renamed Terminal because supposedly that's where they left all the bodies of the fighters who lost. Just piled 'em up here and let 'em rot.' Fin's voice has a distinct tint of fascination to it. 'The Dead Line got shut down eventually, and Terminal was lost again in the last inter-district war – but some say that the station, being set so deeply underground, and then sealed up by that bomb attack in Utheran times, has preserved those bodies to an impossible degree. That some of them don't even look dead.'

The room they are in looks surprisingly small for a former station, and entirely free from the corpses of former knights, well preserved or otherwise.

'I don't see any bodies,' Red says.

'Disappointing, isn't it? It got cleaned up. Now it's used for other purposes.'

'What purposes?'

Fin says nothing.

Executions.

'Why did you bring me all the way here?' Red asks.

The longer this goes on, the more her brain tries to cut in and make her think. She does not want to think. She cannot afford to think.

'It just seems fitting,' Fin replies. 'The story of this place.'

Red begins to relax the fingers around the knife, readying a throw. 'I never had you as a romantic.'

'I never had you as a traitor.' Fin's words float back to her. 'You can die like all the rest of them did down here. You're one of them now. Disgraced.'

The pure hatred in her voice hurts.

Red swallows it away and hardens up. 'You have it wrong,' she says. 'To be disgraced, you'd first have to be in grace and I've never once claimed that. This is who I am, who I've always been. You just couldn't see it.'

'You're a good liar,' Fin quietly replies.

Red shakes her head. 'I never lied to you. You just never asked the right questions. Not until now.'

'No, not until you took my friend's life. Now I get to take yours. It's called justice.'

In Fin's mind, this is all a Caballaria bout. A moldra lagha vengeance fight for the life Red just took. Stupid, honourable knight games? Here and now, when honour should matter the least?

'For Roben?' Red says. 'The soothsayer so bad he couldn't even see his own death?'

There is an awful pause, but Fin won't be drawn out. 'He was good enough to see the truth about you.' The room's damp echo gives Fin's words a hissing undertone. 'Will you really go through with it?'

Red just laughs. The heady freedom of no choices left.

'Then I have two reasons to kill you,' Fin says.

A glint flashes out from behind a pillar, a whir, and with just enough time to register them both, Red twists – but not fast enough. A cycle blade scratches her arm on its spinning way past, scoring open her flesh. A second later and a white-hot fire of pain lines its way through the wound. Her sword arm. Soon her fight hand will be soaked in her own blood.

This is no fast execution. The bitch wants to play.

At least Fin just lost her main weapon. Her cycle blade fetched up against the wall behind Red with an echoing clatter. Risky, silly move.

'I thought this was about honour,' Red spits through gritted teeth, pushing away the pain that sings in her ears. 'You a coward, Fin? Only cowards hide.'

'You did learn to taunt, after all,' Fin says, and finally, she moves out from behind the pillar.

Her gaze is savage. Red knows the look well and welcomes it like an old friend. This is what she understands: complications, doubts, politics, guilt, love, shame. They are all gone. This is simple.

To the death, to the death, to the death, her mind sings at her as she takes her chance and throws the needle knife in her hand, right at Fin's heart, who raises a defensive arm. The knife thwacks into the slender trunk. Her mouth opens in a soundless scream.

Each of them is a weapon down – but Red has another needle knife in her boot.

Fin glares at her. Her eyes flicker to Red's left. It is slight, brief, but instinct collapses Red's legs to get her to the floor. She hears the hiss of another blade pass harmlessly through the space where her vital organs had been only a moment ago.

There is someone else in the room with them.

Fuck! her mind screams. *Not so honourable after all, is she?*

Red rolls away, springing back up on her feet to face her new opponent.

Which is Fin.

One Fin is tensed into a crouch in front of her, whole and unwounded. The other Fin stands a little way away, clutching her forearm, the needle knife sticking out of the flesh.

Two Fins. Apart from the wound, they are exact copies of each other. The hair. The clothes. The look of dead-eyed fury. Identical twins? Impossible – no one can keep a twin a secret for a lifetime.

The new, unwounded Fin disappears with a strange, flat pop.

Red's brain gives a sickening lurch.

'You're a saintsfucked illusionist,' she spits. 'Just like Wyll.'

So all that training he gave her against illusions will come in handy after all.

The unwounded Fin reappears right in front of Red, tilts back on one leg, kicks her hard in the stomach, then disappears. The air in the space she left behind pops again, loud enough to hurt Red's ears.

'Wrong,' says the wounded Fin.

Red scrabbles on the floor, badly winded and desperately trying to breathe. Illusions can't touch. Illusions don't make a sound when they disappear, either.

'What in seven hells are you—?' she wheezes.

'You're not the only godchild in the Caballaria.'

'I've never heard of . . . that—'

'Neither have I,' she hears Fin say, voice pain-ragged around the edges. 'They don't yet have a word for what I am.'

Red's mind races as her eyes search the gloom for Fin's copy. The original Fin cradles her arm. Even with her weapon arm gone, she can still do some damage.

One of them is hard enough. Two of them?

'You're unregistered,' she says, trying to stall her. 'Illegal.'

'Oh shit,' Fin mocks. 'Who will you tell?'

Two powerful godchildren in the same neighbourhood, growing up together – what were the odds of that? No wonder Roben had gone to her. No wonder they had been friends. The lifetime lie alone would be enough to get Fin locked up. Lying as a Caballaria knight? Every bout she has ever fought could be overturned. It would be chaos. Her life would be over.

So now she has three reasons to kill Red.

The air in front of Red gives a horrible crack and Fin's copy appears. She feints, slides in, and Red hauls her protesting body out of range, propelled by desperate survival. She tries to reach her boot for the other needle knife but she is too slow – Fin's copy kicks her hand out of the way. The copy is real, solid, thick human flesh, and fresh as a new-cut flower. Red's arm is slick with blood from Fin's earlier hit. It drips off the ends of her fingers and splatters the floor, taking her energy with it.

The real Fin moves in behind her copy. Slowly, gradually, they work Red into a corner. Every time she tries to break out of it, the copy, implacable, hems her in.

Red is tiring fast. It cuts deep to the bone, slowing her up, no matter how hard she pushes. She tries not to panic, but she can feel it pushing insistently at her guts, distracting her with its rat scratching.

They spring together. They have her. Red heaves with

everything she has, but holding on to her strength is like trying to grasp water. It slips out of her hands, and they have her. They hold Red down, they slide in blood, Fin's and hers, scrabbling for purchase.

Then they start to choke her.

It happens so fast there is barely time to acknowledge the fact that she is about to die. The pressure on her throat blackens the edges of her world, pulling it tightly in to here and to now. Red becomes dimly aware of a howling sound – the last of her blood, roaring in her ears? – but then that crushing pressure on her throat halves in a sudden dizzy loss, and after a sickening black moment, her senses begin to work again.

The howling is the room. Dust and dirt grit Red's cheeks, pushed into a savage wind. Loose chunks of tile and stone fling themselves through the air, battering her body and the bodies crouched over her alike. Red's magic screams out of her and rifles through the room, throwing everything it has at her attackers.

Instead of trying to keep control, she lets go, she lets it all out – her blood, her life, whatever she is, she collapses in its midst, out in all directions at once, she screams it out with everything she is.

If you're going to die, die loud.

CHAPTER 39

Mynchen Arena, Blackheart
Two Days Ago

The knight is on his knees on the sanded arena floor.

His opponent has the thinnest, sharpest edge of her cycle blade hovering at his jugular.

'I yield,' the Wolf of the Wastes growls.

The Fair Fae gives a savage grin and lifts her hands to the sky, cycle blade clutched in one fist. The crowd chants her name like a bestial prayer.

It has been a long and closely followed tournament, a series of clashes over district border disputes. Today's outcome should put a full stop to further violence, although Londoners can always find something else to spill it over. *Stop the fight, stop the joy*, so the saying goes.

Both fighters haul themselves to their feet. Arena officials swim up from the hidden ring and spill into the pit, ready to guide the loser away and give the winner their prize – a newly made patch in Blackheart symbols and colours, immortalising their win. Some knights like to more permanently commemorate their favourite victories by getting the patch design inked on to their skin, but the Fair Fae is unusually averse to tattoos.

The Wolf of the Wastes, still down from the fight, is helped to his feet. With an impatient shove he refuses the trolley that has been wheeled on and limps off in the midst of a knot of medics.

The Fair Fae straightens as she watches the herd of white jackals approach. Leading them is the arena's head adjudicator, there to bestow the winner's patch in person, as befits a tournament of this stature. Adjudicator heads can attract almost as much fame as knights, particularly the more charismatic, and this one is a well-known lover of glows attention. He comes out into the pit wearing an overlay disguising his face, a fact that doesn't immediately strike anyone as odd – though perhaps it should have been noted that he appears to be a foot taller than normal. The overlay is etched in glossy black feather designs that streak across his cheeks and sweep to his ears, drawing the eye further back to the slicked blond hair beyond.

The cameras track him as he stops in front of the Fair Fae, focusing in on his hidden face. The crowd noise dies down expectantly, the better to hear the ceremonial word exchange that will conclude the tournament.

It begins as expected.

'Finnavair Caballarias o'Rhyfentown,' the head adjudicator states. 'You have been declared the victor. Do you accept the will of the saints and we their mortal hands?'

It is only then that people begin to realise that something is different. The head adjudicator's voice is off. Normally a reedy piping that forcibly investigates the ears, this voice is softer and much lower.

The Fair Fae seems to have noticed. She hesitates a moment before replying.

'I do.'

'And do you accept whatever might come next as a consequence of what I'm about to do?'

The capturers are tight on her face.

She blinks. 'What?'

The head adjudicator doesn't reply. Instead he raises his hands to his chin and begins to peel the overlay from his face, tantalisingly slow in revealing his features. He drops the overlay to the pit floor. Every capturer is focused on this impossible, glorious moment.

The King of London is standing in the middle of the arena.

His hands are loose by his sides, his attention on the Fair Fae as if he cannot even hear the crowd around them lose all reason. In all his reign he has only ever been seen in an arena once, when he first took the Sword of London with his Silver Angel. That was nearly twenty years ago, and the Mafelon Massacre has had him famously sealed up in the palace for the last few. The Tricky King does not leave Cair Lleon for anyone or anything.

Ever.

They are talking, he and the Fair Fae, their voices drowned out by the roaring. She is dumbfounded. He is calm. The capturers are greedily focused on their mouths, their eyes, their gestures. The roaring drops to a low rustle hum as the conversation goes on.

Just about at the moment where it starts to become apparent that they know each other well, which would be news enough to splash across the glows for a month, the King leans in, hesitates – as if to ask permission, later speculators say – cups the Fair Fae's sweat-streaked neck, and kisses her.

And eardrums begin to bleed.

★

'What the fuck were you *thinking*?'

Art hugs the wall by the door, his arms protectively folded against his body as he watches an incensed Fin ricochet around the arena dressing room.

'Well,' he muses, 'I realised a while ago that if even *I* don't know what I'm doing two hours ahead of time, how can anyone else? So I sort of made the decision on the fly. It's fool-proof, really.'

'This is not a game,' Fin snaps. 'This is your *life*. You don't play around with your *life*.'

He watches her stomp around a moment more, and wonders what the arena's guards, clustered outside the dressing room door, are thinking of the argument they can no doubt easily hear. They likely have enough going on right now, what with suddenly having to protect the King of London, a.k.a. the world's most unwelcome surprise. He makes a mental note to send an apology to their Knight-in-Green.

'Fin,' he says patiently, 'do you think this is the first time I've ever, since Mafelon, sneaked out of Cair Lleon? Do you really?'

She stops, caught.

'No,' she concedes. 'But it's the first time you've ever done it in front of an audience.'

Each word drips furious worry.

Art pretends to consider. 'Yes, I think you're right. But I'm always in disguise when I go out, and I'm always alone. I know that sounds riskier, but actually—'

'Oh saintsfuck, Art,' she interrupts, 'I'm not really angry about the risk, am I?'

He shakes his head. 'No.'

Her smile is sharp. 'The King and the street fox. What a

wonderful story for the glows. You used me for a political statement!'

'Yes,' he said. 'I did.'

She rounds on him. 'What?'

With a gaze like that, Art wonders how anyone ever faces her down in the arena and comes out alive.

'Yes, I did,' he repeats. 'Do you want me to lie about that? I wouldn't do you the disservice. Everything I do and everything I say is political, Fin. I'm the glowing silver idol of political. Nothing in my life gets to be free of that.'

He watches her digest this.

'Where you're wrong,' he continues, 'is if you think that's the only reason I did it.'

'Evron help me, there's more to deal with?' Fin asks the ceiling. 'What's the other reason?'

I lost a bet with Lucan.

This does not seem like the right moment for levity, however, so instead he says, 'I wanted to get your attention.'

She throws her arms up into the air. 'Success! Congratulations! Why couldn't you have just sent me a gift?'

'I had something bigger to prove.'

'What could you possibly have to prove to me that would warrant you doing something as stupid as this?'

'The fact that I'm in love with you.'

The effect is immediate. Her arms lower. Her mouth opens.

'Oh,' she manages to say.

They watch each other. Art tries gamely to control his breathing.

'We've been doing this for two years,' she says. 'Why haven't you ever said that before?'

So many reasons.

He shakes his head. 'It was too much. Once I'm in love – once I *say* it – that's it. I can't walk away, and it gets complicated for me. I had to sit with it a while. And you and I, we're both busy. We both have other passions. It didn't seem like something that should be said.'

'Then why now?'

'I suppose I finally found the courage. Also, I'm getting old.'

Fin doesn't smile.

'Being in love doesn't excuse your behaviour,' she says, a spark flaring.

'No, it doesn't,' Art admits. 'Yes, it was calculated. It was a taste of how it would be to be with me, properly, the way that I desperately want. It's not the easiest sell, I'll admit. But I'm betting on what I know of you.'

She waits.

At least she isn't throwing anything. 'You thrive on challenge.' Art plunges on. 'How could you not, with the amount you've already faced in your life? Easy wins bore you. I've seen it. Challenge makes you feel alive.'

Fin gives a soft snort.

'I'm right,' he presses.

Her gaze is too wary. 'This is no good, for either of us.'

Art refuses to sag. 'I want what I want. And I want you. I look around at the other people in my life, the sheer joy they get to have, and I want it. I know I'll never have it the same way they do, and for a long time I thought that was why I never tried: because I thought it was impossible. I thought it wasn't allowed. But that's not the reason. This whole time, I've been afraid.'

'Of what?'

'The work it would take to make that joy for myself. Because then I'd have to try, and maybe fail. And I'm afraid of failing. I'm afraid of pain.'

'We're all afraid of that,' Fin says.

'I know. I told myself I'd never fall prey to self-glorifying, but it turns out I did. I just went the other way.' He adopts a mournful tone. 'Oh nooo, it is so hard being me, I am the worst of all time, I deserve nothing but punishment!'

Her mouth twitches. 'Some people quite like punishment.'

'Stop trying to make me blush when I'm making a heartfelt point.'

'My apologies.'

'I've overthought it for so long now that I'm sick to death of my own brain. I've been trying to come up with a solution when there isn't one. The only lesson I've learned from my life so far is this: you can never have any idea, not truly, of where your decisions will lead. That's the thing that is so terrifying about the way humans are made. You know as much as you know in the moment. Then all you can do is take a breath and jump.'

Art subsides. He has nothing left. There it all is, for better or worse.

Fin takes her bottom lip in her teeth, bites, lets go.

'Did you rehearse that?' she asks. 'It was very smooth.'

'I rehearse everything I say so much I've forgotten how to talk like everyone else.' Art pauses. 'Too smooth? It was too smooth, wasn't it.'

She puts a hand on his chest. 'It was honest.'

She must, *must* be able to feel his drumming heart under her palm.

'Is that . . . a yes?' he asks.

She says nothing, but an agony of conflict marches across her face.

'Fin, what are *you* afraid of?' he asks.

'Having my freedom taken from me,' she murmurs.

'You can go when and wherever you like,' Art says firmly. 'Your life is your own. I won't stop you. I don't want to stop you. I like your freedom. It's beautiful to me. All I ask is that when I need you, you will be there. That you'll be my happiness.'

'That's a lot to ask.'

'I know. But in return, you'll want for nothing. I only want to please you. I need you. Fin, I don't want to do this alone any more.'

He is pleading, he is begging. He is opening up his insides and putting every soft, small part of him on display for her to judge and reject. She has his life in her hands. She has her cycle blade to his throat.

She looks up at him, and something in his face sets hers. 'Okay,' she whispers.

He can hardly dare to breathe. 'Okay?'

She nods. Art lets loose a shaking whoop and scoops her up in his arms.

Finally, finally, finally, he gets to have this.

Finally, he gets to be happy.

CHAPTER 40

Terminal, Marvoltown
One Day Ago

When she comes to, it is in fits and starts.

Her brain sputters, blinking on – blinking off.

On and then off.

And then on, steadier.

Red tries to move. She hears a hoarse groaning sound. She realises, in a detached sort of way, that she is the one making it. A moment later, as if everything is on a time delay, rivers of pain flood through her body, sending dopey, juddering signals to alert her that nothing is right.

She manages to pull herself to a half-collapsed sitting position. The ground is cold and hard against her palms. One hand is sticky with congealed blood. Her eyes adjust slowly, and when they see what they see, she wishes they hadn't.

What she had thought was a small, pale stone glowing dully in the darkness just before her is the white of an eye. What she had at first taken for some kind of miniature bike wheel, half-buried in a lumpy mound of rubble, is a cycle blade. Fin's body is the lumpy mound of rubble. The cycle blade is buried in her neck.

The blade she threw that opened up Red's sword arm and

then fetched up in a corner – Red's magic must have picked it up and flung it at her, along with everything else in the room.

No, not Red's *magic*, as if it is a separate entity to be blamed. Red. Red did this.

She forces herself a little closer. The blood around Fin's neck has turned darker, globbier. She hasn't moved in a long while.

She is dead.

You have to be sure. You can't leave yet. What if she wakes up? What if her copy reappears?

A part of Red knows it is far too late for all that. Still, she gathers her legs up, curls herself into a ball with her back against a wall and waits beside Fin's body for what feels like a very long time.

Fin does not move. Her eyes stay open.

Red manages to turn away into the corner just before she vomits. Her ravaged throat screams at her, burning from the acid. She ignores the pain – it can join the queue of complaints her body has, and it can go right at the back – and slowly drags herself across the room to the broken tunnel wall. Terminal station keeps deathly silent behind her. She limps up the dark tunnel and reaches the steps. She climbs. Her feet slip twice. Mercifully, her head remains empty all the way.

That is, until she gets outside and looks up at the sky.

News glows swing across the inky black, flickering through today's marvels. Red stands for a moment, staring dumbly. It could be the night's breeze furring up her skin, but it is more likely the fact that Finnavair, the dead woman underground, the woman Red just killed, is currently splashed across a thick, dark cloud for the whole district to see.

Fin's face is streaked with Caballaria paint and her expression is one of abject shock. The words below her chin read:

THE FAIR FAE CATCHES A KING
Sword of London leaves palace for first time in three years to declare love

Red reads the words, over and over.

Then she sinks to one knee and starts, hysterically, to laugh.

Wyll opens the door. His face drops.

'I need to see the King,' Red rasps. 'Now.'

CHAPTER 41

Cair Lleon, Blackheart
Last Night

There are wolves on the walls.

They lope across the stone, their lacquered faces fixed on Red as she sits in the antechamber. She was deposited here an hour ago by a harried-looking vastos and told to wait.

She has been using the time to stare at the wolves. Their rangy bodies and ringed eyes make her think of Wyll, a similarly piercing gaze locked on his face while his private medic stitched her up in the safety of his training station a few hours earlier.

There had been no one else to go to – no choice more obvious. It looks like all she had to do to get what she'd been after all this time was to give the Death Saint a firm handshake.

'Why won't you tell me who did this to you?' Wyll asked her as soon as the medic was gone.

Red sat mutely on his bed. Her bruised throat had been a good excuse not to talk, until Wyll, producing an electric pen and pad, ordered her, despite her injuries, to write out exactly what had happened. It was hard to blame him. She looked and felt like shit.

'I will find out, Red,' Wyll said, searching her face.

She just stared back, safe in the knowledge that the only two people who could tell him were dead.

Please, she wrote out painstakingly. *Just get me an audience, as soon as you can.*

Please.

He read it through. 'Why does it have to be in person?'

Can't trust anyone in the palace to tell him. I have to tell him myself.

'You can't trust me?'

Yes. But this is for him only.

'Can't you even tell me what it's about? I can't just request an audience with the King of London without that. Not even I can do that, do you understand me? I know you think I'm all powerful, but the palace—' He trailed off as she began to scribble.

Finnavair. Betrayal.

Wyll looked up from her shaky handwriting, surprise marching across his beautifully cut features.

She continued writing.

Do you trust me, *Wyll?*

She had never used his familiar name with him before. It felt so much weightier written out than when spoken aloud. As he read his name, he stilled. His lips parted, just a little, as if he liked seeing it.

Bizarrely this, this deliberate misuse of their fragile new intimacy, felt like the worst thing she had ever done. She might have just killed two people, but at least they saw it coming.

'Yes,' Wyll said finally. 'I trust you. Try to rest. I'll arrange it.'

And so he had.

Red's thoughts are interrupted by a voice. 'This way, please.'

An imperious-looking vastos has appeared at the doorway of the palace antechamber.

Red is clad in the Red Wraith outfit designated for her pre-bout sequestered training. Perfectly fitted to her form, its dark, heartsblood red with accents of black and burgundy is showier than her regular training outfits and less showy than her public bout outfits. It is still one of the most impressive sets of clothes she has ever owned. Clandestine and unofficial though it might be, this is still an audience with the King of London.

This is still the most important moment of her entire life.

The only thing missing from the outfit are weapons. No weapons are allowed in Cair Lleon, even ceremonial ones. The only exception to this rule are the guards' guns – and they are everywhere, at the corners of every room and hallway. Only the suicidal would try anything on palace grounds.

It is three o'clock in the morning, and yet every vastos Red has seen in this vast labyrinth is impeccably turned out. So many of them. So many more than she could have ever dreamed of. They say the palace never sleeps. She had always assumed it to be exaggerated.

She follows the vastos out of the antechamber, another vastos quietly falling into step behind her as they walk. Always two escorts everywhere, one in front and one behind – to make sure no one gets lost, they tell her. Having someone shadowing her gives her nerves, already jacked up to terrifying levels, an extra tremble she could really do without.

A door approaches.

Behind it . . . the end of all things.

The vastos in front knocks. A voice comes from within, indistinct encouragement. The door is opened. Red walks through. The door is closed behind her.

She catches sight of a delicately decorated room in black and gold lacquer, dotted with standing screens and sweetly fluted tables, before her attention focuses on the only other person in the room.

The King is sat in a comfortable-looking armchair, a squat cup filled with amber liquid by his elbow. Without the lava-glass crown on his head, he looks like a normal man. She has only ever seen him filtered through a capture or a glow, the weight of a Kingdom on his face. He looks so much younger than she expected in person, and it is disconcerting.

So very young.

But old enough.

'Good evening,' he says, breaking protocol. 'I'm sorry to keep you waiting. There's so much damn ritual around everything in this place. You'd think I'd have the power to get rid of it all if I wanted, but I have to admit that the palace holds all the cards. I'm just the pretty face on the game box.'

He smiles. His eyes turn sweet when he smiles. It sends a repulsed kind of shock right through her.

This is not how it should be. She had not expected to be in some small, pretty room with a crownless, softly spoken man. She had expected to find a suspicious, paranoid weakling, wrapped in all the layers of protection he is famous for hiding behind.

She has succeeded in removing Wyll, the most dangerous and deadly obstacle in her path, but the room should at least be filled with guards, their guns ready cocked. The King displays no power. Why has he hidden it all? Why is he so relaxed?

Is it some kind of trap?

'Wyll has been talking about you to me,' continues the King. 'He's very impressed, and what impresses Wyll impresses me. I hope that doesn't embarrass you. It seems like everyone is talking about you. They say you're one of the most exciting Caballaria knights to come along in years.'

Red has lived this moment inside her head so many times, with so many permutations that she had convinced herself that not one thing about it could take her by surprise. She is wrong. After all this time, she is finally, finally standing right in front of him, the sole object of his attention. He studies her keenly as he talks about her, interest and curiosity aroused plain on his face. He sees her, really *sees* her.

And he has absolutely no fucken idea who she is.

'I'm told you have some important information for me,' he says. 'Why don't you sit down?'

There is the politest hint of a prompt in his voice and Red realises she has not yet moved or uttered a word. No one sits in front of a King like an equal. No one does that. Why is he asking her to do that?

Slowly, Red sinks into the chair opposite him.

His hand reaches out. She sees the famed tattoos covering the skin of his fingers, a tiny black-inked symbol for every win he has had as King. There are thirteen symbols so far, as everyone knows. He always decides the symbol himself. Placing a bet on what symbol he will choose for each win has become another regular ritual at the betting bars over the years.

The fingers push forwards an erasable writing pad and an electric pen towards Red.

'I can talk,' she croaks.

If he notices her lack of 'Sire', he doesn't show it.

'As you desire.' He nods. 'But please don't strain your voice. Parnere said that your throat will take time to heal and I'd rather he didn't blame me if it takes longer than it should.'

Parnere. Apparently even the Sorcerer Knight's private medic gets to be on familiar naming terms with the King.

'So, can you tell me something of what this is about?' he asks.

Red tries to speak over the screaming of her heart. 'I have a dispute with someone in Cair Lleon.'

'What kind of dispute?' he asks.

'Moldra lagha.'

'I see.' The King's mouth tightens. 'Who is it?'

It's clear that he is waiting to hear Fin's name. It's clear that Wyll has warned him to expect it.

'It's you,' says Red.

She watches his expression with every ounce of concentration she has.

He'll scream for his guards now, she thinks.

He doesn't.

Every following second is agony. After an eternity, his mouth opens. 'You look a little bit like someone I used to know, now I can see you close,' he says.

There it is.

'She was my mother,' Red tells him. 'You killed her.'

There is nothing on his face. Nothing at all. No shock, no anger, no denial.

Red feels herself beginning to break into tiny little pieces. 'Please tell me who I am,' she says. 'Please, you must know who I am.'

The beg in her voice should shame her, but all is long past shame.

'How old are you?' asks the King at last.

'I'm eighteen,' she says.

'When is your birthday?'

She tells him, and watches the truth pass through him like a ghost. Eight months from the night that Belisan fled the palace as a fugitive, Red was born.

'Why have I never known about you?' he asks.

Still so monstrously calm.

'Because she didn't want you to know about me. She was afraid of what you might do.' Red clutches the arms of her chair. 'And you murdered her.'

'That is not what happened.'

'Don't you lie!' she shrieks suddenly, and her bruised throat pulses in pain. 'I was there, *I saw you do it*!'

It is the first time she sees him falter. Horror, true horror, passes across his face.

'You . . . you can't have been,' he stutters. 'Why were you there?'

'Lord Welyen found out about me. He took me – he *kidnapped* me. He was too much of a coward to do it himself, so he used my mother, made her contact you to draw you out. There was a woman holding a butcher's knife to my throat in my mother's eyeline, while Lord Welyen sat two tables away from her. She could see me the whole time she talked with you.'

Red pauses. The knife prickles at her throat even now. She can still feel the implacable force of the stranger guarding her, her thin steel arms around hers, locking her into place. The incandescent fury that she had felt, the screaming energy in her to escape, all did nothing.

Then she had watched the stranger in the knight's costume raise a gun to her mother's head, and her mother reel back in an awful *wrong* way, a snap-and-twist kind of way that the eight-year-old Red somehow knew – although she'd never seen a gun fired before – was not the kind of movement that anyone could walk away from.

She still doesn't remember what happened next, only that the woman holding her was on the floor now, clutching her hip with her mouth stretched open in comical agony. Red's hands felt like they were doused in fire. Without moving a muscle, she had overturned the tables nearest her and smashed all the drinking glasses, leaving the liquids splashing across the cushions.

It was an unbelievable mess, but the entire hallway was chaos, people running from the shots and the death, and no one noticed what she had done. No one noticed a child running blindly through the crowd and out into the night. She made it all the way to the Evrontown border before the shock wore off, before she even understood what had happened or where she was.

That was the first time her magic kicked, but it kicked too late. She broke free from the woman who had held her struggling in place while her mother was threatened, the woman who had tried to take her power from her, she *won* – but she won too late, and her mother was dead, and her life was ruined.

From that moment on, she would make sure she never, ever felt so powerless again.

From that moment on, *she* would be the knife at the throat.

'I don't understand,' the King whispers. 'I don't understand.'

'My mother was a threat to you,' Red says, 'because she was more powerful than you.'

'She wanted to kill me—'

'She didn't care about *you*! She didn't want anything to do with you! She just wanted to protect me, from you and from Lord Welyen. But she couldn't. He found us.'

The King is very still. His head drops a little, gently. He

presses the heels of his hands against his forehead, and then he begins to cry.

It paralyses her.

It shouldn't. She has fantasised about this moment for ten years. She has prepared herself for every possible reaction. She has told herself that no matter what he did – denied it, turned to violence, blubbered for his life – she would be implacable. Ice, not fire. Death, not life.

But the King's pain is very raw, and it sends a shock through her that nothing, nothing at all, not a thousand hours of vengeance fantasies could have prevented.

The room is still and quiet as he weeps and tries hard not to. His skin is tired around the mouth. His body is slender like a stag. He has crooked teeth. One eyebrow is just a little thinner than the other at the end. There is a tiny shaving cut on his jawbone. He must have done it in haste, just before this meeting with her, and not even noticed. The King hurried to make this meeting, hurried to look presentable for some knight he'd never met before.

He is not a monster. He is just a man. A soft, vulnerable man, as easily punctured as anyone else. The air tastes sour, of sadness.

A knock comes on the door behind Red, shattering the quiet.

The room explodes.

Glass disintegrates. Tables are hurled through screens, ripping their leaf-thin skeins to shreds. Red has her hands around the King's neck, though she hasn't moved from her seat. The pure terrified agony in her, relentless years of it, a lifetime of it, squeezes hard. His legs kick. He chokes. But he doesn't struggle.

That is what stays with her afterwards, how he doesn't struggle.

A part of her understands that she is crying too, now, furious, wordless weeping leaving her breathless herself as she crushes her father's throat.

'I didn't know about you,' he wheezes, pushing the words out on his last breath, 'I didn't know. I would have—'

His eyes squeeze shut as the door to the room opens with a splintering crash.

Whoever they are, they are too late.

CHAPTER 42

Cair Lleon Clusterloc, Blackheart
Now

The clusterloc of Cair Lleon holds only the most important of prisoners.

It has some very comfortable rooms, for a prison: lavishly furnished suites as indulgent as any other in the main palace, the only signs of confinement being a complete lack of windows and heavy locks on the outside of the one door.

Then there are the other rooms. The ones with transparent, double-panelled flecter-glass walls, impossible to break. Spartan, heavy metal furniture bolted to the floors, with nothing that can be smashed and used as a weapon. Ceilings are laced with strip lights that never turn off.

The last is the worst: no shadows or darkness to fold over your ugly sharp edges. Crouched in the glarebright of your crime, on display in a human torture zoo. A set of snake-iron chains, so minutely articulated they look like rope, tethering you to an iron staple as thick as a forearm set at hip height into the wall. A godchild prison: keep your body lit and your brain fogged, keep your magic crushed down behind your spine, glazed behind you where it's too hard to reach, almost too hard—

Then again, what would you do with it if you did manage to pull it out of you? There's nothing to throw or destroy. You have no rage left, and no reason.

You've fulfilled your life's purpose and you are empty now.

The door lock gives an insectile *chirrup click* and opens to admit a woman in a long, dusky-coloured coat that lips at the heel backs of her boots. The door is immediately closed behind her and she stands just inside the room, an expression of mild curiosity on her clean apple face as she gazes down at its occupant.

Red crouches in the corner nearest the wall staple. The woman is the first visitor she has had since she was put in here – how many hours ago now? It could be days, for all she knows; in here where the sun never sets. She watches the woman cross to the immovable little table and take an immovable little seat. She arranges her coat just so, taking care not to crease it as she sits.

Red moves, just a little, resettles. The chains slither and the sound crashes around the tiny room.

The woman regards her for just a moment.

'Si Dracones,' she greets her.

Red's heart gives a gentle squeeze. They have her last secret now, and it is an odd sensation. She would feel lighter, she is sure, if she could feel at all. She'd feel as if her limbs have been weighted for the last year, and only now does that weight crumble and slide off her skin like cakey slabs of wet sand.

'Do you know who I am?' asks the woman.

Of course she does. The Lady Orcade Welyen has a very recognisable face, one the glows have favoured for years. They like her cheekbones and her pale hair. Whole swathes of society model their fashion on hers. She is an icon.

She is also the sister of the man who helped kill Red's mother. The man who took her and held her captive and forced the worst event of her life into motion.

'Interesting family you have,' says Red dully.

Lady Orcade laughs. 'I could say the same thing about yours. The Dracones produce such forceful characters, don't you think?'

There are more lines on her face than the glows show, but they increase the magnetism of her physical presence.

'It's cost me some effort to get a chance to talk to you alone,' she says. 'A debt or two called in. It comes with the upbringing, I suppose. We're nothing much more than glamorised traders, and glamour is just one big mass delusion. If people all decide tomorrow that something is worth nothing, it becomes so. Belief is the greatest force in the universe. Like your belief in the right to vengeance. Look at all you've accomplished because of it.' She ticks her fingers. 'You became a godchild knight. Impressive in itself. Then you secured the mentorship of the most powerful knight in the country. Then you ended the Artorian era armed with nothing more than a pair of magic hands. I've been trying to get him killed for years, and here you are, snatching victory from under my nose.'

She glances at Red.

'Oh look,' she says. 'I think I finally have your full attention. Don't worry, there are no capturers in here. No eavesdroppers. We can be quite candid. I so rarely get the opportunity, and I don't want to waste it.'

Red's mind pushes against the fog she has descended into, sluggish against the faint warning bells ringing of the danger she is only just now beginning to sense.

'Why would *you* want him dead?' she asks.

Lady Orcade taps at her mouth with a gloved finger.

'No reason, really. To see if I could? I get bored, you see. So I play games. With myself, mostly, as I rarely come up against a good opponent. My brother and I played a very long game, quite a good one. But he lost in the end.'

Red stares at her.

'A game,' she repeats.

'Yes, people do tend to get confused when I say that.' The Lady offers Red an encouraging smile. 'You know, when I was a child, I did think there was something wrong with me. Everyone around me seemed to be half mad with various desires. Everything they did was designed either to attract something they wanted or repel something they didn't. It was obvious, but they acted as if their motivations were some great secret that no one else could see. I can't really imagine how you all live like that, it sounds exhausting.' She pauses. 'But as I said, I do get horribly bored. I should be honest about that. And you're the most interesting thing to happen for a very long time. I felt it when I had you in my arms. I thought, here's a special little girl. But then, when your mother got shot and your magic came out . . .' The Lady's face mists over. 'The destruction you caused – it was like a little bomb going off. No one had any idea you could do that! Marvellous.'

The arms around Red like a vice of iron. The knife she has felt slicing into the thin, vulnerable skin of her throat all these years. The arms and the knife that helped her mother die.

'It's really no good getting upset,' Lady Orcade says, watching her scrabble upright, jerking mindlessly against her chains and mouthing wordless shouts. 'The drugs they fed you, well, they aren't exactly approved for general use, but they do appear to work. Apparently they depress the part of your brain that connects your emotions to your magic. I don't pretend to understand it, myself.'

Crush her windpipe, Red's mind urges, but it is a weak flare of defiance, a juddering spark that dissipates fast.

Lady Orcade smoothes a wrinkle from her coat. 'You could thank me for helping you. I doubt you'd have become a knight without me.'

'What are you talking about?'

'Oh. I hoped you were cleverer than that. Well, the besotted Wyll might have paid your way, but I had people watching out for you – guiding you. Making sure you passed training.' Her head tips. 'Si Timor is an old friend of the family. Your tutor Frome? I knew his father. Debts called in, like I said. It's really quite a small world at the top.'

Red utters a hollow laugh.

'Oh come, that victory is still yours,' the Lady reassures her. 'Please don't take insult from my modest support. I just got so excited. I'd been looking for you without any luck for years, and then not only do you resurface but you do it splashed across my glow screen. I was just so curious to see what you were here for. I had high hopes, I admit, and you have more than fulfilled them.'

Red slumps, defeated. 'What the fuck do you want from me?'

Lady Orcade's hands fold neatly into her lap. 'As you may imagine, some rather heated discussion has been taking place on your myriad possible futures. There's one where you might become Queen.'

It sounds like a joke, at first, but she doesn't have a smile on her face. Just a patina of polite interest.

'I'd have thought you'd have already set my execution date,' says Red.

'Moldra lagha,' the Lady replies. 'If that's the story we go with, it stays your death, doesn't it?'

'Godchildren don't get anywhere near the Sword,' Red flatly replies.

'No? Tell me, who now holds the most power in this Kingdom? You, as technically you are the current rightful Rhyfen candidate?' She cants her head. 'Or Si Wyll, perhaps, as the King's extremely able champion? Either way, it's godchildren everywhere you look, isn't it?'

Red is silent.

'I'm curious,' she hears the Lady say. 'How do you feel about being Queen, Red?'

She spits. 'I'd rather die.'

'That may happen,' Lady Orcade agrees, 'but let's see if we can keep you alive a little while longer, shall we? After all, I was married to your grandfather. Call it a residual familial fondness, if you like.'

She stands, clasps her hands together and gives Red a bright, kindly look. 'Have a little patience. You have a new purpose on the way. Life is about to get very interesting for you, Mordred Dracones.'

Her coat hem sways, dusting the floor. Her boots give out quick little clicks. The door shuts behind her, and Red sinks, exhausted, to the floor. She hadn't even realised how tight she had been holding every muscle.

She sits alone, lit in bleached electric light, and waits to see if Wyll is coming to kill her.

ACKNOWLEDGEMENTS

Boundless gratitude to the saints who provide invaluable free internet resources – dirtysexyhistory.co.uk, Gutenberg for that concise dictionary of Middle English, oldenglishtranslator.co.uk, and a dozen other sites on subjects ranging from 'how the hell do urban power grids actually work anyway' to 'is it weird that I don't understand the structure of the criminal justice system?' It's not their fault that I took only what suited me and then bent it all out of logical shape – I claim poetic licence, an artist's most constant friend.

Thank you to Antonio Lulic for being the kind of person who says yes to a tour of the hidden tunnels underneath Euston and takes me on long bike rides to the stranger parts of the city. Thanks to the band Tool, particularly for the song 'Right In Two'. You sort of wrote parts of the book for me, there.

Grateful as ever to my agent Sam Copeland, always my first reader and therefore the most nerve-wracking. Your opinion means all.

Very grateful to Jo Fletcher and Molly Powell for your passion and enthusiasm for *Knights On Bikes* (I'm good at working titles) and to Jo in particular for your keen editorial eye and staunch support. Grateful to Ajebowale Roberts, Ella Patel and all at Jo Fletcher Books and Quercus for working to get this book out there during unprecedented times.

Thank you to early readers Samantha Shannon, Jay Kristoff and Krystal Sutherland – you gave me such relief with your encouraging feedback. Thank you to Alwyn Hamilton for your plot brainstorming sessions and provision of Crosstown doughnuts as the best of work fuels. Thank you to Katie Webber and Nina Douglas for your wonderful cheerleading.

Thank you to my sister, my mother, my father and my step-mother for your love and support. And to the wily one, for yours.

Laure Eve
London,
March 2021